PILGRIM SOUL

GORDON FERRIS

CORVUS

First published in hardback in Great Britain in 2013 by Corvus,
an imprint of Atlantic Books Ltd.

This paperback edition published in Great Britain in 2013 by Corvus,
an imprint of Atlantic Books.

10 9 8 7 6 5 4 3 2 1

A CIP catalogue record for this book is available from the British Library.

Paperback ISBN: 978 0 85789 762 6
E-book ISBN: 978 0 85789 925 5

Printed in Great Britain by CPI Group (UK) Ltd, Croydon, CR0 4YY

Corvus
An imprint of Atlantic Books Ltd
Ormond House
26–27 Boswell Street
London
WC1N 3JZ

www.corvus-books.co.uk

'If there were enough like him, I think the world would be a very safe place to live in, and yet not too dull to be worth living in.'

'The Simple Art of Murder', Raymond Chandler,

The Atlantic Monthly, December 1944

For Kathryn and Helen

ONE

There's no good time to die. There's no good place. Not even in a lover's arms at the peak of passion. It's still the end. Your story goes no further. But if I had the choice it wouldn't be in a snowdrift, in a public park, ten minutes from my own warm fireside, with a two-foot icicle rammed in my ear. This man wasn't given the option. His body lay splayed in cold crucifixion on Glasgow Green, his eyes gazing blindly into the face of his jealous god.

I looked around me at the bare trees made skeletal with whitened limbs. High above, the black lid of the sky had been lifted off, and all the warmth in the world was escaping. In this bleak new year, Glasgow had been gathered up, spirited aloft, and dropped back down in Siberia. So cold. So cold.

I tugged my scarf tight round my throat to block the bitter wind from knifing my chest and stopping my heart. I looked down on his body, and saw in the terrorised face my great failure. The snow was trampled round about him, as though his killers had done a war dance afterwards. Around his head a dark stain seeped into the pristine white.

A man stood a few feet away, clasping a shivering woman to his thick coat. Under his hat-brim his eyes held mine in a mix of horror and accusation. I needed no prompting. Not for this man's death. I was being paid to stop this happening. I hadn't. This was the fifth murder since I took on the job four months ago. But in fairness, back then, back in November, I was only hired to catch a thief . . .

'I'd be a gun for hire.'

'No guns, Brodie. Not this time.'

'A mercenary then.'

'What's the difference between a policeman's wages and a private income? You'd be doing the same thing.'

'No warrant card. No authority. No back-up.' I ticked off the list on my fingers.

She countered: 'No hierarchy. No boss to fight.'

I studied Samantha Campbell. She knew me too well. It was a disturbing talent of hers. Of women. She was nursing a cup of tea in her downstairs kitchen, her first since getting home from the courts. Her cap of blonde hair was still flattened by a day sporting the scratchy wig. The bridge of her nose carried the dents of her specs. I'd barely got in before her and was nursing my own temperance brew, both of us putting off as long as appeared seemly the first proper drink of the evening. Neither of us wanting to be the first to break.

'How much?' I asked as idly as it's possible for a man who's overdrawn at his bank.

'They're offering twenty pounds a week until you solve the crimes. Bonus of twenty if you clean it up by Christmas.'

'I've got a day job.'

'Paying peanuts. Besides, I thought you were fed up with it?'

She was right. It was no secret between us. I'd barely put in four months as a reporter on the *Glasgow Gazette* but already it was palling. It was the compromises I found hardest. I didn't mind having my elegant prose flattened and eviscerated. Much. But I struggled to pander to the whims of the newspaper bosses who in turn were pandering to their scandal-fixated readership. With hindsight my naivety shocked me. I'd confused writing with reporting. I wanted to be Hemingway not Fleet Street Frankie.

'They gave me a rise of two quid a week.'

'The least they could do. You're doing two men's jobs.'

She meant I was currently the sole reporter on the crime desk at the *Gazette*. My erstwhile boss, Wullie McAllister, was still nursing a split skull in the Erskine convalescent home.

'Which means I don't have time for a third.'

'This would be spare time. Twenty quid a week for a few hours' detective work? A man of your experience and talent?'

'"Ne'er was flattery lost on poet's ear." Why are you so keen for me to do this? Am I behind with the rent? Not paying my whisky bills?'

She coloured. My comparative poverty was one of the unspoken barriers between us, preventing real progress in our relationship. How could a reporter keep this high-flying advocate in the manner she'd got accustomed to? My wages barely kept me; they wouldn't stretch to two. Far less – in some inconceivable medley of events – three.

'The *Gazette*'s just not you, is it? An observer, taking notes? Serving up gore on toast to the circus crowds. You're a doer, not a watcher. You're the sort that joins the Foreign Legion just for the thrill of it.'

'Not a broken heart?'

'Don't bring *me* into this. What shall I tell Isaac Feldmann?'

Ah. Playing the ace. 'Why didn't Isaac just call me?'

'He wanted to. But he's from the South Portland Street gang. This initiative's being led by Garnethill.'

In ranking terms, Garnethill was the first and senior synagogue in Glasgow. It served the Jewish community concentrated in the West End and centre. I'd only ever seen it from the outside: apart from the Hebrew script round the portal, more a pretty church façade than how I imagined a

3

temple. Isaac's place of worship was built about twenty years after Garnethill, at the turn of the century. It looked after the burgeoning Gorbals' enclave. Jewish one-upmanship dictated that they called the Johnny-come-lately the Great Synagogue.

Sam was continuing, 'I've worked for them before.'

'They?'

'A group of prominent Jewish businessmen. I defended them against charges of operating a cartel.'

'Successfully?'

'I proved they were just being business savvy. The local boys were claiming the Jews were taking the bread from their mouths, driving their kids to the poor house and generally living up to their reputation as Shylocks. But all the locals managed to prove was their own over-charging.'

'I suppose I should talk to them.'

'Oh, good. I'd hate to put them off.'

They came in a pack later that evening, four of them, shedding their coats and scarves in the hall in a shuffle of handshakes and shaloms. They brought with them an aroma of tobacco and the exotic. Depending on their generational distance from refugee status, they carried the range of accents from Gorbals to Georgia, Bearsden to Bavaria, sometimes both in the same sentence. As a Homburg was doffed, a yarmulke was slipped on. I recognised two of the four: a bearded shopkeeper from Candleriggs; and my good friend Isaac Feldmann, debonair in one of his own three-piece tweed suits.

'Good evening, Douglas.' He grinned and shook my hand like a long-lost brother.

'Good to see you, Isaac. How's the family?'

'Ach, trouble. But that's families, yes?'

I guessed he meant his boy, Amos. Father and son weren't seeing eye to eye on life. A familiar story. I envied such trouble.

'But business is good?'

'Better. Everyone wants a warm coat. Come visit. I can do you a good price.'

'I don't have the coupons, Isaac. Maybe next year.'

I grew conscious that the other three men were inspecting me. I turned to them.

'Gentlemen, if Miss Campbell will permit, shall we discuss your business in the dining room?'

Sam led us through the hall and into the room at the back. We played silent musical chairs until all were seated round the polished wood slab, Sam at one end, me at the other, then two facing two. I placed my notebook and a pencil down in front of me. I looked round at their serious faces. With the hints of the Slav and the Middle East, the beards and the lustrous dark eyes, it felt like a Bolshevik plot. None of your peely-wally Scottish colouring for these smoky characters. Sam nodded to her right, to the big man stroking his great brown beard.

'Mr Belsinger, the floor is yours.' She looked up at me. 'Mr Belsinger is the leader of the business community.'

'I know him. Good evening, Shimon. It's been a while.'

'Too long, Douglas. I've been reading about your adventures in the *Gazette*.' His voice rumbled round the room in the soft cadences of Glasgow. Shimon was born here from parents who'd pushed a cart two thousand miles from Estonia to Scotland seeking shelter from the Tsar's murderous hordes.

'Never believe the papers, Shimon. How have you been?'

I'd last seen him just before the war in the wreckage of his small furniture store in Bell Street. Some cretins had paid their own small act of homage to Kristallnacht. All his windows were in smithereens and his stock smashed. But the perpetrators hadn't been paying real attention; the legs of the daubed swastikas faced left, the wrong way for a Nazi tribute. Unless of course they really meant to hansel the building with the gracious Sanskrit symbol. We caught the culprits, a wayward unit of the Brigton Billy Boys led personally by Billy Fullerton, who wanted to show solidarity with his Blackshirt brethren in the East End of London.

'Getting by, Douglas, getting by. But we need your services.'

'You want me to write an article?'

He looked at me through his beard. A rueful smile showed.

'We could do with some good publicity.'

'You need more than a *Gazette* column.'

No one had to mention the headlines in these first two weeks of November: 'Stern Gang terrorist arrested in Glasgow'; '800 Polish Jews held in South of Scotland'; 'MI5 searching for Jewish terrorists'; 'Irgun Zvai Leumi agents at large'.

The factions fighting to establish a Jewish state in Palestine were exporting their seething anger and violence to Britain. Poor thanks for trying to midwife the birth of a new nation already disowned by every other country in the Middle East.

Shimon nodded. 'Not even Steinbeck could improve our standing. But that's not why we're here. We are being robbed.'

'Dial 999.'

He shook his head. 'They don't come, Douglas. Your former colleagues are too busy to bother with a bunch of old Jews.'

Isaac interjected from the other side of the table: 'They came the first few times, but lost interest.'

Tomas Meras leaned forward, his bottle glasses glinting from the light above the table. Tomas had been introduced as *Dr Tomas*, a lecturer in physics at Glasgow University.

'Mr Brodie, we pay our taxes. We work in the community. We are *Glaswegians*. We expect an equal share of the services of the community.' His vowels were long and carefully shaped, as though he polished them every night.

I knew what they were saying. It wasn't that the police were anti-Semites. Or not *just*. They were even-handed with their casual bigotry: anyone who wasn't a Mason or card-carrying Protestant got third-rate attention. Jews were at the bottom of the pecking order when it came to diligent community law enforcement, alongside Irish Catholics. On the other hand crime was rare in the Jewish community. Self-enforcing morality. Glasgow's finest were used to leaving them to their own devices until whatever small dust storm had been kicked up had settled.

'First few times, Isaac? How many are we talking about and what sort of thefts? I mean, are these street robberies or burglaries? Shops or houses?'

Shimon was nodding. 'Our homes are being broken into. Eight so far.'

'Nine, Shimon. Another last night,' said the fourth man, Jacob Mendelsohn, waving a wonderfully scented Sobranie for emphasis. As a tobacconist, he could afford them. It went well with his slick centre parting and his neat moustache. A Cowcaddens dandy out of central casting.

'Nine is an epidemic,' I said.

They were all nodding now. I looked round at these men and marvelled at the capacity of humans to uproot themselves and travel to a far-off land with weird customs and languages and make a home for themselves and their families. How did these innocents or their forebears fare when they encountered their first Orange Parade or Hogmanay? What use was their careful cultivation of a second language like English when faced by a wee Glesga bachle in full flow? Urdu speakers stood a better chance.

I thought about what they were asking of me. It didn't seem much, yet I wondered if my heart would be in it. I used to be a thief-taker but I'd moved on. The world had moved on. Did I care? Was I still up to it? I wouldn't give my answer this evening, but in the meantime . . .

'Gentlemen' – I flipped open my reporter's notebook – 'tell me more.' I began scribbling in my improving shorthand.

TWO

Sometimes I like to just sit in a pub, a pint in one hand, a book or newspaper in the other, fags at the ready. Time to myself but surrounded by other folk. A social antisocial. Wanting to be part of something but not tied to it. It summed up what I was and what I'd become.

It was the night after I'd met the Jewish gang and I wanted to digest their plea for help. I'd talked about it with Sam when they'd gone but her enthusiasm was getting in the way of my personal analysis. I needed quiet time to give her and them my answer. I worried that my decision would be driven solely by the money. Not that money in the pocket is a bad motivation.

It wasn't that I needed to weigh up the morality of the challenge. The poor sods must feel their persecution would never end. The British were hardly in the same league of villainy as Hitler and his gang, but our troops were throwing them back in the sea off their promised land and banging up eight hundred veterans of the Italian campaign in case one or two were Jewish terrorists.

The job needed doing and if the Glasgow cops didn't have the time or inclination to catch a thief, then I saw no reason in principle not to help these good citizens. I just wanted to be sure I knew where I was going with this latest diversion. I was beginning to lose my bearings. If I ever had any. No job seemed right for me. No clear path. How long could a grown man go on being a dilettante?

I'd had enough of sore feet and trenches, and had the medals to prove it. And despite the blandishments of the top brass there was no going back to the soul-sapping work of a policeman. But four months into the newspaper game I was frustrated. Sam – cool, perceptive Samantha Campbell – with her lawyer's insight had stripped back my illusions to reveal some sort of would-be knight errant, handier with a gun and his fists than with his dreaming pen.

And yet, with this offer from Garnethill, was I seriously contemplating becoming a *private* detective? Would it be one skirmish, and then back to reporting? Could it be a career move? Did I *have* a career? Or was I just one of life's drunks, stumbling along, oblivious and falling into situations – scrapes usually.

I looked round the pub at my fellow drinkers. There were a few loners gazing into their glasses or examining the runes of the racing pages. My future selves? I hefted my glass and pondered having another, but I'd had enough of introspection. I walked out into a night as dreich as a child's funeral. I pulled my hat down and pulled up my coat collar against the cold drizzle.

I zigzagged up the hill to Sam's house and let myself in. She called down from the lounge.

'There's some cold ham under a plate, if you haven't been to the Tallies.'

'Thanks.' I hung my coat and hat up, went down and made a ham sandwich. I took it up to join her. She looked up from her book with a smile. The Light Programme hummed softly in the background.

'Well, Douglas?' She meant, had I decided.

I shrugged. 'Why not, Sam? Why not.'

I made an early start on Monday with a plunge into the great pool of the Western Baths Club. It had become a ritual, a penance and my salvation. A cure for hangovers and a banishment of the blues. By eight o'clock I was bashing through the swing doors of the *Gazette*'s newsroom as though I had a calling. No sign yet of Sandy Logan, former blue-pencil maestro in the sub's chair and now acting editor in the absence of Eddie Paton.

My aim was to clear the decks by lunchtime and then visit some of the crime scenes for my new employers. My *supplementary* employers. I reasoned that whatever came out of it – twenty quid a week for a few weeks not being the least of it – I was also garnering material for the crime column. I won every way you looked at it. I felt eager, like an old bloodhound with a fresh scent. I was even whistling as I typed.

With no boss around this morning, I could press on with a final draft of a piece I'd been working on about corruption in local politics: a seemingly bottomless cesspit. During his reign before the war, Chief Constable Sillitoe banged up so many city fathers for graft that he was warned by the government that if one more went down, they would disband the council and run it from Whitehall.

From my recent personal experience things hadn't improved, though two of the venal councillors had received a grislier come-uppance than a mere prison sentence. I was now exploring other fishy contracts awarded without public tender to the good cousin of the ways and means chairman.

By one o'clock I was walking past the bustling shops in Sauchiehall Street. I turned up on to Renfrew Street just so I could pass Mackintosh's School of Art. Not just for the fancy windows and portals. The girls at art college had always been more interesting than the bluestockings reading English. Bohemian Scots. Educated but wild at heart. A potent mix. Another climb up Thistle Street on to Hill Street and I was walking along the ridge of Garnethill.

Up here the criss-crossing streets were formed of the same grand red sandstone terraces, but, being perched on a hill, there was a brightness, an expansiveness to the place that was missing in the flatlands south of the Clyde. The folk themselves seemed less huddled, more prosperous. Maybe they were just fitter from clambering up and down hills all day.

I walked into the echoing stone close with its smell of carbolic soap and climbed two flights of spotless clean stairs. I had a choice of doors and peered at the name plates: Kennedy or Bernstein. Applying my great investigative powers I knocked on the latter. I heard bolts sliding. The door opened and I was looking down at a tiny man with watery eyes blinking through thick specs held together at the bridge by Elastoplast. He wore two cardigans, baggy trousers and slippers.

'Mr Bernstein? It's Douglas Brodie, sir. I'm working for Shimon Belsinger and his colleagues. Investigating the thefts. Shimon said he'd warn you.'

'*Ja, ja*. Come in, come in.'

He shuffled off down the narrow corridor of brown-painted walls. I followed, breathing used air mixed with cooking smells. We emerged into a sitting room. A massive three-piece suite hogged the floor. Lost among the cushions and antimacassars was a tiny woman. She wore a curly russet wig that belied her mottled and sagging skin. A much younger woman occupied one of the big chairs. A big-eyed child curled in her lap, thumb firmly jammed in her mouth.

The old man turned to me. 'This is my wife, Mrs Bernstein. My daughter, Ruth, and my grand-daughter, Lisa.' His voice softened when he mentioned the baby. His accent was thick and guttural with 'wife' coming out as a 'vife'. He spoke slowly to make sure he'd said it right.

I took a chance and replied in German. 'Good afternoon. I'm here to see if we can catch the thief.'

The old woman's head jerked up. The young woman smiled. The old man's shoulders dropped and he said,

'Belsinger told me you spoke German. But why do you have a München accent?'

I smiled. 'I practised with Isaac Feldman and his wife, Hannah – rest her soul – when I was studying at Glasgow University. It upset my tutors.'

Now the old woman broke in, using her native tongue, and I recognised the softer accent of Austria. 'They say you were an officer in the British Army. You saw it all.' The question was loaded with meaning: *You saw what they did to us . . .*

'After the surrender I was assigned to interrogate *Schutzstaffel* officers; senior SS camp commanders, doctors and Gestapo.'

Three pairs of adult eyes bored into me. I had brought horror into the room and they didn't know whether to examine it further through my memories or to banish it and me before it could swallow them up. The child sensed tension and burrowed into her mother's arms. This time it was the young woman who spoke, in English with a Glasgow lilt.

'Come on now, Mama, Papa, Mr Brodie is here to help. We don't want to hear war stories, do we? What do you want to ask us, Mr Brodie? Papa, let him sit. Where are our manners?'

I took out my notebook. 'Tell me what happened?'

Bernstein began, 'It is a short story. We go to *shul* on the Sabbath. The Garnethill Synagogue. Every week, same time.'

'Sometimes we go to my sister's first, Jacob.'

'Yes, yes, yes. But when we go straight there it's at the same time.'

'Except on Hanukkah or Passover of course. Then we—'

The old man flung up his arms and switched to German. '*Mein Gott*, Mrs Bernstein! *Usually*. That's all Mr Brodie wants to know. Usually. And when the theft took place, it was a usual Sabbath.'

'I was just saying. Explaining it right.'

Bernstein turned to me and gave me a look of complicity. *Women? What can you do?*

I took the baton. 'So, when was this?'

'The twelfth of October. I sold a fine little Austin the day before.'

'You're a car dealer?' He nodded. 'You all went? The house was left empty?'

'Ach, yes. But we locked up. Every window. Every door. Even the doors inside, you understand?'

'How long were you gone?'

The old woman said, 'We sometimes make it a nice day. After we walk down to Sauchiehall Street and maybe have some tea and cakes.'

The old man rolled his eyes. 'But not this day, Mrs Bernstein. Not that day. We just came home for *Seudah Shilishit*, the third meal.'

'I'm just saying. Sometimes—'

'But this day, we – came – home. Straight home. No diversion. It takes us ten minutes to walk there.'

'So you were gone . . .?'

'Two hours, maybe two and a half.'

'And what happened when you got home? What did you find?'

'A nightmare! That's what we found!' said Mrs Bernstein. 'Our lives thrown upside down, that's what happened. My jewels. My mother's jewels. My best china. Except these cups. They were a wedding present and I kept them in a box . . . All gone. And my earrings, my lovely earrings . . .' Her old eyes filled and she stumbled to a halt.

The old man walked over and sat beside his wife on the couch. He took her hand and rubbed it, shushing her all the time. I'd witnessed scenes like it a dozen times when I was a copper working out of Tobago Street in the thirties. It wasn't the cost of an item, or its value. It was their story, their connection with the living or dead. For these old people, who'd fled fascism and left so much behind, it was a further severing of ties.

I listened to their outrage and their hurt. I learned that a uniformed policeman had visited a few days later and taken a perfunctory statement but he'd never come back. They'd never been told what was happening.

'Mr Bernstein, did the burglar break in? Was there any sign of damage to the door?'

'Nothing. Not a mark. It was all locked up like I left it.'

'Who has keys?'

He looked at me as though I was daft. 'Only me. And of course Mrs Bernstein. You don't think I am careless with my keys?'

'Good. What about visitors in the past month or two?'

Mrs Bernstein chipped in, 'My sister Bella came round. Such a lovely daughter she has. But no man yet. She needs—'

'Mrs Bernstein!' said her husband. 'Mr Brodie wants to know who has been here. He doesn't want their personal history.'

'So – Mr Bernstein?' I asked.

'Apart from my good-sister Bella, no one.' He shook his head and his glasses gave up the ghost. They fell in two bits on to the carpet and there was confusion and exclamations until they were joined back together by fresh Elastoplast.

'Papa? There was a gas man, you told me.'

'Ach, what news is that?'

'When was this, Mr Bernstein? And why was he here?'

'Papa, it was before the burglary. About a week or so.'

'Mr Bernstein, did you let him in? How did you know he was a gas man?'

Old Bernstein's jaw jutted out. 'He had a board with a sheet of paper on it. He looked at the meter. Am I stupid?'

I left them, apologising as I did. Apologising explicitly for my old police comrades and for their cavalier attitude. Apologising implicitly for what had happened in Austria and across Germany and Poland and Russia without the West lifting a finger until it was too late. We'd hanged ten of the top Nazis at Nuremberg last month, but it hardly compensated for the hell they'd visited on millions.

THREE

I did two more interviews that afternoon, all within walking distance of each other and of the Garnethill synagogue. It seemed the gas board had been unusually solicitous lately. I was explaining my findings to Sam that evening.

'That's a pretty clear pattern, Douglas.'

'It's only three out of nine, and I don't want to draw conclusions, but . . .'

'See, you're a natural.'

'You mean I should ditch the reporting life and go back to sleuthing?'

She coloured. 'I wasn't trying to push you down one track or the other. It's your life.'

I paused and decided to use the opening. 'Would it make any difference to us if I did? I mean if I was earning more?'

Sam turned away. 'It's not that, not at all.'

'Then what is it, Sam? We could turn this house of sin into a happy family home.'

She rounded on me, her eyes glittering. 'House of sin, is it? That's the worst proposal I've ever had.'

'How many have you had lately?'

'As in *I'm an old spinster and I should grab the chance because it's likely to be my last*?'

Bugger. 'That's not what I meant!'

We were poised like boxers, waiting for the next blow. I took a deep breath.

'Samantha Campbell, I love you. I want to marry you. Why are you crying?'

'I'm not. Well, I am. You made me.'

'Tears of joy, then?'

'Shut up, Brodie.'

I stepped forward and held my arms open. She welded herself against me. Her heart hammered against my ribs. I could smell her hair. Her voice vibrated in my chest.

'We only met in April.'

'Long enough to know me.'

She pushed herself back and studied me.

'I'm not so sure.'

'We don't have to rush it. Just have the intent.'

'If I got married I'd have to give up my job. There are no married women in our chambers, not even secretaries.'

'And I couldn't support us both on my pittance. Hardly even the coal bill for this grand place.'

She turned away. 'It's not that. We'd manage. Somehow. But I worked so hard to get here. I don't want to give it all up. I promised myself and I promised my parents I'd get silk. Hah! The way I've been flapping around all year I'll be lucky to have a job by Christmas.'

'We could keep it quiet.'

'They'd find out. And I don't want a Gretna Green do, thank you very much!'

She was right. Neither did I. We were better than that. I hoped.

She wiped her eyes, poured us each a glass of whisky and we put the argument aside for another day.

The next day I spread my search to the south side, over Glasgow Bridge and into Laurieston. Into another world. Radiating out from the imposing synagogue in South Portland Street is a network of streets and courts studded with shops garlanded in Hebrew. Posters in Yiddish adorned spare walls, and distinctive hats and beards and long black coats stood out among the whey-faced natives. The smells were richly different; leavened bread and sugary cakes; barrels of herring standing outside for inspection. And everywhere a sense of bubbling life, language and accents competing and clashing in a joyous babel.

I called in on Isaac Feldmann's tailor's shop. I nodded to the ageless and familiar mannequins in his window and went inside, the bell heralding my entrance. Isaac stuck his head out from behind the curtain to the back room.

'Douglas. It's you. Welcome. Come have coffee. Meet my boy, Amos. See if you can talk some sense into him.'

'It's been a long time, Amos.' I shook the young man's hand. I'd last seen him as bright-eyed teenager before the war. This was a man coming into his prime. Tall, with an assured manner and his mother's great eyes behind the specs. I wondered what his younger sister Judith looked like now.

'He's a doctor, Douglas. A doctor in the family!'

'Congratulations!'

Amos flushed. 'Not yet, Father. Still two years to go, Mr Brodie. If I finish.' His voice was smart Scottish, the product of good schooling.

'Ach, listen to him. Of course you will finish. Your mother would turn in her grave.'

'That's not fair, Father. I have to make my own way.'

'And what is that? What nonsense are you telling me?'

I'd obviously come at a bad time. Amos sighed and explained to me: 'I'm thinking of going to Palestine. It's where we belong.'

So this was the family trouble Isaac had mentioned.

'Well, Amos, they certainly need doctors over there.'

Isaac picked up the thread. 'See! Douglas is right. It's a bloodbath over there! At least wait till it settles.'

'That could be years away, Dad! I want to be there at the start.'

I asked gently, 'How would you get in, Amos? We're blockading the ports.'

Palestine was a cauldron. Arabs and Jews competing for the same strip of desert, each claiming ancient rights. No give either side. All or nothing. And the poor bloody British Army stuck in the middle trying to keep the peace while the infant United Nations tried to find a solution. No sign of a Solomon. It seems I'd touched a nerve. Amos turned on me.

'Yes, you are! And it's shameful! After what our people went through!' He calmed himself. 'Mr Brodie, the ones that are left need a home. Israel is our home.'

'I can't argue with that. The world should die of shame for what the Nazis did. But it needs to be done by agreement. By law.'

His dark eyes blazed behind his glasses. 'Pah! My people were gassed and burnt in ovens waiting for the law. Laws don't apply to Jews. People do what they like to us. And we let it happen. Never again!'

I had only one argument. 'But, Amos, you're killing the peacekeepers. Are you going to join one of the gangs? Take up a Tommy gun? What about your family?' I knew he had a wife and young daughter.

'Go on, answer Douglas! You'll join Lehi. Become a murderer. Is that what we raised you for?' Isaac was on his feet, stabbing a finger at his son.

It summed it up. The disputatious peoples of the Middle East had fought for centuries over which strand of monotheism was best. Fought each other; fought themselves. Within the Jewish tribe, the latest argument was about Zionism – the creation of a Jewish State – and how to achieve it. While we were at war against Nazism, the Middle East was having its own convulsions. And now it threatened to be the new battleground for the world.

'Never Lehi! They supported the Nazis, Father.'

'So which is it to be? The gentle souls in Haganah? How

about the peaceful Irgun Zvai Leumi? Or the angels in Palmach?'

Isaac was ticking off on his fingers the amoeba-like factions spawning terrorism across Palestine and now shipping it to Britain. They'd captured a member of Lehi – we called them the Stern Gang after their dead founder – in Glasgow last week. God knows what he was up to. They'd bombed our embassy in Rome last month.

'Stop, stop! I know you think I'm mad. Well, I'm not. I'm just angry, Father. Don't I have a right?'

Isaac let his arm drop. His face collapsed. I thought he was going to weep.

'Amos, no one is angrier than me. I just don't want to lose you.'

I left Isaac and his son embracing in tearful reconciliation, but I didn't think it was the end of this debate. In the meantime, however, I had a much simpler Jewish puzzle to solve.

FOUR

By Wednesday night I'd interviewed all the robbery victims. I had a clear enough picture of the crimes and I was rehearsing my findings with Sam before explaining to Shimon Belsinger and his pals.

'The thief was picky. He followed public displays of wealth.'

'Folk flaunting it?'

'Not necessarily. But deducing who might have money. Car dealers, shop owners. Businessmen. Professional classes.'

'But that could apply to non-Jews.'

'The timing helped. He would know they'd all be at prayer.'

'But again, why not Protestants or Catholic businessmen on a Sunday morning?'

'Sundays are dead. A thief would be more obvious. Whereas . . .'

'The Saturday Sabbath . . .'

'Then there's the refugee aspect. The Jews fled here with all the jewellery and gold they could carry.'

Sam was nodding. 'Adds up. How did he do it? Shimon said there was no sign of break-ins.'

'Each theft was preceded by a visit from the gas board. Or rather someone pretending. Everybody opens the door for the gasman. He'd have been able to confirm there was stuff worth nicking. He'd establish the layout for the raids, and probably took impressions of the keys. I looked at some of the keys; they felt waxy.'

'You've cracked it, Douglas! All you need is a name.'

'I'm going to follow the loot. Unless the thief is stockpiling his personal treasure cave with trinkets to admire, he'd have to fence the stolen goods. Anywhere in Glasgow – other than Hyndland and Bearsden – you'll find pawnshops and small jewellers.'

'That's your next step?'

I nodded. 'But I'll need help. Seven years ago I knew every fence in the East End and the Gorbals. Some of them might still be in business. But looking round Laurieston today, the pawnshop business has being doing a roaring trade. New shops on almost every street. And Garnethill was never my patch so I have no contacts there.'

'So?'

'It's time I bought Duncan Todd a drink – or three.'

'How will he take finding out you've become a gumshoe?'

'Not well.'

I got into the newsroom early next morning. I went over to the empty secretary desks, picked up a phone and dialled Central Division. Finally, I got put through to Detective *Inspector* Todd, Duncan having been bumped up a month ago after endless years as a sergeant, on the strength of his showing during the recent crime wave. I took some small pleasure and pride in having a hand in his long-overdue recognition.

'*You're* in bright and early, Duncan. Trying to impress folk now you've scaled the heights?'

There was a sigh. 'Brodie, if Ah could go back to my wee quiet corner here, nobody minding what Ah did, nobody caring if Ah lived or died, Ah would. Like a shot.'

'Away! You're loving it. And the money's handy, is it no'?'

'There's that. But Sangster's running me ragged. He still thinks you put one over on him, and that Ah helped. But he can't quite see how. It's festering in his wee brain. Ah expect

to see pus oozing oot his lugs just before his brain explodes wi'
all that pent-up confusion.'

'I want a ringside seat for that. In the meantime, can I buy
you a beer the night?'

'Thought you'd never ask. Ah need to get Sangster aff ma
chest. Someone who'll no' clype back to him. See you at
McCall's. Six on the dot.'

I was hanging about waiting for the doors to open. I got in
the first double whiskies and a brace of supporting pints.
Duncan must have been waiting round the corner. A minute
after I sat down he was immersing himself in strong liquor. I
got to the point:

'Dunc, amidst all your arduous duties cleaning up after
your boss, have you been involved in any of these thefts
among the Jews in Garnethill and South Portland Street?'

He licked his lips and sighed as the Scotch went down. 'Not
me, Brodie, but Ah heard about some goings-on.'

'There's been nine burglaries in a month. Why's no one
doing anything about it?'

'Ah assume that's a rhetorical?'

'As in, *because they're Jews*?'

'Christ, Brodie, Ah hope you're no' gonna quote me? Ah've
only just got used to being ca'd Inspector. It could be a gie
short promotion.'

'No names. No pack drill. Besides, this isn't for an article.
I've been asked if I can help. You know, take a wee peek.'

'Oh, God. Is this you with your Sherlock hat on again? Can
ye no' just leave things alone, or just write aboot them? Ye
know it only brings trouble.'

'You're wrong, Dunc. The trouble's already there. I just lift
the stone.'

'Aye, and then you poke away at what's beneath.
Disturbing bugs, snakes, toads. Could ye no' have taken the
Chief Constable's offer and done it legit? We need a' the good

cops we can in this talent-free backwater. Some of the guys Ah work wi' make Sangster look like Lord Peter Wimsey.'

'It's a one-off, Dunc. Not a career move.'

He looked at me sceptically. 'Oh aye?'

'And I'm not competing. Just sharing your burden.'

'Ah'm all for that. As long as you don't steal my job. So what do you want?'

'The amount that's been nicked could start a new jeweller's. The stuff must be going through somebody. Who's the likely fence?'

'Unless it's gone south, of course.'

'England? London? Sure. But unless things have changed, when it comes to dumping hot goods Glasgow's average criminal mastermind tends to stray no further than the city limits. Debts to be paid. Drinks to be drunk. Women to be wooed. Instant gratification.'

'For that sort of priceless information, it must be your round, Brodie.'

'Again?'

That evening the first real gales of winter hit. Just to remind us of our fragile grip on the Earth's surface, furious seas smashed the coasts and drove ships aground. Hurricane winds whipped off roofs, flattened garden sheds, felled trees and sent old ladies' shopping flying down the street in a whirlwind of spilled spuds and soggy brown pokes. Sam used the storm as an excuse to seek refuge in my arms that night. More gales, please.

Afterwards I was falling into a sweet sleep when she touched my shoulder.

'Douglas? Are you awake?'

'I am now.' Women have a special sense of timing with their wee chats: when we're at our most vulnerable.

'Two things I meant to mention. This place is like a tip. I used to have a housekeeper but she went up home –

Tomintoul – to look after her mother. She's back now. Her mum died. And she's starting here again. Three days a week.'

'That's nice.'

'She'll iron your shirts too.'

'Very nice.'

'Only a pound a week. Is that OK? Ten bob each?'

'I'll cut back on the caviar. What's the second thing?'

She was silent for a long moment. That got me worried.

'I had call from an old friend of mine. Iain Scrymgeour. He's a lawyer working for Shawcross.'

'Hartley Shawcross? In the Nuremberg trials?'

'Iain and I were intrants at the Faculty of Advocates at the same time. Farquharson Stable. Same as me. Iain was a high-flyer. Wants to be an MP eventually.'

'He thinks Nuremberg will make his name?'

'It's Hamburg now. The first of the Ravensbrück trials. In the British sector. High-profile and on the side of the avenging angels. It will look good on his CV when he stands for parliament. We've kept in touch.'

'That's nice.' I immediately disliked this bloke.

'Are you really listening?'

I'd turned over on to my back and reached for my cigarettes when the reference to Ravensbrück came up. I lit one and we passed it between us.

'Shoot.'

'He wants me to help him.'

'Do some research?'

'Prosecute. Out there.'

'In Hamburg? At the war crimes trials? Are you serious?' I was wide awake now and it wasn't the nicotine. Memories were flooding back.

'The first trial starts on the fifth of December. He's run off his feet. He's already asked for help from our chambers. I don't know if he suggested me or they offered me.'

'Can you say no?'

'Not really. You know my chambers have been nagging at me to go back to Edinburgh. I've had a rotten year and they want to bring me back under their wing.'

'I thought you were all self-employed? Why do they care?'

'If I'm not doing well, I don't get new briefs. It's a downward spiral. And they don't like having low-earners on the team. Bad for the stable's reputation.'

'How does that fit with Hamburg?'

'It's a solid slab of work with guaranteed fees from the government.'

'Not a punishment?'

'More a test. I'll be on the other side.'

'Prosecuting war crimes? God, I hope it's not a growth business.'

Long after she had fallen asleep, I lay trying *not* to remember my own post-war confrontation with madness and depravity. Interrogating murderers and seeing them tried. Samantha Campbell was tough, but this might test her to the limits.

FIVE

She was up and away first thing so we didn't discuss it further. I headed into work just in time to take a call from Duncan. He had the names and addresses of three slippery entrepreneurs known to be actively passing parcels in central Glasgow. One was a major pawnbroker, and the second the proud owner of a pair of jewellery stores. It meant that in both cases they could nicely combine the brokerage of hot goods with the retail. They made a turn buying and selling. The third fence tripled his chance of facing awkward questions at the Pearly Gates by fronting the fencing with an illegal bookmaking business and arranging dog fights.

Duncan explained about the third man: 'Sanny Carmichael thinks there's safety in numbers. That he's running so many crooked scams the polis will get confused and give up. He's no' far wrong. And he's got a wee arrangement with the local station that gets him a phone call to warn him he's being raided.'

I knew Sanny. 'It's only polite, Duncan. Otherwise they'd get accused of being unfair to hard-working criminals.'

I'd had a run-in with Carmichael before the war when we raided one of his unlicensed bookies. He was operating it from a pair of ground-floor tenements in the Calton. I decided to start with him.

The rain had stopped and the winds had died down by the time I set out from the *Gazette*. But the water was still puddling the streets and flushing the gutters. I'd checked with the *Gazette*'s sports editor. There was a big meet at Ayr over the weekend. Carmichael would have set up shop in one of his known haunts around the Trongate.

It didn't take me long to pick out a couple of spotters, doing sentry duty on opposite corners of a busy street of tall tenements above shops. The spotters were the least casual street-corner smokers I'd seen. They twitched and paced. Their heads were on swivels and their caps were pulled down. I could either be furtive myself and wait to see which shop or close was being used and run the risk of kicking off a panic when I was spotted. Or I could go straight at them, hoping I looked less like a cop than I used to. I tucked the newspaper under my arm, racing page on display, and nonchalantly approached the nearest. I could feel his eyes running up and down over me and then sweeping beyond me to see if I had back-up. Cops on a raid never arrived solo. He took the fag from his mouth as I got close. I took out my own packet and walked up to him, waving a fag as I got close.

'Got a light, pal?'

'Aye, sure. Here you go.' He held out his red-tipped cigarette to light my own. As I puffed mine alight from his ember, I said quietly, 'I've got a sure thing in the three thirty.'

'They a' say that. An' maistly they're wrang. But it's your dosh. Nummer twelve, the grocer's shop. In the back. Don't hing aboot.'

'Thanks, pal.'

The only gamble I was about to take was whether Sanny was still personally involved at the makeshift bookies. I needed his expertise and street knowhow. Duncan had told me that though he was getting long in the tooth he was still very much a hands-on crook. He liked to keep a close eye on his wealth and how it was accruing. I was also gambling that I wouldn't get my head kicked in when I started asking him questions.

As I walked towards the grocer's I saw men like me entering and leaving. They left with lighter wallets but without evidence of purchase: no string bags of spuds and carrots. I pulled the door open and walked in. A man in a suit stood admiring the tinned goods and keeping an eye on the door. He saw my paper and nodded me through a door by the counter.

It was a bare room with a wooden table and a few chairs. A wireless whined off-tune in the background. On one wall a number of newspaper pages were tacked up displaying today's fixtures at Ayr. Four punters in caps and coats stood squinting at the form guides, the odds and the conditions, as though they had relevance. They sucked pencils and scribbled on their own newspapers or fag packets, doing mental arithmetic to ensure they were picking winners. They might as well have been examining chicken entrails.

But what interested me most was the group of three men round the table. Each wore a coat and a bunnet. Each was smoking. Two bruisers were pretending to read the paper. I knew it was pretence. Their lips weren't moving. Old Sanny sat in the middle staring at the punters through red, darting eyes. A big leather bag was perched in the front of him. The clockbag. Just as I stepped in, one of the four men analysing form stepped forward to the table.

'Florin each way, Constant Dreamer, two thirty.'

Sanny pulled a little pad forward, scribbled the details and tore off the slip. He removed the carbon and tucked it into the next pairing. Then he handed the top copy to the punter and thrust the carbon into the compartment on the clockbag for that race. He dropped the two coins into the open bag. Later, when the race was 'off', the clock would be locked. It was supposed to give the punters confidence, but mostly it was to stop the bookie's runners from making a little side money by taking a later bet – perfect forecasting – from a pal.

Throughout, the old man's eyes flicked his gaze between the bag, the punter and me. When the punter stepped away, I was left staring into Sanny Carmichael's face. He raised an eyebrow.

'Ah heard you wuz back, Brodie. Kicking up trouble.' His voice was a rasp going over wood, his face a lump of pumice, grey and pitted.

'I don't go looking for it. How's it going, Sanny?'

'No' bad. Have you had a hot tip then? Want a few bob on the nose? I could make you good odds. Old times' sake.'

'I'd like a word, Sanny. Some friends of mine have been turned over.'

'Oh aye? An' who might these pals be?'

'Let's put it this way: they're from the Garnethill area.'

Sanny studied me for a while; then he looked either side at his cronies who'd long since put their papers down. 'So these are *Sheeney* pals, ur they? Fuck's sake, Brodie, have ye lost the end of yer willie? Shot off by the Boche?'

His pals sniggered at his great humour. Sanny stared at me, waiting for me to dig a bigger hole for myself.

'Everything's intact, Sanny, thanks for asking. But yes, the leaders of the Jewish community are my pals. Do you have a problem with that? I'm helping them run down a thief.'

'An' what makes you think I'd know anything aboot thievery? A man could take offence.'

At the word, his guard dogs perked up, as though Sanny had said 'rabbits'. Their juices were running at the thought of some action. Preferably some violent action.

'A man who wants no trouble in his life wouldn't dream of giving offence. I just want a word.'

Carmichael's brain whirred for a while; then he turned to his men. 'Mind the bag. Let's take a wee donner, Brodie. I could do wi' some air.'

We walked out into the street. Sanny seemed to have got shorter. He was barely up to my shoulder. The cold air rushed at us and he pulled his coat tight.

'First right, Brodie.'

We walked past his corner scout, who looked at us askance, querying what his boss was up to. We turned round the corner and into a quiet side street. Carmichael walked purposefully along the road and pushed into a crumbling café. A warm fug of smoke, hot fat and sweaty clothes wrapped itself around us like a sticky blanket. There were six tables. We had a choice of six. Carmichael steered towards the one farthest from the window and door. A swarthy man in a manky pinny nodded at Carmichael and inspected me.

'Twa teas, Bertie. The big yin's paying,' said Sanny as he took a seat. Two mugs of tea materialised, hot and grey, like thin kaolin. Carmichael filled his with sugar.

'Now, whit's goin' on, Brodie?'

I told him about the nine thefts and the cocky gasman. Carmichael stirred his tea throughout the explanation. I kept waiting for his spoon to come to a halt in the syrup.

'. . . and your name came up, Sanny, as someone who might be aware of – shall we say the *flow* of goods?'

'Is that a fact? And who gave you ma name, might I ask?'

'Inspector Duncan Todd.'

'I ken Todd. So he finally made inspector? No' a bad lad. A left-fitter, mind. And he's wrang aboot this. But, haud on, Brodie. Why the fuck should Ah tell yous anything?'

'For a quiet life, Sanny. Todd needs to meet his quotas. New inspector? You know how it is. I talked him out of raiding your very well-known set-up here on the strength of you giving us a wee nod in the right direction. It would be seen to be a help, Sanny. And you could be left in peace.'

He sat back and chewed his tea for a while. 'That's a kind o' blackmail, Brodie.'

'Between friends? It's more a kind of *you help me, I help you*.'

He leaned forward. 'Once a cop, always a bloody cop.' I waited. Sanny drummed on the table with his fingers. 'Ah've heard McGill's got some new stock in.' There was a hiss from my cup. He got up and walked out, leaving his fag floating in my tea.

I had a name. Interestingly it was one of the other names Duncan had given me. Whether it was the right name or not, I'd aim to find out on Monday.

SIX

Over the weekend Sam and I began tidying up the house in advance of the first inspection by our new housekeeper.

'I'd be ashamed to let Izzie Dunlop see this place. The state of it.'

'Isn't that the point?'

'Just carry the hoover upstairs, Douglas, and don't be difficult.'

The rest of the time we spent dodging questions about Sam's impending assignment in Hamburg. I could tell she was both anxious and excited by the challenge. I didn't want to terrify her by recounting my own experiences. She didn't want to talk about it in case it turned out as horrible as she expected.

On Monday morning I set out for McGill's. The pawnbroker is an essential part of Glasgow life. He oils the machine that permits the working man – or more often, the non-working man – to live from one week to the next in the absence of five bob for food or a shilling for the electric. He's the bridge that connects one slim pay packet with the next, when an unsuccessful flutter on the dogs or a successful session on a Saturday night in the Drouthy Drover has left a mortal dent in the readies.

As often as not it's the woman that wears out the path between her home and the sign of the three balls. The man

34

has a sure bet or loses his job, and his wife has to do some conjuring to make half a crown stretch two days. No wonder old women used to get branded witches; their financial legerdemain was simply magic. Off she'd trot on a Tuesday with some gewgaw of value only to her heart. For a ten-bob loan she'd exchange the worn gilt wedding ring or the treasured marcasite earrings handed down from her mother. It would put warm oats in a child's belly and coal in a fire. It would buy a piece of leather to mend a hole in her only shoes, and still let her pay the insurance man threepence a week to make sure she didn't get buried by the council.

Then the heat was on to make sure her feckless man didn't drink away the next pay packet or lend it to a pal who had a 'sure thing' at Doncaster. It would send her on Friday night, shawl about her head, to the gates of Dixon's Blazes or John Brown's, a wee rock splitting the flood of men launched homeward by the whistle, searching her man out among the thousand cloth caps and picking his pocket before the bookie did it for him. The wedding ring would be back on her finger on Monday. Till the next crisis.

McGill's had a prime corner position on Bath Street. It made no pretence about its purpose. It was, in many ways, a social necessity, a lifeline. I stood across the street peering through the dirty windows at lines of shelves displaying the mementoes of a thousand lives. Some of the treasures would have been there for years, surety on a loan that was never repaid, of a broken life that never quite got mended. Symbols of little failures, burst dreams and ruptured marriages. Eventually, each discarded piece would become the property of McGill's and be made available for sale. The perfect place to launder stolen property.

I took out the list again and ran my eye down the most distinguishable stolen items. Anything with gold or diamonds would likely stand out among the bric-a-brac of the average pile of Glasgow collateral. Even so, I knew it could be like looking for a teetotaller in a crowd at Hampden. Yet it was all I had.

I crossed over and pushed in the door. Bells tinkled in the back. I looked around. This was no rainbow's end. The smell of must clogged the nostrils. There was hardly a bare surface in sight. The floors were littered with piles of chairs, nests of table and brass coal scuttles. A man popped out from behind a curtain. It wasn't Aladdin. For one thing he wore pince-nez, for another he wore a cardigan with leather patches on the elbows. He peered at me. I guess I didn't look like your average borrower.

'Are ye after something, mister?'

'I might be. Can I just look around?'

'Aye, sure. Help yersel'. But if ye brek onything, it's yours an' ye'll huv to pay for it.'

'Fair enough.' I started to walk round the shelves, trying not to kick the lamps and odd golf clubs littering the floor. Most of the stuff was junk, much of it coated in a skin of dust, abandoned long since by the owners. Nothing of real value. Nothing that remotely fitted the description of any of the stolen valuables. There was one glass case, almost opaque with dust and dirt, but it held little of interest. The contents had lain undisturbed since Kilmarnock last won a Scottish Cup Final: '29, as I recall. I consoled myself by asking why I thought I'd strike lucky first time. The city was full of shops like this, and anyway, the stolen goods would be long gone.

'Mr McGill?'

'Aye?'

'Is this all you have? I was hoping to find a wee bit of jewellery. Something nice, for the wife. It's her birthday just before Christmas.'

He stared me up and down. I was wearing one of Sam's father's old suits, altered to fit by Isaac Feldmann. The cloth was good wool and better made than anything from Burton's. My broad Ayrshire accent had been softened by my spell among the petite bourgeoisie of Glasgow University and commanding a company of lilting Highlanders. In my bearing there was the legacy of my police training. Obviously.

'Yer no' polis, are ye?'

'Not at all. I've been south for a while. Army.' As if that explained anything. But it seemed to satisfy him.

'I've got some stuff roon the back. Gie's a minute.'

He went through his curtain and appeared a minute later carrying a large wooden box. He laid it on the counter and made a performance of opening the lid. A piece of dark blue velvet lay over a collection of bumps. He took out the velvet and smoothed it on the counter. My eyes fell on the uncovered contents. The box was lined with ridges in the same blue velvet. Carefully seated on the ridges were glowing items of precious metals and stones: garnets and rubies, silver and gold, marcasite and pearls. And ivory.

I gazed in. 'That's more like it.'

'Aye. This is ma best stuff, so it is.'

'Had them long?' I began sifting through the items trying to keep the interest out of my voice.

'Varies. Some just come in. Others a wee while. Ah only show this to *discerning* customers.'

I began picking out items and setting them on the velvet cloth. One by one I ticked off mentally the list in my pocket: the ivory wolf with diamond eyes; the ruby ring in its baroque gold setting; the hat pin with the massive amethyst head. The cufflinks of silver and ivory inset with a silver Star of David. The dangling earrings with perfect matching pearls. Old Mrs Bernstein would be pleased.

I was aware that with each item I brought out, the man behind the counter was becoming increasingly still and silent. I looked up at McGill. The pince-nez weren't the only reason

37

for his eyes being wide. His mouth was gawping. He wiped the back of his hand over his lips.

'When did you get these, Mr McGill?'

I saw him swallow, twice. 'Ah've hud them a while, so Ah huv.'

'No you haven't. When did you get them in? And who brought them?'

'Look, pal, it's a' legit. Ah just bought the lot the other day. Ah can do you a guid price.'

'Could you? How about a farthing for the lot? And then I can return them to their owners and you can hand yourself in to Albany Street. Ask for Detective Inspector Todd.'

McGill all but collapsed. He reeled back and grabbed the counter.

'Ah thocht you werenae polis?'

'I'm not. But I used to be. Now I'm a reporter for the *Gazette*. Your wee shop could maybe do with some publicity?'

'Aw no. Gie's a brek, mister. Ah don't ask questions when stuff comes here. Ah jist take it on trust. Ah mean it's no as if the folk coming by have receipts or nothin', is it?'

'A name.'

'What?'

'Give me a name. Who brought these in? Tell me a name and I will take these, and give you a receipt.'

The glasses were off now. He was rubbing his eyes like a kid. I hoped he wouldn't greet.

'Ah cannae, Ah jist cannae. The fella'll kill me, so he will. He's a baddie, right enough. Ma life will no' be worth a sugar moose.'

I sighed and carefully rolled up the booty in the velvet cloth. It was an expensive tube. 'Well, I'm taking these back to their owners anyway. I'll give Inspector Todd a call and he'll come and get you. Oh, and I'll make sure I send you a copy of the newspaper tomorrow to Turnbull Street. You'll love what I say about you.'

I turned and walked towards the door.

'Wait! Wait a minute! Christ! For Christ's sake, pal. You're gonnae get me killed!'

I shrugged.

He lurched forward over the counter. 'OK. OK! Ah'll tell ye.'

SEVEN

'**D**uncan? It's Brodie. I've got a name for you.' I was calling from the phone in Sam's house. She wasn't home yet.

'How about Inspector?'

'The name of the thief. I talked to one of your fences, Sanny Carmichael, who clyped on one of his business rivals: McGill the pawnbroker. I encouraged McGill to whisper in my ear. Oh, and I retrieved some of the stolen goods. Unless you have any objection I'm just going to hand them back to the owners.'

'Fine by me. Saves paperwork. We never took much interest in their departure in the first place. But we might need the bits and pieces as evidence to lock up the thief. Hang on to them for a couple of days, would you? You say McGill gave you a name? Ah hope you didnae hurt him too much?'

'Duncan, you know I was never one of the *beat them till they confess* brigade. I used moral persuasion. That and threatening to unleash you on him. And maybe a wee column about his dodgy emporium in the *Gazette*.'

'You might as well have hit him. So, the name?'

'Craven.'

'*Paddy* Craven?'

'The very man. I never ran across him in my day, but I recall the reputation. McGill says that as well as being a thief he's a hard man.'

'That's Paddy all right. An all-round villain and complete bampot. Only finished a seven-year stretch about six months ago. A wife and three kids who've seen little enough of him in the past twenty years. Ah thought he was trying to mend his ways. Got a job, Ah heard.'

'It wouldn't be with the gas board, would it?'

'Could be, now you mention it. Why?'

I told him about some of the burglaries.

'God help us. That's the kinda ballsy thing Paddy would get up to.'

'Do you know where to lift him?'

'Might as well start at his hoose. Lizzie will be delighted to see me again.'

'Lizzie, the wife?'

'Common law. But aye. Shame. Used to be a nice lassie. But concerning Paddy . . . will McGill testify?'

'He was near greetin' at the idea that Craven might find out.'

'Ah'm no' surprised. Craven disnae gie a toss about who gets hurt. And somebody always gets hurt wi' Craven around.'

'Sounds like you're going to struggle to get cooperation.'

'Either he helps or he goes inside with Craven.'

'That should encourage him.'

'Does that mean you're off the case? Crime solved? The Glasgow police force is no longer redundant?'

'Break out the streamers.'

'Easy money, Brodie. You could be tempted again.'

'I'm hanging up my badge. And my spurs. Quit while I'm ahead. Pity, the pay's good.'

Sam and I were sipping celebratory whiskies in the kitchen while she donned an apron and attacked two slivers of rationed chicken. I wielded a knife on the tatties and carrots. A scene of domestic bliss. I smiled. It felt good. I'd succeeded in this new role, I had money in my pocket, and Sam and I had settled into an easier relationship than I'd thought possible a month or two ago. Scratchy friends; sporadic lovers; marriage a distant prospect if at all. Perhaps a bit too random for my tastes, but overall a delicate confection of shared needs and common views – on most things.

Just a pity Hamburg was looming large. The dread of it was mounting in me, almost as if I were going. She'd been sent travel documents and was due to fly out on Thursday, ready for the start of trial a week later on 5 December. She was to be back for Christmas and then go out again until February. We were talking about anything else but her trip.

'You should have stretched it out a bit, Brodie. Made it look harder.'

'There's a bonus coming, so I can't grumble. And maybe they'll give me a call if they need help in future. Find the lost ark. That sort of thing.'

'Did it give you a taste for it?' she asked casually.

'For sleuthing? It hardly seemed like a proper job. It all fell in my lap. It's not usually that simple.'

'Maybe you've got better at it.'

'Nah. Just a fluke.'

But her question had coincided with my own thoughts. Was it just like old times? No. I had to answer to nobody, except the men who'd employed me. Was that better or worse than acting within a police hierarchy for the general public good? Oftentimes when I had been out playing detective properly, it had seemed like I was battling my bosses more than the criminals. This part-time, private work was free of such restrictions. No politics. No paperwork.

The downside was that I had no formal authority to act. Unlike England, there was no provision in Scots law for carrying out a citizen's arrest unless it was to help a policeman needing assistance mid-collar. The only authority I had was my personal one. I'd been finding lately that knowing what you're doing, or where you're going – or giving the impression of it – carries people along with you. Most folk are a bag of uncertainties. They're ready to follow someone with an idea; even a bonkers one. Take Adolf.

I had no plans to start a mass movement in the beer halls of Glasgow. My rhetoric would have made no dent on the practised nonchalance of the average bar fly. *Is that right, pal? If you say so. Now what about that new centre forward for Motherwell* . . .

I was happy to be the founder and only member of my gang. But I was just beginning to understand that fourteen years of higher education, police training and being a commissioned officer in the army had given me a certain weight and authority in my dealings with my fellow man. Especially the bad men, where the moral choices were clear-cut and the consequent actions obvious.

'I can hear you thinking, Brodie,' Sam said. She pushed aside a strand of blonde hair with the back of her hand and tumbled my hacked vegetables into the stew pot.

'I was thinking that it's not a bad life at times.' I grinned. She smiled back at me. I walked over and put my arms round her.

'Get off, you big oaf. I'm cooking.' But I could tell she didn't mean it. So I kissed her. Maybe tonight the moon would turn blue again.

The next day, I was well into writing up a version of events surrounding the catching of a thief when I was summoned across the newsroom to take a phone call. It put an end to yesterday's brief moment in the sun. No wonder we Scots are natural pessimists.

'Brodie, it's Duncan.'

'Perfect timing. I'm just finishing my article. Have you caught Paddy Craven?'

'Catching's no exactly the right word. We *found* Craven.'

My stomach lurched. 'OK, Duncan, I'm sitting down.'

'He burgled one house too many this morning.'

'Fell off his ladder?'

'Knifed by the man whose house he broke into.'

'Shit.'

'Shit, indeed.'

'I suppose it's an occupational hazard.'

'You might say that. It's a mess round there.'

'A fight?'

'Not exactly. More like an accident wi' a mincing machine. The owner got a bit carried away. Says he went off to work but returned home because he forgot something. Disturbed Craven in the act. The man says he was terrified. Not as terrified as Paddy Craven must have been when he got a carving knife in his belly.'

'Carried away?'

'Six stab wounds, then kicked Paddy's teeth in. Or maybe the other way about.'

'Good God! Who was this bloke? Sweeney Todd?'

'One of yer Jewish fraternity. Maybe they've stopped turning the other cheek.'

'Are you charging him?'

'With what? He finds a burglar in his own hoose and he defends himself.'

'Six times?'

'Anyway, that's the end of that. Rough justice. Rougher for Craven's wife and weans, even if he was an old rogue.'

'For the record, who was this knifeman?'

'Victor Galdakis.'

'Polish Jew?'

'Lithuanian, he says. At least Ah think that's what he said. English bad. Scots even worse. Runs a couple of stalls in Barrowland, he says.'

'What about our pawnbroker pal, McGill? Are you going to bring him in?'

'No point. He's mair use to me where he is. Ah know how to get hold of him. Besides, Ah might need a wee borrow . . .'

I put the phone down and walked back to my desk. I was breathing fast, as though I'd done forty press-ups. My forehead was wet. I opened the window to let chill air in. It was as if Duncan's news had set something off. Maybe I was getting squeamish in my old age.

I called Shimon Belsinger and arranged to see him and tell him how conclusively the case had been closed. One week, from start to finish, perpetrator found, justice meted out, payment on result.

Late morning we met in a café on the Byres Road. Shimon hunched over a milky tea, listening intently, stroking his great beard.

'You've done well, Brodie. My colleagues will be pleased.' He reached inside his overcoat and pulled out an envelope. 'This is your fee and your bonus.' He smiled. 'You should have taken your time. Earned a bit more.'

'Miss Campbell made the same point. But that's how it goes at times.'

'This man. The Jew who killed the thief. Do you know his name? Is he at Garnethill?'

'Galdakis, Victor Galdakis. DI Todd says he's Lithuanian. He has a flat in the Gorbals. So maybe he goes to Isaac's synagogue.'

'His business?'

'Stallholder. That's all I know.'

'We should find him. We should thank him.'

'I suppose so.' It seemed a wee bit tasteless to applaud a frenzied killing, but I understood the broad sentiment.

'Dr Tomas will know him. Tomas studied at Vilnius. He knows all the Lithuanian Jews. The ones that made it here.'

'Just warn Tomas not to creep up on him.'

EIGHT

In the afternoon I went back to the day job with plenty of material. This would please Sandy Logan, my temporary editor standing in for the injured Big Eddie Paton.

Eddie was out of hospital now and convalescing at home, but when I'd visited him last week I'd found him threatening a part-time return. It was a remarkable turnaround. I'd doubted we'd ever see him back. He'd lost several stone in weight and, with it, his bounce. And nom de plume: *Wee* Eddie from now on, bless his ink-stained heart.

I felt irrationally guilty; the self-styled Glasgow Marshals had been after me that day, back in September. The Marshals were a wild gang of vigilantes recruited from the ranks of jobless and homeless demobbed soldiers. Fizzing with a sense of injustice, they'd been framed for several vile murders and thought I held the key to proving their innocence. But I'd been elsewhere the day they stormed the newsroom and took it out on Eddie Paton's poor wee head.

Ever since, I'd done my best to support Sandy and Eddie by cranking out a decent crime column every edition. All the time in the absence of my mentor, the doyen of crime journalism, Wullie McAllister. Wullie was another casualty of the summer of madness; he'd got too close to the wicked creatures who'd committed the murders and framed the Marshals. He'd been abducted and beaten to within an inch of his life and lay, mouldering and vacant, in the Erskine convalescent home.

It had been a torrid summer, right enough.

At my desk I bashed out an article on the violent death of a thief. At breakfast tables all over Glasgow, it would raise a chorus of sanctimonious variations on *that's what ye get for* . . . It might take their minds off the front page about the Jewish refugee ship *Lochita* off the coast of Palestine. I wondered if Isaac and his son had come to verbal blows over it. Some four thousand rioting illegal immigrants had set upon our poor bloody soldiers, and one of our boys had died. How would the War Office explain that to his mum?

I slid carbon copies into Sandy Logan's hands. A short while later he wandered over to drape his long limbs over the filing cabinet by my desk and peer down at me. He took his pipe out of his mouth and pointed at my draft.

'A thoughtful piece, Brodie. Even-handed. One might say equivocal.'

I nodded. 'I hoped our readers would be similarly torn. But I doubt it. It seemed harsh punishment for nicking some trinkets.'

'The ultimate price. I think this needs a follow-up.'

'How?'

'Go and interview the man, this Lithuanian. Bring us remorse, rage, sorrow, pride . . . bring us *emotion*, Brodie. We'll run this tomorrow and say there'll be a second piece on Thursday. Human interest.'

'I'll drop by on my way in tomorrow, Sandy. Catch Mr Galdakis before he leaves for work.'

Come Wednesday, I wrapped my coat round me, pulled down my hat and set off into driving rain. Last week's gales were heralds. We were in that suicidal period between autumn and full winter when the Westerlies just sweep over Glasgow each day and dump the Atlantic on us. Galdakis lived on Bedford Street, south of the river. I would have hailed a taxi but Sandy said the paper was economising. I found a tram to get over Glasgow Bridge and then trudged through the puddles across Laurieston. I was curious to meet a man so handy with a knife. I also had one niggling thought that kept cropping up: why was Galdakis robbed in the week, and not on the Sabbath like all the rest?

Early morning and the broad streets were cleansed of people. Some sheltered under shop awnings in the forlorn hope of the rain easing off for just five minutes. The house I was looking for was above a haberdashery. I found the door and walked into the dank entry, shaking the rain off like a terrier. Galdakis was on the first floor. I left wet footprints and a trail of drips all the way up the stairs. I took off my hat, bashed it against my coat, put it back on and rapped on his door. It took a couple of knocks before I heard movement. The door edged open. A thickset face peered at me, the eyes wary and on a level with mine.

'Mr Galdakis?'

'Police? I seen police.'

I took a gamble. 'I work with Inspector Todd.' Which was almost true.

The eyes kept flicking at me and behind me. 'What you want?'

'A few more questions, please. Just five minutes.'

The door swung open and he stood back to let me in, framed in the open door of the room he'd just left. I caught a glimpse of tossed bedding. He wore a stained singlet and trousers. His belly bulged above and below a broad leather belt. Ahead was a short dingy corridor leading to a closed door. 'Go in front,' he said. I stepped past him, my nostrils twitching at the heavy smell of sweat and boozy breath. He followed me. I felt my shoulders hunch as he marched close behind me, his heavy boots clumping on the lino.

'In here?' I asked.

'Yes.'

I pushed at the door and entered an icy sitting room. I

stood dripping and shivering on the lino. A wooden chair lay against the wall, its legs snapped and twisted. A pair of sagging armchairs had been pushed to one side against a small sideboard. A chunky metal safe had pride of place on it. Temptation enough for a 'gasman' to break his habit and come calling during the week, thinking Galdakis was at his market stalls. He must have been watching the house.

The dark-patterned wallpaper was stained along one side as though a bucket of water had been thrown at it. The fireplace was barren and cold. There was one grimy window with half-pulled curtains. Through the dirt and the gap I could see a desolate back green.

Suddenly I didn't want to be in this space. I moved closer to the wall. My heart was racing again. Flu?

I turned to Galdakis and inspected him properly. A big man, about my height but heavier. A sullen Slav face in which the eyes glittered and probed. Though his paunch strained at the broad brown belt, it was clear that he was no fat pushover. The shoulders and chest spoke of hurling bales of hay high up on to wagons or wrestling yaks. I took off my hat and perched it on the mantelpiece to drip. I pulled out my notebook and pencil. He looked at them warily as if they were guns.

'This is where you fought the intruder?'

A grin crept over his broad face. He nodded.

'What time was this?'

'I told Inspector. 'Bout nine in morning.'

'You'd gone to work?'

'I come back. Forgot keys for chain on my stalls.' He was slowly pacing past me, examining the wall, glancing round the room, as though he was thinking of buying it. Or enjoying the reminiscence. He was moving silently now, his big feet seeking out each step like a bad actor in a pantomime. *Behind you! cry the kids.*

'Did you know the man? Had you seen him before?'

'He come before. He say: Look at gas. I not think so.'

'You were suspicious?'

'I not fool.' His mouth twisted in a malevolent grin.

'Where did you get the knife?'

'Always have knife.' He patted his chest where his jacket pocket would be. Suddenly I was glad to meet him in just his grubby vest.

'You live alone?'

He nodded.

'Were you afraid, Mr Galdakis?'

He stopped pacing and looked at me, puzzled by the question. He shook his head and grinned at me again.

'I see you broke a chair. Was it a big fight?'

He shrugged. 'Not so big.'

'Can you describe what happened?'

He shrugged again. 'I come home. Door not locked. I come in quiet. I hear him try numbers.' He pointed at the dial of the safe. 'He come out. I hit him.'

'With the knife?'

'Yes.'

I imagined how Paddy Craven must have felt stepping into the dim hall and feeling the hammer blow of a knife to his stomach. He would have been thrown back into this room with the force of it.

'He fell in here? Then what? What did you do?'

'I come in. I kick him. I angry.'

'Of course. But why did you use the knife again?'

'My house.' He pointed at his chest. 'He thief.'

'You stabbed him *six* times. Did you know that?'

'I angry.'

'Mad.'

'Mad as hell.'

'Did he fight back?'

He pursed his lips in contempt and shook his head. I stared at him, his bulk and his bad breath filling the room. Anger would take you only so far. After a few stabs you would

50

be operating on some different emotion. I remembered Sandy's request.

'Are you sorry you killed a man?'

'Thief!'

'Are you sorry you killed a thief?'

'No.' He mimicked spitting on the floor. 'Pig.' I scribbled a shorthand note.

'You are from Lithuania?'

He examined the question. 'Yes.'

'Jewish?'

He nodded.

'Which synagogue.'

'I no like going.'

Fair enough. I'm a lapsed Protestant.

'When did you leave Lithuania?'

'When Russians come.'

'At the end of the war?'

He nodded.

'What was your job? In Lithuania? What did you do for a living?'

He shrugged. 'Farm.'

'Now you have two stalls in Glasgow? At the market. Where did you get the money?'

His broad face creased in thought. 'I bring little money.'

'Lithuanian money?'

'Gold.'

'Where did you get the gold?'

Now his brows were corrugated. His response was truculent. 'Why you ask? I save money. All my life. What this mean? Why police ask this?'

'Did I say I was police, Mr Galdakis? I'm not.'

As his brain absorbed this he stepped towards me. He moved fast for a big man. 'Who are you?'

'I'm from the *Glasgow Gazette*. My readers want to know all about you.'

'No! You not tell! You not write 'bout me.'

His face was a foot from mine, his mouth contorted in anger, his breath a blowtorch. He knocked the notebook from my hands and grabbed the lapels of my coat. My hands were down by my sides. It left me only one alternative. My head was already pulled back as far as I could from his stench. I jabbed forward. The ridge of my brow caught him full in the nose. He staggered back and fell over one of the armchairs. He went crashing into the valley between the two chairs and flailed around until he dragged himself upright. Blood was pouring from his nose.

'I kill you! I fucking kill you, bastard!'

He jumped on to the chair, roaring and screaming. He leaped down at me swinging his meaty fist towards my face. Maybe my head-butt had dazed him. Maybe he was just slow, but I seemed to have plenty of time to step to one side and punch him on his big fat cheekbone as he blundered past. This time he crashed to the bare floor and lay groaning. I curbed my urge to kick him. When had that become my instinct? I waited, rubbing my knuckles. He got on to his hands and knees and then sat back against the stained wall. He held his face and nose with one hand and leaned on the other.

'You bloody bastard. You bastard you.'

I picked up my notebook and pencil and put them away. I remembered my hat. I put it on and touched the brim to him.

'Don't worry about getting up. I'll see myself out. Good morning, Mr Galdakis.'

As I walked down the stairs and out into the fresh air I felt the familiar aftershock of the adrenalin. My heart rate slowed as if I'd got something out my system. I sucked in the oxygen and decided to walk back to the newsroom to clear my thoughts, the first of which was how to explain to my readers that an interview had turned into a rammy. The second of which was to wonder exactly what emotions Galdakis had revealed in this piece commissioned by Sandy. Remorse wasn't one of them. Just raw, thuggish anger. Some men are born mean, some achieve meanness, some have meanness thrust upon them. Galdakis ticked all three.

My third thought was to wonder what Galdakis was hiding.

NINE

Sandy nabbed me as I walked past his glass-windowed office at the entrance to the newsroom. It faced Eddie Paton's office, so that between them they could cudgel or caress the reporters as we came and went. Sending us over the top in search of a scoop and bandaging us up on our return, mauled from the front line.

'How did it go, Brodie?' Sandy asked me.

I told him. He looked at me for a while and shook his head.

'I think we'll not mention the small fact that you put the heid on him, Brodie. Ever since you joined us – and I'm not necessarily saying you're the *cause* – it's been mayhem around here.'

'It's the nature of the job. If you want a crime column you're going to have to consort with criminals. They're not nice people.'

'Are you saying this fella, Galdakis, is a criminal?'

'He killed a man. OK, it was a thief. But this wasn't self-defence. He butchered him.'

Sandy nodded. 'Look, write it up and we'll see what we can make of it. Drop it in, and I'll peruse it. Then finish off the story by having a wee chat with the pawnbroker.'

'McGill?'

'It started with him. It should end with him.'

'That's tricky, Sandy. Duncan Todd isn't pressing charges. He prefers McGill on the outside. Finds him useful.'

'Go and see him anyway. We want colour. Maybe he's feeling remorse. Somebody should.' He shook his long head. 'Aboot something.'

I wrote up my encounter with the angry knifeman without mentioning that the author had given the interviewee a Gorbals kiss. It might put off other people from being interviewed by me in future. My reputation was colourful enough.

I decided to leave my interview with McGill to the following day. It turned out to be a day too late.

I had a restless night and was glad Sam had opted for her own room. My nightmares were bad enough company for me. Sam's announcement that she was off to the Hamburg trials had picked the scab off some of my more troubling memories.

I woke groggy. Thursday morning began in confusion and descended into chaos. Sam had packed the night before and was ready for the taxi that would take her to Central Station and then down to Euston. From there she'd be taken to RAF Hendon for the military flight to Hamburg.

'I'll be back in no time.'

'For Christmas.'

'You can start getting the decorations up.'

There was a knock at the door.

'Your taxi's early,' I said. Why was my heart suddenly pounding? It wasn't me going. I opened the door. A woman stood on the step.

'Hello,' she said.

Sam called from behind. 'Oh, Isobel, it's you! It's lovely to see you again. Come in, come in. Douglas, this is Isobel Dunlop.'

I'd forgotten about the new cleaner. Jutting shoulders on a wiry frame, a hook for a nose. A sparrowhawk whose piercing grey eyes were already taking X-rays of my guilty relationship with Sam.

'Good morning, Miss Campbell. And this would be your

lodger, Mr Brodie?' Her accent was Highland. Tomintoul indeed. I now knew her mother had worked for Sam's parents and the two girls had played together as they grew up.

'Och, Izzie, don't you go all formal on me. I'm still Sam. Give me a hug.' The two embraced. 'It's been ages. I'm so sorry about your mum,' Sam said.

'Aye, well. We all have our time. You're looking well, Sam. A bit skinny for my liking, but otherwise . . .'

'You're a fine one to talk. There's not a pick on you. I'm going to commission some of your famous broths for the pair of us. When I get back, that is. I'm sorry about rushing off like this.'

'Never you worry. I'll have the place sparkling for when you get back.'

They'd edged into the hall so that when the doorknocker clacked again, the three of us jumped.

'That'll be the taxi this time. Oh, goodness. I'm not ready for this.' Sam's face was red. Mine felt hot too. I wasn't ready for this either. And how were we to say farewell? A big kiss from the lodger in front of the housekeeper?

We fumbled through goodbyes by my carrying her case out to the waiting taxi and handing her into it. Her eyes registered something like panic. Mine should have shown a manly determination to be bright and breezy. But she saw the anxiety behind it.

'It'll be all right, Douglas.'

'Of course it will. Phone me when you get there.'

She leaned forward before I closed the door and kissed me lightly.

'Be nice to Izzie,' were her last words.

I went back inside and could hear Isobel Dunlop already attacking the top floor with a hoover. It was fine. We needed some curb on the dust piles. And Sam would only be gone for just over three weeks. Three weeks, three days. I'd survive, though I might have come down with the flu if my hot flushes were any indication.

I went up to my room. I sat on the edge of my bed until the sweating stopped and my breath came more easily. This wouldn't do. I flannelled my face and body, put on a tie and gathered my jacket. A notion struck me. I went over to the sideboard. I pulled aside my socks and took out a box. I pushed aside my campaign medals and picked up my old cap badge of the Seaforths. I rubbed it against my lapel and thrust it into my left jacket pocket.

I set off for the Western. I swam my morning lengths and, rejuvenated, headed towards the *Gazette*. Might as well call in on McGill's on my way. It was just past nine as I turned into Bath Street. There was already a crowd round the pawnbroker's. A bit early to be needing a wee borrow, surely? Then I realised that a number of the crowd were wearing uniforms. A squad car stood outside. My mouth went dry. I quickened my pace, feeling my stomach muscles tense.

A constable was blocking the door, and I could see others milling about inside. A familiar head turned round and saw me. A spasm warped his face. He raised his eyebrows and shook his head as if in weariness. He came to the door.

'Did you *smell* this, Brodie? Or did you happen to *know* something about this?'

'Good morning to you, Detective Chief Inspector Sangster. It's good to see you. I might be able to answer one of your questions if I knew what *this* is.'

Sangster sighed, 'Let him in,' to the constable.

I followed him inside. The Luftwaffe couldn't have done a better job. Or a bull. There was hardly a display unit left standing. My feet crunched on broken glass and pottery. The carefully stacked piles of junk were tumbled together like flotsam after a deluge.

'Stock-taking?' I asked.

Sangster sighed again. 'Spare me your wit, Brodie. Through the back.'

A uniformed officer stood by the door behind the counter. I hesitated. I didn't need this. I'd had enough. I started towards him, knowing what I'd find. The officer moved aside. Lying sprawled on the floor was McGill. He was as smashed up as his store. His head was partly severed. The great gaping wound in his throat still wept blood. Behind, on the wall, a safe door stood open. The safe was empty. An officer was dabbing at it for fingerprints.

'So, Brodie, what extraordinary coincidence brings you and this pair wee man thegither?'

There was a crunch behind us. 'Ah think Ah can answer that, sir.' Inspector Duncan Todd joined us.

Sangster narrowed his eyes. 'Now Ah'm really worried. What the hell brings you here, Todd?'

'Ah jist heard about this at Albany Street, sir. Brodie and I had been talking about McGill the other day.'

'Oh aye, and why would that be? What are you twa up to?'

I stepped forward. 'I was following a lead, Sangster. Some of your Jewish parishioners were being burgled and you weren't taking their calls. They asked me to take a look. Inspector Todd suggested I had a word with McGill here. I came here on Monday. I found McGill had acquired a number of the missing items and that he'd bought them from a certain Paddy Craven.'

Sangster's face whitened. 'Craven! Who got knifed the other day?'

'Tuesday, sir. In a burglary that went wrong,' said Duncan.

Sangster looked from one of us to the other, wondering where to start.

'Jesus, Brodie, can you no' lea' the polis stuff to us?'

'I'm a reporter. It's what I do.'

'So what's your reporter's theory about this then?' He indicated the bleeding body of poor McGill.

'McGill has a place upstairs. Somebody got in, forced him down here to open the safe, and cut his throat to shut him up?'

'Who?'

'Well, we know it wasn't Paddy Craven getting his own back for McGill clyping on him,' I said.

Duncan said, 'Maybe Craven was working with someone else? And they took the hump?'

'Or McGill knew something or someone else involved in the thieving?' I suggested.

'You huvnae written about McGill for the paper?'

'I was about to. It's now a job for the obituary boys.'

We tried a few other formulae, but without any evidence we might as well have blamed Jack the Ripper.

A little later, Duncan and I stepped outside, leaving Sangster to it. We began walking towards the city centre.

'Anything you're not telling me, Brodie?'

'Only that we've grabbed a bit of string and found a tiger on the end of it.'

TEN

I t was a long day. I waited by the phone until past midnight. My worries piled up. A train derailment? A plane crash? The morning Royal Scot should have got in by four thirty. Sam was to be whisked up to Hendon and flown to Hamburg on the evening military flight, which got in around nine o'clock our time.

By midnight my anxiety had turned to anger. I was furious at the world. Another rotten trick. Finding her, making me fall for her and then wresting her from me. Laughing at our mortal antics. Slapstick clowns on life's stage. I paced up and down like a madman, throwing back the Johnnie Walker and smoking till my throat was raw. I forced myself to pick up a book. I had no idea what I was reading.

The phone jolted me from my doze at one thirty. I leaped out of the armchair, knocking my book to the floor. I stumbled downstairs and grabbed the phone.

'Sam?'

'Thank you, caller. Please go ahead.' The cold, international operator's voice was replaced by hers. Distant and tinny.

'Douglas? Can you hear me? It's me. Sorry. Sorry. Just got here. Gales over the North Sea. I feel like I've been on one of those big dippers at the shows.'

For a moment I couldn't speak. 'I was that worried. Are you OK?'

'Wabbit. But I'm in my hotel. Iain met me and we're getting down to it tomorrow. The real thing starts next week.'

We talked some more, but I heard the weariness in her voice and let her go. I didn't mention McGill's death. Two murders in a week didn't make for a social call.

Three weeks two days.

I drifted through the weekend, trying not to hit the bottle too early. I even went to the pictures on Saturday for diversion. *The Big Sleep* with Bacall and Bogie. It left me wishing I had some of Marlowe's luck with women, not to mention solving murders.

Sitting in the dark by myself, I was a wee boy again, in the Plaza or Regal, mouth gawping, staring up at the huge flashing screen on a Saturday morning. The minors' matinee. For years I thought it was only for kids of miners like my dad. Each school week dragged by until at last I was running, with threepence hot in my hand, down the Bonnyton Road to the High Street. Jostling with my pals in the queue. Buying an ice lolly for a penny.

On into my teens, watching grown-up pictures. Transfixed by other lives, other trajectories; the impossible glamour and sophisticated drawl of Clark Gable, Garbo, Joan Crawford. The canyons of New York, an open-top Chevy Speedster under blue California skies. How did I end up pounding the beat in Glasgow when the Wild West beckoned? My life choices always seemed to be a response rather than a calculated decision.

Sam phoned me on Sunday evening sounding in better spirits but complaining about the cold. Her hotel was by a frozen lake near the centre of Hamburg.

'I should have brought my mother's old fur, Douglas. I'd wear it to bed.'

'Now there's an image to leave me with . . .'

On the Monday after the slaughter of Craven and McGill, another random piece of jigsaw landed on the board with a thump. The piece, in the shape of a distraught young woman, turned up at the newsroom. I could see her talking to one of the secretaries: Morag Duffy. Morag pranced over to my desk. She made sure that her left hand hung over my filing cabinet – casually. On her ring finger a tiny gem emitted a faint light on a gold band. For a while back in the spring, when Sam and I weren't talking and I was slumming it in a bedsit, I'd been winching Morag. She was young and bonny and fun, but I couldn't shake my interest in someone more challenging. Love makes us idiots.

Morag had sought refuge from my callous spurning of her affections by taking up with a policeman: the brave sergeant who'd comforted her in the newsroom after the assault by the Glasgow Marshals. She was to become Mrs Murdoch on St Valentine's Day. I wondered if the blushing bridegroom had had any say in the matter. Morag had her entire life planned out, right down to the pattern of her net curtains.

'There's a woman asking for you. She's in tears.' She meant: *You've done it again, Brodie, you've broken another poor lassie's heart. But look at me: I couldnae care less.* The daft thing is that her blatant display got to me. I felt a pang of jealousy. I'd traded in – so to speak – Morag's curvy enthusiasm for an uncertain relationship and a pair of adamantine eyes.

'Who is she, Morag?'

'She wouldnae gie her name. Said it was *personal*.' It was amazing how much innuendo Morag could put into one word.

'Is the wee conference room free? Can you show her in there, please.'

I gave it a minute, got the nod from Morag across the room, and headed for the room. I found a woman sitting at the table clasping and unclasping her hands, as though washing them. She twisted at a wedding ring. She was small and plain, her brown hair mostly hidden under a green Paisley scarf. Late twenties perhaps. Her face was stricken, her dark eyes rubbed red.

'Hello, there. I'm Douglas Brodie. You wanted to see me?'

She nodded stiffly. 'Thanks. Ah'm ... ma name is Ellen Jacobs.'

I sat down opposite her. 'How can I help, Mrs Jacobs?'

She looked at her hand. 'It's Miss, actually. Ah'm no' married. It jist keeps the ... Look, it's about this man that was killed.'

'Which? I'm afraid we've had a spate.'

'Paddy Craven.'

'You have my fullest attention.'

'And also this pawnbroker.'

'McGill?'

'Aye, him. Look, the thing is, Mr Brodie ...' She took a deep breath. 'Ah'm a jeweller. Ah work from home. Ah do work for the other jewellers with shops. Paddy Craven came to oor house with some stuff a wee while ago. It wisnae the first time.'

'Stuff?'

She looked on the point of tears again. 'Ah didnae ask Paddy too many questions. Ah need the work. He'd bring in some old jewellery. Used stuff. Ah would put them in new settings or at least clean them up, mend them if needed.'

'I see. Shouldn't you be saying this to the police? I know a copper who'd be glad to hear it all. A decent man.'

That set her off properly. It took a while with hankie and sniffs to get back to the story.

'Maybe, but first Ah hud to see you. Ah've read about you. Ah always read your wee column.'

'Thank you. Now what is it you're telling me?'

'In case it isnae obvious, Ah'm Jewish.'

It was, but from where? Her accent was local but there was something else in it. Was she here because of guilt? She'd read about the thefts and had realised she was party to these crimes against her own people?

She reached into her bag and came out with a piece of

cloth. She set it down on the table and opened it carefully, uncovering two lozenges of glittering yellow metal. Each was about an inch and a half long and an inch wide, with the thickness of a florin. The edges were rounded and they were without markings. She picked one up and placed it in my hand. It was heavier than it looked. I rubbed my thumb over it, enjoying the smooth weight. I wanted it.

'Gold?'

She nodded.

'Paddy?'

She nodded again.

'Why are there no assay marks?'

She picked up the second small ingot and rolled it between her fingers. Gingerly.

'Ah suppose it was stolen, Mr Brodie. The thing is, when Ah was using it, you know, melting it to make rings or to hold jewels, Ah tested it. There's still some traces of amalgam.'

'From old jewellery?'

'Gold fillings.'

She must have seen my cogs weren't meshing. She waved it at me.

'Teeth, Mr Brodie. From the camps.'

I dropped mine.

ELEVEN

She burst into tears properly this time. I was my usual hapless self in front of tearful women. I proffered my hankie and called out to one of the secretaries to bring us some tea. By the time it arrived Ellen Jacobs had pulled herself together somewhat. Though the secretary gave me a funny look. Morag would have primed her.

I tried. 'They could come from anywhere.'

She shook her head. 'That's what Paddy said. Ah didn't know what to do. How to stop.'

'He could have stolen them from a dentist or . . . a mortician?'

She raised her eyebrows at me, as though I was being stupid or slow instead of self-deluding.

'No' like this. You need a furnace. And they're unmarked. Ah *know* where they come from. You wrote about the thefts among ma . . . among the Jews. And the papers are full o' the other stories. Out there in Germany. At the trials. It's all coming out. And here Ah am, wi' this!'

'How many did he steal?'

She played with one. 'About eight.'

'And he stole them from a Jew, here in Glasgow? That doesn't make sense, unless the Jew was in a concentration camp and managed to steal the ingots in the first place.'

'That's what Ah think.'

'Do you know who Paddy stole them from? Do you know the address?'

'He never told me anything.'

'Wait here a minute, please.'

I left her alone and found Alan Clarkson, the head of administration. I asked him to retrieve my package from the office safe. I then went back to the conference room. A short while after, Alan came in bearing a cloth. I gently unwrapped the velvet package and laid out the jewellery collection on the table in front of Ellen Jacobs.

'Do you recognise any of these?'

Her long slim fingers reached out and with sure movements, like a bird pecking at seeds, picked out four items and laid them to one side. Three pairs of gold earrings and one ring, each clean and glittering on the dark velvet. Some had small pearls set in them. The ring held a turquoise. They were striking pieces, modern and stylish.

'These are mine,' she said, unable to contain a certain pride in her voice.

'They're lovely.'

'Not now,' she said and raised her anguished eyes to mine.

'Did you take them to McGill's?'

'No. Paddy did a' that side of things. Ah made the jewellery and put an estimate on them. Then he took them round to McGill's. Depending what happened Ah was to get twenty per cent. But as you can see, they didnae sell well.'

'And now he's dead. And so is McGill. You never met him? The pawnbroker?'

'Once, when he was trying to price some of the bits and pieces too low. He was jist trying it on, so he was.'

'Who do you think killed the pawnbroker?'

'Ah don't know.'

'Did Paddy have a pal? An accomplice? Someone wanting to get even?'

'Ah jist don't know. He could have. But Ah never met anyone except Paddy.'

'One last question, Ellen. Did you make keys for Paddy? From a mould?'

Her already flushed face went scarlet and the tears oozed again. She nodded.

I had no choice. I called Duncan Todd. He came straight round. He went through the same questions I did, but this time Ellen Jacobs was less given to weeping. Maybe Duncan had a gentler way with him. Maybe she'd unburdened everything with me.

Duncan was pursuing a point. 'Are you sure Craven didnae give you any clues about where he got this?' He pointed at the yellow ingots.

'He never telt me names. Or addresses.'

'How did he choose his targets?'

'He kept his eye out. Always looking for folk wi' money. Businessmen, stallholders, that kind of thing. He had a job as a gasman. Did you know that?'

'Yes. And he went after Jews in particular?'

'Aye. He said Jews had all the money.'

'Did he know you were a Jew?' Duncan asked.

'Ah suppose so.'

'Did you no' mind?'

She flushed. 'Not until this!' She pointed at the gold.

I picked up on this. 'How did you get into this, Ellen? You don't seem like a crooked jeweller.'

She winced at the adjective. 'Ah live in the Gorbals. Do you think Ah choose to?'

'You go to Isaac Feldmann's synagogue?'

She nodded. 'Not since this. But Ah know Isaac.'

I kept pressing. 'What about family?'

'Ma mother lives wi' me. Just the two of us. We got out in '35 when they took away our rights bit by bit. Made us wear a yellow star in the street. Ah was just a wee girl. Ma father stayed on to try to keep the business going. He was a pharmacist. He said even the Nazis needed pills. Maybe more than anyone. He never got out.'

Her anger wiped the guilt from her face. She had more reasons than most for trying to climb out of the slums, make a life for herself. One of the new Scots. A descant to an old tune.

'Where from?'

'Berlin.'

'*Sie sprechen gutes Englisch. Obwohl mit einem Gorbals Akzent! Wo haben Sie es gelernt?*'

'*An der Schule. Und hier. Offensichtlich. Und Sie? Ihr Deutsch ist gut.*'

'Aw right, you pair, that'll dae. Speak Scots.'

I shrugged. 'University, then the army. I was based in Lüneburg for a few months after the armistice. I got to know whom we'd been fighting. And why.'

'Lüneburg? The Belsen trials?'

I nodded, surprised she knew the connection. She held my eyes for a beat and then turned to Duncan. 'Are you going to arrest me?'

'Ah'm thinking aboot it. You are an accomplice. Hell, you cut keys for him! Any reason why Ah shouldnae?'

She looked down. 'Nane at a'. But can Ah speak to ma mum? She disnae speak English very well. She'll be that worried.'

Duncan and I looked at each other. He shook his head.

'Just leave your address. When Ah need to find you, Ah'll come and get you.'

She looked surprised. I stared at Duncan. Getting soft in his old age? Or didn't fancy the paperwork? Another question occurred to me.

'Why did you come and tell us all this, Ellen?'

She stared, big-eyed, at me, then at Duncan. 'Because this is wrong.' She poked at the golden tablet. 'Dead wrong. And Ah'm feart. Feart Ah'll be next.'

'Why would anyone want to kill you?'

'Cos they're annoyed? Or they think Ah've still got some gold? Who knows? But it's a' too close for ma liking.'

'Have you told anyone else about this, Ellen?'

She reached out and picked up the ring she'd made. She rolled it through her fingers.

'Ah told ma rabbi. Maurice Silver. Yesterday. He telt me to speak to you.'

TWELVE

There was no doubt Isobel Dunlop knew how to punish dirt. Every surface was scoured. If I took a long enough lie-in I'm sure I would have been ironed and starched where I lay. We didn't talk much. I called her Mrs Dunlop. She called me Mr Brodie. She came in on Mondays, Wednesdays and Fridays and did three hours each time. Hitherto I'd sent my shirts off to the cleaners, but now, without any overt transaction that I was aware of, that duty had been taken over by Isobel. The costs seemed to balance out. And it was nice to be relieved of porridge-pot cleaning duties. However, in a stupid, guilty, little-boy way, I was glad Sam wasn't around so that I wouldn't feel embarrassed at Izzie finding two dents on my pillow.

On 4 December, the day before the start of the trials, Sam fought her way through the international call system.

'You've been hiding your light under a bushel.'

'You've just been slow to recognise my talents.'

'I've been ploughing through these dossiers on the defendants. I keep finding reports by a certain Major Brodie. Any relation?'

'My alter ego.' I'd been waiting for this. I'd recognised the names of some of the Nazis on trial in Hamburg. I had been their first-line interrogator in the summer and autumn of 1945.

'Iain says they're models of clarity.'

'I'm amazed you're amazed, Sam.'

'Big head.'

'Good luck tomorrow.'

'It's terrifying. But we're well prepared. My brain is gowping with details. Horrible details.'

So was mine. I kept trying to switch away from the subject but it was like sticking your fingers in your ear and going *la la la* to block out a brass band in your bedroom.

The first snow of the year hit us on 6 December, a day after the start of the trials. It proved a false harbinger. By mid-month the weather softened again and we were all beginning to think we'd get away with a mild one. I was roundly thanked by the Garnethill elders for catching the thief and for the return of at least some of the valuables. I held on to the few items hand-crafted by Ellen Jacobs. It didn't feel like the end of this tale.

My life fell into a routine through December, with Isobel's visits punctuating the passing of time. Sam phoned every so often, on each occasion sounding wearier as though she was adding a brick a day to the hod she carried. In my mind I was pacing through the trial with her, wishing I were there to help, but guiltily glad I wasn't. I missed her. Missed the smell of her neck and hair. One time she called, a little accusatory:

'You never mentioned you were at Lüneburg,' said Sam. 'For the Belsen trials.'

'It never came up. And it wasn't something to chat about over the porridge. It was all part of my post-war secondment.'

'But I thought you were only involved in the interrogations.'

'One thing led to another, Sam. It was quicksand.'

'So you know exactly what I'm doing out here?'

'I know, Sam. I know.'

And in my dreams each night I was reliving it, so that each morning was like crawling from my grave.

*

71

Ellen Jacobs phoned every few days to see if there was any news. About anything. She was still fearful, and she and her mother had gone to stay with a cousin for a couple of weeks, over in Govan. But with each passing day and no visit from any of Craven's pals or enemies she was getting less anxious. She planned to move back home for Christmas. Duncan and Sangster had got nowhere with the McGill murder. The prints didn't match any on file, and no one had seen anything. Temporary blindness was a contagious disease in Glasgow.

Eddie Paton was back working part time while his head healed. It was a slow business. He was a sliver of his old self. You could see where his wife had taken in the tartan waistcoat and the trousers without cutting off the material, just in case he became Big Eddie again. On present progress it seemed unlikely. He was smoking more than ever, and his left eyelid had a tendency to twitch when he got excited.

And whether my writing had improved or Eddie was less engaged, he rarely put a blue pencil near any of my drafts. Some mornings he'd barely emerge from his fug-filled office. I could see him toying with drafts and old stories, but often just staring into space. I was tempted to go in, grab him by the lapels and shake him. Tell him to snap out of it. But I'd seen other men with the same introspective look. It was probably how others saw me at times. You just had to get over it.

The news about my predecessor Wullie McAllister was worse. His brother Stewart and I visited him at the convalescent home out by Erskine. I'd borrowed Sam's car and picked Stewart up. Afterwards we sat by the Clyde in the car, windows rolled down, watching the ships go by. More refugees bound for the promised land.

'He's not going to get any better, is he?' Stewart asked.

I shook my head in denial. 'He's got more colour to him.'

'But he doesn't even recognise me.'

I didn't answer for a while. 'You're getting the worst of it,' I said.

The two men had lived together as brothers. Yet their ties weren't blood. The title was for convenience and propriety. A very queer relationship.

I told Sam about our visit that night when she called.

'Douglas, if I ever end up doolally will you promise to push me off Ben Nevis?'

'Will the top of Hope Street do? It might be all that I can manage.'

'Just make it quick.'

'Does that mean we're going to grow old together?' I broke into Burns:

> *'John Anderson, my jo, John,*
> *We clamb the hill thegither;*
> *And mony a cantie day, John,*
> *We've had wi' ane anither:*
> *Now we maun totter down, John,*
> *And hand in hand we'll go,*
> *And sleep thegither at the foot,*
> *John Anderson, my jo.'*

'Have you been at the poetry bottle again?'

We were heading rapidly towards Christmas and the turn of the year. It meant I was rising in the dark and going home in the dark to the great echoing house. We'd closed down all the rooms except the kitchen, one bathroom and my bedroom. My mind was closing down with it, room by room, as I tried to barricade myself off from the past. For sanity I kept up my morning swim though it was getting harder and harder to leave the quilt and face the cold plunge.

Sam was due back in seven days.

In my constant search for news stories I was patrolling the streets by the light of gas lamps in the mid-afternoon.

Like a Dickensian ghost. Between restless nights and the cosy warmth of the newsroom, I found myself jolting awake at my desk at times. As though my brain had switched off, then on again.

Often enough the hunt for a column led me south of the Clyde. As we neared Christmas I noticed lit candles in some of the windows of tenements around South Portland Street. The soft glow threw the nine-branched menorah in clear silhouette against the net curtains. Isaac Feldmann had told me that only eight candles counted; the central or side one was the *shamash* – the servant – used to light the significant others. Each night the number of candles would grow by one. When I saw four lit in the window above Isaac's shop I went in.

'Happy Hanukkah, Isaac!' I called out to the empty shop. I heard rustling from the back and at last he shambled out, muttering away until he saw me.

'Ach, Douglas, thank you. You remembered it's our Festival of Lights?'

'You think I learned nothing from you and Hannah? I just wanted to wish you well.'

'Thank you, thank you. You know that this year we light the eighth on Christmas Eve? Double blessings for all of us.'

'Maybe it means we will be kinder to each other.'

'Jews and Christians? Why not? We are all children of the book.'

'Except the Orange Order and the Blackshirts.'

'Even them, Douglas. Though they don't know it. Is this a social call? Come. Have coffee. I have some real beans.'

'You must have come into the money, Isaac.'

We sat in his back room, swaddled and muffled among the bales and shelves of cloth. The coffee was hot and sweet, and as different from Camp Coffee as a real egg from powder. It was the first time we'd met since my sleuthing and the murders.

'They are still talking about you, Douglas. Some of them want to hire your services again. There is always something. A lost cat, a lost wife, lost money . . .'

'I don't do cats. And nobody can bring back a lost wife if she's not willing.'

'But they also talk about this man who killed the thief.'

'Galdakis?'

'Him. No one knows him. He just appeared about a year ago, they say. Money in his pocket. But he never comes to synagogue. At least not ours. They are not even sure he's Jewish.'

'Hmmm. He said he was, but he didn't go to *shul*.'

'You met him?'

I told Isaac about my run-in with him.

'He is *bescheuert*,' he said.

'As we say around here, a total bampot. A malignant one.'

I found myself using the Hanukkah candles as a countdown to Sam's return. When the sixth was lit – not counting the *shamash* – on the Sunday before Christmas, I was waiting up for her. She'd confirmed the night before but the weather was atrocious again. It was edging towards midnight when I heard a car draw up outside, a door slamming, a voice, and then short quick steps. I dashed down the stairs and was at the door to open it for her. I grabbed her case, flung it behind me and held out my arms. She gripped me like a lifebelt.

When I felt her muscles ease I pushed her back to see her face.

'Sam, dearest, why are you crying?'

She couldn't find the words, just buried her face in my chest and I felt her body heave as sobs crashed through her. Slowly she came to a halt and pushed herself back.

'I seem to be rubbish at flying, Douglas.'

I stroked her hair and laughed. She laughed too and we left everything in the hall and went up to my room. My bed wasn't cold but she was shivering for a long time until my body heat calmed her.

'Bad, Sam?'

'Bad. I thought I'd read enough, seen enough in *Pathé News*. I knew about what they'd done. But nothing prepared me for the reality.'

'Nothing can.'

Next day was easier. She phoned Izzie to come round and the pair of them tackled a big wash, giggling like girls. It was good to hear her laughter from the wash-house. I left them to it and went into the newsroom.

When the clock hit five, I sprang for the door. Morag was holding the phone out to me. I shook my head and saw her deal with the caller. I elbowed my way past the rush of secretaries and dashed home. Sam was pale but already getting back to a version of her sparky self. We made tea of Izzie's tattie soup, and had just adjourned to the lounge to take our first sip of the evening when the phone rang. I took it. It was Duncan.

'Brodie, Ah think you should be here. You could maybe help.'

'Where's here, Duncan?'

'Bedford Street.'

'Galdakis?'

'Aye, him, possibly. That's why . . . Look, it disnae matter. Ah'm sure you've better things to do. Like washing your hair or listening to ITMA. You said Sam was due home. But . . .'

'Duncan, I'm on my way.'

THIRTEEN

I t took me twenty minutes to cross the city centre and get to the scene of the crime, for that's what it was. The bobby barring the downstairs entry simply asked, 'Mr Brodie?' and let me through. I walked upstairs and paused at the door. It was wide open. The wood was splintered at the lock, smashed open. No gasman subtlety here.

I stepped inside. Duncan was pacing the front room, the room I hadn't been in, which looked out on to the street. It had a hole-in-the-wall bed and a small kitchen. The room had been wrecked. Amidst the debris a familiar figure kneeled over the body spread-eagled in front of a cold fireplace.

'Come ben, Brodie. Is this your man?'

My man lay staring at the ceiling, heavy arms trailing above his head like a baby relaxing. But no one relaxes when they're impaled on a pitchfork.

The kneeling man stood up. It was Jamie Frew, police doctor.

'It's yourself, Brodie. Still chasing trouble?'

'Not as much as you, Jamie.'

I stared down on the massive bulk topped by the round face. From the centre of his chest grew a near vertical wood pole. The three tines were buried so deep that they were almost invisible. His shirt was stained and torn in other places. Blood had pooled around his chest and soaked into the runkled scrap of carpet.

'It's him all right. Is that really a pitchfork?'

'It would appear so, Brodie,' said Jamie. 'He's got further sets of puncture marks on his arms and abdomen commensurate with—'

'—a pitchforking. Christ,' I said. 'So we're looking for an angry farmer?'

'Ah knew Ah could rely on you to lighten the mood, Brodie.'

I looked round the room. It had been quite a fight. Pictures ripped off walls, smashed chairs, table upended and a trail of blood across the floor suggesting Galdakis had dragged himself to where he now lay.

'Any sign of a knife?' I asked.

'No. Why?'

'He liked his knife. Could use it.'

'We'll have a look.'

'What's the other room like?'

'Take a look.'

I walked down the short corridor and into the back room. The furniture had been repositioned since I'd last visited. It was neat but dusty, and it still felt empty and damp. The safe gaped open and empty on the sideboard. I walked back.

'What happened, Duncan?'

'Call from a neighbour a couple hours ago. Said there'd been a fight. A big shouting match, then a lot of crashing about and swearing. Then quiet.'

'The rest is silence, right enough. What do you reckon? Front door bashed in?'

Duncan nodded. 'Ah'm assuming you don't simply walk up to somebody's front door wi' a pitchfork and ask to come in for tea.'

'One man or many?'

'Neighbours heard two or three voices all shouting.'

'What were they shouting?'

'She doesn't know. Says it was some foreign words. Ah don't think she meant sweary words that she was pretending never to have heard.'

'And I don't think it was the ghost of Paddy Craven. But he might well have been cheering them on.'

'Retribution?' asked Duncan.

'Could be. Or just theft. They emptied the safe.'

'It wisnae quite empty.'

'Oh?'

'Sergeant? Gie me that envelope.'

Duncan took it and gingerly fished out a stained slip of paper. The blotches were dark brown.

'It's a pawn slip,' he said.

'McGill's?'

'Oh aye. It could have been planted.'

'Or just left where the raiders found it. But *you* think not?'

'Ah think Galdakis knifed Paddy Craven and found this slip on him. He put two and two thegither. He stuck it in the safe and then went after McGill.'

'Why? Craven didn't manage to steal anything from Galdakis. Unless it was his second trip.'

'Sheer badness? He knifed the thief six times. Maybe he carried his anger through to the fence? We're looking for the missing link.'

'Don't bring Sangster into this.'

Duncan guffawed. Jamie Frew hid a smirk.

'Enough, Brodie. Look, you met this guy. Any ideas?'

'You've got prints from McGill's. So that's an easy check with this fella's. But can you get your photographer to take a mug shot, before he goes off? There's a bunch of folk I'd like to run it past. If you could get me half a dozen copies that would be even better.'

I felt no sorrow at the death of Galdakis, but it would fair put a damper on the rest of the evening with Sam.

We tried to pick up some of the lightness we were beginning to feel at her homecoming but even a wicked man's death casts a shadow.

'But why, Douglas? Why was Galdakis murdered?'

'One of Paddy's pals finishing the job of cracking the safe?'

'With a pitchfork?'

'Revenge for Paddy?'

'If my memory serves me, Craven was a soloist.'

'His wee wife, then?'

'Against a gorilla? Your description, Douglas.'

We sat stymied for a bit, and then Sam took us down the next path.

'Why would Galdakis go after McGill?'

'Anger at the world? Out to get everyone involved in trying to steal from him? I don't know. But when I met him I definitely felt he was hiding something. Wish I knew what else was in that safe.'

I got into the newsroom late the next morning. Christmas Eve. I paused at Morag's desk. Something was nagging at me.

'That phone call last night, Morag. Who was it?'

'Oh, it was yon lassie. The one that calls you every week.'

'Ellen Jacobs? Did she say what it was about?'

'No. But she sounded a wee bit het up. And was really sorry she couldnae get you.'

I walked on to my desk. I sat and doodled for a while feeling a gnawing worry spreading through me. I don't believe in coincidences.

It was no coincidence. Mid-morning, I saw Duncan's figure over by the secretaries. They were pointing my way. I walked across and ushered Duncan out into the stairwell. He looked ashen.

'Have you got the photos already?'

He shook his head. 'No' yet.'

My mouth was dry. 'Spit it out, Duncan. Is it the prints? Did they match?'

'We're still waiting on them. Should hear this afternoon. It's no aboot that. Or rather it is, but it's different.'

'It's about Ellen Jacobs, isn't it?'

His eyes widened. 'Huv ye heard?'

I shook my head.

'Well, then. She's been found deid. This morning. In a phone box by the Broomielaw.'

I felt the world go still. Then a roaring in my ears. Then Duncan grabbing me by the arm.

'Brodie! Brodie! Are you a' right?'

I gulped in air. 'I'm fine. Fine. Oh, shit! What time? I mean, when do you reckon she died?'

'Hard to tell. The poor wee lassie was a' bunched up on the flair of the box. The cord was roon her neck. It was freezing cold. Must have been last night.'

'She called here at five yesterday.'

His eyes lifted to mine. 'Did you speak to her?'

'No. I missed the call.' Refused her call. 'You should have locked her up, Duncan. For her own good.'

'Aye maybe. Wi' hindsight.'

He looked away. A thought struck me. Surely not.

'Did you do it deliberately? You didn't want her locked up until you saw if anything happened to her?'

'Not at a'.'

'You used her as bait!'

'Naw, naw. It wisnae like that, Brodie.'

'What was it like?'

'Tak' your hands aff my coat!'

I released him. I lowered my voice.

'What *was* it like, Duncan?'

'Ah just though Ah'd let things run. See what happened for a bit. Christ, Brodie, there were twa murders! An' we hudnae a clue about either. Sangster was on my case.'

I left him standing in the hall. I went back in, grabbed my coat and walked out into the cold damp streets. The shops had fairy lights on. A brave attempt at jollity. A group of Salvation Army singers stood outside Central Station singing their hearts out and collecting for the homeless. Peace on Earth. Goodwill to all men.

I walked for a long time, finally seeing the point of the cilice. Eventually I took my guilt home. At four in the afternoon a police sergeant appeared at the door.

'Sir, Inspector Todd sends his compliments, sir. He says to tell you that the prints match. He says you'd understand.'

'Oh, I do, Sergeant. I do.'

'And this is for you, sir.' He drew out an envelope and handed it to me.'

'Photos?'

'Yes, sir.'

I parked the packet on the mantelpiece unopened. I didn't want to see the death mask of a killer. Not on Christmas Eve.

FOURTEEN

On Christmas morning I woke in a blaze of determination. I was going to be Mr Positive personified. I brought Sam tea in her room, stoked the boiler and had a bath. I turned the wireless up and sang along to carols until Sam pleaded for respite.

I left her determinedly stuffing a flat-chested chicken with chestnuts and sausage meat while I drove down to Kilmarnock in her Riley. Nearing the town limits I took the Western Road and then down Bonnyton Road to the square. I saw the curtain twitch and by the time I'd stopped the car and walked to the entry, my mother was locking her front door. Her face was scrubbed and shining, her hair newly permed and glowing soft white. She had her Sunday coat and hat on, a parcel under her arm and a big pot at her feet. We hugged as best we could given the obstacles.

'Happy Christmas, Mum.'

'And you, son. This is such a treat, Douglas. Such a treat. Are you sure Samantha disnae mind? She's only just back from Germany.'

'She's looking forward to it. You know she likes you.'

'She's lovely, Douglas. Don't you let her get away.'

'Chance of getting her would be a fine thing.'

'Just be patient, son. You're not the easiest lad to get to know.'

'What's that supposed to mean?'

'Don't be obtuse, Douglas. Take this pot. It weighs a ton.'

'Clootie dumpling?'

She nodded.

'Smashing!'

She beamed. 'Now then, see that bag over there?' She pointed at the hessian sack half full and bulging at the front door.

'The coal bag?'

'Get it into the car boot. That'll pay for my Christmas dinner.'

'Mum, there's no need. You'll have better use of this.'

'Douglas, this is a mining community. We've got more coal than we know what to do with. I'm on a miner's pension. This is a bonus, if you like.'

'Och, Mum . . .'

'You're not ashamed that your old mither is showing up at Samantha's nice hoose wi' a bag o' coal, are you?'

'Of course not. Let's think of it as an early first foot. OK?'

I noted she was still insisting on using Sam's full name. She just liked saying it. It sounded posher to her gossipy pals than Jeannie, Jessie or Annie.

I placed the pot on the back seat and manhandled the coal sack into the boot. I got Mum on board and we set off back up the Glasgow Road.

'Thanks, Mum. The coal's a generous thought.'

'Wheesht. Is this as fast as we can go?'

Sam had been busy. She'd dug out the painted balls and figures from her own long-ago Christmases and festooned the hall and tiny tree she'd set up in the lounge. She cooed over the dumpling and the coal. Mum settled in as though she'd been born to the grand life.

The smell of cooking blessed the house. We stripped the chicken to the bone and set upon the dumpling. We washed them down with tea and port, as the taste suited. We turned on the wireless and listened to more carols.

Mum had knitted a cardigan for Sam and socks for me. I'd blown some of my detective bonus on a silk scarf for Sam and a blouse for my mother. The last present was a small parcel from Sam to me.

'Go on, Douglas, open it.'

I undid the brown paper to reveal the small box within. I opened it and took out the card. In her fine hand she'd written: 'To Douglas, on our first Christmas. Love Samantha xxx'.

First? That sounded hopeful. I unwrapped the tissue paper and found a pair of silver cufflinks bearing lustrous blue opals the size of my fingernail.

'Sam! They're magnificent! Far too much, just lovely. I . . .'

'Second-hand, Douglas. Sort of. The stones were my dad's. I had them reset.'

I walked over, leaned down and kissed her. My mother's eyes glowed.

It was a day for building memories to draw on when hope's on the wane. It ended in style, with my mother safely tucked up in a bed under Sam's warm roof, and Sam tucked up in mine.

'Merry Christmas, Sam.'

'Shhh . . .' She pointed at the ceiling where my mother lay in the room above.

I drove my mother home to Bonnyton the next day.

'You should just ask her, Douglas.'

'We've talked. She says no.'

'Why? I think she loves you.'

'She's got a career. She's worked hard to get where she is. She'd have to give it up if she got married. It's how it works in her business.'

'I think you'd be worth it.'

'You're my mum.'

*

I picked up a *Daily Record* on the way home. In the world at large, the Clyde would get off to a jaunty start to '47 with £73 million of new orders. This was offset by the parlous state of the national economy: coal rationing, booming black markets and grasping landladies putting the squeeze on poor tenants in slum accommodation. Out in Palestine our boys continued to be piggy-in-the-middle. One of our Arnhem heroes – a major – was kidnapped and flogged by the Jewish terror brigades in retaliation for a birching of one of their own. Biblical revenge.

When I got back to Sam's we let the world crowd in again. I took out the six photos of the dead man from the envelope left by Duncan's man. He looked less mean and explosive in death's repose. I called Shimon Belsinger and Isaac and they came by in the afternoon to collect them. They would pass out the photos to see what their people might know.

Sam wasn't due back to Hamburg for a couple of weeks. But she'd brought back enough paperwork to keep her busy. I didn't ask to see any of it. She didn't offer. But over the coming days we began to talk more about her trial. I told her about the similarities with the Belsen court and defendants last year. But there's a limit to how much horror you can discuss without feeling you were trying to trump the revolting with the obscene.

Hanukkah was over, so was Christmas, and we were in no man's land leading up to Ne'erday. The gentle, brief celebrations were over and preparations for the real thing – the four-day Scottish bacchanal – were commencing. Sam and I were simply waiting. The news from Shimon came back on Sunday. It was what I feared.

FIFTEEN

Inside the Statue of Liberty in Manhattan harbour is a bronze plaque bearing Emma Lazarus's sonnet 'The New Colossus'. It closes with the ringing appeal:

> *'Give me your tired, your poor,*
> *Your huddled masses yearning to breathe free;*
> *The wretched refuse of your teeming shore.*
> *Send these, the homeless, tempest-tost to me:*
> *I lift my lamp beside the golden door!'*

They could have nailed the words up on Glasgow Bridge at the entrance to the Gorbals, where they would have been equally relevant, and just as poignant. Or, as the self-aware Gorbals-dwellers themselves would have pointed out, at the exit.

The Gorbals straddles Wards 18, 19 and 20 for the purposes of electing councillors in Hutchesontown, Laurieston and Kingston. In reality the Gorbals is a nation state, operating and existing quasi-independently. Hardly redolent of Venice or Genoa, but certainly a law unto itself, a defined enclave within which its inhabitants blink into life, grow up, get into bother, reproduce and die, passing on the spluttering torch of ignorance and over-reproduction to the next luckless generation. Some of course get away and make it big in Canada or New Zealand, there to sing maudlin songs of home, nostalgic for a place that only existed in rose-tinted memory.

But from what I hear about New York, the Gorbals is no worse than the Lower East Side, a raucous anthill of new arrivals clambering over each other to survive and prosper in a strange land. For many of the huddled masses that fall to their knees on Ellis Island, an earlier staging post is Glasgow.

These days the Clyde is filled, nose to tail, with urgent steamships. They can't get out of Scottish slums and Scottish weather quick enough. Some stay; they run out of money or fall in love or become too weary to take another step, climb another gangplank. Whether transients or stickers, they fill the Gorbals to bursting point.

I crossed the bridge into this teeming ghetto. Isaac Feldmann met me in front of his Great Synagogue and showed me through to a small back room. Five people were already clustered round a low table, in the centre of which lay the much-fingered photos of the thuggish knifeman. Shimon Belsinger rose to greet me. I also shook hands with Dr Tomas Meras, one of the men I'd met at Sam's back in November. Another wore the raiment and bearing of a rabbi. Isaac introduced him as Maurice Silver. He took my offered hand in both of his and bobbed a shalom at me. We held each other's gaze.

'I'm sorry about Ellen Jacobs, Rabbi.'

'Not as sorry as I am, Mr Brodie. Let us talk later.'

Two other men shifted in their seats and rose to greet me. I caught the names August and Konrad. Isaac asked Dr Tomas to talk first. As before, Tomas spoke in the clear deliberate English you'd expect from a lecturer in physics at Glasgow University. He pointed at the photos.

'There are now over twelve thousand Jews in Glasgow. Most arrived in the past decade. We come from all over Europe. We know our own. I am from Vilnius in Lithuania.' He leaned over and stabbed the photo with his finger. 'This man is not Lithuanian. I talked to Lithuanians who saw him, who talked to him at his stall. He is Polish.'

'Go on.'

'Nor is he Victor Galdakis, Mr Brodie. We have independent corroboration from two sources. Both are here today.' He indicated the two men sitting at the table. 'August is one of my own countrymen. He *knew* Victor Galdakis. The *real* Victor Galdakis. They were in the same camp at Treblinka.'

The news hit me like a waterfall. Yet a part of me wasn't surprised. I turned to August. He was nodding vigorously and making sign language. Rabbi Silver leaned forward and picked up the thread.

'August had his vocal cords crushed in the camp. A guard dog. I will translate. He tells me the real Victor was a small man, always smiling. He was an optician by day and a violinist in his spare time. He did not survive. He says he thinks this man killed him.' He pointed at the photo. 'He thinks he saw him once, but did not learn his name. And then this man was moved to another camp.'

'Is Victor Galdakis a common name in Lithuania? Is it like John Brown here?'

Tomas shook his head. 'It's not uncommon, but not as common as all that. More importantly, we *know* who this is, and where he went after Treblinka.' He again stabbed the photo, as though he could hurt it. 'Konrad, please tell Mr Brodie what you know.'

I turned to Konrad. In his drawn face were huge staring eyes, unblinking, as though he was gazing through me into another world.

'I saw this man.' He pointed at the photo with clear distaste. 'Ivan Draganski. *Dragan*. He was not a Jew. He was a *Rapportführer* at Ravensbrück.' He spat the word. It hit me like a bayonet to the belly.

'A camp marshal,' I said. Mix four deaths with Nazi gold and what do you get? Havoc. Only the details would be news.

Konrad nodded his head with certainty. 'He came from Treblinka where he was a *Blockführer*, we heard. He was sent to us on promotion. He had two pips and a bar on his uniform collar.' He touched his thin shoulder.

I nodded. 'Roughly the same as our sergeant. His earlier rank equates to a corporal.'

The others were inspecting Konrad quizzically. But for me the words were a key to a secret door. A tunnel back into the nightmares of last year in north Germany.

We set up camp in Bergen, a couple of miles from the concentration camp at Belsen. They brought in the Nazi prisoners in chains and under guard. Most were men. Most were senior SS officers who'd been running the camps. A few women came through and some doctors. My job was to sift the testimonies and decide who should be sent to trial for war crimes, just fifty miles north of Bergen, at Lüneburg.

In the first analysis it didn't take much interrogation. Unless they'd managed to discard their uniforms, anyone with the double lighting flash and the *Totenkopf* – death's head – insignia on their collars was sent for trial. Anyone who'd removed their collar tabs or sleeve markers were also assumed to be SS until they could prove otherwise. The same went for any officer sporting one or more oak leaves. A full colonel and above was deemed to have been sufficiently steeped in the blood of innocents, one way or the other, to be culpable of war crimes.

This steady fashion show emphasised how much the Nazis loved their uniforms, and how they were always fussing about with it. From field grey to black, from SS rank to Wehrmacht, from shoulder-boards to collar patches and sleeve diamonds, it suggested an army more taken with appearance than combat. Which was far from the truth. On reflection, thinking of our kilted warriors, maybe pretty uniforms made for better soldiers?

But my job went further than separating the sheep and goats. We wanted information. We were tracking down the top men, the ones who unleashed hell, and we were following every lead. In exchange for useful information, we were prepared to write on their notes that they'd been cooperative. It might be enough to save them from a hanging.

I realised the rabbi was talking to me. I broke out of my reverie. 'I'm sorry?'

'I was saying that justice has been done to this man, Mr Brodie.'

'I doubt that, Rabbi. If he was anything like his pals, he got off lightly.'

The rabbi inspected me carefully. He turned to the others. 'I have some words to say to Mr Brodie. May I beg your indulgence?'

The other men murmured and nodded and took their leave. The rabbi and I were left sitting together. We knew the subject matter. He began.

'Ellen told me she'd talked to you, Mr Brodie.'

'We let her down. She was terrified by the murder of Paddy Craven and then the pawnbroker. You know the whole story?'

He sighed. 'She was not a bad woman, Mr Brodie.'

'Brodie will do, Rabbi. I agree with you. It's not easy making a new life.'

'Not when the old one comes back to haunt you.' He smiled. 'Call me Maurice.'

I took a breath. 'She tried to call me the night she died. Probably from the phone box they found her in.'

He was nodding. 'I know. She called me too.'

'What!'

'You know she was staying with a cousin for a while after you met her? She came back just before Hanukkah. To celebrate with her mother. She came to see me. Told me she thought she was being followed.'

'Did she know who it was?'

He shook his head. 'I called one of our people. I asked him

to keep an eye. He did. He saw a man waiting outside Ellen's house.'

'When?'

'Two days before.'

'Did he know this man? Did he get a description?'

'He did better. He followed him. Back to his market stall.'

'Galdakis's stall?'

'It would seem so.'

'Why didn't your man act?'

'Galdakis – *Draganski* – hadn't *done* anything at that stage. My man didn't know why he was following Ellen.'

'When she phoned you. That night. What did she say? What did she want?'

'She was terrified. She lived on the third floor. She'd looked out through the curtains and saw the man. He was walking up and down and looking up at the window. Ellen panicked and left the flat. She went out the back door of the entry, through the green and round to the phone box. She said she was trying to speak to you. I told her to stay where she was. I thought she'd be safer in a phone box than going back to her house. I called my man. He rushed round . . .'

'And was too late. Did your man see anything?'

He shook his head. 'He just found her.'

'Then he went after Gal— Draganski.'

The rabbi shrugged. 'I cannot say what happened next.'

'You *must* say!'

He sighed. 'Brodie, I am going to make a phone call. Depending on what I hear, I will get back to you in a day or so. See if he agrees to speak. It is the best I can do.'

SIXTEEN

It was New Year's Eve and the newsroom was winding down. There would be no papers till the 4th because of the way Ne'erday fell on the Wednesday followed by a second bank holiday and a slack Friday.

My first draft of the article spelling out Dragan's foul background and impersonation of the real Galdakis prompted a meeting in Eddie's office. Sandy stood gangly in the corner with his arms folded. I sat in front of Eddie's desk and Eddie glowered at me over the top of his paper piles.

'Ah mean it's good stuff, Brodie. Don't get me wrong. It's just awfie . . . ?'

'Awfully what, Eddie?'

'Dreich. Can we no' get a bit o' cheer in? Ah mean it's Ne'erday the morn. Nothing to look forward to?'

'I hear Iron Brew's going back on the shelves.'

'Ah never missed it. But a' this stuff about the concentration camps again. There's enough o' that on *Pathé News*, is there no'? When will it a' stop?'

'When there's no more horrors coming out of the woodwork, I suppose. Until then, what should we do about it? Just ignore it? Stick some photos of pretty girls on your front page and hope it all goes away?'

'It's no' such a bad idea at that, Brodie.' Eddie sought and got an answering chortle from Sandy. 'But look, oor readers will be getting confused wi' all these murders. I mean, who's killing whom? An' why?'

'We don't know everything yet. We've got four deaths. Craven, McGill, Ellen Jacobs and Draganski. We know that Dragan killed Paddy Craven. At the time it was a householder protecting himself against a burglar. Then Dragan found out about Craven's accomplices: McGill the pawnbroker and Ellen Jacobs the jeweller. And he killed them. The police have matched the prints found at both murders with Dragan's. What we don't know is *why* Dragan did it. Or who killed Dragan. We're pretty sure the link is the ingots made from tooth fillings.'

'But you've nae actual proof? Not even that the gold comes from – well – ye ken – the camps,' said Sandy.

Eddie sighed. 'OK, have another go at this. We'll run it after the holidays. Don't mention the Nazi stuff. We're just guessin' and we don't want the good burghers of Glesga panicking in the streets.'

Sandy chimed in. 'Keep it simple. Make it understandable to the average man in the Govan tram. In other words, me.'

I simplified and sanitised the story for the *Gazette* readership but couldn't make sense of the reality of it. Sometimes there's no solution to a problem and you just have to put it aside and let it simmer, wait for something to turn up. Besides, Hogmanay rolled across Scotland like a minor Black Death, leaving bodies strewn in its wake.

Sam and I were in no mood for revels. We repelled all first footers and simply toasted each other in single malt before sliding into bed. Outside, even in smart Parkside, we could hear the shouts and singing from drunks and optimists until the wee hours. We fell asleep clutching each other like castaways, full of foreboding for tomorrow.

The day after Ne'erday, the phone rang in the hall.

'Brodie? It's Maurice Silver.'

'Yes, Rabbi?'

'Maurice, Maurice. My man is ready to meet you.'

'What's his name?'

'He'll explain when you meet.'

'He's going to talk about Dragan and Ellen Jacobs?'

'Let's say it's about murder.'

'OK, murder interests me.' God help me. 'Where and when?'

'Tomorrow. At Brown's Bar in the Gallowgate. Twelve o'clock.'

It was just before noon on Friday. My tram was ploughing through rain-sodden streets. I sat oozing water on the top deck. I peered through the rivulets on the windscreen at the long stretch of the Gallowgate. Between bomb damage and neglect it was a journey into a dystopia of decay and misery.

I shook myself. I needed to snap out of this mood before it took proper hold and dragged me into the glums. All I needed was a ray of sunshine in January in Glasgow. Which was like hoping for a ray of sunshine in January in Glasgow. The memory of a hot summer was like a child's dream.

In theory Hogmanay was over; double bank holiday on Wednesday and Thursday and then back to pit clothes and porridge on Friday. Fat chance. Alba was nursing a sore head and planning on getting a line from the doctor should any foreman be around to request it. But some hardy editors had managed to get a few skimpy newspapers out. Maybe the Fourth Estate was better practised at revelry. However, the headlines had turned gloomy again. A US Flying Fortress was overdue at Prestwick. The coal crisis was mounting. And in terms of ill omens, it was hard to beat the news that in Palestine the Jewish terrorist brigades had found a new way of suggesting we'd outstayed our welcome: flame-throwers.

I wondered about the choice of venue: Brown's Bar in the badlands of the Gallowgate. A Catholic bar. But then I couldn't think of a Jewish pub – per se – in Glasgow. Brown's reputation surrounded it like a grubby halo. If you knew a couple of verses of 'The Fields of Athenry', or fancied sporting the green on a Saturday before an Old Firm game, this was the place to muster. Get tanked up on a few pints of heavy with your green and white scarved pals. Rev up the vocal cords. And march off with flutes playing to face the old enemy. It depressed the hell out of me.

I'd thought about taking Duncan Todd along for protection. Not as a policeman, but as a card-carrying left-footer. But I was still in the huff with Todd over Ellen Jacobs. Which was silly; I was just as guilty. If only I'd taken that phone call. So I travelled alone, feeling like Gary Cooper wondering for whom the bell was tolling, but lacking an Ingrid Bergman to soothe my worried brow.

I was asking myself why I was doing this. For Ellen? I owed her something. Or for the news story? Really? The rabbi had made it clear that anything that was said by whoever it was I met would be, must be, off the record. Curiosity? It's not a good reason to get killed. No one was paying me for this, either. Occasionally I felt someone else was in charge of my mind. Freud's conflict between Id and Ego no doubt, though I couldn't now remember which was which. I just felt hijacked.

I got off within sight of Brown's. The pub sat squat and ugly just round the corner from Barrowland, the 'Barras'. I pulled my collar tight up round my neck, jammed my hat further down and set off into the east wind. Captain Oates heading into oblivion. Was Brown's preferable? It was closer. And I presumed it was providing a hair-of-the-dog service for its loyal clientele.

I pushed in the door and was instantly minded to step back out and take my chances in the filthy weather. At least the rain was fresh. The sour smell of Hogmanay beer and fags hung in the air like mist from a midden. I looked round. A few old boys cheating at dominoes. Others propped at the bar gazing into their pints, wondering where the last three days had gone. In the corner, some young lads you wouldn't want to mess with after a few pints on a Saturday night. Especially if Celtic had lost. Or if they'd won. No sign of anyone in a skullcap or tugging at his prayer shawl.

I ploughed my way through the damp sawdust to the bar, getting taller as I walked on clogged-up shoes. The man behind the bar was unwavering in his intent to polish his pump handle before noticing me. I waited, feeling the eyes of regulars feast on my back. They knew the game and wanted to see who would break first. I had a ridiculous impulse to cross myself but worried I'd be considered to be taking the piss. Finally the barman feigned surprise and drifted over.

'Yes, pal?'

'A Bell's. Double please.'

He measured two shots into a glass and set it down. I splashed the same amount of water into it. I placed half a crown on the bar and waited for my tanner change. I should have brought a paper to hide behind. A little later I heard the door bang. Steps scuffing towards me. A man in a cloth cap and an eye patch appeared alongside me. The barman moved to greet him.

'Usual, Mal?'

'Same as the big fella here. He is paying.' The transaction complete, Mal turned his one good eye to me. 'Over there.'

He set off and I followed, under the contemplative gaze of the barman.

SEVENTEEN

We sat facing each other over a shoogly table. It was like drinking with a pirate. Someone out of the cast of *Treasure Island*. One-eyed, scar-faced and grinning like a madman, Mal – if that was his name – had a face for the gibbet. Had leaped *off* a gibbet just as the noose was coming his way.

'Mal?' I queried.

'Malachi. Mal's what they call me round here.' The accent was Yiddish-Scots, but the grammar precise.

'Blending in, then?'

'It helps. That and the face.' He grinned and his face didn't get any less piratical. '*Salut.*' He downed the glass of whisky in a oner.

'Did Rabbi Silver explain who I am?' I asked.

'That you are a reporter? Or a detective? He told me you were a little of both. He did not say why you are still investigating these matters.'

'What matters?'

'Life and death, Mr Brodie.'

'Just Brodie is fine. Let's get to the point, Malachi. You were shadowing Ellen Jacobs. You know who killed her. A former SS guard in the Ravensbrück concentration camp. Draganski, or just Dragan to his many victims.'

Malachi sat grinning as I reeled off the facts, as though I was talking about how I'd put up some shelves at the weekend. I ploughed on.

'Ellen Jacobs confessed to her rabbi about her activities. In particular she told him that the small ingots Paddy had stolen were made from gold fillings. Tooth fillings. There's a connection. This is where you pick up the story, *Malachi*.'

'Rabbi Silver said you were also a *soldier*.' He made it sound like vampire.

'So?'

'We want to go home. To Israel. You and your buddies are throwing us back into the sea.'

'And your buddies are using flame-throwers on our boys.' I laid the paper on the table. He glanced at it and shrugged. I planned to hit him on the next shrug.

'Mal, Israel doesn't exist yet. Until the UN agrees, Britain has a mandate to enforce. Oh, bugger this. I didn't come here for a lecture. If you want to play games set up the dominoes.' I got up and grabbed my hat.

'OK, OK. Sit down.'

I sat back down, slowly. He went on. 'I heard you were an interrogator? After the war. You met some bad people?'

'The worst.'

'So, you put these bastards away?'

'I did the first sift. Picking out the rotten fruit. Then sent them for trial.'

He nodded. 'Did they hang? Like the last lot? At Nuremberg?'

'Some. I was at the Belsen trials.'

He grinned. 'I wish I could have seen them swing.' Then he frowned. 'Some got away.'

'Like Dragan, you mean?'

'Him. Others.'

'Small fry slip through the net.'

'Landing in Glasgow.'

'Where they come to a bad end. Tell me what happened to Dragan.'

'My throat is dry.'

I stared at him. I got in two more doubles and sat back down. I held his glass back. 'Let's hear it.'

'OK, OK. I will talk.'

I slid the glass over. He held it between his hands and gazed into the honeyed depths. He went on.

'How many gold pieces did Ellen tell you about?'

'She mentioned eight.'

He shook his head. 'There was more. Much more.'

Light began to dawn. Ellen hadn't quite made a full confession.

'There was more than one robbery?'

He grinned. 'Three. Dragan would have been the fourth.'

Malachi put his hand inside his jacket and pulled out a dirty hankie. He opened it enough for me to see the dull glitter of several small slabs. Then he put it away.

'From Dragan's safe?' I asked.

He nodded.

'Did you find the pawn slip in it or plant it?'

'It was there. I left it for the police. So that even stupid coppers would make the connection.'

'But you're saying there are *three* others like Dragan out there? Nazis? From the camps?

He nodded. My brain was racing.

'Is that what Dragan was after at McGill's? The other gold? He was trying to get the gold back for his pals?'

'We think so.'

I digested this for a while. 'Why did she lie to me?'

'She thought she'd said enough.'

'Why are you telling *me* this? Why not tell the police?'

He shook his head. 'It was police that did this.' He pointed at his eye and the long scar that ran down from his ear.

'Here?'

'Warsaw.'

'You were in the ghetto?'

He nodded.

I said, 'It's different here. *They're* different here.'

'Are they? They have uniforms. It changes them. Who can we trust?'

'Why do you think you can trust me? I'm not of your tribe.'

'You were in Germany. At the camps.'

'I was doing my job.'

He leaned close to me and fixed me with his good eye. It's amazing how concentrated a glare you can achieve with one eye.

'You *saw*, Brodie. Didn't you? You *saw*. I think you are on our side, Brodie.'

I shook my head. 'A number of people have reached that conclusion. They're wrong. I'm on my own side. If our objectives cross, or our views coincide, then fine. But it's coincidence.'

'So tell me: fascism or communism?'

'Don't start. One's as bad as the other. It's just a matter of timing.'

'Timing?'

'Whoever's winning. Both are vile. Both end up with dictators.'

'Pah! It is unthinkable to compare them. Marx makes it clear. Communism is the resolution of the conflict between man and nature and between man and man. It is the riddle of history solved.'

'Mal, if I'd known this was the quality of chat in a Celtic pub, I'd have changed allegiance. Between Marx and Trotsky, Sinoviev and the rest, Jewish intellectuals seem to have a lot of blood on their hands in your great Bolshevik experiment.'

'Well, let us agree that fascism is currently the one in the doghouse. We need help to find Dragan's cronies. Agreed?'

'To stick pitchforks into them? A peasant's tool against the oppressor? Marx would approve.'

His face went hard. 'With whatever we have! With bare hands. You know what this man did at Ravensbrück and Treblinka!'

I shook my head. 'We have laws here. They must get a trial. I won't help you unless you agree to hand them over to our police. We took care of them at Nuremberg.'

He sat and considered for a while. Finally: 'OK. We will do this. You will start now?'

That was too easy. 'We haven't discussed price. My services don't come free.'

'Sure. The rabbi said you work for money.'

'Why sneer? Marx defines me as a wage labourer. I sell my services in order to live.'

He eyed me up, looking miffed that I'd been reading his hero. 'They will pay you the same as before. OK?'

I hesitated. It wasn't that the money was insufficient. It was the job that was different. Very different. Before, it was to catch a thief. Now there'd been four murders and they wanted me to help catch escaped Nazi cut-throats and to deliver them to . . . whom exactly?

'I'm not sure, Malachi. You're talking about a manhunt. That needs men, lots of men. These guys will have gone to ground, especially now Dragan's been killed. One man – me – won't make much of a difference.'

'Brodie, you are a local. You know this city. You have contacts, can ask questions as a reporter. Also, *we* have men. I have men. Others like me. Keen to find *Nazis*.'

'Still . . .'

He leaned close again. 'Brodie, we have documents. From Dragan's house. I can show you.'

'What sort of documents?'

'Official documents. Red Cross. There is a . . . *Netz*?

'A network?'

'Yes. They call them *Rattenlinien*.'

'Rat lines?'

'They say that there are well-established rat lines from Germany through Italy and Spain to South America.'

'And you think they run to Scotland too?'

'Sure. You see the boats in the Clyde? Next stop America.'

'Show me!'

'I don't have them with me. I can bring them. You will be surprised.'

He didn't know me.

EIGHTEEN

'They're coming here? Sunday night!'

'Well, they couldn't come on Saturday, could they?'

She threw the dishtowel at me.

'Sam, they're part of the same crew that Shimon Belsinger brought to inveigle me into getting involved. You were happy to invite them then.'

We squared off across the kitchen table that evening after my meeting with Malachi. The notion of *Rattenlinien* through Glasgow chilled me to the marrow. It felt like a personal invasion. My past hunting me down.

'It's hardly the same business any longer! Shimon and his pals just wanted you to track down a thief. Not mass murderers! The stakes are far higher, Douglas. Too high!'

'You're the one who tells me I shouldn't walk away from trouble. It's what I'm good at – so you tell me.'

'This is *four* murders, Douglas! You could be next!'

'I intend standing aloof. Giving orders. Setting Malachi's army on them.'

'You? Aloof? I'd like to see that. And why would you trust this man – this *communist* – who stuck a pitchfork into someone?'

'It saved a trial.'

'So now the pair of you want to do me out of a job?'

'The only way I'd lead this manhunt is if our goal is to hand these scum over to the polis.'

'Why don't you just hand it over to them now?'

It was a good question. I only had irrational answers tied into personal vengeance and guilt.

So I said, 'The wages are good. Let's hear them out. Shimon and Isaac are coming too. To represent their synagogues.'

On Sunday night, Shimon Belsinger, Isaac and Malachi took seats at Sam's table. The three men were cut from very different cloth. Alongside the solid upright bulk of Shimon and the tailored trimness of Isaac, Malachi looked shifty and lean. His patch and scars spoke of back alleys and dirty deeds. Sam wasn't intimidated by his piratical stares and sneers for the bourgeois trappings. Perhaps I shouldn't have mentioned his politics to her.

'Shall we start with introductions? I like to know who's in my house. I know Mr Belsinger and Mr Feldmann, of course.'

'My name is Malachi Herzog.'

'And who or what are you, Mr Herzog?'

Malachi looked startled, but then grinned. 'I am a Marxist, Miss Campbell. What are you?'

Before Sam threw him out, I sat forward.

'Rather than debate dialectical materialism, can I suggest we focus on the Nazi escape routes? Malachi, you said you had documents. That you would share them with us. Please.'

Sam looked miffed at not getting a verbal battle. So did Malachi. He pulled at a gas-mask case round his body. He dug out a brown envelope and laid it on the table. From it he produced a small pile of papers.

'This is the passport Dragan used. It is in the name of Victor Galdakis. You will see it is a full displaced person's passport issued by the International Committee of the Red Cross.'

He slid the document to Sam who flicked through it, studied the stamps and signature and passed it to me. I picked it up.

'It looks like the real thing. I saw plenty of these after the war.'

Malachi interjected. 'It *is* the real thing. Look at these.' He placed other papers alongside. We examined them.

'Good grief, this is the seal of the Vatican,' I said. 'The Pontificia Commissione di Assistenza – the Vatican Refugee Organisation.'

'And this is a letter signed by Bishop Hudal,' Sam chimed in. 'It's in Italian but I get the gist.'

'Let me see.' I took it and read it aloud in a halting translation. 'This is to testify – certify – that Signor Victor Galdakis is a true friend of the Church and is to be accorded all necessary help . . . without let or hindrance . . . And so on, and so on. Enough backing to get him into the kingdom of heaven.'

There were other letters in German, Italian and French, all supporting the refugee status of the impersonator.

'How did he come by these? Do you know?'

Shimon spoke. 'We don't have answers, Brodie, just more questions. There is talk of these escape routes running across Europe.'

Isaac nodded. 'There is considerable panic in our group. When we heard about Draganski, that was bad enough. But to learn there are others out there! *Mein Gott!*'

Malachi leaned forward. 'We know there are. And we think there may be a big fish. Someone important.'

Sam asked, 'What makes you think that?'

'These papers. They are expensive to obtain. Someone has gone to a lot of trouble for a junior SS guard. He had gold ingots. So did others. Surely only the top Nazis got their hands on gold? We think minions like Dragan could have been hired as guards. To protect someone much more important.'

The room went quiet for a moment while we looked round at each other.

Isaac lifted the passport and waved it at me. 'Douglas, I know you have been through much. You have seen much. For you, these Nazis are *shadim* – demons. We are asking a lot of you. But we need your help. Find the big fish!'

I sat with Sam after they'd gone. Horrors that I'd stuffed away in the dark corners of my mind were slithering out.

'What was I saying about evil seeping into our lives?' she asked.

'It's why I should act.'

'Not just the money, then?'

'If Herzog is right – and I believe he is – then I know what we're looking for. I met them. The type.'

'*If* you believe Herzog. I don't like him.'

'Because he's a commie?'

'Partly. I loathe what they stand for. Stalin is just as much a monster as Hitler. But apart from that, I just don't like *Mal*. Even his nickname means bad. He's trouble.'

'I agree. Have you heard anything about these rat lines at the trials?'

'No. Nothing. Of course we're dealing with the ones we caught, not the ones that got away.'

'That's not to say none of them knows about it.'

'But just to mix up our metaphors thoroughly – rat lines and big fishes – do you really think Glasgow is part of a Nazi escape route? I mean, *Glasgow*?'

'Why not? Some of them will have been planning this for a while. Germany lost the war when they were defeated on the Eastern Front in '43. Hitler wouldn't admit it. He'd rather burn the house down about his ears. But not all of his scummy pals were ready to join their boss in the last bunker. They'd be tucking away gold for a rainy day, and making exit plans.'

*

I went for a swim after work the next day, so that by the time I got home, Sam was already back. She had news.

'I gave Iain Scrymgeour a call. He's in Edinburgh till next week. He says he's heard about your ratty lines. At least about the ones to the Argentine. The idea of a Scottish link had him spitting out his porridge. But he agrees it's feasible. There's no reason why there shouldn't be a northern escape route. He wants to hear more.'

'I'll give him a call.'

She gave me a strange look. 'You can do better than that.'

'How so?'

'He wants to meet you.'

'Edinburgh?'

She cocked her head to one side. Wondering how I'd react. 'No, actually. Hamburg.'

'Don't be daft.'

'Neither Iain nor I have time to question the defendants about this. We're running to stay on top of things as it is. You could come out and see what you can dig up. We have a captive audience.'

'I'm not going to Hamburg.'

She ignored me. 'There's another thing. Iain had asked me about this back in December. I didn't want to raise it with you. I knew it would upset you. But he's asking again.'

'Go on.'

'You know some of the folk you interrogated are facing trial. I've told you how much Iain admired your reports. He says your corroborating testimony would make a difference. He's right, Brodie. If you can get a witness in the stand describing events it's worth ten times the value of a bit of paper.'

'But it all happened over a year ago.' That sounded weak even to me. An unexpected surge of anxiety swept through me, as if I were being threatened. Bile rose in my craw and I had to swallow to cut the gag reflex.

She eyed me sharply. 'What's the matter, Brodie? Have you forgotten? Forgotten them?'

Forgotten the instigators of my nightmares? Forgotten how ordinary they looked and how extraordinary their vile deeds?

I said slowly, 'No, Sam. I haven't forgotten.'

As much as I tried to, I hadn't erased the images. I'd stilled some, obscured others, and caged away my emotions. But when it came to the men and women I'd interrogated, their faces popped up in vivid detail like jack-in-the-boxes.

'There's a third reason. You could keep me company.' She smiled in what she thought was a seductive manner. But it was as seductive as the smile from a dental nurse holding a pair of pliers behind her back.

NINETEEN

I lay on my lonely bed in the dark. Only the light from my cigarette punctured the night. Outside a steady rain drummed on the streets and sluiced my window. Sam's suggestion had upped the ante. Yet I was calm. As if I were accepting my fate; that no matter how hard I tried to put distance between me and my past, it wasn't going to work. It was annoying. I'd long since stopped believing in a higher power and yet here I was acknowledging that I'd been dealt a hand and had no choice but to play it. I couldn't throw in my cards and leave the table.

Could I?

Was I really not master of my fate? Is there no self-will for any of us? Or just me? It didn't seem tolerable. I *wouldn't* tolerate it. I came to a clear decision. In the morning, I'd simply say no. Let this cup be taken from me. I wasn't going through another war crimes trial. I wasn't going to bloody Hamburg. They couldn't pay me enough to compensate for the guaranteed future of sleepless nights and daytime nightmares. I drifted off to sleep, full of resolve.

Sam and I collided at breakfast. I was about to tell her about my decision.

'Oh Douglas, Izzie was doing our laundry yesterday. Boiling the hankies. She says she found some of yours with blood on them. Nose bleed?'

I started. 'Yes. Yes, the other day. Sorry. I should have put them in cold water. Did they come out?'

'They're fine. Look, must dash. I'm in Edinburgh this morning. I have a review with the top brass in Farquharson Stable.' She gulped down her tea, kissed me on the cheek and shot up the stairs.

As the door slammed I examined my left hand. The thumb was covered in tiny bruises. Pinpricks. I licked it. I reached in my pocket and pulled out the Seaforth cap badge. I rubbed the stag's head gently and fingered the motto: *'Cuidich 'n Righ'* – 'Help the King'. I slid it back in my pocket. As the thunder of Izzie's hoover roared down the stairwell I made for the door before she started questioning me too.

I went off for a swim and then headed straight into the *Gazette*. At Sunday's meeting with Shimon and Malachi I'd left it that I would let them know if I was prepared to pursue this case further. My answer was no. I was going to pass on this one. In the same determined vein I planned to see Sam this evening and get her to call Scrymgeour to say I wouldn't be coming out to Hamburg to testify, far less go on a wild-rat chase.

I spent the morning shaping an article on the black market in counterfeit Co-op coupons. If it weren't for the constraints of column inches, not to mention deadlines, and subs killing my darlings, this job would suit me. Maybe I should give it a bit more time? Use it as a springboard to a full writing career: short stories, novels . . .

It was nearly noon and I looked up to see what the commotion was at the door. I was just in time to see Eddie pointing directly at me. Alongside him was a much taller figure. In uniform. Police uniform with lots of glinting silver on his shoulder and his cap peak. God, what had I done? And why did it merit arrest by the top man?

Eddie saw me looking and summoned me with his hand as though he was conducting traffic. I got to my feet, slipped on my jacket and walked towards trouble. Eddie was flushed and stretching up and down on his toes.

'Ah, Brodie. This is Chief Constable McCulloch.'

McCulloch pulled off his leather glove and held out his hand. 'Mr Brodie, it's good to meet you in person at last.'

I shook his hand. 'And you too, sir.'

So I wasn't being arrested. I'd seen his photo plenty of times in the papers and viewed him in the flesh years ago, before the war, at a parade in the city centre. He would have been a superintendent then. I had been a uniformed sergeant before shifting across to detective duties. He and I had spoken once, by phone, last September. At the bloody end of the Glasgow Marshal vigilante case. He'd offered me a job. I'd declined. Had he come in person to twist my arm?

'I wonder, Mr Paton, if I could steal Mr Brodie from you for a short while? Is there somewhere we could talk? Privately?'

'Of course, sir. Right this way, sir. Elaine! Get some tea thegither for the Chief Constable. Follow me, sir.' Eddie all but bowed as he retreated like a flunky leaving his king. I exchanged a look with McCulloch, and followed them out. Eddie showed us into the conference room and left us to it, McCulloch having declined tea in favour of privacy. We sat. He took off his cap and remaining glove. He was a big well-set man, I'd say in his early fifties. Bald head, amiable face but scrutinising eyes.

'What can I do for you, sir?'

'Well, you can start by calling me Malcolm. What do you prefer, Mr Brodie?'

'Brodie is fine . . . Malcolm.'

'Good, well, Brodie, I'm not here to try to convince you that you should take up my offer of a job. Though it's still on the table if you change your mind.'

'Thank you. I've got my hands full here. Taking a back seat.'

'Really? That's not what I hear.'

I wondered whom he'd been talking to, and how much he knew. I smiled inscrutably.

'You have been busy, Brodie. And now's my chance to thank you in person for – shall we say – your help in dealing with the Glasgow Marshals. Not to mention the Slattery gang before that.'

'It wasn't something I went out looking for.'

'It just came your way, eh? And it seems you have friends in high places.'

'Really? I'm only aware of those in low places.'

'Well, let's just check a few things. You *are* Mr Douglas Brodie, formerly Major Brodie of the Seaforths? You *did* carry out special duties in Germany after the war including interrogation of some senior Nazis? And you were directly involved in the Belsen war crimes trials.'

'Guilty as charged.' How the hell did he know about Belsen? It wasn't something I ever talked about, even to myself.

'You've also been . . . how shall I put this? . . . helping us with some enquiries into some thefts among the Jewish community? And related murders?'

'Just from a reporter's perspective.' Duncan been blabbing? Sangster?

'Indeed? In that case, I have the right man. I received a call this morning from the head of MI5.'

TWENTY

was in real trouble.

'You know who that is?'

'Your predecessor. Sir Percy Sillitoe.'

'Exactly. He told me about the possibility that this fair city of ours is harbouring escaped Nazis.'

'How did *he* hear?'

'Sir Percy took a personal phone call last evening from the British legal representative at the Hamburg trials.'

I felt the tidal wave of fate lapping at my knees.

McCulloch was continuing: 'Do you know what he asked Sir Percy to do? And therefore why I'm here?'

I sighed. 'I'm beginning to guess.'

'They would be very grateful if you would make your way to Hamburg. You can travel with your colleague Advocate Samantha Campbell.'

Colleague? What sort of euphemism was that? Was he trying to make this sound like a wee holiday? A jaunt with my girlfriend down the Elbe? It might be more tempting in springtime, but it would be bloody freezing just now. And I didn't imagine it would involve a lot of jolly beer-swilling and lederhosen-slapping.

'Malcolm, I'm honoured and, frankly, astonished that you've come in person to deliver this message. I have to ask why. You're a busy man. A phone call would do. In fact Sillitoe could have called me himself and saved you the bother.'

'He wanted me in the loop. Correctly. This is my city. As for this personal invitation, would it have worked if I'd called you? The last time I phoned you to do something you turned me down. You have a certain reputation for stubbornness, Brodie. Percy made it clear that he won't take no for an answer. Besides . . .'

'Besides?'

McCulloch's face suddenly lost its openness and charm. He bared the steel. 'We've had four deaths, Brodie. Four! If there's a viper's nest in Glasgow, I want it ripped out and the creatures crushed underfoot!'

'Right.' The force of his anger seemed to reverberate round the room. 'I can understand your interest. But why is Sillitoe engaged?'

'Why do you think? He's MI5. His department is responsible for rooting out and returning these escapees for trial by the British authorities. If there is an international network operating in Britain with links to the Red Cross and the Vatican – good God, the mind reels just talking about it – he wants to know about it. Wants to stop it. This is a threat to the safety of the kingdom.'

'Why doesn't he just ask for the information from the Hamburg legal team?'

'Ah, the very point I made to Percy myself.' He smiled. 'It seems the team out there have very little knowledge of these rat lines. Just a few snippets. More whispers than hard facts. They're also up to their legal eyeballs preparing for the next round of trials and don't have the time to spare on digging into this matter. They're short-staffed and need a hand. You have the German, Brodie, and can have a second go at chatting up the accused. Find some facts. Some *names*.'

'Why are any of these detainees going to talk to me?'

'I assume they will have little say in the matter. It'll be up to you to get them to spout, of course. Brodie, we're desperate for leads. You're our best hope of stopping more killings.'

'Then you're in bother.'

He ignored me. 'There's another reason for your going out there. The legal team and indeed our government are being pressured by the Polish authorities. The Poles want to take over the trial.'

'Why?'

'Overtly? It's all about statehood, showing they're a competent democratic government again. They're not. The communist parties – backed by the USSR – staged a vote last year. Poland is a satellite of Russia in all but name. In a week's time there will be parliamentary elections. They will be rigged. The communists, manipulated by Stalin's agents, have flung all opposition in prison.'

'What impact would this have on any trials?'

'The Poles would kill the process or, at best, delay it for years.'

'Why would they kill it?'

'There's a lot of uncomfortable history out there. A lot of Poles and Russians were willing accomplices in getting rid of their Jews.'

'But what good would *I* do?'

'We want quick justice in the British occupied zone. Calm things down and move on. They think it will considerably strengthen our case if you take the witness stand to support your own reports. Confirm identities and statements. Cometh the hour, cometh the man, Brodie, eh?'

The waters were now up to my neck. I tried one last lunge for the lifeboat.

'I don't *have* to do this, Malcolm, do I? I have the choice?'

He looked at me, startled, head on one side. 'I suppose so. But it's your duty, man.'

'Malcolm, don't, just don't, talk to me about duty. I've more than done my bit.'

'We all have, Brodie. These are demanding times.'

I bit my tongue. Demanding times? Was he comparing his

sacrifice of sitting behind ever-bigger desks with endless cups of tea with my six years of running around the Continent being shot at?

'I'm trying to lead a quiet life.'

'Can I say you're not making a very good job of it?'

We looked at each other and laughed. I tried again.

'I'm not explaining it right. Sure, it would be nice to lead a tranquil existence. My feet up. My nose in books. But it's more than that. If I get bored with it I want to *choose*. *I* want to decide what *I* do . . . not take any more bloody orders from on high.'

My rising volume and choice of words shocked me. It was like my inner Brodie talking. Where the hell did that come from? But it was also liberating.

'Rubbish, man! Do you think God handed out talents but didn't expect you to use them? Besides . . .'

I was beginning to dread his *besides*. He had the look of a man holding a hidden ace in a high-stake poker game. What now?

'Yes?'

'Sir Percy wanted me to remind you that as a demobbed officer you're on the reserve list. You can be called up at a moment's notice. He's been in touch with the Army Department. Your papers are on the way.'

I collapsed back in my chair. 'I'm being – called – up? *Again?*'

'But to sweeten the deal, you're being promoted, Brodie. For the duration of this special mission, you will be given the acting rank of lieutenant colonel. Congratulations. Apparently a uniform is already on its way, together with travel documents. 'Fraid it might not be the Seaforths. They're at full strength. Pity. They say you could have been one of them if you'd stayed on . . .'

My brain was short-circuiting. A half-colonel? But not my old regiment? Back in uniform? McCulloch was still explaining.

'. . . but it's only for a short stint. It's the rank that counts when you're dealing with these international legal matters. Lots of red tape about. Gives you easier clearance. Smooths the way. Full pay, of course, at the new rank, and some deal being done about your army pension contribution.'

He must have read defeat in my eyes. As well as shock. The waters rose over my head.

'Splendid. I knew we could rely on you.' He got up. I got up. He shook my hand and left me standing alone in the conference room, incredulous at what had just taken place. Back in uniform? They can't do this.

TWENTY-ONE

'Colonel Douglas Brodie has a ring to it.'

'Shut up, Sam. I've been conscripted.'

'I love a man in uniform. I wonder which you'll get? I hope it has a kilt.'

'This is your fault for stirring things up with your pal Scrymgeour.'

'It'll be interesting. And we'll be together. We've talked about going away for a wee jaunt.'

'North Germany in the middle of winter? I was thinking more of Rothesay in the summer.'

I got up and poured another big splash into both our glasses. I began pacing the lounge. I put my tumbler on the mantelpiece and poked at the smouldering briquettes. It provoked a pitiful flame and only a brief burst of heat. Coal rations had been cut again and this was a big house to keep warm. Mum's Christmas contribution had long since been consumed. As had her dumpling.

I gave it one last try. 'I have a job to do here. Wee Eddie's short-staffed.'

'Get away with you. Eddie would love to have his star reporter out in Hamburg. "Read all about it! News from the trial of the century! Our man in the witness stand!" The *Record* is always headlining this stuff. So can the *Gazette*.'

I stopped pacing. 'How would this work, Sam? I mean, let's think about the practicalities. Say there's a dozen or so of these defendants, each locked up in his wee cell. They're on trial for their lives. They've already seen the big bosses strung up. Why would they talk to me about escape routes when – quite obviously – they don't have access to one themselves?'

'You've answered your own question, Brodie. *Play ball with us and you might save your neck.*'

'We can't make that sort of promise, Sam.'

'Not a promise, more a suggestion. A hint, if you like.'

'You're a ruthless woman at times, Samantha Campbell.'

'*All* the time, Douglas Brodie. Your turn to get the coal in.'

Next day I phoned Shimon and Isaac and told them that I would be pursuing this case but they could save their money. My new paymaster was the Crown.

'When will you be back, Brodie?' asked Shimon.

'I don't know. February? March?'

'Will you call me on your return? Tell us what you found? This is vital to our community.'

'I know, Shimon. I know. I'll be in touch.'

Isaac's concerns were different.

'This will be hard for you, Douglas.'

'It's a short stint. I know the ropes.'

'It's because you know the ropes that I am concerned for you. It is too much for one man. We have asked too much. I'm sorry.'

'I'm fine, Isaac.'

'No, you're not. I've seen your eyes.'

I swallowed. Was it that obvious?

'I'll be with Samantha.'

'That's the only blessing. Take care of each other.'

'We will. Which reminds me: how's Amos? Is he still intent on life in a kibbutz?'

'The arguments get worse, and go nowhere, Douglas. He is a stubborn man.'

'He didn't fall far from the tree, Isaac.'

'That's the trouble. I would do the same. Maybe I will.'

'Don't say that! I'd miss your coffee.'

'I'd send you some. Go with God, Douglas.'

By way of preparing us for the north German plains, winter hit Scotland with a vengeance. It snowed for two full days across the west of the country. All the major towns and cities had power cuts, partly because of pylons downed in the blizzards, partly through government efforts to save supplies.

In sharp contrast to Manny Shinwell's shambolic Ministry of Fuel and Power, the War Office moved with uncomfortable speed and efficiency. They'd had practice. On Saturday morning, within four days of McCulloch's visit, I took delivery of a thick brown envelope covered in official red sealing wax, and a large parcel, similarly sealed and stamped 'Priority War Office'. They arrived, special delivery, at seven o'clock in the morning. I signed for them and took them in.

I emptied the envelope on the kitchen table and picked through the instructions and travel warrants; first class all the way to Hamburg. Sam had already received her identical set. No sign of return tickets for either of us, however. There was a separate envelope in good-quality white paper. I used a kitchen knife and pulled out a folded foolscap document and a second smaller envelope. The foolscap had red wax seals. It was a commission, my new commission as a lieutenant colonel in His Majesty's armed forces.

I sat down, staring at the paper. My father hadn't lived long enough to see my first commission as a one-pip lieutenant in his old regiment. It had been one of the proudest days of my life. This commission – unlooked-for, unwanted and unwarranted – churned up a whole ragbag of emotions from guilt to wonder to pride. My immediate thought was to phone my mother to share in this casual achievement. My next was that it would terrify her, that she would worry sick about me being back in the army. Mostly I felt this wasn't real, in the sense that I hadn't earned it. Would I? What was being asked of me? How much of me did I have to provide in return? But I couldn't quite hide from myself the small thrill it gave me.

I placed the smaller envelope to one side and turned to the box. I picked it up, placed it on the table and began hacking with the bread knife at the wax and string. I tore away the brown paper and gingerly opened the cardboard box. Please don't let it be the Black Watch. Or the Signals. Fine regiments both, but . . . The 'friendly' rivalry between the Black Watch and the Seaforths was now ingrained in me after too many pub fights in my NCO days. And while the Signals Corps were some of the bravest men I'd met, they carried radios. I was a rifleman.

Sam would be disappointed. I was amused and then touched. The moment I saw the black beret and its silver badge with the distinctive emblem and the words 'Fear Naught', I relaxed. I would be proud to wear this.

Sam came in. 'Show me, show me.'

I stuck the beret on, pulled it to a jaunty angle and turned to her. 'What do you think?'

She put her specs on and peered at the insignia. 'It's a tank.'

'That's a clue.'

Her face fell. 'No kilt?'

'Not even a Kilmarnock bunnet. Sorry.'

I turned back to the box. Under the beret was a black holster. I took out the gun. The Enfield No. 2 revolver. Empty and no sign of a box of .38s. For safety they would be sent separately, I assumed. Unless they thought I didn't need bullets. Which would be ironic for a Royal Tank Regiment man. Also a pity; on this trip I'd feel more comfortable with something that went bang.

I hauled out the khaki jacket. I'd forgotten the weight of the heavy wool. It had the correct crown and star on each shoulder and collar insignia and buttons to match the beret.

'Go on. Put it on,' she said.

I hoped they'd got the size right. It would be a real test of the system. They must have checked my service record. And my swimming was keeping my weight down. More or less. It was a neat fit. Not new, but well cleaned and cared for. I did up the jacket and Sam helped me slide the black leather Sam Browne belt and cross-strap in place, looping through the holster. She stood back and inspected me as gravely as Monty himself.

'You'll do, laddie. You'll do. How does it feel? Take a look.' She pointed at the mirror upstairs in the hallway. I walked up and stood in front of it. I was startled. It wasn't me. It was the wrong headgear and the wrong jacket. Certainly the wrong buttons and wrong rank. But, Christ, it felt right. What the hell was happening? Was I enjoying being wrapped up in the comfortable embrace of old rituals? Was I relieved at once more being told what to do rather than working it out for myself? Or did I just relish the promotion?

Sam joined me and put her left arm round me from behind.

'It suits you. But you're improperly dressed. No, not your troosers. You've no decorations.'

She fingered the gap on my chest. Then she put her right arm round and slid a strip of material in place. 'This was in the box.'

It was a row of medal ribbons. They'd got it right. All my tours of duty. The red, white and blue of the France and Germany medal. The green, white and red symbolising Italy. And the sandy ribbon with red and blue stripes for Africa.

It also held the little strip of purple with white either side. The Military Cross, handed out to eejits and show-offs. I fingered each and triggered snapshots from every campaign. But it was like I was watching *Pathé News*; it wasn't me in the pictures.

'What about this letter?' Sam handed it to me.

I sat down on the steps and opened it. It was in fine black copperplate. I looked up at her. 'It's from my old boss in the African campaign, Gordon MacMillan. He's a major general now.'

'Tell me.'

'It says, "Dear Lieutenant Colonel Brodie – Dear Douglas! It gives me much pleasure to have you back with us, albeit under different colours . . ." It goes on for a bit . . .'

'Tell me.'

'If you'd stayed in, as I advised you, you would already be wearing these badges of rank and, in due course, would have made field officer rank and above. You still could.

Wear this uniform with pride. It belonged to a good man. If you perform this service on behalf of your country half as well as Lieutenant Colonel Bill Ferguson we will not be disappointed in you.

Yours sincerely,
Gordon MacMillan
Major General
Director of Weapons and Development, General Staff
War Office
London'

I paused, trying not to let my feelings overcome me. MacMillan had led from the front at Tobruk and was now safely behind a desk somewhere. I remembered him last at Bremen after Tom Rennie, the CO of the 51st, got killed.

Rennie had given me my major's crowns. I took off my beret.

'Well then, Miss Campbell, shall we catch a train?'

We left that night on the sleeper to Euston. I slept fitfully on the bottom bunk, as ever mildly amazed at how my life could take a turn, remembering the journey I'd taken in reverse last April. Called to Glasgow from London by the lady now in the bunk above, Advocate Samantha Campbell, and asked to help prove my old pal Hugh Donovan innocent of the murder of a young boy. She'd needed all the help I could give her. The odds and the system were stacked against him and us.

The real killer was long dead now. I'd seen to that. And the corrupt policemen who'd concocted the evidence against Hugh were queuing up for gruel in Barlinnie alongside the cut-throats and thieves they'd put away over the years. I'd heard Muncie, former Superintendent Muncie, was spending much of his time either in the prison hospital or in solitary between attacks on him by his fellow inmates. It should have brought me satisfaction. Instead it just left me empty.

Now here I was, heading south again, on my way to reprise the worst period in my life. Once more to sit opposite malign intelligence and twisted reasoning. Facing such amoral certainty made me doubt my own standards. Even my sanity. Was wickedness always just below the surface in everyman? And why should it be my job to confront it? The wave of self-pity made me nauseous. I had a stupid moment of anxiety when I realised I'd left my old cap badge behind. I had a new one, hadn't I? In its proper place.

When I had drifted off to sleep, rocked in my hurtling cradle, my dreams turned black. The old powerlessness settled over me and I woke gasping and punching the base of the bunk overhead, fearing I'd been buried alive.

'Douglas? Are you all right?' came the urgent whisper, then the hand from above, digging down through the cloying earth, dragging me to the light.

'Sorry. Bad dream. I'm OK.' I held her fingers until sleep carried me off again.

TWENTY-TWO

We rolled gently into Euston at six thirty. In the narrow confines of the compartment we sluiced our faces, bumped into each other and fought our way into day clothes. I shaved and donned my uniform and we sat on my bunk turned back into a seat – hers we had stowed away – sipping hot sweet tea until life returned to our brain cells.

We stepped out on to the platform and were saluted and whisked into a staff car driven by a young WRAF.

'This is for you, sir.'

Shells for my service revolver. I tucked them away.

The drive to RAF Hendon took half an hour through busy London streets. Snow had come south too. Dirty grey mounds lined the pavements. I could see the changes already. This city had more life than a year ago, more double-deckers, more cars and certainly more people. Fewer in uniform.

We swung into the RAF station and instantly left the suburbs. A vista opened up: white fields surrounding a long grey strip of runway. A few planes sat round the far right of the field next to a huge hangar. We pulled up at the officers' mess, a black and white faux Tudor building facing the airfield.

It felt natural to be sitting at the long brown tables tucking into bacon and eggs surrounded by fellow officers, albeit in RAF blue. Sam seemed completely at ease too. She'd already made this journey once and smiled at the fuss being made of her by the CO and his staff.

We took off over London and turned east. We could now see the staggering extent of the bomb damage. Great swathes of the docks and east London obliterated. It would take decades to rebuild. I dug into my bag and pulled out the cartridge box. I loaded my revolver. Sam glanced at me and then looked away with a frown.

We crossed the North Sea, taking the same route as Bomber Command just a couple of years ago. We picked up the coast of Holland, just north of my own last battlefields. Every mile from the Normandy beaches to the Rhine crossing costing us blood. By the end, the 51st had lost over 1,200 officers, killed, wounded or missing, and over 15,000 men.

We hugged the dotted line of the Dutch coast until the pilot announced we were over Germany and into British-controlled air space. Below was worse than anything we'd seen over London. Towns and cities had been steamrollered. Only the seams and slices of tarmac left a clue to former civilisation. Our plane droned on into the late morning, heading northeast up the bend of the coast.

Suddenly we were over water again, a great wide estuary: the Elbe, the gateway to Germany's biggest port city. Now Hamburg was a great wasteland dissected by the grey wind of the river. Our plane took a northerly dip and headed towards the edges of the concrete moonscape. We landed just after noon on a patched-up airfield in the middle of acres of rubble. Sam and I were stiff and sore from sitting, and we tumbled down the steps into a snell wind blowing from the north. It was below freezing and all round the airfield were piles of cleared snow. British bombers and some aircraft with American insignia were parked haphazardly round the landing strip. The hangars and control towers were pockmarked and damaged. Bomber Harris's boys hadn't missed much.

Another round of saluting, another staff car, and we were driving south. The sun was already dipping into the cold sky of this short winter day. All around, tumbled buildings. Windows gaping blindly. Cratered roads punching the springs and bouncing us around in the back seat. Suddenly a road sign swam into view. I focused on it until I could make out the German script. Hamburg.

'How far now, Sam?'

'About five miles. A part of the city called Rotherbaum. In the centre of town, near Lake Alster.'

'Where's the courthouse?'

'In a big old building aptly called the Curiohaus.'

'Are we rooming there?

The driver cut in from the front seat.

'You've got a nice gaff, sir. If I may say so. You and the lady. A hotel we've taken over for senior officers, sir, like your good self.'

Sam snorted. 'A decrepit pub by a big bloody cold lake.'

It was a fair description. We were suddenly driving alongside a vast frozen plain. Mist hung across it. A faded watercolour from a palette of greys.

We drew up outside a small hotel. A sign bearing a snarling grizzly hung over the doorway. Though built of wood, the Bear had come unscathed through the firestorm of bombing that reduced much of the city to ash. Saved by the lake. Its old dark timbers made it look more like a Goering hunting lodge. I was surprised not to see a black and red flag dangling from its pole.

We got out, and an arctic chill engulfed us from the lake. I stared across the dull expanse and felt my life force sucking away.

Our driver grabbed our suitcases from the boot and we followed him into a dark lobby. A tall young officer shot up from an armchair, folded his newspaper and came towards us. He hit the spot in front of me and snapped a salute.

'Sir, welcome to Hamburg. I'm Lieutenant Collins, sir. I'm your liaison officer while you're here.'

'Thank you, Lieutenant. You'll know Advocate Miss Samantha Campbell?'

The young officer turned to Sam and managed to salute and blush at the same time.

'Yes, of course, ma'am. It's nice to have you back. I'll get your driver to put your bags away. Can I get you a drink, sir? And ma'am? Before we dine. Unless you'd like to freshen up first?'

'A drink would freshen us up, Lieutenant. Yes, Sam?'

'Takes the chill off.'

Collins left us to it. He would meet us in the morning but said that Sam's lawyer pal was planning to drop by for dinner at seven. We had a couple of hours to kill. The barman splashed liberal doses into our glasses. Mess standard measures were doubles but here the measuring glass had been dispensed with. For safety we added the same amount of water. I found I'd got a thirst and the first couple hardly had time to wet the glass. Sam was barely less restrained. We sat on our bar stools and caught our breath.

'I could get used to this life . . . Colonel.' Sam smiled.

'Stick with me. Rank has its privileges. Though we'd better keep an eye on our mess bill.'

'Also on our headaches. We've got work in the morning.'

TWENTY-THREE

We retired to hang our clothes, freshen up and change for dinner. I was looking forward to confronting Scrymgeour. Thanks to him I'd been shanghaied back into the army and dumped in this arctic bombsite. But I needed to watch myself. I had an instinctive and petty envy for his privileged background: head boy at Fettes College, a double first at Edinburgh and then casually taking silk as though born to it. As no doubt he was. What did he know of tenements and tatties? I was pretty sure he could trace his lineage directly to the bearer of William Wallace's standard and before that the pastoral staff-holder of St Columba.

Then there was the small matter of being an old 'pal' of Sam's. How pally were they? She'd said he was single. I knew from my studies that his surname was Old English for 'swordsman'. Hah. I could see the pair of them in Edinburgh in a year or two's time holding cocktail parties in their six-bedroom townhouse in Charlotte Square while upstairs in the nursery their nanny looked after the next generation of lawyers and standard-bearers.

I tightened my tie, shot my cuffs out and went down. Waiting for me in the hallway was Sam, deep in conversation with a civilian who looked just like I imagined: tall and angular, auburn hair and specs and high winged collar as though he'd had no time to change other than slip on a casual jacket since leaving the courtroom. A bulging briefcase stood between his legs. They turned as I arrived. The man looked bone-weary but still came up with a smile. He stuck out his hand. Long thin fingers with a strong grip. Just the job for carrying a flag.

'You must be Douglas Brodie. I'm Iain Scrymgeour. Delighted to meet you and glad you've come.' He maintained his hit rate: posh Edinburgh accent with only the faintest undertones of Scotland.

'Did I have any choice? Pleased to meet you, Iain. Call me Brodie.'

'Sorry if you felt a bit railroaded. I can assure you this will really help us along. You should get something out of it too.'

'I already have. I've been conscripted.'

He had the grace to look abashed. 'Yes, well, the War Office moves in mysterious ways. Sorry about the rush, too. It's always like that round here. Seat-of-the-pants stuff most of the time. Look, I'm starving. Shall we cadge some dinner?'

The dining room continued the theme of hunting décor, this time with the added presence of startled deer heads ranged round the walls. I could imagine the local Waffen SS in here singing the '*Horst Wessel*' and pounding the tables with their tankards. More whisky helped. And the conversation. I continued to give Iain a hard time. Apart from Sam I didn't get much opportunity for crossing swords with smart people. Far less actual swordsmen.

'This is just for show, Iain. Everyone knows your defendants are guilty of something unspeakable. Even in the name of medical science it was inhuman. How do you respond to the accusations that this is victor's justice?'

'One could say why the hell not? But we're sticking to the letter of the Geneva Convention on military trials. It's fairer than any of them deserves. Christ, you saw it first-hand, Brodie. Surely you agree?'

'I didn't see them do it. Isn't that the test? There's no doubt the crimes were committed. You're the prosecutor. Your job is to prove the accused did it.'

'Spot on, Brodie. We're making history here. Down the line, we want the next generation to say we did it right.'

'On which point . . . why the hurry?'

He peered at me over his glasses. They kept slipping off his now shiny nose, unveiling his weary eyes. He'd only been back a few days but already looked like he could sleep for a month. At least he was a worker.

'Samantha mention that we're under the gun? Bloody Poles trying to barge in and take over. New communist government trying to throw some muscle around. Also a bit of understandable revenge against the Nazis. Real reason? A bloody cover-up. Not washing dirty linen in public and all that. Some of the Poles and their Soviet paymasters could just as well be in the dock for war crimes as their former Nazi allies. Basically they want us out of here so they can draw a veil over everything.'

'An iron one presumably. Why don't we let them?'

He raised his eyebrows. 'Devil's advocate, Brodie? You mean, does it really matter? Wouldn't it be nice to pack up and go home and let them get on with it?'

'They don't deserve your expensive services.'

'Government rates, sadly. But I take your point. Sam and I have debated this umpteen times. What happened here – I mean in Europe – changed everything and nothing. Parts of the continent have swapped one totalitarian regime for another. If we give in to the Soviets, if we just walk away and cede any ground, then we've only won part of the war.'

'And this trial is important?'

'It sheds light. Dictators can't stand democratic sunshine.'

'Like vampires,' I suggested.

They both laughed. Nervously, I thought. 'Exactly.'

It was an argument I instinctively supported, but I wasn't about to agree. 'You sound like you're running for office, Iain.'

He smiled. 'Mayor of Hamburg?'

Sam kicked me.

I pulled in my horns. 'How's the trial itself going?'

Iain leaned forward. 'We've got a momentum going and I reckon we can tie up this first trial in a matter of weeks. Justice done and we can all go and get on with our lives.'

'*First* trial?'

'Gosh, yes. Of many. As we catch them and bring them to court. That's why the first one's so important. Sets the standard, the modus operandi and the pace for the subsequent.'

I saw his point. 'My priority is try to put a stop to the killings in Glasgow. What's yours?'

'Nailing the defendants. Your notes are fine records of a difficult job. I assume you wrote in German as you went along and then typed them up afterwards in English?'

It took me back to the fifteen-hour days, every day of the week, dealing with a constant stream of paranoia, invective and claims of innocence. There wasn't a time when I wasn't cursing my lack of shorthand, or my rusty ear for the language. It was like attending an intensive, unremitting conversational German course. I heard every accent from the Urals to the Rhine, from Hamburg to Vienna. I heard every excuse and dodge and lie invented. I realised Iain was waiting for my answer.

'We had teams of secretaries in the room. Brilliant girls. My favourite was called Hillary. She kept verbatim notes in shorthand. I'd go over the notes afterwards with her and dictate a draft. She'd have the transcript ready by the next day. I'd amend it and she'd type a final. We'd get the prisoner back in and have them sign the statement. Top copy in those files, I assume.'

'But it was your analysis that really shone through. It wasn't just a transcript.'

He sounded like he meant it. Maybe he did.

'They weren't the most cooperative of defendants. I had to work round and through their answers. Make interpretations. Then persuade them to sign up to them.'

Iain was nodding. 'We want you to stand up and confirm your notes and their statements. Give some colour. We'll ask questions and firm up on the evidence.'

Some colour? Is that what they wanted? All I could remember is grey, pasty pink, the colour of human skin left to rot on skeletons.

'Is there a problem?'

'The defence is doing its job. Trying to pick holes in every case. Making claims about statements made under duress. That's where your first-hand account will be invaluable. You know the ropes, Brodie. You were at the Belsen trials at Lüneburg.'

'Not as a member. I ran the support unit for the court president, General Berney-Ficklin.'

'Great background for this, Brodie.'

'A bellyful.'

'*That*, I can appreciate. These are for you.'

He leaned down and lifted up his briefcase. It was a weary gesture as though he was carrying more than the simple weight of the bag. He placed three fat files on the dining table. He might as well have placed them on my shoulders. As their names appeared I fought the urge to get up and walk out: Schwarzhuber, Ramdohr, and the lovely Binz. I opened the first pages of each and gazed at their photos.

'Recognise them?' Iain asked.

'Of course. Have they changed in the flesh?'

'Thinner, greyer, fewer smiles? One other thing, Brodie. You need to meet one of our key people here, Vera Atkins.'

'Special Operations Executive?'

'Three of her agents were murdered at Ravensbrück. One survived, Odette Sansom. Odette's here too. Both extraordinary women.'

'A miracle. I look forward to meeting them. And, Iain, I'll do all I can to punish the beasts who murdered our people. But to return to my primary goal: what do you know of these escape routes? The rat lines?'

'Just gossip. We lost a very big rat a month ago. Fritz Suhren.'

'The camp commandant?'

'Gave us the slip. We've got everybody out looking for him. I'm just maddened by the thought that he could be in Argentina by now.'

'Or the Gorbals,' Sam chipped in.

'God spare us,' Iain replied.

'What's my access to the prisoners?'

'They're all yours. The prison – and indeed this whole trial – is under our jurisdiction.'

Sam stifled a yawn, and I realised how tired I was. I'd sunk a brain-pickling volume of whisky. Iain was staying up on sheer will power. We called it a night and fell into our respective rooms.

I dumped the three files on the dressing table and hung up my clothes. I was too tired even to try the connecting door to Sam's. But when I stripped and got into bed, my brain switched on and began grinding away at the memories stirred up by those three names. After a while I gave up and got out of bed. I put the table lamp on, and moved the files into the pool of light. I picked the folders up one by one, and flicked them open. I knew these people. Knew what they did.

I read for a bit until my eyes hurt. I closed the files and lay down on my bed. I smoked and thought about the morning. I assumed I would be awake until then.

Next thing a bell was shrilling in my ears. I stumbled across the room and grabbed the phone. It was Lieutenant Collins.

'Good morning, sir. I'll be at your hotel with a car in half an hour, if that's all right, sir? Mr Scrymgeour says he will see you at his office. Oh, and he asked you to kindly remember to bring the files.'

I mumbled a reply and put the phone back in the cradle. I looked up. The mirror showed an old man with red eyes and wrinkled brow. My hair was plastered to one side. My mouth was full of bar-room sawdust. I had thirty minutes to restart my heart and hope my brain would follow.

I picked up the phone and got the front desk. It was a shock to hear German, and automatically to answer in kind. Hot tea and toast was on the way. I peeked out of the door and saw the signs to the bathroom. I grabbed a towel, crept along the corridor and stuck my abused body under a hot shower. Within twenty-five minutes I was marching down the corridor in full uniform, files under my arm, thinking that I might live after all. But it would be pain-filled.

Sam was waiting, polished and perfumed, her eyes clear, her hair shining. A rebuke.

'Long lie, Brodie?'

'Been studying the files. And good morning to you too, Miss Campbell. Shall we go?'

I marched towards the door, shoulders back, head up. Inside, my heart was hammering like a child's on his first day back at school after the long summer holidays. Which was ridiculous. There was no Latin teacher waiting for me, swishing his tawse, limbering up to punish the first sloppy translation of the day. These creatures had no hold over me.

TWENTY-FOUR

t was a short drive to Rothenbaumchaussee and the impressive Curiohaus, all red tiles and stolid German façade. I fingered my medal ribbons and played with my badges of rank to remind myself I'd moved on. I was all grown up. This was the real world and I'd passed all the tests. Then why was I breathing so fast?

Scrymgeour's office was tucked away in the back of this building commandeered for the trials. Lieutenant Collins led the way past heavily armed guards and through locked doors. The lobby and halls were filled with uniforms and suits, all bustling about their duties.

We walked into a barn of an office. For a second it felt like the *Gazette*'s newsroom. Phones going, folk chatting, constant movement. Desks crammed together, piled with papers. Filing cabinets spewing folders. A group of secretaries, desks abutting, belting out discordant medleys of clacking keys and tinkling returns. People marching purposefully in and out, clutching files and clipboards as if it were a war room.

Scrymgeour was sitting at a desk on the far side, already hard at it behind his defensive walls of papers. He smiled and stood up to greet us.

'Let's start with a look at the wall of infamy.'

He guided us over to one wall to which papers and pictures were pinned in a higgledy-piggledy mass. Red tape criss-crossed the wall, linking various photos and type-covered cards and sheets to each other. The outline of the hierarchy was familiar from my post-war work at Bergen and Lüneburg. At the top was a photo of the commandant, the absconded Fritz Suhren. No wonder he was smiling.

To his left and with only a dotted line to him, was the Political Department, home for the Gestapo and the Kripo – the Criminal Police. Their solid reporting line ran up to Himmler himself.

Reporting directly to Suhren was his deputy, Schwarzhuber, and under him the entire team of SS supervisors and guards.

'How many SS, Iain?' There was a worrying lack of names.

'We think about a hundred and fifty to two hundred. Not counting the Kapos. Could be another few hundred of them. But unnamed.'

Ah, the lovely Kapos. Sporting their green triangles of power. Drawn from the ranks of temporary preventive custody prisoners – *befristeten Vorbeugungshäftlinge*. Criminals and thugs every one, sharing the camps with blameless Jews, homosexuals and gypsies. The Kapos were perfect material for deployment as camp enforcers. Saved on trained SS manpower. Clever Nazis.

I turned to other parts of the chart. There was the usual Administration group, which maintained the huts and the ovens, and ran the warehouses where they stored the shoes, glasses and belongings of the people who had no further need of worldly possessions. Then came the Employment Department that organised work gangs and hired out the slave labour to local businesses like Siemens. They worked in conjunction with the Central Construction Board who built the extermination facilities.

The final grouping was medical staff: photos of doctors and pretty nurses in splendid uniforms or white coats, ministering to sick wardens and experimenting on healthy prisoners.

It was a simple but efficient structure and testimony to the German penchant for hierarchy and control. In my mind I was already working out the line of questioning. I'd borrow the photos and use the personal files to talk them through the hierarchy and elicit ideas about where their pals might have scarpered to.

'A lot of gaps, Iain.'

He sighed. 'Bloody Suhren. He burned a stack of the records. Then the Red Army trashed the place looking for loot. We've got requests in with the Berlin team to find central records of each camp. But nothing so far. We're a bit stymied.'

'Are you in touch with other units as well as Berlin?'

'Oh yes. We've got the word out. We get calls every day: Brits and Yanks – French even – saying they've got a suspect and asking for a description.' He screwed up his face. 'Which is the missing bit unfortunately.'

I tried to be encouraging even as my spirits sank. 'You've got better data on the lower orders,' I noted, pointing at the middle of the chart, which had a number of photos and names.

He grabbed it like a lifebelt. 'That's right. Suhren started at the top with his incineration. So we can corroborate that your man Draganski was one of the SS guards.' He patted, with satisfaction, a small grey card at the bottom of the chart with the name, rank and number of the man who'd been assassinated by pitchfork in Glasgow. It was a small but significant step.

Sam touched the blank grey cards at the top of the chart.

'How do you even know there was a person missing?'

'We don't. We've extrapolated positions based on other camps' chain of command. Inspired guesswork tells us there should be someone there, but we're not sure. That's where Brodie's detective skills come in.' He grinned at me.

'I may need an Ouija board. So, to sum up, you think there's maybe six senior staff missing. Two medics and four SS?'

'Give or take a couple either way.'

'But no names.'

'No. Not a trace. We haven't had time or manpower to interrogate the ones we've caught.'

'And maybe thirty or so lower-order staff missing?'

'Looks like it.' He gazed at the blanks gloomily.

'What's this other group?' I pointed at a single large sheet standing by itself.

'You might say that's the alumni. Ravensbrück was a training camp. As far as we can tell over four thousand *Aufseherinnen* – women guards – passed through these portals and on to hone their skills in other camps.'

'Four thousand! How many have been caught, Iain?'

He looked rueful. 'We don't know.'

'Good God! Show me to your Augean stables. I stand a better chance of cleaning them than getting names of SS rats in Glasgow!'

He flushed. 'That's not quite the end of it, Brodie. Might as well have the full horror show. Ravensbrück was the administrative centre for forty or so sub-camps. Places like Grüneberg, Neubrandenburg, Barth, Leipzig-Schönefeld, Magdeburg, Altenburg and Neustadt-Glewe . . .'

'Enough! I get the picture. This is a waste of time. A wasted trip!'

I could hear myself getting more Ayrshire as my anger rose. I felt duped, stupid. I should have known things were a total mess, that it would be impossible to cut through the chaos so soon after the entire continent had been ravaged from east to west and back again. I might as well pack up and head home. I could claim I was deceived, and avoid stirring up the dirt pond that was festering in my head. Scrymgeour seemed to read my thoughts.

'Look, Brodie, you can still get something out of this,' he pleaded. '*We* certainly will via your court testimony. You should at least be able to confirm the Scottish rat-line theory.'

'But there's no obvious way of linking the missing to Glasgow! Nor do we have a clue who's flown and who's still here.'

Sam touched my arm. Her face was stretched with anxiety. 'You can fill in these top gaps, Brodie. You know you can. They've captured enough of the Ravensbrück senior staff for you to get them to explain their reporting lines and who they worked with.'

She was right. I could do *something*. Deep inside, I needed to admit that I was looking for a way out. I blew out a big breath and rubbed my face. It was sweltering in here.

'Well, I'm here now. It would be a shame not to renew old acquaintances.'

Iain and Sam's faces relaxed.

I went on: 'Tell me. Do the ones in custody know Suhren scarpered?'

Iain shook his head. 'We've said nothing. But I'd be amazed if they hadn't heard.'

'Can I use his escape as part of my interrogation? Can I mention it?'

'Why not? You're going to say he used a rat line?'

'It might help. Let me make some notes of your rogues' gallery.'

I took out my reporter's notebook, which suddenly seemed so out of place here. I jotted down what sparse details we had on the missing persons. I wished I'd had this shorthand skill back in '45 during my earlier interrogations. When I had all I needed, I rejoined Sam and Iain at his desk.

'One other thing, Iain. You didn't by any chance pick up any gold from any of your defendants? Ingots?'

'I said the Red Army got there first. Locusts. The safe was emptied. But we found a cache in the medical wing. About a hundred pieces.'

'Can I see a couple?'

He came back with a handful of glitter. I turned them over on his desk top. Some had the full Third Reich and swastika markings. Others, like the ones Ellen Jacobs had shown me, were smooth and blank.

'That ties in.' I handed them back.

'Here, keep one. Wave it at the prisoners if you like. Jog their memories.'

I took one and slipped it into my pocket. 'I'll make a start on the interrogations as soon as possible. And can you set up a meeting with Vera Atkins and her agent in the camp, Odette Sansom? That could be invaluable.'

'I'll fix it.' He scribbled a note for himself. 'Regarding the interrogations, where do you want to start?'

'I'll start at the top and work down. In the absence of the commandant, I'll begin with his deputy.'

'You've got till one o'clock each day. We have to get them into the courtroom prompt for two.'

Ian made a phone call and within five minutes Lieutenant Collins was in front of me, saluting.

'Collins, both our arms are going to get tired. Can we stop all the formalities while we're in the office?'

'Certainly, sir.'

'Including the *sir* bit. What's your first name?'

'Wilfred. Everyone calls me Will.'

'How's your German?'

Collins visibly relaxed. 'Cambridge. A first in modern languages.'

Of course. 'What a waste. Where's the prison?'

'A short ride.'

TWENTY-FIVE

E ven in full uniform and with all the right credentials Collins and I had to jump through hoops to get into the prison. Checkpoint after checkpoint. Eventually we were striding down a long concrete corridor lined either side by metal cell doors. A British soldier stood guard outside every cell, looking in. The authorities hated the idea of someone cheating a good hanging. There had been enough suicides among the accused.

We stopped outside one door. I nodded to the guard. He took out his key ring and turned one lock after another until he was able to swing open the heavy grill. Gazing straight at me from his seat on his bed was the man I'd helped to put in this situation over a year ago. SS-Oberststurmführer Johann Schwarzhuber, Deputy Commandant of Ravensbrück concentration camp.

He didn't know me at first but his face was unforgettable: eyes the colour of ice, features so elongated he could have modelled for Modigliani. He'd always been slim-built but now he was scrawny. He wore dark civilian clothes: a creased jacket, shirt and trousers. His skin was matt grey as though dust had stuck to it.

The soldier guarding him shouted, 'Stand for the senior officer! Attention!'

I outranked Schwarzhuber by three levels. He glanced at my shoulder insignia. I watched the ingrained habits of military discipline kick in even after a year in custody. He struggled to his feet and made a clumsy attempt at standing to attention. As he did so I tweaked his memory, in German.

'Well then, Schwarzhuber, justice catching up with you at last?'

A spasm crossed his face. He recognised me and my voice but not in this uniform or rank. Then it settled. His body relaxed.

'Major Brodie. Or rather, *Lieutenant Colonel* Brodie. The war has been good for some.'

'Not for *anyone*, Schwarzhuber. And certainly not you. Let's go.'

I nodded to the soldier, who stepped forward and clicked chains on hands and feet. Then with Lieutenant Collins taking his other side we marched him out to the end of the corridor and into a small cell with a table and four chairs. I had the prisoner sit on one side of the table. I took the other. Collins sat behind me and the guard stood behind the prisoner.

'Let me read your file.'

I made a point of sitting silently while I flicked through page after page, including my own notes from so long ago. It came flooding back. Learned his trade at Dachau and Auschwitz before taking charge of the gas chambers at Ravensbrück in early 1945. I wondered if I could keep my hands off him this time.

'You don't seem to be quite so relaxed, Lieutenant Schwarzhuber? Not like our first meeting. Why is that?'

'What do you want?' There was no 'sir' attached. He'd dropped any pretence of acknowledging my rank.

'Not sleeping? Is it the thought of being hanged? I imagine it does tend to keep you awake at night.'

'Are you just here to gloat?'

'A little gloating is allowed. A little *Schadenfreude*, don't you think? Not just that. I'm here to give testimony against you.'

'Ha! You think they need testimony? You think they need evidence? You are confusing this charade with a court of law.'

'Justice will be served, I'm sure. No matter how we get there. I have some questions. Let's start with the easy stuff. Your chain of command. You were the *Lagerführer* – head of supervision of the camp at Ravensbrück? Who did you report to?'

'You know this.'

'Please remind me.'

'SS-Sturmbannführer Fritz Suhren.'

'Did you know your boss has escaped?'

He shrugged. 'He's not here.'

'Who helped him?'

'Good Germans.'

'*Good* Germans would shoot him on sight for fouling their name. Sadly there's too few of that sort left.'

'Really? Do you refuse to obey orders, *Colonel*? We soldiers have no right to question our superiors, or else where are we? A rabble.'

'That's a worn-out defence. Look where it's got you. Got the whole German nation! Don't you feel any guilt for what you did personally? You were in charge of the gas chambers!'

'It was my job.'

I stared at him. He didn't blink. His thin mouth was set.

'It says here you were a drinker?' I tapped the file. 'Drowning your conscience?'

'We were cleansing the fatherland! Our race had been weakened.'

'Is that why you lost?'

'You've Stalin to thank, not your precious Montgomery or Churchill! Even the Wehrmacht hadn't enough bullets to kill every Russian yokel at Stalingrad. If not for Stalin's peasant pig-headedness, Germany would have won!'

'Leaving Europe a charnel house!'

'Prospering!'

'Unless of course you were a Jew. Or a homosexual. Or a little slow. Were you a little slow, Schwarzhuber? Slow to realise you were beaten?'

He stiffened. His eyes were wild. I pressed home.

'We know that plans were laid to allow criminals like you to get out of the country. Why didn't you? Why are you taking the rap?'

'There were no plans.'

'Ah, it seems you weren't important enough. You were only a lieutenant.'

'An *SS* lieutenant.'

'And you think that's better? Good God. So why were there no plans to help a *mighty* SS lieutenant escape?'

'There were *no* plans.'

'Or you would have heard?'

'Certainly.'

'You had access to gold. Jewish gold. Why didn't you use it?'

He dropped his stare. He peered at the table. 'I want a cigarette.'

I pushed my pack across to him and lit the cigarette he pulled out. 'Keep it.' I pointed at the pack. He grabbed it. I let him take in deep lungfuls. He smiled.

'Why are you smiling?'

'Himmler said these were bad for us.'

'Himmler was wrong about a lot of things. But at least he had the courage to kill himself. Why didn't you?'

A flush appeared on Schwarzhuber's sallow face. 'I have been prevented. Give me your gun and leave me for twenty seconds. You will see how an officer dies!'

'I don't waste bullets. So, let me understand. You were not important enough to be given a cyanide pill like Himmler. You weren't important enough to be told about the escape routes. You're small fry. Cannon fodder. While you swing on a rope your old comrades will be swinging in a hammock in Argentina.'

'This is not true!'

'Which bit?'

He sat back, his eyes darting about the room. He grabbed another cigarette and lit up. I waited.

'What's in this for me?' he asked.

'If you give me useful information, will it save you from the gallows? I doubt it. But I could ask the hangman to set the rope right. Not short like the Americans prefer it. I heard one of your Nuremberg gang took twenty minutes to strangle to death. Better the long drop. Knot under here' – I pointed at the side of my neck – 'so that as you fall, you'll just hear a click and that's it. You'll join your Führer in hell.'

His face went into spasm. I thought he was going to have a fit. I went for the kill.

'Of course I could only arrange that while you're in the British sector. The Polish Free Army want you for their trials. They seem quite bitter about what you did to their country.'

He sat, panting, thinking. Something seemed to break in his face. Finally he shrugged.

'What does it matter?'

I waited.

'The commandant . . .' he started again.

'Suhren?'

'Suhren told me to get to Zurich. Or Rome.' He snorted. 'Right across Germany. Through the Russian lines. Or the Americans. It was out of the question. And . . .'

'And?'

'We did not believe it would happen. We did not hear about the Russian advance. They told us the Eastern Front was holding. Another lie. Ach, you know, Colonel Brodie, belief becomes a habit. Like these.' He held up his cigarette. 'Until it's too late.'

'Did he mention a northern escape line?'

'Yes. From the coast. It made sense. South were the Americans and the Russians. But he didn't talk much about it.'

'Keeping it for himself? Did he give directions?'

He smiled. 'No. I didn't press him. It seemed disloyal to even be talking about it.' At last some regret.

'Pity for you. Loyalty seems to have been one way only.'

Afterwards I felt dirty and drained. As though I'd been sick and then had to clean up my own mess. Bargaining with a man over whether he dies slow or quick on the end of a rope. I got nothing more out of him. But it was a start. The Scottish rat line began to take on deadly substance.

I pulled myself together for the court session in the afternoon back at the Curiohaus. It was jammed with sour-smelling humanity. Sam told me the public galleries held 150 or so. It seemed every seat was taken. The good burghers of Hamburg were here to see what they claimed not to have known about for so many years. I took a seat to one side of the upper gallery with a clear view of the whole court. The local Germans gave my uniform a wide berth.

I looked down. On one side were the jammed ranks of prisoners, mainly women, each with a huge number attached to her breast. Flanking them were British WRAC guards. Our poor girls' faces showed how much they were hating their proximity to such evil. In front of the prisoners sat a line of defence lawyers. Facing them, across the short floor of the court, were the wigged and gowned prosecutors, including Advocate Samantha Campbell. She sat beside Scrymgeour, files at the ready, earning her modest fees.

Forming the linking bar of the horseshoe between defendants and prosecutors was the bench of court members. They faced the tall windows of the Curiohaus. General Westropp, the court president, sat in the middle of a line of uniformed British officers and one wigged lawyer. It gave the sense of a tightly packed kirk with the dock serving as a pulpit for grudging penitents.

But for Sam's presence, it was as though time had reversed. The layout and the attendees were different, but it might have been Lüneburg and the Belsen trials of over a year ago. General Westropp rapped his gavel for silence and the first defendant was brought to the witness box: Warden Greta Bösel. She was perhaps late thirties, dark hair swept up and back under a hat. Just another hausfrau on a shopping trip, apart from the big number 7 on her breast. They gave her headphones for the simultaneous translation of questions.

Sam stepped forward and I felt a surge of pride as she quietly and efficiently exposed the woman as an uneducated sadist given the power of life and death over her betters. Power used to crush women who'd lived in nice homes, who could play piano, read Schiller and Goethe, and discuss Nietzsche without seeing it as a licence to slaughter the *Untermensch*.

Sam called a witness: a frail bird of a woman who had to be helped into the witness box. Her hair was grey. She looked about sixty.

'What is your name, please?'

'Ruth Silverstein.' Her voice was cracked and slow.

'What is your age?'

'I am twenty-nine.'

'You were a prisoner in Ravensbrück concentration camp?'

'I was taken there in May 1944 with my daughter.'

'What was your daughter's name?'

'Rachel. She was called Rachel.' A memory lightened her face.

Sam's voice softened. 'How old was Rachel?'

'Just two. Her birthday was in March that year.' She smiled. 'We had balloons.'

The court was still. Not breathing.

'Do you recognise the woman in the dock?'

Ruth looked up and stared at number 7. She nodded.

'Do you know her name?'

'Oh, yes. I know *her* name. She is Greta Bösel.'

'Why are you so sure?'

Ruth Silverstein said it quietly, so quietly that the whole gallery leaned forward to hear. Sam asked her to repeat it.

'Because she killed my daughter, Rachel.'

Sam let the words hang in the air until they'd been absorbed by every ear in the court.

'Ruth? Do you mind if I ask you how the defendant killed Rachel?'

Ruth turned to stare at Bösel. She inspected her, scrutinised her. Her voice grew firmer. 'We got off the train. We were all tired and thirsty. The children were fractious, crying. *They* were waiting for us. *She* was. With dogs. The wardens took the children from us. They said they would be given food, water.'

'Did they?'

Ruth shook her head. 'There was a lorry with its back open. Steel sides. The guards took the children over to it. When they were all there, the wardens started to kill them. Some used iron bars. Some picked up the kids by their legs and swung them against the side of the truck. They smashed them. Then they threw them on the truck.'

The silence was wrecked now. There were gasps and stifled cries of *Nein* from the German spectators. Ruth waited for quiet. She lifted her finger and pointed at Bösel, whose head was down now. She spoke slowly, making every word draw blood from the defendant and the spectators.

'Greta Bösel took Rachel. Hers was the last hand Rachel held. I saw Rachel ask her something. Bösel smiled down at her. Like a kind lady. Bösel was laughing as she swung my little girl against the truck.'

Later, Sam and I were crunching along the bitter shore of the lake, arm in arm. Our coats were tightly buttoned against the freezing mist that hung over the dead water.

'You were brilliant, Sam.'

'No. I always do my homework. The rest is easy. The evidence speaks for itself.'

'It's the way you deliver it.'

'Is it ridiculous to say I almost felt sorry for her?' she said.

'Bösel? As long as it's only *almost*.'

'*You* hate them. I can see why.'

'Hate? I'm not sure that's the emotion. Hate's something you feel for another person. The Nazis are a stunted branch line of human development. Like Wells's Morlocks. You don't hate cold-blooded reptiles.'

'Was that how you saw Schwarzhuber?'

'He's had almost two years to contemplate his crimes. Two years wasted. Not a hint of contrition. We should have lined the buggers up and shot them while we had the chance. Said he'd been given orders and carried them out. That's what a soldier did. Surely *I* understood that. A *fellow* soldier!'

'Why does that upset you so much?'

I took a deep cold breath. 'Damn it, because he had a point. The last thing I needed going into battle was some squaddie saying *I don't fancy this fight, sir. I think I'll stand this one out.*'

'This wasn't a battle.'

'No. But who in uniform gets to choose? When? Look at the last war, at the Somme or Passchendaele. *On my whistle, go and commit suicide, there's a good lad. Or face a firing squad for cowardice.*'

Sam squeezed my arm. 'Nothing useful then?'

I calmed down. 'I filled in a couple of gaps on the hierarchy. Schwarzhuber knew who'd got away all right.'

'Did he say *where* they might have gone?'

'He'd heard of the escape lines to Rome and Zurich, and on to Spain. Franco's regime was very welcoming and if he'd had the chance he'd have gone to Barcelona. Or Argentina. He fancied Argentina. Likes horses. Says General Perón is one of *them*.'

'Fascists?'

'The world is split in three: fascists, communists and us.'

'Us being the sane ones? Soft old Western capitalists?'

'Not so soft. We won, didn't we?'

'Did we, Sam? Did we?'

We walked together for a while, silent with our thoughts.

'Are you all right, Douglas? Is this too much?'

'It needs doing. Come on. I think we've earned that first drink.'

We had and we did and it wasn't the last. And I shouldn't have asked for a bottle for my room. But it got me to sleep. Eventually. I dreamed of broken dolls.

TWENTY-SIX

We'd planned an early start. I set my alarm for the morning. It came with a jolt, and I struggled to free myself from the knotted sheets and the bloody images. The mattress was soaked with my sweat. I shaved, showered and forced some toast down to quell the nausea.

This morning I faced Ludwig Ramdohr, Gestapo. I wasn't afraid of him. I was afraid of how I'd react. With my temper running so hot I wondered about leaving my service pistol with the guard.

I forced myself to think about how useful this session could be. Ramdohr would have had a unique view of all the personnel running the camp, including the doctors. He had access to all their personal records. He had also been a detective before the war. It didn't mean we were going to be matey and clubby, two old professionals comparing notes on how detectives operated differently in Gallowgate and Ravensbrück. But it was a convenient entry point. We were – according to his file – of a similar age.

Lieutenant Collins and I went through the usual security rigmarole and took our seats in the interview cell. Ramdohr was brought in, hair thinner than I recalled, but the square face familiar enough. I deliberately spent time reading his file. It unsettles a man trying to read damning notes about himself upside down.

It reminded me that our Ludwig showed an aptitude for heavy-handed interrogation that would have won him plaudits from the more thuggish members of the Glasgow police. But even the polis would have stopped short at drowning prisoners to screw confessions out of them. Most of them anyway.

I looked up at him. Ramdohr seemed uncrushed physically by his time behind bars. He'd recognised me immediately but made no mention of my new outfit and rank.

I started gently, mindful of my blood pressure. We went through his Political Department and I fleshed it out with names and ranks. Then I put my pencil down and sat back.

'Was there anyone you trusted? Among your comrades?'

'It wasn't my job to trust people. That was the first lesson I learned. Didn't you?'

'I think we went to different schools. In particular, what did you think of Suhren, the commandant?'

He shrugged. 'Loyal enough. That was my job. I had to test for it.'

'How? I see you were inventive.' I tapped his file. 'Liked playing with water.'

He smiled, perhaps in fond memory. 'People don't like drowning. Or thinking they are. They prefer to breathe and talk.'

I decided to try one of the names I got from Schwarzhuber.

'Exactly how loyal was Dr Walter Sonntag?'

'The nerve man?'

'The nerve man. His file says he removed nerves, bones, muscles. To see what happened. Tried to give them to other prisoners. Transplants, he called them. "Like grafting a rose" was the phrase he used.'

Ramdohr smiled. 'Obsessed. He'd do anything for the Führer.'

'He got away.'

'I thought so.'

155

'One of the lucky ones?'

'Just smarter than the rest. Smarter than me. He got out before the Reds arrived. Spirited away.'

'The rat lines.'

'*Ja*. Down a sewer.'

'Did you know where the entrance to this sewer was?'

He shook his head. 'Above my pay grade.'

'Did you know where it came out?'

'South America. New York. London. Somewhere nice. You'll never find them.'

'So we'll hang you instead.'

That got through. His lips became lines. 'Is there an alternative?'

'I'm not the judge. But I can talk to him.'

'You're lying.'

'Even if I am, what have you to lose? Tell me about the gold.'

'Ah. It's always the gold.'

'Did Walter get his hands on gold? Gold from teeth. From jewellery. From your victims?'

'There were several at it. Suhren, of course. Sonntag certainly; once he knew the Reds were coming.'

'Where did they get it?'

'Why, from the dentist, of course.'

It was so blindingly obvious that I didn't speak for a while. I flipped though my notepad. I looked up.

'That would be Hellinger. Dr Martin Hellinger.'

'That's your man.'

As luck would have it Hellinger was in the prison hospital. He'd cut his wrists, but had made a mess of it and would live. I'd get to him when they brought him back.

I kept at Ramdohr without a break until midday. I'm not sure which of us was more wrung out. Collins and I wrote up some brief notes over a plate of ham from the canteen and I prepared for my first inquisition in the witness box in the afternoon. I was to be grilled about my eighteen-month-old report on Schwarzhuber.

I had a very different perspective down in the well of the court. More claustrophobic. I was able to view Schwarzhuber directly opposite me, standing in the dock with guards either side. He wore headphones as I was answering in English. He allowed that maddening sneer to play about his lips as he listened to my answers. It didn't take me long to confirm the details of our first meeting. Then the defence lawyer went on the attack.

'Lieutenant Colonel Brodie, it was a confusing time back in June 1945 when you were interrogating the defendant, was it not?'

'Confusing for whom? Not me.'

'Your certainty is admirable. The whole of Europe was in turmoil. Officers like the defendant were dragged before you and made to sign anything in the interests of expediency. Is that fair?'

'Not in the slightest. I asked questions and wrote down answers.'

'You speak German. Fluently?'

I answered in German long enough for Counsel to cut me off.

'Let us assume that's a yes. But returning to your notes from that time. These are not verbatim, are they?'

'No. They are in a sense minutes of our discussion.'

'And like all good minutes, they say what the minute-taker wants to get across? Is that correct?'

'This wasn't a board meeting. We weren't dealing with policy matters. I asked Obersturmführer Schwarzhuber his name, rank and unit. He told me. I asked him how many victims had died under his command. He gave me an estimate. I asked him whether he personally oversaw the gas chambers. He said he had. Did he stand by the crematoria and order his men to shovel bodies into the flames? He said he did. I asked—'

'Thank you, Colonel. We get the picture.'

'I haven't finished. Your defendant gave me his answers. We wrote them down. In his role as deputy commandant, he was directly responsible for the murder and incineration of thousands of innocents. That was the statement he signed.'

Counsel dug into the details and tried to find weak spots: *The defendant simply took orders and passed them on. He had no choice. There were thousands of prisoners; how could he have seen what was happening to all of them . . .*

I began to find Counsel's probing unsettling. I was hardly an objective interviewer back then. I'd fought these men for five years. The liberation of the camps had sent shock waves of revulsion through the West. Schwarzhuber and his like came in front of me tainted beyond redemption. My reports were always going to be skewed to convict.

And God knows, I'd seen at first hand, back in Glasgow, how evidence could be cooked. How an innocent man could end up in the condemned cell.

But with Schwarzhuber I had no need to exaggerate.

By the end of Counsel's inquisition I felt I'd been through the mangle. His clever probing had uncovered my own growing view that there were no certainties any more. I walked stiffly from the court desperate for clean air. It wasn't just the stuffy reek of packed humanity I was trying to get away from. I'd been soaked in horror since I flew in. It had poured on me remorselessly every day. I went back to the hotel alone while Sam ploughed on. I should have waited for her to join me before hitting the bar, but my throat was dry.

Wednesday and Thursday followed the same pattern. I interrogated three of the smaller fry, who knew nothing about anything, except that they expected to hang. They were probably right. I put in a couple of appearances in the witness stand to underscore and corroborate my first interviews some eighteen months ago. And at day's end I tried to erase the images with Red Label, that convenient scouring agent for filth in the mind's U-bend.

Friday came too soon. I was renewing acquaintance with 26-year-old Aufseherin Dorothea Binz, Deputy Camp Warden. Binz was a kind of anti-she. The negative of all that I appreciated in a woman: softness, sweetness, kindness, tenderness; the necessary counterweight to our barbed manhood. La Binz was all dark, hard, and warped. She was licentious to the point of absurdity, reportedly performing lesbian acts in full view of the camp inmates and her SS lover Edmund Bräuning. It wasn't interrogation Binz needed. It was exorcism.

I'd met one of her protégées, Irma Grese, in the Belsen trials. They called her Die Hyane, the beautiful beast: just twenty-two and addicted to torture and slaughter. I had a hand in sending Irma to the gallows in December 1945. Her mentor, the blonde Dorothea, would surely follow her on to the trapdoor.

She was already seated in the small interrogation room when I arrived. Her face lifted to mine and recognition dawned. Was that fear? I was struck again at how ordinary she seemed. A blonde but with disappointingly coarse features. Blue eyes like Sam's but without the intelligence. Her dull, country-girl looks would have been perfect on billboards advertising milk or honey, if she weren't so sulky.

I sipped at my strong tea and wished it were gin as I read through her file. The last time I'd interrogated her, she'd said little or nothing. She was contemptuous and sneering. This time I decided to go for the jugular. It wouldn't be nice. I hoped Will Collins, sitting behind me, had a strong stomach. The file mentioned an affair with another woman, Dr Heidi Triedelmann. It would be worth seeing how she reacted to my disclosure of her love life.

'Fräulein Binz, it has been a while. You remember me? My name is Brodie.'

'I remember *you*.' She spat the word.

'Have you heard from Edmund recently?'

'What? What are you talking about?'

'Your boyfriend SS-Obersturmführer Edmund Bräuning? Your lover boy.'

Her face contorted. 'Where is he?'

'Dead. We hanged him.' I heard a gasp behind me from Collins.

Binz shot out of her seat and lunged at me. 'You bastard!' The guard grabbed her and pulled her down.

'And I suppose you won't have heard from your little protégée Irma either. Have you?'

Her eyes were wild.

'Fräulein Grese took the drop a year ago. I personally made sure of that.'

'So? What do I care?'

'You're next, Dorothea. And the instructions will be to make it slow. A very short drop.'

'Fuck you!'

I sighed. 'Shame that Dr Triedelmann won't be joining you.'

'What?'

'Your other little sex pal, Heidi, got away. She was sent down a rat line. They made sure that the best Nazis, the ones they wanted to survive, got away. Live and fight another day, eh? But no one cared what happened to you. Did they?'

'Shut up, shut up!'

I sat back and lit a cigarette. I was no longer sure if I was probing her for answers or just to rile her. What she'd done was sickening but what I was doing didn't seem much better. I could feel Lieutenant Collins's eyes on my back. I'd been innocent once. Binz was breathing hard and staring at my pack of cigarettes.

'Want one?'

She nodded.

'OK. We're going to play a little game. I will give you a cigarette for every useful answer you give me. I will take one back if you are evasive or I think you're lying. Ready to play?'

Her eyes flicked between mine and the fags. Her tongue moistened her lips. She nodded.

I got corroboration of some of the new names on my list and pointers to others. Binz knew about escape routes but not how to find one, far less a northern one to Scotland. She also knew about the pilfering of gold. Had even done a bit herself.

'Why not? Everyone else was doing it.'

'Where did you get it?'

She shrugged. 'Sometimes direct.'

'You mean you stole it directly from the prisoners?'

She laughed. 'They weren't going to need bangles where they were going.'

I stared at her brazen face, her pitiless eyes, and I reached across and slapped her as hard as I could.

She screamed and fell off her chair. Collins leaped forward and pulled me back. The sergeant jailer helped her to her feet and back into her chair. 'Shut up or you'll get another from me,' said the sergeant. My red handprint tattooed Binz's shocked white face.

I reached over and picked up the five cigarettes she'd won and crushed them. I threw them at her; then I got up and marched out. My head was pounding. Anger blazed in my chest. I stormed down the corridor and through the metal doors until I got outside. I walked faster and faster until I was running down the street. I floundered to a halt in a small park and threw up. Collins found me with my head in my hands sitting on a damp bench. He got out his fags and gave me one. He lit me and we sat quietly, embarrassed by my outburst, sandbagged by her poison.

'Sorry, Collins.'

'It's fine, sir.'

'It's not what a first in languages prepares you for, is it?'

'No, sir,' he said quietly. 'But I haven't been through it. Sorry I held you back, sir.'

'You did right. Thank you.'

We walked back to the car. I felt hollowed out. I got to my room, lay down on my bed and shivered as though I was coming down with malaria.

I woke to someone shaking me. I shot up in confusion, my arms raised to defend my face.

'Douglas, Douglas, it's all right. It's me. It's me. You're all right.'

'God, Sam. I was out.'

'You were shouting. In your sleep.'

She eased back and sat by my side. I sat upright and leaned towards her. I embraced her and felt her slim arms round me, holding me tight, until the pain between my eyes lifted.

'You're shaking, Douglas. It's all right now.'

I was a child wrapped in his mother's arms.

'What time is it?'

'Nearly six. We've got dinner at seven with the court president, General Westropp, and his pal from the Judge Advocate General's unit. I can call it off. Say you're poorly. I'd love to miss it myself.'

'I'll be fine. It's passing.' I unpeeled myself and gazed at her worried face.

'Are you sure?' she asked. 'This is taking too much out of you. I'm finding it hard enough.'

'It fair stirs things up, doesn't it?'

She nodded. 'Some tea?'

'Something stronger.'

TWENTY-SEVEN

The days blurred. I was waiting for Dr Martin Hellinger – the dentist – to be released from hospital. His wounds had turned sour but they were expecting him to live – I hoped at least long enough to tell me about his depraved alchemy: turning teeth into ingots. He was increasingly my main hope of a breakthrough. All roads led to the dentist.

Over the next week, I interrogated twelve other prisoners. The interviews were variations on a palette of black and grey. My brain was marinated in a dismal stew of foul deeds and feeble excuses. My questioning of the defendants was getting more and more derailed. I was shouting accusations at them as much as I was seeking answers.

Each evening I drank too much, and each night I paid for it in lost sleep and violent dreams. Sam woke me twice more in successive nights. My shouts had terrified her in the adjoining room. By tacit agreement – or maybe it was simply Sam's decision – we'd suspended normal relations for the duration. Somehow the situation and the context of our work weren't conducive.

She too was feeling the strain. Each morning her bright eyes looked duller, her fine skin paler. I looked worse. I was permanently tired, usually had a headache and always a sense of growing despair. Not about our mission; despite my mental fragmentation we seemed to be getting somewhere. Maybe because of it. I was scaring the hell out of the prisoners as well as Sam and Will Collins.

There was respite in the form of the interview I had with Odette Sansom. In a sense it put the whole wretched business in better perspective. Back in August, while I was running around Scotland reporting on the antics of the vigilante group, the Glasgow Marshals, Odette was being awarded the George Cross for bravery by our king. Now here she was, supping tea with me, after testifying against the SS guards at the trial.

She was a bonny woman, my age, with a shock of curly brown hair. Her softness and sweetly accented English belied her steel core. She was French-born but had married a lucky Englishman and moved to England in 1931. They had three daughters. She gave up sweet domesticity for the perilous life of a British agent.

'What did you do with your girls, Odette?'

'I made them very safe. I put them in a convent.'

'And then marched off to war?'

'Not war, exactly. I joined the Resistance in Cannes. As a courier. To do my bit for France. That is all.'

'All? It was extraordinary bravery. They caught you.'

Her brows furrowed. 'Gestapo. They tortured me and sent me to Fresnes prison. In Paris.'

'Why didn't they just shoot you?'

She laughed. 'It was my cover. My SOE boss in Cannes was Peter Churchill. I told the Gestapo he was my husband and also the nephew of Winston.'

'They *believed* you?'

'They didn't know what to believe. So they sent me to Ravensbrück. And there, too, they were a little wary of losing a . . .'

'Bargaining counter?'

'Exactly.' She grinned.

165

'I heard a bizarre story about you and Fritz Suhren, our absent camp commandant.'

'Suhren arrived in early '45 and I kept the Churchill story going. Just before the Russians liberated the camp, he drove off with me to surrender to the Americans. He thought they would not hang him if he had looked after a relative of Mr Churchill.'

'When we catch him again, he'll find he was mistaken.'

Her face clouded. 'I hope so, Douglas.'

'Did he mention rat lines to you?'

She shook her head. 'Not by that term. But he talked about getting away, getting to South America.'

'Did he say how?'

'Only that he'd been too late to abandon his post and go to Spain. It's why he threw himself on the Americans' mercy. But there's one thing. While we were driving he stopped in a wood and took out a box from the back of the jeep. He buried it.'

'Good God! What was it?'

'He laughed when I asked. He just said insurance.'

'Do you know where?'

'Not a clue. I was pretty dizzy with it all. I couldn't have told you whether we were driving north or south.'

'Did you meet Hellinger, the camp dentist?'

Her mouth pursed with distaste. 'He was a creep. I never met him but I know what he did.'

'What did he do?'

'It was common knowledge. He hung around like a ghoul waiting to rip out gold fillings.'

'You never saw him in action?'

'No, but I heard about him from Vera. She got hold of Schwarzhuber in Minden prison and got him to confess to what happened with our SOE pals.' The tears welled up and she dabbed at her eyes.

'I'm sorry, Odette. Please stop.'

'No, no. It needs telling. They treated Denise, Lilian and Violette abominably. They took them out to the crematorium barely alive. Poor Denise and Lilian had to be carried on a stretcher. Suhren was in charge. He had them shot in the back of the head.'

'Hellinger?'

'He removed their gold fillings.'

We sat transfixed with the unspeakable images. I gave her a cigarette and we talked quietly until the light faded and we'd exhausted our different experiences of dealing with the Nazis. She left me feeling like a fraud for my angst and outbursts. She'd survived hell. I'd merely been a spectator.

As the days passed I completed the top and middle layers of the hierarchy on Scrymgeour's blackboard. We now had a complete picture with names and ranks, and we knew who was missing. We even had names and some photos of the SS commandants of the sub-camps. We just didn't know where they'd gone. The names were sent to Berlin in the hope of some cross-checking. Some of the missing might have been picked up in other zones. Though nobody knew what the hell the Russians were up to.

We had several confirmations of the existence of *Ratten-linien* across Europe. And from the snippets I was picking up, we had a growing certainty of the existence of an escape route through north Germany and on to Scotland. If only I could get my hands on bloody Hellinger.

'It's the weekend tomorrow, Douglas.'

'So it is. I intend sleeping through it.'

We were sitting in the Bear's saloon, gin and tonics in hand, and catching up on the newspapers flown out from Britain. The news was of twelve-hour gales and floods, followed by snowstorms. We'd already had the hurricanes and rain. We'd be buried in snow in the morning. It felt like the end of time.

'Well, you can't. I won't let you. It's your birthday tomorrow.'

I stared at her. Then I checked the paper. The latest was yesterday's, 23 January. Rabbie Burns's birthday – and mine – was tomorrow. I would be thirty-five. Halfway through my three-score and ten. The tipping point.

'That's all I needed. Another intimation of mortality.'

'Rubbish. We're going to celebrate. The Black Watch garrison is holding a Burns Supper. We're invited.'

I groaned. 'Not the Black Watch. Have you seen how those guys fight?'

'Well, no. But I understand they're quite good at it.'

'That's how they throw a party.'

It was a mad, glorious riot of an evening. My one regret was being in the wrong uniform. Sam and I were made honoured guests in a full-blown, bagpipe-blasting, kilt-swirling ceilidh. Haggis had been flown in along with crates of 56-proof Glen Grant straight from the distillery. Once the colonel found out I was a Seaforth Highlander in disguise and that we'd fought together in the 51st, I had no choice but to lead the highland dancing.

I soon found how out of shape I was, but it didn't matter. The Black Watch officers had kidnapped every secretary, every QARANC nurse and WRAC officer for miles around. Even so, Sam stood out. I don't know where she'd hid it but a long frock and sequined jacket had appeared from her suitcase. By the light of the roaring fires, fuelled by Scotch and Burns's verses, we danced like linties till the small hours.

We sprawled in the back of our staff car on the drive back to our quarters with smiles on our faces. For the first time in weeks I'd broken out of my downward spiral. It was a reminder of how good life could be if you let it. How good Sam and I were together. Given half a chance.

'Thanks, Sam. You were right.'

'Of course, I was. Silly man.' She squeezed my hand in the dark and whispered. 'By the way, I've been saving your present till we got back to the hotel.' She smiled meaningfully.

TWENTY-EIGHT

We had Sunday to recover and took it easy on ourselves. For a day at least I felt I was regaining some balance. On Monday morning I found that the birthday bash had given me a much-needed burst of energy. The way I'd been feeling lately it was unlikely to last so I decided to seize the day. Collins was waiting for me downstairs on as usual. Seven thirty on the dot. I stormed past him.

'Come on, Will.'

'Sir?'

'We're going to the hospital. If Hellinger won't come to us, we'll bloody well go to him.'

We drew up outside the building. It had lost part of its left wing but the rest stood firm. A great red cross was painted on its front and in the quadrangle in front. Two soldiers stood on lazy guard duty on the steps. They sprang to attention as Collins and I strode up and through the doors. We grabbed a Queen Alexandra's nurse and had her steer us up two flights and along a corridor. Two more soldiers sprawled in chairs outside a room, smoking away, tunics loosened and ankles crossed. All they lacked were hammocks.

Collins called out, "Ten-shun!'

The squaddies leaped to their feet. One dropped his rifle and scrambled for it before standing blushing with his mate on either side of the door. I walked up to them and gave them my senior officer eyeball-to-eyeball inspection. I found them wanting.

'Do you normally throw your rifle around, Corporal?'

'No, sir!'

'Stand easy. And that doesn't mean sit on your arse. Clear?'

'Sir!'

I pushed open the door and walked in. A man was sitting in his pyjamas and dressing gown reading a book. Cigarette smoke curled leisurely up and away from a brimming ashtray. His specs obscured his eyes until he looked up, surprised at the sight of two British Army officers marching in. An army nurse was flattening the top sheet on the bed. She straightened up.

'Good morning, sir. Do you have an appointment?'

'Yes, nurse. And it's long overdue. You can leave us. Thank you.'

She looked as though she was going to object, glanced at the man in the chair, and walked quickly out. We turned to the man. I spoke in German.

'Obersturmführer Dr Martin Hellinger?'

His mouth was open and his eyes were round with fear. Did he think we'd brought a firing squad? He took off his glasses and rubbed his eyes. He managed a nod.

'Good. I've come to talk about teeth.'

Collins and I pulled up chairs on either side of him. Other than the panic we'd induced he didn't look that poorly. Pale-faced and scrawny, but far from death's door. He was swallowing hard and breathing fast.

'Show me your arms.'

He stuck both arms out in front of him. I yanked up the dressing gown and pyjama sleeves. Red weals ran across both wrists. But they were healed.

'So, Hellinger, feeling better, are we?'

He gulped and nodded.

'Speak, man!'

'*Ja, Herr Colonel.*'

'Hellinger, we have testimony from a number of witnesses that you were responsible for removing the gold fillings from the poor wretches in Ravensbrück camp. Before that, you were similarly employed at Sachsenhausen and Flossenbürg. Correct?'

'I was just a dentist. I—'

'You committed war crimes. You are a stain on humanity. You will hang.'

His face looked as though it would melt in fear. He shook his head as if to deny his bleak future.

'My job is to make a final assessment and recommendation about what happens to war criminals like you. Do you understand?'

He swallowed and nodded.

'I have the power of life or death over you and your kind. Usually I am implacable but I have been known to be lenient. I have been persuaded to recommend long prison sentences instead of a slow hanging. Do you understand?'

'*Ja, Herr Colonel.*'

'It all depends on how much cooperation I get. Clear?'

'Yes, sir.' He was nodding for his life now.

'Let's start. See how this goes, shall we? See if you can save your neck. What did you do with the gold you took from people's mouths?'

His eyes fluttered. 'I melted it down.'

'Where?'

'We had a little furnace, next to the crematorium.'

'Handy, eh? Was this your responsibility?'

'Hauptsturmführer Suhren ordered me to do it. He said they had one at Auschwitz.'

'Just fillings or other sources?'

'All the gold jewellery ended up in the pot. Silver in another.'

'What did you do with the melted gold and silver?'

'We made ingots and sent them to Berlin.'

'Did you stamp them?'

'With the eagle and the swastika.'

'All of them?' I dug in my pocket and pulled out a small yellow slab. It glittered in the morning light. Hellinger's eyes were drawn to it like a magnet. 'Why are there no markings on this one?'

'Can I have some water?' he croaked.

Collins got up and brought him a glass. He choked as it went down. I held the ingot in my palm, waiting.

'Suhren kept some aside. He didn't want them marked.'

'What for?'

'Escape. He thought the Red Army was coming.'

'He was right. How many of these did you make?'

'Many. I don't know.'

'Dozens? Hundreds?'

'Hundreds.'

'Did Suhren talk to you about escape? Did he say how?'

Hellinger looked from me to Collins and back again.

'Is this what you want to know? How he got away?' His look of fear was draining away.

I leaned closer. 'It could save your life.'

A flicker of emotion crossed his lean face. Hope? Cunning?

'Can you promise me prison if I tell you?'

'If the information is good enough.'

'How can I trust you? I don't know you. I don't know what powers you have.'

'You don't. But what are your choices?'

I could see his brain whirring, assessing.

'He talked about escape routes.'

'Rat lines?'

He shrugged. 'If you like. He said the ones to Rome and Switzerland had been blocked. He would have to go north.'

My mouth went dry. I tried to be casual.

'I've heard that. On the coast. Where exactly?'

He looked out the window, and then back, flicking his eyes between us, assessing us, assessing his chances. 'Cuxhaven.'

'At the mouth of the Elbe?'

'Yes.'

I nodded. 'Address? Contact?'

He shook his head. 'I don't know who. But Suhren told me if I wanted to follow him I should go to a certain bar near the old harbour.'

'That makes sense. A sea route out. Name of the bar?'

'The Angel's Wing.'

We emerged from the hospital and I turned to Collins. He was grinning like a fool. I punched him gently on his shoulder.

'We did it! We bloody did it, Will!'

'You did, sir. You bloody did!'

'Right. Talk to me, Will.'

'Sir?'

I switched to German. 'I've not heard *you* speak German. From now on, we only speak German. Let's hear it.'

'How's this? I'm afraid my accent isn't as good as yours.'

'Christ, man, you've even got a posh German accent!'

'Sorry.' His young face coloured. 'I spent a year in Germany before the war with my parents. Father was at the embassy in Berlin. So I picked up the accent among the kids there.'

'Well, it will have to do.'

'Have to do for what, sir?'

'For our trip to Cuxhaven, of course.'

TWENTY-NINE

I found Sam at her desk in the offices behind the court. It was barely nine. She was preparing for the afternoon session.

'You're mad, Douglas! What are you going to do, just waltz in to this bar and ask about their arrangements for escaped Nazis?'

'Sort of. I've got Collins out looking for old clothes. German clothes. And a boat.'

'A boat! You're going to storm ashore from a boat? Guns blazing? You tried that before, remember. On Arran.'

'And I seem to recall that it resulted in the rescue of a certain damsel in distress.'

She had the grace to blush. 'You're a big stupid hero, Brodie. And I'd like you to stop now.'

'No heroics this time. Will Collins and I are going on the run. We're a pair of SS officers looking for a way out of occupied Germany.'

Sam put her hand to her mouth. 'You'll never get away with it.'

'Why not? We both speak good German. Though I might have to add a duelling scar to Collins's face to go with his *Hochdeutsch* accent.'

Iain Scrymgeour had wandered over and was tuning into our conversation.

'Samantha's right, Brodie. It's bloody mad. But it might work. Worth a try. Need any help?'

'Gold. I need more of these.' I took out the sliver of gold and let it blaze. 'Or silver.'

'How much? We've got a safe-full somewhere.'

'Thirty pieces?'

Sam gave me a scolding look. Scrymgeour smiled.

'Anything else?'

'Collins is out looking for a boat. You don't happen to have one handy, do you?'

I caught up with Collins back at the hotel. He came to my room, arms full of clothes. Mostly smelly. Bartered for food in the local market. He was grinning like a schoolboy preparing for the Christmas play.

I dug through the pile. They looked like the miscellany worn in the gallery of the courtroom. Collins and I were about the same size, though he was slimmer. We tried it on, including the flat caps. We looked in the mirror. Two honest Germans ready to go about their business. Collins, with his blond flash of hair and blue eyes, would have made old Adolf go weak at the knees.

'You all right about this, Will?'

'Absolutely! It's my first action. It's why I joined.'

'Volunteer?'

'Stupid, isn't it? I wanted to do my bit. But . . .'

'You end up nursemaiding a crazed old war horse.'

'No, sir! Not a bit, sir.'

'It's fine, Will. But let's hope we *don't* see any action.' I was sticking to German. 'What about the boat?'

'Iain got hold of me. He's been in touch with our unit down by the harbour. We can have our pick. Tugs, fishing boats, a motor torpedo boat . . .'

'I've been looking at the map.' I pointed over at my bed where I'd spread one out. It showed the whole length of the Elbe from Hamburg through to its mouth. Cuxhaven was at the tip on the west bank. We walked over to it.

'I reckon it's about eighty miles upriver. We need something quick. I want to get going now and be there by evening.' I glanced at my watch. 'It's eleven a.m. Target arrival is eight o'clock. Something that does nine or ten miles an hour?'

'Tight, sir. What about by car?'

'Where's your sense of romance, Will? Fair point, though. But the roads are a mess all the way up. Snow. Ice. Bomb craters. Roadblocks too. A boat is quieter. Comes in from the sea. They're keeping the harbour open and the mid-channel is clear. Our story will be that we nicked it at Hamburg docks. If we're asked.'

'What *is* our story?'

'Let's work it out as we go. Here. Have some.'

I walked to the table and dug into a small bag. I pulled out a handful of glittering tablets, some gold, some silver. Collins took them, grinned at the feel of them and put them into different pockets of his faded jacket. I did the same.

'Stick your service pistol down the back of your pants.'

'Won't our guns give the game away?'

'If we've reached the stage where we have to draw them, it won't matter whether they're stamped with the Union Jack and a bas-relief of Churchill. Let's go.' I grabbed my gun and the map.

In the car to the docks we sat side by side and began to invent. In German.

'We need names,' I said. 'Choose a good German name. Fling in a von if you like. Goes with the accent.' After a little pause for thought I offered: 'OK, I'm Dieter Schulz, SS-Sturmbannführer Schulz. Who are you?'

'Drexel. SS-Hauptsturmführer Ernst von Drexel.'

'And a promotion to captain! Good for you, Ernst. And let's get used to first names. Call me sir when there are people around, and Dieter when it looks like we might be accidentally overheard. Let's start right now. OK, Ernst?'

'*Jawohl*, Dieter.'

'We need a past. A dirty past. How about the SS Totenkopf Panzer Division? A right bunch of bastards if ever there was one. Fought like madmen on the Eastern Front but guilty of atrocities wherever they went. The first recruits were SS camp guards, but later they were just the normal maniacs and zealots.'

'Sounds like our sort of people. How do you know about them?'

'My job after the surrender. I had to have a fair knowledge of all their units. Some were notorious. Like the Totenkopf. Fought like machines.'

'What happened to them?' he asked.

'Eastern Front. They got hammered outside Vienna and did a fighting retreat back to Linz just in time to surrender to the Americans.'

'So they're in POW camps?'

'Maybe. But not an American one. The Yanks handed them over to the Russians. I doubt we'll ever hear of them again.'

We swung into the docks and caused a ruction at the guardhouse until we produced our army identity cards. Scrymgeour had laid the way. A bulky sergeant escorted us down to the harbour. Ice extended from the shore out beyond the marina. But a gap was being kept clear all the way out to mid-channel. We gazed over the assembled boats.

'I'm tempted by the torpedo boat but it's a bit loud and obvious. And we might get blown up by one of our eagle-eyed RAF guys.'

The sergeant pointed at a wooden cruiser with a stubby cabin, sitting at the end of the pier.

'We've had that one out, sir. *Der Schwan*. She may not look much like a swan but she's a goer. Bit like my old lady, sir. Har har.'

'I'll tell her you said so, Sergeant.'

'Don't you worry none, sir. I told her mysel'. She just larrfed.'

He had his men run out the fuel wagon along the pier and filled her up. He showed us how to start and stop the big diesel engine. Steering was easy: a wheel.

'Any experience in boats, Ernst?'

'Rowing blue, Dieter?'

'Of course you are, Ernst.'

We unhitched from the pier, coiled the rope and set off into the wide basin. At first we had to negotiate wrecked boats and tangled jibs of cranes, but once we were out in the middle of the Elbe, we opened up. The diesel engine thumped away like a foundry.

For the first time in days, weeks, I felt the chains drop from me. The bitter wind lacerated my face but told me I was alive.

Collins steered and soon our bow wave rose up the sides and flung spray back along the deck. We were getting a good ten knots out of her. Estimated time of arrival in Cuxhaven: eight o'clock. Just in time to have a drink at the Angel's Wing.

THIRTY

We took turns at the wheel and made steady progress. Here and there we had to dodge half-sunk barges and small warships. Ice floes bumped against us and ground under the hull. *The Swan* groaned, slowed and then powered through. We hadn't expected so many impediments. When darkness fell in late afternoon, we had to be more vigilant. Thankfully it was a clear sky. The moon was three-quarters full and lit the wide river in front of us. Nevertheless we both kept our eyes straight ahead, looking for tell-tale masts jutting out of the water.

We passed lit shores on either side. Just a few fragments of the lights that would have blazed from riverside towns before the war. At one stage we were intercepted. A fast motorboat cut across our bows and trained a searchlight on us. We lost half a precious hour while they came alongside and we proved our identity to the Royal Navy team on board. They wished us *bonne chance* and we sped on our way.

The great grey expanse became wider as we headed towards the mouth. The shoreline curved steadily round to the left and ahead we could make out where the land ended and the North Sea took over. By half past eight we saw the lights of a town way to our left. We checked our position. It had to be Cuxhaven. We began to steer towards it. By nine we were entering the small harbour and looking for somewhere to tie up.

There were no lights on the harbour wall and none ahead, as though there was still a blackout. Our heavy boots echoed between the sea walls. The dark mass of the town loomed up at us and now we could see the odd street light and glow from a window. We passed ruined houses and heaps of rubble, courtesy of the RAF. A street stretched out in front of us. Our boots resounded over its cobbles until we found a café. Light seeped out behind curtains and the door. We walked in.

There were a handful of people sitting, smoking, supping beer. They turned as we walked in. The room went quiet.

'Good evening, gentlemen. We're looking for a bar. It's called the Angel's Wing.'

They looked at each other; then the man behind the counter said, 'Sure. Just down the road. First left, then right. Can't miss it.'

We thanked them and walked out into the night.

'How did that sound, Ernst?'

'Fine. But it's the strangers thing, isn't it? We stand out.'

'Like a tart at a vicarage.'

We walked on through quiet and narrow streets. An occasional shadow flitted past the crossways. After we took the right turn we could see dim light ahead from a low building. A sign above the door showed a white wing.

'Ready, Ernst?' I felt for my gun in my rear waistband. I hoped we wouldn't need them.

Collins nodded. I took a deep breath and pushed open the door.

It was a small dark bar. A cosy fire threw flickering light round the handful of faces that had turned to the door. The air was sour with smoke and old beer. Not quite as homely as McCall's but certainly of the same genus.

'Good evening, all,' I said cheerily in my best Bavarian accent. It got some muttered responses but they still kept staring at us, as if waiting for us to break into song. We walked to a small table away from the fire and therefore away from the other drinkers. We sat and waited.

The barman lifted the bar flap and came over. 'Yes, gentlemen? What can I get you?'

His eyes flicked over us, registering the military bearing, Collins's blond locks, my wariness.

'Two beers. Thirsty work that trip up from Hamburg.'

'Hamburg, eh? River?'

'Easier than the roads. And the ice wasn't bad.'

He nodded and went off to get us our drinks. I reached for my cigarettes and realised I'd left them behind. Senior Service stands out among the local weeds, even with the black market. I called out to the retreating barman.

'Bring us some cigarettes too, please.'

He came back with a tray bearing the two long glasses of beer and fags. As he turned to go, I gripped his arm.

'We want to pay with this.'

I held out between finger and thumb one of the gold ingots. It caught the light and the barman made a soft sound, sucking his teeth.

'Put it away.' His voice was low enough not to be heard across the room. I nodded in understanding.

'We're hungry. Do you have anything to eat?' I asked.

'Bread? Cheese? A little ham?'

'Bring it. Thanks.'

We sat quietly eating and drinking. The other customers had picked up their chat again and it could have been a normal pub anywhere in Europe. But I noticed the barman slip away through a back door. He was gone for ten minutes.

A little later the front door opened and a man came in. A big guy, bull neck and barrel chest, with the rolling gait of a seaman. He wore a heavy grey pullover with a crew neck. He took off his cap and nodded to all before sitting down in a corner. The conversation dropped off again. This time it didn't pick up. One by one the other drinkers said their goodnights and drifted off. Finally it was just Bull-neck, the barman and us. The man looked up and raised his glass to us.

'*Prost!*'

'*Prost,*' we answered. He got up and walked over to us.

'I'm the owner of this place. I hear you might have difficulty paying, gentlemen?'

'No difficulty. As long as you accept these.' I placed the small rectangle on the table between us. The firelight caught it and made it glow.

'These? You have more like it?'

'Enough. We want to take a holiday.'

'I hear you have a boat. What's wrong with that?'

'Out of fuel, no maps, broken compass, and nowhere to go. Otherwise you're right. Can you suggest someone who might help?'

'Maybe. But I need to know who I'm dealing with.'

'So do we.'

'I'm Günter Hoffmann.'

'Dieter Schulz.' I nodded at Will.

'Ernst von Drexel,' he said.

We shook hands and I felt the power of those huge arms coming through the grip. I hoped we weren't going to have to wrestle. I decided to up the pace.

'Shall we stop pussy-footing, Günter? You know why we're here. Can you help?'

He didn't answer, just simply began to roll up his thick jumper. His arm was bare underneath. Was he getting ready to fling a punch? When he got to the biceps a tattoo began to appear. He stopped halfway. He didn't need to go any further to uncover the death's head.

'So,' I said. 'We're among friends.'

'Maybe. What's your story? Or should I say, what rank?'

I looked at Collins and nodded to him. I went first. 'Sturmbannführer Dieter Schulz.'

Collins followed. 'Hauptsturmführer Ernst von Drexel. At your service.' I'm sure if Collins had been standing he'd have clicked heels and bowed. Easy does it, boy.

'SS?' asked our new pal.

I pointed at his tattoo and smiled in complicity.

'1st battalion, 3rd Unit Panzer Division.'

He grinned. 'The Totenkopf. Who was your commander?'

'Obergruppenführer Priess. Hermann Priess.'

'Last engagement?'

'Linz. The Reds forced us back from Vienna. We chose to surrender to the Americans rather than those animals.'

Günter grunted. I looked grim.

'But we were betrayed. The Americans handed us back to the Soviets. That's why we – shall we say – left.'

Once more he stuck his great paw and shook both our hands. 'Welcome. How did you find us?'

'We bumped into a certain Fritz Suhren. He was also on the run.'

A frown crossed Günter's face. 'When was this?'

'About a year ago. He told us he'd put himself in the hands of the Americans but they were going to try him. So he escaped.'

'Ah, that figures. He came through here about then.'

I grinned at Collins. 'That is great news! So Suhren got away?'

'Yes, yes.'

I tried it out. 'So, a boat to Scotland, was it? Is that how it works?'

His face darkened again. 'You know a lot about us.'

'Suhren was a talker with a drink.'

He was nodding all the time. 'Ja, a drinker. But then who isn't, eh?' He laughed and we all joined in.

'How many of us have you saved, Günter?'

'About twenty. Haven't seen any for a while though. You're the first this year.'

'We thought we could lie low. But they're closing the net. It was time to get out. Warmer where we're going. I mean South America. Not frozen Scotland!'

He laughed but I wondered if I'd pushed things too far.

'So, Günter, what happens now?'

'We wait. I have to get in touch with someone. It takes a bit of fixing. We will give you a house. You will have to stay put. No going out. Sometimes there are British patrols. You understand?'

'How long?'

'A week. Maybe two.'

I weighed up the situation. We could hang around and get the pick-up. We could follow it all the way through to Scotland. Roll up the whole network. But every hour, every day we spent here was high risk. They would check our story. There would be other questions. One of us would talk in his sleep; me probably. I needed names of the twenty who'd gone through already. How many were still in Scotland? I'd made my mind up to jump Günter and drag him back to Hamburg for interrogation, but suddenly he was on his feet.

'OK, boys. I need to fix some things. I'll be gone for a little while. Stay put and I'll be back soon. Then we can get things moving. OK?'

He slid out of the bar. For a big man he could move fast and silently. Now we waited. We talked in a low murmur. In German still. The barman watched us and occasionally smiled.

Half an hour went past and we heard the sound of a truck trundling along the cobbles. It stopped outside and I heard doors open and close. Then it went quiet. Steps sounded on the pavement. At least two sets. They stopped at the door. I also heard a door creak behind the bar. The barman had disappeared.

'Guns out!' I whispered fiercely. 'Get hold of this table.'

We heard running steps outside.

'Now!'

We lifted up the solid oak table and crashed it on to its side to form a barrier just as the front and back doors slammed open.

'Front's yours!' I called to Will and faced the rear.

Men with shotguns burst in from both sides, weapons up, swinging about, seeking targets.

I put a bullet in the man who'd crashed through the back door. Collins got off two shots. I glanced round and saw a man tumbling to the ground. There was a roar from the back door and Günter barrelled through, blasting away with his shotgun. We ducked and the table rocked as the blast hit it. I dived to the side and got a shot in under the flap over the bar. Günter bellowed and fell back clutching his leg. His shotgun boomed again and smashed through ceiling plaster.

A fourth man made it through the front door, exchanged shots with Collins, and dived back out. In the echoing silence I heard him running off on the cobbles.'

'Get him! Don't let him take the truck!'

Collins sprinted to the door. I scrambled to my feet and charged the bar. I slid over the surface and found Günter sprawled on the floor, cursing and trying to reload.

'Drop it! Drop it, Günter, or your balls are gone!'

My pistol was aimed directly at his groin. He got the message and lowered his shotgun. With his left hand he was gripping his thigh. Blood soaked his trousers and ran through his fingers.

I heard shots and a cry. I prayed it wasn't Collins going down. I twisted and took aim at the open front door. Collins walked in, grinning. He gave a thumbs-up.

'Well done, man. Let's get this pig out of here. On the truck.'

We wrestled Günter out through the bar flap, dragging him by his feet. His head bumped on the flagstones and then crashed on the doorsill. His groans cut out. Outside, a man lay face down by the door of the truck.

'Good shooting, Will.'

We dragged Günter over the cobbles and flung him on the open back of the truck. It was like hauling a sack of coal.

'Drive, Will! I'll look after Hoffmann.'

I jumped up on the tail. Collins climbed into the cabin. He tried the engine twice before it spluttered into life. Then we were off, rattling and banging, careering round the corners, heading for the harbour. Something like glee coursed through me. We hurtled out along the dark line of the pier. I prayed we didn't skid off into the drink. Günter was awake again, groaning. His leg was thick with blood. We slammed to a halt by the dear old *Swan*.

Way behind us flashlights split the dark. Shouts bore down on us. Together we grabbed our unwilling passenger and dragged him off the truck and on to the ground. The tide had gone out and the deck of the boat was some six feet below. By luck we'd left enough play in the mooring lines or *The Swan* would have been dangling from the pier. We looked at each other. The hue and cry was closer. We took shoulders and legs and swung him over. He seemed to fall for ever before landing with a massive thump and a yelp on the mound of tarpaulin. I tugged at the lines and together we wrenched them clear.

'Jump!' I called. We landed on deck, and sprawled in a heap. Gunter was alive and groaning. I didn't feel sorry for him. I just wanted him alive long enough to give me some names.

'Bind his leg. I'll get going.' I darted to the wheelhouse. The boat was already swinging out from the wall but we were being pushed backwards by the tide towards the enemy lights. I turned the big motor over and it rumbled into life. *You beauty*. I pushed the throttle halfway open, not wanting to stall, and started steering us away from the wall. We were making progress but it didn't seem enough. The shouts were getting closer and the first shots were fired.

Steadily we began to gather speed. I put the throttle full forward and heard the engine groan and lurch. A bullet shattered the window behind me, but I could see the line of the end of the harbour wall. Ever faster we pulled away and finally we were chugging out to the main river. I kept the throttle wide open until we were sure we weren't being followed. I thumped the wheel. This was what it was about. Not endless rounds of interrogation.

'We did it, Will! We did it! Well done, man!'

There was no answer.

'Collins! Will! Are you all right back there? Has he stopped bleeding?'

I called a couple of more times. I could see Günter lying flat on his back. Collins had turned a rope round his thigh above the wound. I couldn't see Collins. Then the cabin door pushed open. Collins slumped across the frame.

'Sorry, sir. Sorry. Caught a stray.'

I knocked the throttle back and let the boat steer its own course. I knelt down. I dragged him further inside.

'Will, Will? Where are you hit? Point to it.'

He brought his arm up and levered himself on to his side. 'Back. In the back,' he grunted.

I turned him to the light and could now see the hole in his old jacket and the surrounding stain.

'Will, you need to hold on. Can you lie down in here? Let me help.'

I eased him fully into the cabin and pulled him so that he could lie out fully. He was moaning softly now, and I could see the blood leaking all round him. I found a rug and jammed it under his head. There was no exit wound on his chest. I was helpless to stop the internal bleeding. I turned back to the wheel and gunned the engine to its max. I was careless of obstacles. His one chance was getting back to Hamburg as fast as possible. But it was eight hours away.

I kept glancing at him. He coughed once or twice and blood

came up. Then he lay quietly for some time. I though he was gone. His eyes flickered and he called to me.

I shut the throttle down and knelt by him. His hand was out, groping. I took it and held it. I eased his blond mop back from his forehead. I lifted up his head and shoulders and cradled him in my lap.

'Sir?'

'Douglas. It's Douglas.'

'Douglas. It was worth it, wasn't it?'

'It was, Will. It surely was. Now just hold on. We'll get you home.'

He smiled and gripped my hand tight. Then slowly it slackened and his body sank in on itself in a great sigh.

So many men under me had died. I'd thought I was inured to it. It seemed to get worse. I thumbed the wet from my eyes and laid his head down gently.

I left him there and went out to see how Günter was. He was alive. His leg seemed to have stopped bleeding. I undid the rope so his leg didn't drop off and stuffed the wound with a silk flag from the locker.

'Cold. Cold,' he managed.

I went back into the cabin and took the blanket off Collins. I tossed it over Günter. Then I dragged the tarpaulin right over his body. If he lived, I'd make bloody sure he coughed up every sordid detail of the northern rat line. To make Will Collins's death worthwhile.

I went back into the wheelhouse and pushed open the throttle. If we hit a wreck, so be it. *The Swan*'s bows bit into the water and flung white spray back at me as we sped on to morning.

THIRTY-ONE

made an untidy landfall. To be precise I rammed the pier. But it got attention. The sergeant and a squad of men came running. They found me lying in the wheelhouse half dazed from the crash, half mad from lack of sleep. They got me to my feet, and I dangled between two troopers.

'Take care of him,' I croaked as they manhandled Collins's still body out on to the pier. 'Be gentle.'

'We will, sir. We will. What about this fella? Who's he?'

I turned and looked back at the pile of tarpaulin with Günter's head sticking out. He wasn't moving. I called out to the man uncovering him. 'My prisoner. Is he dead?'

'Not quite, sir.'

'Get him to the guardhouse. Get him a medic. Before he dies I want some information from him.' I turned to the sergeant. 'The biggest mug of tea you can manage. With a big splash of something strong in it.'

It took two days before Günter was well enough to be interrogated. I was waiting for him on Friday morning in the little room next to the cells. He'd been transferred here the day before. And it was here, in the cells, that I missed Will Collins most. I even turned to look for him sitting behind me.

They brought in Günter Hoffmann. He was limping and his left leg was heavily bandaged. They plonked him down on the hard chair opposite me, on the other side of the table. He looked diminished. I was back in my true colours. Günter's lip turned up when he saw me, saw my uniform.

'I knew it,' he sneered.

'How? Not that it matters.'

'The pair of you. Especially the pretty boy. You didn't look like you'd been on the run for over a year. I've seen enough coming through.'

'Was that it? Too healthy?'

'The Totenkopf Division. You said the commander was Obergruppenführer Priess. He was the *second* last. At Linz it was Brigadeführer Becker.'

'Don't tell me you were there?'

'No. But my brother died with them on the Warsaw front.'

'I made a bad choice, then.'

He smirked.

'But I have you. And I'm here to offer you a choice. Your neighbours in the other cells are camp guards from Ravensbrück. They're on trial for their lives. Next week a number of them will be found guilty and they will be sentenced to hang.'

'What's that got to do with me?'

'You can choose to die with them on the scaffold, or you can tell me all about the northern rat line.'

'You can't do that! I'm a civilian!'

'You're whatever I say you are. For the moment, you're a spy. Your Nazi pals murdered our spies in Ravensbrück. Tomorrow I can prepare papers which show you were an NCO at Ravensbrück. We have enough witness testimonies to go round. I can have an inch-thick file made up for you showing the atrocities you committed.'

'That's illegal!'

I laughed. At first it was a forced laugh. But then it became genuine. I finally pulled myself together.

'I had no idea you were a comedian, Günter. Let's make this simple. We won. You lost. You take your medicine. And, by the way, I might just have you hanged anyway for the death of my friend.'

I watched him think. I watched the fear settle on his face and the realisation grow that I was deadly serious. The interesting thing is, I was. I was perfectly ready to concoct a case that would send this man to the gallows. What a long way I'd fallen.

'So even if I tell you something useful, you might still do me in?'

'Depends on the quality. Roll the dice, Günter. Roll the dice. I don't really mind where they fall.'

I waited, arms folded, gazing at him, watching him do the calculations. Sweat beaded his brow and he reached for the cigarettes I'd placed in front of him.

'Ask me,' he said.

I reached for my pad and pencil.

'Who set up this rat line?'

'Our schoolmaster, Josef Erlichmann. He ran the Hitler Youth. He knew my opinions. Knew my brother died fighting the Reds. He said some good men needed help to leave the country. To keep up the fight against the Bolshies. He gave me money to arrange a boat.'

'Where did a teacher get the money?'

'He'd been approached. He said there was an organisation.'

'Called?'

'No name. I know nothing about it, except the papers came from Switzerland.

'When did it start?'

'Early '45. He brought the first one to me. I hid him in my cellar under the bar. It took three weeks for the documentation to come through.'

'Documentation?'

'Passports, references from the Red Cross.'

'The Vatican?'

He nodded.

'Then what?'

'We had to wait for the weather. Then the boat left on the night tide. It was a fishing boat. Plenty of fish in the North Sea.'

'Where did it go?' Though I could guess.

'Scotland. Edinburgh.'

'You mean the port of Leith?'

'Exactly.'

'That wasn't their final destination.'

'No. They were taken to Glasgow, then the Americas. You see, I asked if I could use the route. You know, in case they came after me. Left it a bit late, didn't I?'

'Someone was waiting at Leith?'

'The teacher had a transmitter. He could warn them when the boat went north.'

'Who was the local contact in Leith?'

'I've no idea.'

'You used the same boat, same fisherman?'

'Yes.'

'What's his name?'

'Doesn't matter now. You shot him.'

Bugger. If I believed him. 'One moment.' I got up and walked out of the cell. 'Sergeant!'

The duty NCO ran over. 'Sir?'

'Get a platoon together and send them to Cuxhaven immediately. I don't care how you get there. Boat or bike. Both is better. Just get there as fast as you can. They're to pick up the local schoolmaster, Josef Erlichmann. And the barman at the Angel's Wing. Find out the names of the fishermen friends of the prisoner. Bugger it. Bring them all in. Every man who owns a boat. At the double!'

'Sir!'

I went back into the interrogation.

'You said in the bar that you'd sent about twenty through?'

'It was twenty.'

'How many got all the way through?'

'All the way?'

'America. North or South.'

'How would I know? There was a hiccup in the line last year.'

'What do you mean?'

'We were told to stop sending anyone. Back in February or March.'

'Why?'

'The line got stuck or something. I never heard why.'

'Was that the time when Suhren went through?

'Just before.'

'How many of the twenty had you sent by then?'

'A good dozen.'

I imagined a conveyor belt running from occupied Germany through Cuxhaven, north to Leith, through Glasgow, then boat to New York. Somewhere past Cuxhaven the belt had jammed. A contact arrested?

'But a further eight showed up *after* the suspension of the line? Like Suhren?'

'That was the trouble. They kept coming and we couldn't send them on.'

'What did you do with them?'

'I hid three in my cellar. Suhren was one. The others were scattered around the town.'

'But you eventually got them out?'

'The teacher had to plead with someone. He argued it was better to get them to an unoccupied country than let them get caught here.'

'What are their names?' I had my pencil poised.

He looked uncomfortable. 'I'm not good with names. Honest. I'll do my best. Can I have a bit of paper and a pencil? I work best that way.'

I tore off a sheet and dug out another pencil. I drew a line across the middle and pushed the paper and pencil over to him.

'This is the really important bit, Günter. Above that line, I want a list of the dozen who went through before everything got stuck, last February. Put the second batch of eight below it. The ones that got stuck here for a while.'

I sat and folded my arms. Günter laid his big arms on the table and took up the pencil. His tongue came out as he concentrated. I felt like an adjudicator at finals.

'No pressure, Günter. Give me names and you can live.'

THIRTY-TWO

The court met on Monday 3 February to deliver its sentences. It hardly seemed possible, but the numbers of spectators in the Curiohaus appeared to have doubled. The air was steamy, the tension palpable. One by one the defendants were made to stand and the verdict and sentence read out.

Schwarzhuber, Ramdohr and Binz were sentenced to death by hanging, as were three fine members of the medical profession: Rosenthal, Schiedlausky, and Treite. A fourth wasn't around to hear his fate. Dr Adolf Winkelmann had decided to skip his rendezvous with Albert Pierrepoint by dying the previous Saturday. His sixty-year-old heart had given out under the pressure of the trial. I wish I could say it was due to the guilt of knowing he'd sent some 4,500 women to the gas chambers, but he'd never shown remorse. Five others including Greta Bösel got the same judgment and sentence. All eleven would be taken to Hameln for execution, two by two on the gallows. Very economical.

Martin Hellinger, the dentist, was sentenced to fifteen years in jail. He looked up at me as the verdict was read out and gave me the barest nod. I handed Günter Hoffmann over to our Military Police. They could do what they liked with him. The platoon I'd sent to Cuxhaven had come back without Erlichmann the schoolmaster; he'd vanished. Of the fourteen grumbling fishermen they rounded up, none admitted to trawling further north than the Dogger Bank, far less excursions to Leith.

That night, Iain, Sam and I met for a celebration drink. It felt more like a wake. Which of course it was. A pre-emptive one for the condemned and a belated one for Will Collins. I found when I was writing to his father that I'd got out of the habit. All I could do was assure him that his son's death hadn't been in vain. Had it?

There should have been some sense of triumph or at least relief that justice had been served. But remembering the ashen faces of the women with the numbers on their chests as they were told – one by one – that they would hang brought only despondency. As if we were compounding their inhumanity with our own.

Late in the evening I found myself telling Scrymgeour that he wasn't as much of a prick as I'd expected. He put his arm round my shoulder and told me neither was I. Sam smiled on us like a fond aunt.

It wasn't quite the end for Sam, Iain and me. There was no sense of exultation or even release. The legal team had a colossal amount of paperwork to finalise and cross-reference to help with the next trial. I was trying to make sense of what I'd wrung out of Günter.

I sent a confidential message to Sillitoe at MI5 telling him of my breakthrough and asking him to watch Leith. But I could give him no details. The Firth of Forth offered a long shoreline, north and south. The escapees could have landed anywhere.

Günter had managed to come up with fourteen names out of the twenty: eight above and six below my line. Günter couldn't recall the names of four of the first batch of twelve, the ones that might well have already passed through Scotland. Of the names below the line one was Draganski, the other Suhren. In addition there were two mystery women identified below the line.

'You really can't remember their names?'

'It's not that. I never knew them. Nor their ranks. One was in charge. It was obvious by her bearing. *You* know what officers are like. She came with a younger woman. They refused to talk to me. I think the schoolmaster knew. They were given priority.'

'What does that mean?'

'Their documentation came through in three days. The teacher was always calling his contact to see if the line was reopened. He wanted them gone.'

'This Draganski. Why did you go to such trouble for a junior SS guard?'

'It wasn't for him. He was guarding a more senior officer.'

'Suhren?'

'Langefeld.'

I checked the other names he'd given me. 'Hauptsturmführer Klaus Langefeld?'

'That's how it worked.'

'Do you know Langefeld's background? His SS role?'

He shook his head.

'Who were the other senior officers?'

'I didn't always get their rank.'

I telegraphed the names to Sillitoe, but it was pointless. They were hardly going to use their real ones, and I had no descriptions except Suhren's. I sent all fourteen names off to our team in Berlin asking urgently for details, including photos if possible. I included Dragan to check how much he might have changed by the time I encountered him in Glasgow. Günter had mentioned hair dye and beards but it would be hard to change the shape of a face. I told Berlin to pay particular attention to the second batch, the eight who might still be stuck in Scotland; though we knew Dragan was now a permanent fixture there. I asked if they were aware of any senior woman or women on the run who might fit the sketchy outline of the Cuxhaven pair. After that I could do nothing more than wait for details to come through. I phoned and sent telegrams daily. Berlin seemed to have no sense of urgency that more deaths could follow in Glasgow as the cornered rats fought to save their skins. I was equally worried that the rat line could unblock at any moment and the escapees could get through to freedom in the Americas – rendering Collins's sacrifice meaningless. It would be particularly galling if Suhren got away after what Odette Sansom had said. After what he'd done to her three SOE colleagues.

'I could get over to Berlin and shake them up personally, Sam.'

'It would be counter-productive. You know what wee clerks with power can be like. Iain's already getting complaints about you.'

So I had to sit out, going stir crazy in this cold hut by the desolate lake. The brief surge of hope and enthusiasm that had come with my birthday celebrations and the break-through with Hellinger had evaporated. Had died with Will Collins. I was drinking too much again, and now I had little to get up for.

The days mirrored our moods. The sun hadn't been seen across northern Europe for days. We heard there were ten-foot drifts throughout Scotland and England. Hamburg matched it foot for foot. We got up in the dark; it grew grey; then it went dark again. They were skating on the Alster, even building fires on it and roasting chestnuts hoarded from last autumn. But there was no indication that life and light would ever return to this blighted land.

We were in bad shape. Or at least I was.

'You can't keep blaming yourself, Douglas.'

'Who else can I blame, Sam? Will Collins didn't have to die. I could have sent fifty men to round up Günter Hoffmann and his pals instead of just the two of us. I might even have caught the schoolmaster.'

'You didn't know who you were looking for till you got there.'

'You were right, though, Sam. I was playing the hero. It was self-indulgence.'

Sam too was changed by it, more introspective, more hidden. We'd been gone barely a month but it felt like I'd done a five-year stretch at Barlinnie. I felt engulfed by the churned-up past. I walked through each day with a pack of black dogs snapping at my heels. If I stumbled and fell, they would tear me apart. At night we kept the connecting door open between us. Sometimes we slept together, spooning in the dark. But it was simply good to know she was there, a few steps away.

On 14 February I found a note in my diary and fired off a congratulatory telegram to a certain Police Sergeant Murdoch and his new bride Morag. Sam and I spent the rest of St Valentine's Day holed up in our igloo while the winds howled outside and sabre-tooths fled in front of the advancing glaciers.

At least the information was dribbling in. Across all fourteen names a pattern emerged. About a third of the names were NCOs or camp wardens, *Aufseherinnen* in the case of females. Possibly the guardians of the bigger rats. The rest were former SS officers or medics at Ravensbrück, its subcamps or other camps. Together they formed a roll call of the most terrible places on earth: Auschwitz, Belsen, Treblinka and Buchenwald.

Finally we were done. The last pack of papers came through from Berlin. I could have tried to send them by air courier but nothing was getting off the ground. As fast as they cleared the runway another blizzard took it out. Sam and I were packed ready to go by any form of transport – truck, train or plane – the moment there was a break in the weather. I'd be my own courier. But we couldn't even leave the hotel, far less Hamburg.

We listened to the wireless whenever we could get a signal. Through the whines and the static, we learned it was no better in Britain. Atlee had cut power to nineteen hours per day. Factories were shut and the home fires had ceased burning. It wasn't an attractive destination but we were desperate to get there. I wanted reprisals for Collins.

My patience snapped on the nineteenth and we made a break overland by a series of trains to the Channel. We got as far as Ostend only to find the service suspended because of pack ice off the coast. Europe was marooned. They sent ice-breakers into the harbour on Friday, and on Saturday morning we caught an overcrowded ferry to England. By evening we were toasting each other in the bar of the officers' mess at RAF Hendon.

'Douglas, I don't want to say it, but you're not the man I set out with.'

I looked up at the mirror behind the bar. Looking back was a scrawny old man in an ill-fitting uniform. I pointed at him.

'See. You hit thirty-five and it's downhill all the way. You're a wee bit ethereal yourself, Samantha Campbell, if you don't mind my saying so.'

Her lovely face was hollowed out, her cheekbones beneath her specs emphasising her deep-set blue eyes. She'd had no weight to lose but now she was fragile, wisp-thin.

'Let's get ourselves home, laddie. A gallon or two of Isobel Dunlop's Scotch broth will soon fill us out.'

The RAF did us proud. They cleared the runway twice next morning so we could take off, climbing above snow clouds to blue sky and sunshine. We hoped for a slow flight just to bask in the warmth and light. But by one o'clock we were diving into the clouds again and coming into land over the ice-age landscape that used to be Ayrshire.

Glasgow was a whiteout. The taxi from the station took three goes at the hill up to Sam's. The house was stone cold. At least it was dust-free: Izzie had kept up the assault in our absence. As darkness fell, Sam and I pulled our chairs closer to the puny flames and nursed our whisky.

'Now we're back, Douglas . . . Look, I don't know how to put this. One of my friends is a doctor.'

'Who'd come and take me away in a straitjacket?'

'Of course not. But you could get pills. Help you sleep.'

'I've got this.' I held up my glass.

'That's another thing.'

'I'm drinking too much?'

'*We* are.'

'Look, it'll calm down now. It's finished. I can pass this over to the police. I'll talk them through it, translate it. It's all the information they need. I'll tell Shimon and Malachi that the police or MI5 – or whoever the hell they like – will handle things from now on. Let them take it from here. And I'll see if they'll demob me again.'

'You looked good in uniform. Shame you have to hand it back.'

'There wasn't a kilt.'

It was no night for passion and we went to our separate rooms. I jolted awake with the unfamiliar silence. The old Bear Hotel had creaked and groaned and the wind had howled over the frozen lake. Now there was nothing. I padded to the window and scraped a hole in the ice. Outside it seemed to be daylight, though my watch disagreed. A half-moon silvered across great scoops of snow. The streets were flooded with it. As I watched, new flakes began tumbling again, and soon the moonlight was obliterated in a white storm. I stood at the window for a while, feeling like a little boy, strangely excited for morning.

THIRTY-THREE

A soft touch on my face startled me until she spoke.

'Douglas, Douglas. I have to go out now. Are you all right to leave?'

'Where . . . I mean, what time is it?'

'Eight thirty. You're fine. Take the day off. I'll phone the *Gazette* and say you've got the flu.'

I rolled on to my back. 'I never get the flu.'

'Stay there and sleep it off.'

'Is that an invitation?'

'That sounds like the old Brodie. No time, dear. I've got meetings over in Edinburgh. I'm staying there tonight. I need to report back and persuade them to let me stay working in Glasgow. They owe me.'

She left me lying there and a little later I heard the front door open and close. I was drifting in and out of wakefulness now, brain buzzing and flitting. Faces kept crowding in. Laughing faces, sneering and mocking. I recognised some of them as creatures I'd interrogated, but most were unfamiliar. I kept pushing them back until I woke again shouting at them, hurling abuse at them, denying their existence. I was bathed in sweat. Maybe it *was* the flu.

I forced myself upright, and sat on my bed until the room stopped swaying. This wouldn't do. I had a job to finish. A baton to pass.

Cocooned in gloves, hat, overcoat and scarf I plunged into

ankle-deep snow and began trudging down the hill, skidding and hanging on to railings.

Eddie must have been looking out for me. He shot out of his office.

'Ah thocht you were doon with the flu, Brodie? Your landlady phoned us.'

'I'm a quick healer, Eddie. What's the news?'

He followed me right through the newsroom to my desk. I sat down and Eddie loured over the filing cabinet at me.

'Well, Sandy and me have just aboot managed to cobble thegither the odd crime column in your absence. Maybe without the majestic Brodie flourishes, but no' bad a' the same. So, where's your scoop, Brodie?'

'What scoop?'

'Christ, man, you've just been out there in Germany at the trials of the century and you ask me what scoop? Were you no' taking notes or anything?'

I sprang to my feet. '*Taking notes?* We were taking notes all right! I've got enough filth and tragedy and evil to fill the *Gazette* from front to back for a decade! Is that what you want?'

Eddie staggered back. Behind him, the room had stilled. My face was hot and I could hear my heart pounding in my ears. I gathered myself and took a deep breath.

'Eddie, sorry. I'm tired. It was hard work. Look, give me a couple of hours. I'll knock out something. A day in the life of a prosecutor. I'll do a court scene. Something that tells the readers what it's like. OK?'

Eddie was still looking at me as though I was a ghoul with my head under my arm.

'Aye, right. OK Brodie. You sure you're feeling OK? Ah mean, take the afternoon off if you're no' feeling weel.'

I sat down. 'I'm fine, Eddie. I'll get a column together for you. Two hours.'

*

It took me less, and I produced enough for ten columns. It poured out of me. The packed courtroom of the Curiohaus. General Westropp chairing his military panel. The bank of accused women reduced to cyphers. Eeny, meeny, miny, mo. The public gallery packed with middle-class Germans come to gawp at the working-class thugs who'd let the side down. The defence counsel claiming their clients were innocent lambs, forced to obey orders.

I wrote of my own role, standing in the witness box in my smart uniform, swearing the correctness of my written reports. Pointing out the defendants and confirming their identities. I wrote about the spleen and the bile and the empty eyes of the men and women I interrogated.

But I didn't reveal that some of their number had got away. Or that rat lines ran across the Continent, north and south, easing the passage of war criminals to safe havens. I certainly didn't disclose that some of these escapees had been given written permits and safe travel documents by a rogue bishop. That one of the escape channels was called the Vatican *Rattenlinie*. That another seemed to end up here, in Glasgow.

I didn't give Eddie the scoop he wanted. That somewhere in our city, under the virginal snow, was a rats' nest of sadists and evil-doers.

I handed in my much-too-long draft to Eddie and in return was given three phone message slips. One was from McCulloch's office. Eddie poked it.

'That yin's urgent, Brodie. You can use the conference room to ca' him back if you like.'

The second was from Isaac, no doubt operating as the conduit for his pals. The third was from a Whitehall area number.

THIRTY-FOUR

Sitting in the conference room and weighing up the respective importance of the three slips, I decided to start gently. I made my first call to Isaac.

'I've been worried, Douglas.'

'That I'd forgotten you?'

'That you'd be harmed by this. We asked a lot of you. Too much, my friend.'

His tone was genuine and concerned. For a ridiculous moment my eyes stung.

'It's kind of you, Isaac. But I'm back and I'm fine. Can you call Shimon? Arrange to meet later? At your place?' I thought of Isaac's snug back room as a little sanctuary. It would be good to have somewhere safe to meet.

I then called London. A woman answered; I asked for the extension provided on the slip of paper and gave my name. A second woman answered, this time with a newsreader voice.

'Kindly hold on, Colonel Brodie. I'll put you through.'

Still Colonel? That was nice. But at the same time worrying. There was a pause, a couple of clicks and a 'You're through, sir'. Then a man's voice I recognised from the parade ground of the Glasgow police college, and later, as a detective sergeant, on a private mission that nearly got me killed.

'Brodie? *Colonel* Brodie, I should say.' Sir Percy Sillitoe's even tones were unchanged from a decade ago. Perhaps more BBC. London does that to a man.

'Yes, sir. You want a briefing?'

'If you please, Brodie.'

'May I ask one thing? Am I still in the army? Am I still commissioned?'

'For the moment anyway. A technicality. It just seemed easier all round. Official secrets and all that. So . . .?'

I took a deep breath. This wasn't the moment for an argument. I switched into my debriefing mode, learned in the police and reinforced in the army.

'You got my telex?'

'A breakthrough, you said. We warned the local bobbies in Leith but it's a needle in the haystack if we don't know what they're looking for.'

'I know. Worth a try.'

'But you've got names, Brodie! Descriptions. That's the stuff!'

'And some photos. We found out that the northern rat line had been used by twenty escapees."

'Christ!'

'Indeed, sir. We have fourteen names, plus two mystery women. What we don't know is how many have already passed through en route to South America.'

'Any guesses?'

'The rat line got stuck about a year ago. I don't know why. I think around a dozen had passed through Scotland by then. Since then a further eight were dropped off at Leith and may still be here. We've accounted for Draganski. And we know three other caches of ingots were stolen by Paddy Craven before he ran into Dragan's knife.'

'So perhaps seven at large. Including the camp commandant Suhren. Highly dangerous, especially if they feel cornered. You have descriptions, you said?'

'At Cuxhaven they changed hair colour, grew beards and were given top-quality passports. And presumably some gold and silver to speed them on their way. We think Fritz Suhren had hidden some loot and retrieved it when he absconded. He may have been prevailed on to leave some at Cuxhaven to help others behind him.'

'The schoolmaster got away? The link man at Cuxhaven?'

'It means the rat line could be reopened somewhere else.'

'Do we know who's running the line at your end? In Glasgow? Or Leith?'

'No. What about your research, sir? The documentation with the Red Cross stamps, signed letters from Bishop Alois Hudal?'

'It's a delicate matter, Brodie. We don't think the Vatican was directly involved in helping Nazis out of Europe. One rogue bishop doesn't make a conspiracy. The last thing we want is to stir up more anti-Semitic accusations about the Vatican.'

'Sir, on a different tack, I lost a good man. Lieutenant Will Collins. He was fearless. I shouldn't have risked him. He earned a medal. A big one. It would be important for his family.'

'I heard. He will be honoured. You might have earned one yourself. But don't beat yourself up, man. No one else could have got us this far.'

'No? Anyway, I'm glad it's over. I'll report to the Chief Constable. He'll take it from here.'

'Ah, yes. Of course, Malcolm and his boys have their part to play. But they'll have their work cut out. I want to take up a little more of your time, *Colonel* Brodie.'

I knew it. 'I'm just a reporter, sir.'

'You're a lieutenant colonel.'

'I can resign my commission.'

'You could, but I'm sure you won't. I know you, Douglas Brodie, remember? From the old days? You handled a problem for me in a way that no one else could. You're not hidebound. I need a different take on this. *Your* take.'

'I'm not MI5.'

'Ah, didn't I mention? I've agreed with the Army Department – General Gilmour personally – that you're seconded to me for this mission.'

I felt the clouds building up again. They can't do this to me. But of course they can. Even if they can't make me, can't force me, they know how to draw me in.

'Does the Chief Constable know all this, sir?'

'Malcolm knows. But only him, Brodie. He won't be telling his officers. It would get . . .'

'Messy?'

That was putting it mildly. An army officer, seconded to MI5, running a parallel operation to the Glasgow police force. And there was the small matter of my erstwhile Jewish employers. I was no longer on their payroll but I'd promised they would hear from me. I knew some of them were terrified by the thought of the Nazi plague following and enveloping them. Others, like Malachi, probably relished the prospect of honing another pitchfork.

'Bloody messy. You're a fine detective, Brodie. And you take risks. That's what you're good at. Go and find these bastards.'

My phone conversation with McCulloch was much shorter and to the point.

'I've been waiting, Brodie. Can you come to my office? Soon as you can, please. Have you eaten?'

THIRTY-FIVE

I picked up my neat folder of information on the escapees and told Eddie where I was going. Eddie was glad to get my surly presence out of his newsroom. He and Sandy were hacking away with their blue pencils at my draft. It was now split into four columns to run on subsequent editions. I left them to it.

The snow had stopped and teams of men were shovelling clear the main roads. Some of the trams had snowploughs fitted, and gritters were at work. The carters had covered their horses with blankets and tied sacks round their hooves to give them purchase. The drivers were hauling on their brakes with both hands to stop them becoming sledges on the hills. When the schools broke up at four, the streets and parks would be filled by roaring battalions of kids, in a thousand snowball fights.

I trudged through the snow and the slush with a sense of quiet desperation. I felt, yet again, driven down a path I didn't want to take. I hated self-pity but here I was wallowing in it. Why me? Percy Sillitoe's words rang hollow: *That's what you're good at.* Maybe once. It didn't seem like it now. Not feeling like this. They needed a brave man with a cool head. Not a wreck with a mind full of terrors.

I splashed down Turnbull Street, kicked my soaking shoes against the steps of Central Division and went in. It still smelt the same: old polish, old sweat and now damp, the floors wet and slippery from the carried-in snow. Ahead was the big oak counter straddling the entrance hall. But before I got there I was intercepted.

'Well, the wanderer's returned.'

'Hello, Duncan. Watch your footing out there.'

'It's in here Ah worry about. You here to see me?'

'No. Summoned by your boss.'

'Sangster?'

'The big boss.'

'You're flying high. Is this all about your wee trip to Germany?'

'Yes.'

'By the looks of you, it wisnae much of a holiday. You look wabbit.'

I pulled him over to the side. We stood close. 'Look, Duncan, I can't talk just now. Can we meet later? Buy you a pint?'

'The Jewish thing?' He tapped the folder under my arm.

I nodded. 'McCall's, six o'clock?'

We parted and I walked over to the desk sergeant.

'I'm here to see the Chief Constable.'

'You would be Mr Brodie, sir? We're expecting you. The constable here will take you up.

We went into the building and took the wing of the senior officers. The Chief Constable's secretary was already on her feet. She went to the door behind her, stuck her head in and then ushered me through.

'Come in, Brodie.' McCulloch came to me and shook my hand. 'Let's sit over here.' He indicated a good fire with two high-backed chairs parked either side. He called to his secretary: 'Bring in the sandwiches, please. Then no interruptions, Miss MacDonald. And I mean none.' He took my elbow and steered me towards the fire. Did I look as though I needed a hand? Between him and Duncan, it seemed like it.

'It's bitter out there. And you look like you need a wee half.'

I sank into a chair. Sandwiches were brought and put by my hand. McCulloch himself set a honey-filled cut-glass decanter and two glasses on the table between the chairs. I waited for my whisky as if waiting for breath.

He let me talk with just the occasional sharp question thrown in to show he was listening. He wanted to hear how I'd narrowed down the field and how we'd raided Cuxhaven. He couldn't get enough of the shoot-out. I couldn't talk about it without drowning in guilt.

'Sorry about your man, Brodie. He was a brave customer.'

'A soldier, Malcolm. A soldier.'

We talked about the rat line and discussed how easily a fishing boat could drop a man off along the shoreline of the Forth. And how simple it would be to lose yourself in the crowd and hubbub of the Gorbals. There was no obvious way of tracking down the Leith contact, though McCulloch had asked his opposite number in Edinburgh to see if anyone had spotted a German fishing boat in the firth.

Then we got on to the meat. I passed him the two lists of names and the batch of supporting details together with a rare photograph or two. I explained about the disruption that had stalled the conveyor belt last year. He agreed it was likely we'd lost the first twelve escapees but that we still harboured at least seven, excluding the dead Dragan.

Sturmbannführer Fritz Suhren, Commandant, Ravensbrück
Hauptsturmführer Klaus Langefeld, Senior Adjutant, Auschwitz
Obersturmführer Rudolf Gebhardt, Doctor, Buchenwald
Hauptsturmführer Siegfried Fischer, Doctor, Treblinka
Aufseherin Hildegard Mandel, Ravensbrück
Woman A
Woman B
Rapportführer Walter Draganski, Ravensbrück [deceased]

It was early afternoon by the time we ground to a halt. The sandwiches had gone and the decanter had taken a hammering.

'Well then, Brodie. It's quite a story.'

I nodded. I was light-headed with the whisky and the outpouring of scenes and emotions.

'What worries me, Malcolm, is the rat line starting up again. The Cuxhaven link got away and we don't have a lead on the Scottish operator. I don't know what the blockage is between here and South America but we need to move fast or we'll lose the seven that are stuck here.'

'It's my worry too. That and their propensity for murder if anyone gets in their way.'

'Cornered rats.'

'Exactly. Probably protecting their king rat, Suhren. It's like having unexploded bombs walking about. Four deaths already. I want no more. But Sir Percy's right. We need to keep this between ourselves. Can you cope with that, Brodie, as you press on?'

'As I press on? Malcolm, to be honest, this has . . .'

'Buggered you? I can see it, man. Give yourself a couple of days. You're exhausted.'

'What are *your* plans now, Malcolm?'

'I'd like to flood the streets. Do house to house. As many men as I can spare. Hell, bring in the army.'

'But . . .'

'But can you imagine the panic? *Nazis loose in Glasgow.*'

'I haven't told anyone at the *Gazette*. I've drafted some general stuff about the trials but nothing about our local problems.'

'Keep it that way, please. We'll do this quietly and methodically. Our priority is your second list, while keeping an eye out for anyone that fits the first batch of twelve – just in case any of them decided they preferred Glasgow to Rio. I'll circulate names and descriptions to my senior officers. The detectives can talk to their snitches. The murders of Craven, McGill and poor Miss Jacobs must have stirred things up a bit.'

'What about the Jewish community? I promised to get back to their leaders. They opened all this up. I owe them some of the facts. They might even be able to help.'

He was quiet for moment; then he nodded. 'Keep it minimal. There's no point lying to them or avoiding the matter. But let's not have a repeat of the vigilantes of last year. The *Jewish Marshals*, for pity's sake.'

THIRTY-SIX

I t was just after two o'clock. I called Isaac's shop before I left Central Division to say I was on my way. He said he had a new supply of real coffee beans. He'd let Shimon know I was available. I crossed Gorbals Bridge breathing in the chilled air to clear my head and sober up. The snow was starting up again, blowing horizontally down the Clyde. As I walked, I tried to work out what to tell these men, and what not to.

Isaac greeted me with a cup of his welcoming coffee. I took it into his sanctuary, warming my hands while we waited for the others.

'You look ill, Douglas. Thin. My Hannah would be feeding you chicken soup.'

'I know she would, Isaac. It's what I need. That and her smile.'

We both looked away from each other's gaze.

'Tell me, Douglas, did it make any more sense? When you saw them again?'

'You mean do I understand why they did it?'

'Yes.'

I shook my head. 'I'd hoped you'd tell me. Why do they hate you, Isaac? Not just the Nazis. Everybody. Everywhere you go.'

He examined his cup for a long time. 'I see it like this. Some people can only define themselves by their enemies.

They need someone to blame when life goes wrong. They won't accept personal responsibility. The Jews are handy. We are easily identifiable. We are a tribe that the Christian tribe can accuse.'

'But we share the same start point. Christ was a Jew.'

'Hush, Douglas. It is our greatest crime, they tell us. And it is cause enough to destroy us.'

'For two millennia?'

'For long before that. The Persians, Egyptians, Syrians, Mongolians – they all tried to annihilate us. It is the way of nations to stamp out all other identities.'

'That makes sense if the nations share a border and one wants the other's land or wealth. Jews don't have a state.'

'Ours is a state without borders. We are a tribe within other tribes, across other tribes.'

'You could say the same about Christianity.'

'But you won, Douglas. You won. Then you took away our lands. You took away our rights and pushed us into work that you didn't want to do. Like lending money. Or into brain work that you couldn't exclude us from.'

I understood the full vicious circle Isaac was drawing. We forced the Jews to become teachers and doctors and thinkers. We forced them to become rich. And then we envied them. We hated them.

'You must think the world is very unfair.'

He smiled. 'It's why we're still waiting for the Messiah. It's why we conclude the Passover Seder with the words *l'shanah haba'ah birushalayim* – next year in Jerusalem.'

'So you can hardly blame Amos for wanting to go.'

He batted his hand at me. 'Ach, I know it. If only he'd wait until things had settled. Until the United Nations gives its blessing to Israel.'

'That's an old story, Isaac. A nation state surrounded by its enemies. History repeating itself?'

'Maybe this time, eh?'

The shop doorbell jangled. Isaac went out and came back with two men, shaking the heavy white clumps from their coats and hats. I rose.

'Shalom, Shimon, Rabbi.'

'Shalom, Brodie,' they said in unison.

We gathered round Isaac's fire in the back room. It was snug among the bales of cloth. I gave them the main bits of news and that I'd come back with names and descriptions of possible Nazis among us. It excited them. Thrilled them.

I tried to skip all the wretched details of the Hamburg prisoners and their dirty deeds. But it wasn't enough for these men. They wanted pen portraits of the monsters now under sentence of death. They'd seen the court sentences in the paper and knew all the names. They wanted to know what they were like so that they could spot others like them. Take action against them before another mass slaughter.

I told them what I could but not what they wanted to hear. The camp guards were outwardly no different to anyone else. No horns. No slavering fangs. No mark of the beast.

Maurice Silver leaned into me. 'Tell me, Brodie, these women, did they show any remorse? They have had time to think about it.'

'Only the remorse of someone caught doing something wrong and knowing that they will have to pay for it. More self-pity really.'

'No penitence?'

'Rabbi, they are missing the faculty that provokes remorse. By their amoral code, they did nothing wrong.'

'I cannot believe that.'

'You must. I wish it weren't true. But I met them. I talked to them. The women were the worst.' As I spoke I had the image of Dorothea Binz in mind. Her cunning corn-flower eyes and her vicious tongue. 'Think of a succubus. Think of Lilith.'

The rabbi sat back, clearly stunned at the notion of a

female demon springing live from the pages of the Talmud. The three men glanced at each other.

Shimon asked, 'Brodie, we have been talking about just such an outcome as you have described. That you would come back with proof of this wickedness among us. You have the names, descriptions – including the boss of Ravensbrück, for pity's sake. We want you to – there is no other word for it – protect us. Of course we will pay you.'

'Shimon, I won't take your money. It would be dishonest. I am one man. There are seven of these creatures at large. How can one man protect you?'

He was nodding. 'We have some men. Around twenty. They will work for you. You will direct them.'

'Do they include Malachi?'

'Yes. He is one of them. Is that a problem?'

'He's a Marxist.'

Shimon shrugged. 'Many Jews are.'

'I fear his ideology makes him a little too enthusiastic. Kill first and ask questions after is his style.'

'He needs a leader. You are a leader.'

I was sagging under the weight of these fulsome plaudits. Too much expected of me from too many folk. If I was supposed to be helping Sillitoe, I needed to rope in some assistance. Maybe I could organise them? Set up patrols of the main Jewish enclaves? But I truly doubted if Malachi was controllable.

'Look, I'll help. But on my own terms. These men: do they have any training?'

Shimon smiled. 'Training, you ask? Some of them are trained to survive in the sewers of Warsaw. Some learned to fight in the forests of Latvia and Lithuania. Others learned how to endure in Auschwitz.'

'I get the picture. Can you arrange for me to meet them?'

'When, Brodie? They could gather tomorrow.'

'Fine. Let's meet tomorrow evening. Seven o'clock. Do you have a place to hold – twenty, did you say?'

Shimon said, 'The hall of the Garnethill Synagogue.'

'Tell them not to come as a gang. Come singly or in twos. As if they were coming to evening prayers. One last thing: no weapons.'

THIRTY-SEVEN

I glanced at my watch. It was five thirty. All I wanted to do was go home and fall into bed. But I'd promised to meet Duncan at McCall's at six. I was parched from the whisky and the coffee. Maybe a pint or two would help. I could get a pie there too. Sam was still over in Edinburgh and staying the night. The house would be empty and echoing, as it had been through all of December. I didn't want to be there by myself with my thoughts.

I set off back over the suspension bridge and then straight up Hope Street. The hill seemed harder. Maybe it was the snow beating against my face. Maybe I was out of sorts having missed my daily swims for weeks. I got to McCall's as they were opening and sank into a chair near the fire, barely able to muster the energy to sup my pint. I must have dozed off. I was being shaken awake.

'Wakey, wakey, Brodie. Ye're like an auld alkie slumped there.'

I rubbed my face. 'Your boss is to blame. Kept pouring his best Scotch down my neck.'

'You're honoured. I might tell Sangster, just to see his face turn green. What'll you have?'

Somehow I never found the time for that pie. I gave Duncan as full a version of events as I'd given McCulloch, as though I'd become a gramophone record. But it was different unburdening to a pal. And later we shifted topics to rugby and politics, football and sectarianism, and then we switched from beer to whisky and Duncan was pouring me into a taxi . . .

I fumbled into the great dark hall, shucked off my coat and scarf and hat and found myself on hands and knees climbing the stairs to my bed. I knew Sam was in Edinburgh but I called her name anyway, and even sang to her as I swayed in front of her bedroom door. I crashed into my own room and dropped like a felled tree on to my bed.

I woke in the dark feeling sick. I checked my watch. Five o'clock. I was still in my shirt and trousers, now hopelessly wrinkled.

I sat on the edge of the bed holding my head. My neck hurt. My eyes hurt. My stomach growled. I just wanted to run away. I could pack now, walk out of the door and catch the morning train to London. I could go back to where I was a year ago. Find a wee flat, slide into anonymity, and start my life again. I didn't need all this chaos and bleakness. No more uncertainty about Sam and me; will she won't she. No more Scottish winters: sunless, aching cold, and scoured by blizzards. I felt the panic grow in my chest, as if I'd stirred up a colony of butterflies. The room seemed stifling.

I got up and threw the window open and dragged in the gelid air. I dropped to the floor and tried doing press-ups. I managed ten before the nausea rose again and my arms became lead. I slumped to the carpet and rolled on my back until my heart slowed and the room stilled. I crept downstairs. There was no need to be quiet but I didn't want to disturb the great silence of the house. I made a mug of tea. I poked aside the ashes in the grate, rolled up some old newspaper and kindling and put a match to it. When it caught, I added a few coals and sat staring at it, mug in hand, sipping the sweet hotness until the panic eased. I could get through another day. One day at a time.

I took off into the dark morning. I walked down the middle of empty streets glazed china-white by moonlight on snow. It was too early for trams or carts and my feet made first tracks. I reached the sanctuary of the Western and found the doors locked. A notice told of the baths' closure until further notice owing to lack of coal for the furnace.

Barred from my refuge I found myself drifting along, squinting at the orange glow of the street lamps, as though I was still drunk. I diverted into Central Station and forced down some tea and fried eggs and bacon. I was at my desk by eight o'clock, bolstered by more tea and the first dizzying cigarette.

I found four neatly typed articles: my original stream of conscious outpourings now knocked into shape and substance by the pencil work of Sandy Logan and Eddie. I took my hat off to these wordsmiths who'd made silk purses from my pig's ear. I did a last pass or two myself aiming to get the facts as accurate as possible.

By noon it was done. I picked up some blank paper and a pencil and got down to planning in preparation for the night's meeting. I had one of the girls type up twenty copies of the SS names and descriptions. I got hold of the biggest street map I could find and started making some calculations and dispositions. I typed up a pile of short instructions. I was finished by six and bundled all my materials together in a newsroom briefcase and set off. Despite some of the tramlines being out because of frozen points and downed cables I arrived in good time at the Garnethill synagogue.

I found Shimon and Isaac waiting for me on the front porch. Shimon took me down the right of the building and through a side door into a warm, good-sized hall at the rear. With the slope of the hill, we must have been directly under the great ornate hall of worship. He flicked on two wall lights. It was enough to make out the stacked chairs to one side and the small tables, one at the back and one at the front. Alongside the front table was the easel and board I'd asked for. I emptied my briefcase contents on to the front table and pinned my large street map on the easel. I took a seat on the edge of the table and waited.

They slunk through the door, singly or in pairs, heavily muffled and wrapped against the bitter cold. They stamped the snow and ice off as they came in. As each arrived, Shimon and Isaac grasped his hand and indicated the table and chairs. Each man walked over, took off his coat and dropped it on a growing pile on the back table. As they peeled off their layers they revealed themselves: all shapes and sizes; some with glasses; some with beards. Some kept their hats and caps on. A few exchanged hats for yarmulkes. Then each man picked up a chair and set it up in front of me, starting at the rear. No early volunteers for the front row.

One figure was different: smaller, slighter and, when the coat came off, revealed itself as a young woman. She kept a scarf round her head and sat separate from the men. I felt her huge eyes on me all the while I waited.

By seven exactly, twenty men and the solitary woman were sitting in front of me in straggly rows. It was a good sign. I liked a prompt start. Some nodded to others. A few murmured to each other. Several were loud and chatty, their voices crackling and fizzing with the consonants of Latvia and the vowels of Czechoslovakia. Pipes started coming out, and cigarettes. There was enough light for me to inspect their faces. There was no pattern other than wariness. Nothing that caricatured them like the Jews in the fading propaganda posters we'd seen in Hamburg and other German cities. Nothing, either, to mark them out as having survived pogroms, ghettos, sewer life or concentration camps. Though if I asked for a show of bare forearms I wondered what we'd see.

I felt my heart race and took some deep breaths to control it. What was happening to me these days? Why did I get so easily worked up? As though I were under attack? I wasn't scared to face an audience. I'd done enough of that. I breathed deeply and concentrated on who was before me. Trying to assess them. A mixed bag, but one little group was different. Six older men sat together at the back, their average age around fifty. They'd nodded to each other as they came in and took up position in two neat rows of three. They sat with folded arms and inspected me. My pulse started to slow again. Shimon came and stood beside me.

'They're all yours.'

It was a moment of déjà vu: standing in front of a platoon, ready to brief them, to give orders that would send them into combat. But this was a ragged crew, untrained and unarmed. It wasn't the same. I stood up from the table. Pushed my head up, shoulders back and clasped my hands behind me to open my chest and make sure my voice carried.

'Good evening. My name is Douglas Brodie. Shimon tells me you're willing to help catch some Nazis. Is that true?'

THIRTY-EIGHT

There was an immediate low rumble of assent. A figure rose at the back. My pirate. I'd nodded to him earlier as he'd arrived.

'Yes, Malachi?'

'We hear you're a *colonel* now.' Said with a good dollop of contempt for anyone in the same British Army that was currently preventing Jewish refugee ships from entering Palestine. 'Is that right?'

'Yes, I'm back in the army again. A *lieutenant* colonel.' As if that made it better. 'A temporary situation while we track down these escaped war criminals. So forget the title. It's still Brodie.'

He pulled a smile. 'Are you going to get us guns?'

'That didn't take you long, Mal. Let me be clear. I'm not recruiting for the army. This will be a low-key search operation. There won't be any guns.'

'Same old story, then? Nazis with guns, Jews with bare hands.'

That got a ripple of nods and murmurs.

'Malachi, first we have to find them. There's no point charging off into the night armed to the teeth, frightening old women. Besides, I think the polis would mind.'

Another man stood up, one of the six older fellas at the back.

'Colonel? We didnae get telt much. Just to come here. And that there were Nazis loose. Can you explain whit's happening?'

'I will, but first tell me about you. The six of you. This is going to be hard work. It could take weeks. Hard pounding of the pavements.'

'You think we're no' up to it?' His eyes were bright and steady. For all his years he had an air about him.

'How can I tell? I don't know you.'

'We all served in the Glasgow Highlanders.'

'Great War?'

He nodded. 'Aye. Lieutenant Lionel Bloom, sir. This is former sergeant David Doctorow. And the other men were in my platoon. Look, here ye go.'

He got up and walked towards me, pulling out a photo from his jacket pocket. He held it out. It was like an official school snap. Then I recognised the setting. It was the South Portland Street Synagogue. They'd set up scaffolding and planking to form eight banked terraces. Each terrace held about twenty soldiers. By the looks of their uniforms every regiment in Scotland was represented. Some in kilts, some in tartan trews, most in khaki. All were smiling out at the camera. I wonder how many got home?

'This is us, sir.' Bloom pointed out the small clutch of men at the back. They were wearing the kilts and tam-o'-shanters of the Glasgow Highlanders. I looked at him, and then at the others sitting at the back. There was little doubt.

'You all made it?'

'No' quite, sir. Mannie got gassed. Wipers.'

Ypres. A slaughterhouse. He pointed to a smiling young man; he looked about sixteen. I smiled. 'Sorry about Mannie. You did well. I need your experience.' Former lieutenant Lionel Bloom marched back to his smiling comrades with his back straight.

Then I gave them the story, albeit a shortened version, of what I'd been doing over in Hamburg. There were nods all round, and faces were coming alight, becoming less guarded.

'Were you at the camps? Did you see what they did?'

'I saw. I won't forget.'

'What are they like now? These Jew-killers. *Dieser Scheisser!*'

I replied in German. 'They were like anybody. No horns. No fangs. But no apologies.'

'Would they do it again?'

'We won't let them. Not this time.' But I wondered how we'd stop them. A whole civilised nation had been in thrall, and they'd poisoned neighbouring countries with their proposed final solution. Why could it *not* happen again?

Another man asked, 'The rats who got away. Do you have names? Do you know them? What are we looking for?'

'Yes. Here.' I pointed at the papers. I explained the two lists and that we were concentrating on the seven we thought were still at bay in Scotland. There might be others but this was a manageable number to start with.

'I have descriptions. Some photos of the senior officers, including Fritz Suhren. He's our main target. But of course if they're here at all they will be using different names. The police have the same information and will be on the lookout. Quietly. No noisy manhunt. They don't want to cause panic.'

'So what can we do that the police can't?' asked Malachi.

'They won't be able to go where you boys go. I want you out on the street corners, in the shops, in the pubs, any place that folk go to. Any place where folk gather for a natter and a wee gossip. I want you to be talking to people, asking them questions, looking for signs.'

'What sort of signs?' asked Bloom.

'Let's think about this. Imagine you're an SS guard or a Nazi doctor on the run. A man or a woman. You don't speak English, or have a heavy accent. You're terrified of being spotted. You've got a pocketful of gold but no pound notes. How are you going to live? Where are you going to live?'

That got the ideas rolling.

'Bribery. They'd pay off people to keep quiet.'

'No, they'd change the gold in Edinburgh before they got here.'

'You're mad. They'd hang on to the gold. Everybody wants gold.'

'What about a house? They need a roof over their heads. We should talk to landlords.'

'Colonel? What language do they use? Are they Germans or Poles? Where do these rats come from?'

I didn't have to consult my papers. 'We are assuming they are mainly German or at least German-speaking. But for example Ravensbrück housed a large number of Polish women, so the guards would probably have a working knowledge. They employed experienced wardens and medical staff. They were trained in other camps and came to run the slave labour set up for Siemens and IG Farben factories. Before they started gassing them.'

The room went quiet again, until the questions started up and the ideas began to flow.

'It should be easy. They only got here in the past year. We know who's come and gone.'

'Pah, that's stupid. Look around. How many of us have been here over a year? Why, they could be hiding among us. Right now!'

That got them going. There was much looking around and switching into and out of different languages.

'Ridiculous! Our rabbi knows us. Malachi knows us. And look!' This man was standing. He rolled up his cardigan and shirtsleeve and brandished his bare arm. Even from fifteen feet away I could see the tattooed number on his forearm. 'Auschwitz!'

'That's something,' another said. 'But tattoos are not conclusive. It wasn't done in all the camps. And some of us saw it coming. I got out in '35.'

I called them to order. 'He's right. Tattoos aren't a definitive test, of course not. The senior Nazis and even the Kapos would be smart enough to have their arms tattooed to camouflage themselves. But it's a start. Everything you've been saying is good. All these little bits and pieces of the jigsaw add up. We will try to meet each day. We'll get together like this and we'll compare notes. We'll hone our ideas.'

I got serious nods of understanding from all of them, even sceptical Malachi. I took out the papers I'd been working on during the day and passed them out. Shimon put on another light in the hall so that the group could read them.

'You'll find brief descriptions of the men and women we're looking for.' I waited to see nods. 'OK, at the top of each sheet is a set of Glasgow streets. Each sheet is different. That's your personal patch. Your responsibility.'

I pointed at the map on the easel. 'Each sheet is numbered and corresponds to a grid on this map. You can see where your patch is and who's next to you.' I got further nods all round.

'Colonel, what do we do if we find someone?'

'I'm just coming on to that. You do *nothing*. Do you hear me? Nothing, except report back to me. You *don't* confront them. You *don't* take any action. You do your best not to let them know you've spotted them. At the bottom of the piece of paper is my phone number at the *Gazette* and my home number at my landlady's. I want you to phone me any time of the day or night if you've got a positive sighting. Is that clear?'

They nodded.

'Malachi, is that clear?'

'Yes, *Colonel*.'

'We will meet each day, unless we agree otherwise. Same time, same place, and you will share your findings with all of us. We will aim to build a picture from bits of gossip and rumour. If we get a sense that there's something worth following up, I may deploy more men in one area. Or change the team so that we get a second opinion. So that we don't scare them off.'

Malachi wasn't beaten. 'OK, but what do we do when we're sure we've found one of them? What will *you* do?'

'Call in the professionals. I have contacts at the highest level in the police.'

'The bloody polis!'

I stepped forward and held his gaze. 'What's your point?'

'You know my point. We don't trust the police. They hate us.'

'This isn't Berlin. It's not Warsaw. Our police are here to protect all of you. All of us.'

There were sceptical looks.

'Gentlemen, let's call it a day. You understand your tasks. It won't be easy and I don't expect an early breakthrough. This is painstaking work and it will take weeks. But I'm sure if we stick at it, it will pay off. Any other questions?'

There were none. They folded their chairs, muffled themselves up and began to slip off into the night. Untrained spies on a mission even I wasn't sure of. I walked to the door and shook each man's hand, until only the woman was left. She was waiting for me. Close up, her lustrous eyes were as old as Jerusalem.

'Hello. I'm Douglas Brodie.' I put out my hand. Hers was small, warm. She held it a moment and then challenged me.

'You don't want me here. A woman?' Her accent was German but her English diction was clear and precise. She was wrong; in that instant, looking into her olive-black gaze, I didn't want anyone else *but* her.

'Not so. Some of these Nazis are women. You can go where the men can't. You've an important role with us. What's your name?'

'Bathsheba Goldstein.' She smiled.

A provocative name to match her smile. I switched to German. 'Where are you from?'

'Cottbus. On the German border with Poland.'

'You got out before the war?'

She nodded. 'My parents sent me to Paris. We had family friends there. Non-Jews. They protected me till after the war. Then I came here. I live with an aunt.'

'Why come here?'

'My parents were taken, murdered. My aunt is all I have left. That's why I want to help.' Steel beneath the softness. I clasped her shoulder. She didn't flinch.

'I'm sorry, Bathsheba. I'm glad you are with us.'

I was sincere. She could be a great help. But I also had to ask myself if I would be so welcoming to an ageing crone. I could see Samantha's smile in the air, like a cynical Cheshire cat.

THIRTY-NINE

I skidded down to St George's Road and then plodded up the hill to Sam's house, experiencing vividly what was in store for me in my dotage. I clung where necessary to the railings as my clown feet skited off the icy paths. I paused at the top and waited till my heart stopped pounding before pressing on. I pushed open the front door and stood swaying, as though my body had taken a puncture. As I wrestled with my coat, the lounge door opened at the top of the stairs.

'Douglas, is that you?'

'Yes. Yes it is. You're back.' Relief washed over me.

Sam walked slowly down the stairs and stopped near the bottom. Her face was screwed up with caution.

'Are you all right, Douglas?'

'I'm tired, Sam, just tired. It's good to see you. When did you . . . ? How were the meetings?'

'Never mind all that. There's some soup in the kitchen. On the simmer. Come and eat.' She helped me off with my coat, then my scarf and jacket, like a mother helping her six-year-old after a tough day at school. She even steadied me as I swayed. Then she took my hand and led me downstairs. I held on to the bannister as I went, and wondered how I was going to get back up this flight.

The heat from the oven and the smell of Scotch broth stirred something in me, an echo of childhood, of sanctuary. I flopped at the table and undid my tie. Sam bustled about and laid a spoon and a steaming bowl in front of me. I wouldn't have objected to her feeding me. We slurped quietly at our soup and I felt warmth and life flow into me. Throughout, she kept a wary eye on me and smiled encouragingly when I looked up at her. When I had finished she took the bowl away and tided things up in the sink. The next thing I knew she was shaking my shoulder gently.

'Douglas? Come on, Douglas. Let's get you to bed, my dear.'

I raised my head from my crossed arms and rubbed my creased face.

'Did you put something in my soup?' I tried to ask, but it came out drunk.

'Wheesht.'

She helped me rise to my feet and I swam through fatigue, out of the kitchen and up the stairs. My feet were those of a deep-sea diver. Sam even gave me a push at one point. She helped me out of my clothes and easily beat off my attempt to bring her down on to the bed with me. I felt the sheets being pulled up and the quilt tucked round me like a winding sheet, and I was gone.

'Room service.'

I grappled with my pillow and turned to the voice. 'What? What's . . . ?'

'Tea, Douglas. Here you go.' I managed to open my eyes in time to see Sam lay a cup and saucer on my bedside table.

I struggled to sit up. My watch was still on my wrist. It was eight o'clock.

'Sam, how splendid of you. Do I have a long grey beard? I feel like Rip Van Winkle.'

'You don't look *that* old. You were needing the sleep.'

I rubbed at my face and sipped some tea. She was looking at me apprehensively.

'How was Edinburgh?'

'A real grilling. They'd heard a lot of it from Iain already, but they were keen to know what I'd learned. I felt I was devilling again. Now they're talking about getting me over to Edinburgh for a big trial. Completely unrelated to Hamburg. That's how it works. How are you feeling?'

'Like I've been a pain in the backside lately, Sam. I'm sorry.'

'Just lately?' Her face softened. 'I'm the one that's sorry. I got you into this mess. If I hadn't got you involved with those bloody thefts last year. And the murders. And then to rope you into the Hamburg trials . . .'

I reached out and touched her lips to silence her. 'You weren't to know I'd be such a big jessie.'

'That's the last thing anyone could say about Douglas Brodie.'

'They don't know me as well as you.'

'I didn't know you well enough – what happened to you with the Belsen trials. I thought you'd just been some sort of reporting officer. I had no idea . . . You should have told me.'

'I didn't want to talk about it. Even think about it. Why should I burden other folk with it?'

'I'm not other folk.'

'What *are* you then, Sam? To me?'

We stared at each other for a long moment. Then she broke into a smile at the same time I did.

'I'm your landlady and this tea is the nearest you'll get to room service. Now, Douglas Brodie, it's time I went to work. Glasgow today then over to the dragon's lair tomorrow.' She stood up, pulled her skirt down, leaned over the bed and kissed me on the forehead.

'Is that part of a landlady's duties?' I called as she sailed out of the door.

Long after I heard the front door close and her shouted *Byeee*, I forced myself up and on to unsteady feet. I felt hollowed out. An empty gourd. I went through the routine that got me to the hall, shaved, fully clothed and warmed by tea and toast and jam. I jammed on my hat and set out into the winter's day.

As I passed his office, Eddie jumped out and grabbed my arm.

'Come by, Brodie.' He pulled me into his fug. 'Sit doon man. Now then, are you going to take some time off or what?'

'I'm fine, Eddie. Really.'

He studied me. 'Oh aye? You're like death warmed up, so you are. Take a few days off. Other folk are coming down with the flu. Why not you? We'll manage. We've got a few more days of your Hamburg stuff to use. Ah'll knock something up if need be.'

'I'm better here. Better working, Eddie. What have you got for me?'

'Well, there's the thieving-from-the-kirks story.'

'Collections?'

'Pews. For firewood.'

I laughed at the image of some rough household feeding their fire inch by inch with a long bench.

'Leave me to it. I'll phone around.'

I picked up my pencil and a fresh sheet of paper. To get me in the mood I began toying with headlines such as 'Purgatory for Pew Pinchers' and 'Fires of Hell for Kirk Robbers' . . .

'See! Ah telt ye! He's been like that for hours now.'

I grew aware of Eddie's voice. Close. I lifted my head. Eddie was hanging over my filing cabinet. He was talking to someone and pointing at me. I blinked and turned my head. There was a small crowd. Two men and, behind them, Sam, looking anxious.

One of the men spoke. 'He's in a dwam right enough.' It was Duncan Todd. Who was he talking about? What did he want?

The other man leaned closer. His face was familiar but thinner and older than I remembered. And there was a white scar cutting through his red hair like a wide and wayward parting that finished up just above his right eye.

He said, 'Hello, old pal. It's been a while.'

I stared at him until he was fully in focus both visually and in the pantheon of my mind.

'Hello, Danny. What are you doing here?'

Sam pushed herself forward. 'I asked him to come, Douglas. We thought he could help.' Her bonny face was lined with concern. Help me? Why were they all here?

'Help? What for? What doing?'

'How about Nazi-hunting, Brodie? Ah'm good at that.' Danny McRae smiled wolfishly at me.

FORTY

S am cut in. 'Let's get him out of here. Douglas? We're all starving. We're going to take you back to the house and give you some tea. OK?'

'Tea? What time is it?' I peered at my watch. It said three in the afternoon. I'd lost half a day. Had I fallen asleep? From all the fuss going on it seemed more than that. My legs started to shake. My feet were drumming on the floor. The shakes seemed to be travelling up my body. I couldn't control it. Panic flooded me. I wanted to run.

'Douglas! Douglas!' Sam wrapped herself around me. I held her tight. My lifebelt. She cooed and stroked until I'd calmed. She faced me.

'Why the tears, Sam?'

'I'm not. I'm fine.' She stroked my face. 'Can you boys help him? Let's get him home.'

Danny and Duncan crowded round me and I felt their arms lift me to my feet. That was nice of them. I swayed but they kept me up. They pulled on my jacket, stuck my hat on my head and threw my coat over my shoulders. They all but frogmarched me out of the newsroom. It seemed very quiet and people were staring. Should I wave?

We stumbled down the stairs and out into the chill afternoon. The freezing air hit me and I slumped, but the boys were still holding me up. Was I drunk? Did I have secret bottle in my desk? Just another reporter whose drinking session had got out of hand? A taxi was waiting with its engine running. Sam went ahead and opened the door. I stopped.

'Wait. Wait – a – minute! Danny! Danny boy. What the hell are you doing here? Heard you were beating up the London polis.'

Danny smiled that ferocious smile again. 'That's me. They deserved it.'

'Good man. Did they do that to you?' I indicated the scar still visible beneath the brim of his hat.

'Naw. I had this done professionally. Gestapo. In France. Ah'll tell you later.'

They poured me into the taxi. Sam and Danny joined me, squeezing me between them. Duncan waved us off. They coaxed me into the house and up to the library. I sank into a deep leather armchair and tried to clear the fog in my brain.

Sam lit a fire while Danny patrolled the bookshelves, picking up one book after another, flicking through it and putting it back. Then Sam returned with a tray of steaming soup and half a loaf. She made me slurp it down and I could feel it warming my very bones. She and Danny took a bowl each. Life began returning to my body. Then, warmed inside and toasting in front of the flickering fire, I let sleep overwhelm me.

I woke to the sound of the clock chiming five. Danny was sitting reading. Sam had her glasses on, peering at the crossword. They looked up as I stirred. It was as though this pair had always been in my life and were now in their proper places. I nodded to Danny and cleared my throat.

'It's good to see you, Danny.'

He put his book down. 'Back with us again, old pal?'

'How did Sam track you down?'

'Through Duncan. As it happens, he and I have been in touch just lately. I get the occasional Glasgow paper in

London. Just to see what this mad place is getting up to. And I found that a certain newshound for the *Gazette* has not only been writing the headlines, but generating them.' He grinned. It was good to hear his Ayrshire accent again. The lilt of home.

'You're a fine one to talk.'

'True enough, Brodie, we've both earned a certain amount of notoriety.'

'You win, Danny, hands down in the infamy stakes. As I recall, you were up for murder.'

He bristled. 'You ken what newspapers are like. It was a set-up by my old boss in the SOE, Major Tony Caldwell. The shit! Pardon me, Sam.'

'It's all right, Danny,' she said. 'From what I've heard that seems to sum him up. What happened?'

'Caldwell recruited me into the SOE. He dropped me in France a month before D-Day near Toulon. He was used to coming out personally to control the wider ops in that part. Seems he took up with a girl – a Resistance fighter. I don't know what happened – row or something – but he killed her. And then stuck the blame on me.'

I saw his eyes cloud.

'Did *you* know her?' I asked.

'Oh aye, I kent her fine. I fell for her too.' He shook his head. 'Anyway, her pals betrayed me to the Gestapo by way of punishment. Can't say I blame them. Ended up in Dachau. With this.' He pointed to his head. 'The Yanks got me home, and after a while I began looking for Caldwell.'

'Did you get him?' I asked.

He stared off into the flames. 'Yeah. Finally. He'd been at it again. Got the taste for it. Five other girls murdered in London. Street girls. But yeah, I got him.'

I didn't ask what he meant. Danny McRae was a persistent sod. We were both detective sergeants before the war, and I'd seen him in action. He was three years younger than me but they called us the terrible twins. And that was just our fellow officers.

Sam said, 'How's the head now, Danny?'

'Aye, well, there's the thing. I've got a plate in here.' He knocked on his head where the scar ran. 'So that's fine. But I still get bad heads. And dreams. Let's call them nightmares.'

'Snap,' I said ruefully. 'Though I don't have a lump of metal as an excuse.'

'Douglas, with what you've been through, you don't need another excuse.'

'Maybe, Sam.' I turned to Danny to change the subject. 'But other than upsetting the polis, what have you been doing down south?' I asked.

He laughed. 'Playing detectives. I hung out a sign. "Finders Keepers". I'm a private investigator. Can you believe it?'

'I can believe anything about you, Danny. I'm doing a bit of freelancing myself. Does it pay?'

'Keeps me in Black & White.'

'Your taste hasn't improved.'

'Ah'll drink anything, as you know, Brodie.'

Sam cut in, 'Before the pair of you take that as a cue to start celebrating this reunion, you need to eat something more, Douglas Brodie. Anyway, it's too early in the day.'

While she was gone, Danny and I inspected each other.

'She's a fine lady, Brodie. You're a lucky man.'

'Am I?'

'Are you going to marry her? You should.'

'She's a hard woman to pin down.'

'You mean you huvnae asked her.'

'We keep dancing round it. But what did she say about me? Why did she get you up here?'

He leaned forward and spoke softly. 'She said you were having a bad time. Nightmares. Shouting in your sleep. That you're just back from the Hamburg trials and that it dredged up a lot of bad stuff.'

'I guess so.'

'I know how that goes, Brodie.' He rapped his skull. 'But it's more than just physical. I've seen a good few brain doctors this past year or so. Psychoanalysed until I didnae know my own name. Even some shock treatment.'

'They plugged you into the mains?'

'It was like having your brain scrambled. Afterwards it goes calm, but in bits. Then over a few days it starts to join up again. You start remembering better.'

'This was the result of Dachau?'

He looked down at the carpet and nodded. 'It was shite, Douglas. Absolute shite.' His head came up. His features were suddenly made gaunt and savage by the tension in his jaw and neck muscles. 'How did they get like that, Brodie? How does anyone – any human being – get like that?'

'I don't know. It's a kind of madness. Mob hysteria.'

Danny shook his head violently. 'Naw, too easy! Lets them off the hook. They wurnae dafties. They knew what they were doing. Bastards! They liked it!'

We were stilled by our thoughts.

'How are you now, Danny?'

'No' bad. The headaches have pretty well stopped. I just get down at times. Whisky works.'

Suddenly I recognised myself. Clever Sam.

'Is there a girl in your life?' I asked.

Pain drifted across his face. 'They're a bloody nuisance, aren't they?'

'Escaped your clutches?'

He got up and poked some life into the fire. 'I seem to know how to pick them. She was a reporter in London. Like you, Brodie. Eve Copeland. Heard of her? She had her own column in the *Trumpet*.'

'You're using past tense.'

He rubbed his face. 'Turned out she was also an agent.'

'As in *secret* agent? Good God, man. Who for?'

He sighed. 'Who do you think? She'd been coerced. Nazis had her parents. Jews. Her real name was Ava Kaplan.'

'How did you find out that – Eve? Ava? – was an agent?'

'Eve. Scotland Yard. But she got away before they did.'

'What happened?'

'It's a long story. She went off to Berlin looking for her folks.'

'And?'

He looked sheepish. 'I went after her.'

'Christ, Danny! And I thought I was a magnet for trouble! Did she find them?'

'Nup. Long since dead. The Nazis had been playing Eve along. So she went after them.'

'Retribution? And I suppose you tagged along for the ride?'

'Oh aye. And we had a wee bit of help from the Irgun Zvai Leumi.'

'The ones that blew up the King David Hotel? You're kidding.'

'The same. But they see themselves as freedom fighters.'

'I can't completely blame them. After what was done to them.'

He eyed me closely. 'That's how I see it. We've got ourselves in a right bloody fankle. We're supposed to be in charge of Palestine, but really we're siding with the Arabs, which means we're trying to stop Jewish refugees getting in. Or, as they put it, *going home*. Our boys get shot or kidnapped or blown up, and all the while we're trying to help them create a Jewish state. Eve's part of their delegation in London.'

'Your girl's part of the Israeli negotiating team?'

He stopped pacing. 'She's not mine, Douglas. She's chosen a different way. But yes, she and her pals are hammering out proposals for the UN. She could be prime minister of Israel one day. A tough lassie. But hie, we're not here to solve *my* problems.'

'You think you're here to solve mine?'

He looked me up and down. 'Not me. *You.* No one else can do it for you. It will get better, Dougie. I promise you. It just takes time. Time and talking about it.'

'Are you some kind of amateur Freud? The talking cure? I don't *want* to talk about it.'

He shrugged. 'Well, don't then. You were always a thrawn bugger, Brodie. Just let me say this: I've been through it. Still going through it. It's like a kind of battle fatigue. Oh, by the way, congratulations, *Colonel.*'

I waved it down. 'A contrivance. Short term. While we sort out this mess.'

'Good. If it keeps you busy. Stops you feeling sorry for yourself.'

I looked at him, seeing briefly the slim young detective from thirteen, fourteen years ago. The shining-eyed energy and sharp intelligence. How we'd recognised each other instantly though we'd never met. The door opened. Sam's head came round.

'I hope you like coney stew, Danny.'

FORTY-ONE

We pushed our plates away and, for the first time in days, perhaps weeks, I felt more than just nourished by the hot food. Danny had talked about some of his escapades as a private eye and had Sam and me laughing out loud at the tales of missing dogs and husbands. It seems I'd been starved for not just meat. I filled him in on the details of the pursuit I was leading in Glasgow. I told him about the twenty-one hunters I'd set loose last night. Was it only last night?

'They sound a motley crew, Brodie.'

'They're keen and well motivated. Maybe over-motivated.'

'I can imagine. And can we just get this clear? I *want* to help. If you'll have me – *Colonel* – you've got twenty-two. I'll fit in. I'm as motley as the next man.'

'OK, *Captain*. But can we drop the titles? It's just going to get in the way.'

'Sure. But we need a leader. You're it, Brodie.'

I suddenly glanced at my watch. 'Damn! We've got a meeting in twenty minutes.'

Sam threw her napkin down. 'Are you totally daft, Douglas Brodie? You could hardly stand this afternoon. You were – as Duncan put it exactly – in a total dwam at your desk. Now you think you can just bounce back as though nothing had happened? You're aff your heid!'

Danny was smiling. 'She has a point, Brodie. You could get

hold of – Belsinger, is it? – by phone and cancel. We could make it tomorrow.'

'Nup. It's no way to start. They need to get used to a routine. I need to be there. Are you coming?' I was on my feet. The dizziness hit, but then died down. I seemed to be nearly under control. Fresh air would help.

'I'll grab my hat,' he said.

'Good. Where are you staying, Danny?'

He looked at Sam.

'He's staying here, of course, Douglas. I invited him.'

Danny grinned.

I groaned. 'I hope you can afford your own whisky. Let's go.'

We hacked and slithered our way down through the frozen streets and up the steep hill to our rendezvous at Garnethill. We arrived blowing steam like a pair of old locomotives. I introduced McRae to Shimon and Isaac and we had just enough time to get our coats and hats off before the first of the group started arriving.

As they gathered in front of Danny and me, I sensed a new mood. There was more talking, more recognition of each other. We got them seated, I counted heads – I made it twenty-three – twenty-four, counting Danny. I spotted two new faces. Swarthy characters sitting either side of Malachi at the back. One wore glasses and looked professorial.

'Mal, can you introduce your new pals?'

Malachi turned to them and said something. Then he spoke up. 'They are Paulus and Emmanuel. Hungarian. They got out in '39. They wanted to help.' First one and then the other got up and nodded.

'Shalom, Colonel.'

'Welcome, both. But please, it's just Brodie. OK?'

They sat down and I noticed a quiet watchfulness about them. Self-contained and wary. They looked handy.

'I'm *also* bringing someone new this evening. This is Danny

McRae, formerly captain in the Scots Guards and then SOE agent. But perhaps there is something special about his background you might want to hear. Danny?'

Danny stood up, calm and assured as ever – cocky even – and briefly described his year in captivity in Dachau. It gripped them and got them on side. One man even stepped up and shook his hand in fellow feeling. Bathsheba's eyes glittered in scrutiny.

I got them to settle down and we began taking reports. As each got to his feet I asked him to call out his name and his map reference, his beat. I asked what languages he spoke, and what he'd been up to today. It was hardly a model reporting session from Central Division, and scarcely a team briefing of NCOs before battle. But it would do.

'I'm Maximillian. I have reference D5.' I pointed at the map area on the easel. He nodded and looked down at a scruffy envelope. His notes. 'I talked to four shop owners today. I got talking to some customers too. Asked them about new people. And to keep an eye out for people that acted differently.'

'Good, Max. Any signs?'

He shook his head. 'Next,' I called.

And so it went. Sometimes there were overlaps of areas. Sometimes there were questions from other members of the team.

'Hey, Eli? You said you'd been in MacDougall's. You know his brother has a butcher's in Partick. I hear he's big in the black market. He's got poachers who bring him meat. We should watch for anyone with cash to spend on meat.'

'*Ja*, I know this.'

We had nearly finished with the men. I looked up to the back of the audience. She sat quietly, watching.

'Bathsheba. Miss Goldstein. Would you please report?'

The girl's eyes widened – which scarcely seemed possible –and she tucked a strand of stray black hair into her scarf. Slowly she got to her feet and the room grew quiet.

She started too low for me to hear.

'It's OK, Miss Goldstein. Please speak up.'

She coughed and found her voice. 'I have K4. I'm asking the shop owners to keep an eye out. Some of them are helpful. Jews own three of the shops and I will see them each day from now on.'

'Well done, Bathsheba. And what languages do you speak?'

'German, a little Polish and, of course, English.'

'Of course. Thank you. Everybody: this is working well now. I have decided we'll meet every second night. In between times, if any of you find out anything, you must phone me at the *Gazette* newsroom or at my digs. You have the numbers on your instruction sheets.'

We didn't finish until after nine. As we wrapped up for the evening, I suddenly felt woozy. I'd been keeping going with sheer will power. Danny and I were the last to leave.

'Who was the girl?' he asked casually.

'The one you were staring at all night?'

'Was it that obvious?'

'Danny, you bored holes in her. You heard me use her name. Bathsheba Goldstein. Got out of Germany to Paris just before the war. Holed up there with non-Jewish friends. Lost her folks and wants to get her own back. Like your girl, Eve.'

'No one's like Eve. But I have to admit, Miss Goldstein is easy on the eye.'

I raised an eyebrow at him, wondering where this might go; wondering, too, if I'd just felt a small and inappropriate pang of jealousy.

We negotiated our way over the rollercoaster hills back to Sam's house. Down Hill Street and up Lynedoch Street into Park Circus. A crow would have done it in a couple of wing flaps. But we were fighting icy pavements and the gravity of our years. I think Danny was slowing his pace for me.

Later, when the lights were out and the house was silent, Sam crept into my room and sneaked into my bed.

'Are you sure this is sensible?'

'It's never been sensible, Brodie.'

'I mean with . . .'

'Are you suddenly worried for my reputation?'

'How it looks. In front of Danny.'

'I'm probably seen as the whore of Kelvingrove. At least by the good matrons of Park Ward. I can almost hear them tutting as I walk by. Net curtains twitching.'

'I could make an honest woman of you.'

'Wheesht, Brodie. I'm off to Edinburgh tomorrow for three days. *Carpe diem. Carpe meam.*'

With the last of my flagging strength, I did.

FORTY-TWO

The days and evenings fell into a pattern. Danny McRae would head off first thing and walk the streets himself. Unbidden, he'd simply adopted the role as my second in command. He got a map and list of the streets and the names of the hunters assigned to reconnoitre them. He made it his business to spend a few minutes with each of them every day. Probably longer with Bathsheba, though I didn't ask. Lucky man.

But it gave me an invaluable pair of experienced eyes and ears out on the streets, sifting and evaluating. He hadn't lost his detective skills. Or his questioning, restless mind. An unquiet heart.

We got into the habit of sharing a bottle in the evening. Sam wasn't around to dilute the topics, and initially we talked of our days in the force, and the girls we danced with and kissed. But halfway down the bottle we usually got round to comparing notes on our respective wars. We'd been in the same theatre for a while with the 8th Army in the desert. It's where he got wounded; he still carried the limp that showed at the day's end.

As the level in the bottle dropped further we began to delve into the damage inflicted on us. The mental damage.

'It's the nightmares,' I said. 'Sometimes I'm scared of going to sleep.'

'I know how that goes. But I couldn't work out whether I was having bad dreams or flashbacks. When they first brought me back here I couldn't remember much of the year before. From the time the Gestapo picked me up.'

'Has it come back? Do you remember it all now?'

'Mostly. It's a bit jagged. But in truth there's not much you'd want to remember.'

The more Danny told me, the more I found myself opening up to him in a way I hadn't ever done to anyone, even to Sam. Especially to Sam.

'And you still get down at times, Danny?'

'Don't we all?'

'Oh aye, but does it get bad? Really bad?' I chose my words carefully. 'To where it all seems . . . pointless?'

'Sure. Lately. Since I lost Eve.' He eyed me carefully. 'You mean ending it? That bad?'

I shrugged. 'But you don't, do you?'

'You just bugger on.'

We were quiet for a bit.

'Can I tell you something?'

'I hope it's not about your sex life, Brodie.'

'Nothing as simple. Look, I thought I was over it. And I was. For a while there. But for no reason, sometimes, I get really het up. Like I'm standing on a cliff and I'm about to fall off. Or like I'm being attacked. I just . . .'

'Blow up? No reason?'

I nodded.

Danny smiled and refilled the glasses. He stared into the fire. The white of his scar glowed like a silk ribbon among his red mane.

'I used to get blank spots. As though I'd got stocious the night before. But without having touched a drop. I'd lose a few hours – a couple of days even. Couldn't recall a thing. But I'd find scribbling. My *own* scribbling on a wee notepad. Some kind of warning to myself. Thought I was going daft. And before Eve . . . Naw, it disnae matter . . .'

'Go on. You're among friends.' I waited.

'The girl that got killed in France. By Caldwell. She came back to me in London.'

'How do you mean? In a dream?'

He shook his head. 'It wisnae like that. She seemed real. Completely real. There was this quack I saw. A big Irishman. One of life's good guys. He said there's stuff goes on in our heads that we haven't a clue about. It's how our brains make sense of things that we can't control. How we deal with traumatic events. And often there's a trigger. Something happens that sets it off.'

'Like me with my funny moments?'

He nodded. 'Sounds like it, does it no'?'

Later, in my cold lonely bed, I lay thinking about what Danny had said. The trigger thing seemed to make sense. But what was mine? Violence? Flashbacks brought on by confronting the Nazi guards at the trial? It seemed to have been going on for some time, probably since I was demobbed, if I were honest. As though it had been building up inside and I'd tried to ignore it. Where was my stiff upper lip when I needed it? But it seemed I wasn't alone. What I didn't understand was why I waited till I got home from Hamburg to fall apart. Force of will keeping me going? Then when I was safe, I could fall over?

I didn't like it but I could comprehend it. Sleep gently drew me into a quieter night than many recently. As though by accepting I wasn't in control, I'd regained some of it.

Inspector Duncan Todd kept calling me or, as he put it, *just passing, thought I'd pop into the* Gazette *for a wee chat*. He seemed unusually determined to keep in touch with what my Jewish platoon – as he called them – and I were up to. It wasn't just his solicitous nature. Todd hated the idea of beasts on the loose as much as Danny and me. To manage his 'drop-bys' a bit better I made a deal that the three of us

– Duncan, Danny and I – would meet a couple of times a week for a pint at McCall's. Todd would explain what the official manhunt was getting up to and Danny and I would share any titbits we got. Besides, it was like old times. The banter was balm. I could see light up at the mouth of the pit. And I had stopped digging.

We eased into March with no let-up in winter's grip. Over 150 roads were blocked across the country. Scotland was facing famine as food and milk supplies failed to get through. The government was trying to get us to eat snoek, a tough pike-like fish from South Africa, but folk seemed to prefer empty bellies. The Silver King night train between Edinburgh and London got stuck in a snowdrift for nine hours. Over in Palestine, the Stern Gang bombed the British officers' club, and Monty issued a 'shoot on sight' order to rioting Jews.

Against this depressing backcloth, I still had the sense that someone else was inhabiting my body, as though I didn't have day-to-day ownership. Sometimes the heebie-jeebies hit for no reason that I could see and I found myself with racing heart and panting lungs. As though some rude ghost had sneaked up on me and screamed in my ear. Danny's presence seemed to help. Knowing that someone as tough as McRae had gone through a similar flirtation with madness kept things in perspective. However, I was learning that rationality wasn't always achievable just by willing it.

But I was safer to sleep with. No jolts in the night. Less shouting. When Sam returned from her stint at the Edinburgh courts she took to creeping into my room each night – to check up on me, she said. And ended up staying the night. The girl was fearless.

She even brazened it out with Izzie. It's hard not to spot damage to sheets and pillowcases by two folk in one bed as opposed to separate ones. It was still *Mr Brodie* this and *Mrs*

Dunlop that but there was also a look in Izzie's eyes that said, *I ken what you're up to, you dirty bugger, don't you take advantage of my pal.*

It was in the second week of platoon meetings that our searches bore the first real fruit. The young man could hardly contain his excitement.

'My name is . . .'

'Joshua, I know. Please continue, Joshua.' I had most of their names under my belt by now, and some idea of their varying personalities.

He nodded, pleased. 'I have the area east of the Necropolis. Near the brewery. Fisher Street. An old man came up to me. I'd spoken to him before. He said a woman moved into the house next door about a year ago. She kept herself to herself, he said. Almost never going out. She drinks a lot. Gin. He's seen the bottles. By herself. An expensive habit. There is always the smell of meat cooking. Steak and pork. Who can afford that? He had only spoken to her once and she cut him off. He thinks she is Polish. It fits, does it not?'

The room fluttered with excitement.

'Good, Joshua. But why didn't the old man mention her the first time you spoke to him?'

'He wasn't sure. Didn't want to make a fuss. But last night there was a visitor. A man. To this woman's house. The walls are thin. There was shouting. In Polish. The old man knows a few words. He is from Byelorussia. But he heard the word gold twice. He didn't see the man but he sounded educated.'

'Educated?'

'Not farmyard Polish.'

Joshua stood waiting as I mulled over the information. The rest of the room was buzzing, looking at him intently. Malachi stood up from his traditional place at the rear, surrounded by his small coterie of hard-eyed men.

'Let's go get her. Question her.'

'No! I will deal with this. Tomorrow, I'll get one of my police colleagues and we'll visit this woman. Do you know when she comes and goes, Joshua?'

'The old man said she rarely goes out.'

'Good.' I looked up to see if she was sitting in her usual quiet corner. 'Bathsheba? I want you to meet me and Joshua first thing tomorrow. Let's say eight o'clock.' I looked at the map on the easel, tracing the streets. 'At the corner of Ark Lane and Fisher Street. No one else. We want no noise. No warning. Understand?'

She looked panicked for a moment, but then nodded her head.

FORTY-THREE

We converged in the dark of early morning on Ark Lane just round from our target. We were so well wrapped up I could hardly recognise any of us. Joshua was shaking with either excitement or cold. Bathsheba's eyes – just visible between the thick scarf round her mouth and the woollen hat pulled down over her forehead – were flickering with anxiety. Duncan Todd stood huddled and grumpy under his layers. I'd managed to get hold of him late last night and after some argument about bringing a squad of his men, he'd agreed to come alone. Danny McRae – uninvited but welcome enough for all that – stood smoking beside him as I issued instructions.

'Bathsheba, you said you speak Polish?'

'Everyone did in Cottbus. We spoke both in school.'

'OK. I want you to go and knock on this woman's door. We'll be right behind you. I want you to knock and speak in Polish. Say you're looking for Irma Grese.'

Her eyes grew even wider. 'Who's Irma Grese?'

'She's one of the ones we hanged after the Belsen trials.'

Her hand shot to her face.

'Are you OK with that, Bathsheba?'

She nodded. 'What happens if she doesn't answer?'

'Keep knocking till she does. If she's innocent, she'll come out. If not, we'll go in.'

'Hang on, Brodie,' said Duncan. 'That sounds like breaking and entering.'

'Not if it's polis. That's why you're here.'

'Christ.'

We slid round the corner and along Fisher Street until we got to the entry. We opened the door and quietly filed into the dark corridor. The door to the back yard was closed. The only light filtered in through the filthy windowpane above the door. I closed the door gently behind me. I moved forward, touching the walls as I went. I took out a torch and played it down the hall. In the middle of the corridor were two doors facing each other. Beyond, a stairwell led up. We wanted the first floor. I motioned to Bathsheba to go in front and pointed her at the stairs. I gave her the torch. She stood for a moment, then nodded at me and crept up, the torchlight showing the way. The four of us gathered at the foot and waited.

I watched as the light shifted up and up and stopped as she found the door. There was a long moment's silence before the first knock, timid at first, then louder. Nothing. She knocked twice, harder, and called out in Polish. I heard the name Irma Grese. It sounded convincing to me.

At last Bathsheba found her nerve. There was a flurry of heavy knocks and shouted demands for the long-dead Grese. Silence followed. She waited. We waited. Then Danny slid past me and started up the stairs.

'Danny!' I hissed. He didn't stop. Bugger. Still the madman. I went after him, closely followed by Duncan.

We had barely rounded the corner when there was huge bang and a flash. Something cracked past my head and we all dived to the floor. Danny was on his feet first and lunging forward, shouting Bathsheba's name. The torch swung drunkenly. Bathsheba slid down the wall, still clutching the torch. I couldn't make out if she'd been hit. I was too busy dragging out my service revolver, wishing, as I did so, that I'd brought the bigger-calibre Webley.

Danny flung himself down, cradled her and grabbed the torch. He flicked its beam up at the door, at the splintered wood. It gave me my chance. I aimed at the hole and fired. The second crash echoed through the stone hallway for what seemed like long minutes. I kept on moving and built up speed as I neared the door. I smashed into it with my shoulder. It buckled and crashed partly open. Something was stopping it from inside. Danny joined me and we shoved our way into the dark corridor. He shone his torch down. It picked up a figure groaning and writhing at our feet. A woman. Blood seeped from her shoulder. Beside her was a discarded sawn-off shotgun.

'Shine the light forward!'

I stepped over her and moved down the short corridor, gun up in both hands. I charged into the first room. Empty. Then the kitchen. Empty. By the time I got back Duncan was bent over the woman, stanching the blood with her own dressing gown. Beyond her stood Danny. He was holding Bathsheba. She had her coat off and Danny was inspecting her arm.

'Are you hurt, lassie?'

'It's OK. I'm fine,' she said.

'You're not. You got hit by splinters and pellets,' Danny said, pressing a large white hankie to her seeping wounds.

The woman on the floor groaned and started cursing.

'What's she saying, Bathsheba?'

'She's calling us names. Says she's sorry she didn't kill me. Not nice.'

'Tell her the feeling's mutual.'

Duncan got up. 'Jesus Christ, Brodie! Where the hell did you get that cannon?'

'It came with the uniform. Self-defence, Duncan. Just in case.'

'Noo Ah'm implicated in a shoot-out. Again! Ah'm gontae huvtae arrest you.'

'What for? I'm a commissioned officer acting under the direct orders of both the head of MI5 and your own Chief Constable. We're dealing with – as you can see – an armed enemy. She shot first. I was protecting my agent here.' I pointed at Bathsheba. 'And not to put too fine a point on it, Duncan, saving your arse.'

Danny said. 'He's right, Duncan. Don't go all bureaucratic on us.' He looked beyond us. Lights had come on under the door opposite and from downstairs a voice called out:

'Whit's goin' on? Ah'm ca'ing the polis.'

Duncan shouted, 'We *are* the polis! Have you got a phone down there?'

'Naw, but there's a box outside.'

Just behind Duncan I saw Joshua's face peering round the corner, worried to bits but desperate to know what was going on.

I shouted at him, 'Joshua, away and find that phone box. Call for an ambulance and a police car. Tell them Inspector Todd wants help urgently. OK, Duncan?'

'Sure. Do what you like. It's clearly martial law aroon here.'

'Don't go in the huff. While we're here, might as well turn the place over, eh?'

We got some lights on and inspected the woman. Duncan had propped her up, sitting with her back against the wall, still clutching her shoulder. She was a thickset creature, late forties, and now drenched with blood. Even a .38 slug from an Enfield through a wood door will do that to a body. If I'd brought Sam's father's .45 we'd have had a corpse on our hands. Which would have been a pity. We needed answers.

As it was, my bullet couldn't have hit anything vital or she wouldn't have had the strength to swear at me. Her steady stream of curses rang out into the lobby, interspersed with spit aimed at me. Bathsheba said something to her and it started the woman off again. Bathsheba took one step closer, grabbed her by her blouse and slapped her across her face. There was a brief wrestling match until Danny pulled her back.

'She called me a Jewish whore.'

'Hit her again if you like,' I offered.

'Behave yourself, Brodie,' said Duncan.

'I will if she will.' I knelt in front of the woman and said in slow English, 'If you spit on me I will put another bullet through you. This time your head. Are we clear?'

Her raging eyes stilled. I held her gaze. She nodded.

'Which do you speak better, English or German?'

She shrugged and spat out, *'Deutsch.'*

I switched to German. 'What is your name?'

'Kebel.'

'Your *real* name. The name you used in the camp.'

Her eyes widened. Her head shook. 'Kebel.'

'Let's try some others.' I reached in my jacket inside pocket and pulled out a piece of paper. It had the list of fourteen Cuxhaven names on it. Eight above and six below. We didn't have names for the two mystery women. I gave the list to Bathsheba. 'There are three *Aufseherinnen* in the first list and one in the second. You see? Read them out to her. Slowly.'

As Bathsheba settled to her task I pulled out my folded sheet containing shorthand descriptions of each of the names. Two in the first list were blue-eyed blondes. Even with a perfect dark-hair job, this woman couldn't mask her brown eyes.

Bathsheba read them out one by one while I watched the woman's face. So did Duncan. Danny had wandered off into the other rooms. I heard drawers banging.

'Handloser? . . . Zimmer? . . . Rheinhardt? . . . Mandel?'

There! A flicker, a wince crossed her pale face as though she'd been slapped again.

'You got her, Brodie,' said Duncan.

I read the description. Hildegard Mandel. Brown hair and eyes. Height 5' 3" – hard to tell lying down, but not tall. Heavy build. From Polish Upper Silesia but of German ancestry. Good enough. I stood up.

'Well, Aufseherin Mandel, it seems your past has caught up with you.'

I'd got her all right. Her face showed fear for the first time. She sneered something at me in Polish.

'She said – go away – rudely,' said Bathsheba.

'Did she now.' I stuck to German. 'Well, here's the deal, Mandel. My name is Brodie. Lieutenant Colonel Brodie. I'm just back from Hamburg where I was a witness in the trial of some of your fellow workers from Ravensbrück. Last year I performed a similar service at the Belsen trial. I have the power to arrange for you to be sent to Hamburg on the next plane to join Irma Grese in the afterlife.'

Her face lost its sneer and became wary. Doubt clouded her eyes. I continued.

'You probably heard that the lovely Irma was found guilty at the Belsen trials. We hanged her just before Christmas in 1945. Now we're working through the Ravensbrück guards. You will be sent to Hamburg for trial. At the end of it, I expect you to swing alongside your foul pals.'

'Go to hell!' she managed, breaking into German.

'Not me, Hilde. That's your destination. Unless . . .?'

She couldn't help herself. 'Unless what?'

'Unless we keep you here. In Scotland. Tried you here. And put you in jail.'

She wrestled with the choice. 'Why? Why would you?'

'For information, of course.'

I thought she was going to spit at me again and I stood back. Just then Danny came back into the hall. He was holding something.

'Maybe she could start by telling us where she got these?'

Danny held out both hands. The gold glittered in the hall light. Small carved slabs of dull beauty.

Bathsheba reached out and stroked one. Mandel's face slumped as though the air had been released from it. She looked up at Danny and then me.

'What do you want?'

We asked some questions but it was like pulling teeth. Then she said, 'I am feeling faint.' She let her head slump. Faint or feint? I let it go. We'd achieved enough for one morning.

FORTY-FOUR

anny, Bathsheba, Joshua and I stepped out into the cold light of morning. It was bitter but refreshing. An ambulance was already drawn up and two men were unloading a stretcher to pick up Mandel. Two armed constables had passed us in the entry ready to escort their wounded prisoner to a secure room at the infirmary. A crowd of nosy Glaswegians was already gathering.

Danny and I lit up.

'One down, Brodie.'

'But hardly a big fish. We'll talk to her again when she's patched up. We'll show her photos. See how she reacts.' I looked at Bathsheba. 'Are you cold? You did well.' She was shaking.

'Freezing. But it was meeting her. I never thought ... I never ...' And suddenly the tears were coursing down her face. 'Sorry, sorry, sorry ...'

Danny beat me to it. He put his arm round her and held her. 'You did brilliant, so you did. You're a brave girl, so you are.'

Eventually she pushed him away and Danny handed her a hankie. 'What's next, Brodie?'

'Mandel said we'd never find the others. So she confirmed there *are* others. She also said they knew we were after them. It's why she fired through the door. She had a row with a man. No description but he sounded "posh" according to the old neighbour. Is that right, Joshua?'

'That's what he said, sir.'

'One of the officers then. Maybe Suhren himself. Is it worth talking to the old man again?'

'I just did. While you were with her. He doesn't know anything else. Said he's glad we caught the bitch.' His young face coloured.

'So are we, Joshua. You've done well here. Really well. Look, Danny, you get Bathsheba off to hospital. Get the wood splinters out and a tetanus jab. Then let's compare notes this evening with the others. I'm not expecting to see you, Bathsheba. Take it easy, OK?'

They nodded and Danny walked off with her, a consoling arm round her shoulder. The man was incorrigible. And – truth to tell – I wished it were me.

I walked on down through the cold streets to the *Gazette*. I hadn't been able to face the newsroom for days, ever since I'd been helped from my desk by Danny and Duncan. It hadn't snowed for a day or two and the mounds by the side of the pavements were turning into filthy ramparts. I dropped into a café for a mug of tea and a fried-egg sandwich. I'd learned the lesson about feeding my demons to keep them quiet.

I walked through the doors into the newsroom and saw Eddie jump to his feet in his smoky office. Eyes turned as I walked across the lino to my desk. A few *good mornings* tinged with a query. I was barely at my desk before Eddie was at my side.

'Are you sure this is wise, Brodie? Could you no' just take a wee while longer off? The state of you the other day . . .'

'I'm fine, Eddie.' And the truth, as I inspected myself, was that I felt better than in weeks. Still an emptiness, despite the egg bap, but the black dog had slunk off to its kennel. I could hear its low growl, but I had a collar and chain on it. For the moment. 'What have you got for me?'

He peered up at me searching for faulty wiring. 'Weeeell, if you're sure, Brodie? OK, there's a story coming in about someone stealing coal.'

'Coal? That's hardly news.'

'This was a trainload, Brodie. Coming in from Cumnock for Dixon's Blazes. It's getting like the Wild West oot there. The driver saw sleepers on the line. When he got oot to see what was going on, they jumped him from behind a snow pile. Left him lying there and stole the train. Got as far as Mauchline and unloaded half the wagons on to lorries.'

'It'll have been sold already.'

'Nae doot.'

'How's the driver?'

'At the Royal. Stitches and frostbite.'

'I'm on my way.'

I got the story from the driver but had been just beaten to it by the *Record* man. I filed it anyway, together with a picture of the abandoned train that our staff photographer had taken from the embankment. I left the office in time for the meeting at Garnethill. When I got there I found a clutch of men already waiting. They were talking excitedly together in a huddle of chairs. Joshua was at their centre, his young face flushed. Danny was on the periphery sucking in the flowing conservation. I walked over.

'Telling them about this morning, Joshua?'

He shot to his feet. 'Yes, sir. But there's something else. Sammy here.'

A tiny man with glasses and flat cap smiled from a mouthful of brown and broken teeth. I knew it wasn't bad dental care. Sammy had been given a good pasting by a bunch of my fellow countrymen wearing orange sashes. They'd decided if you weren't Protestant you might as well be some sort of Catholic. His original name was Schmuel Finkelstein. Now it was Sammy Fowler. Like many Jews he'd changed his name to blend in when he arrived in '38 from Vienna. He'd also picked up English with the broadest Glasgow accent possible. But camouflage hadn't helped him against the Bingo Boys.

Sammy seemed embarrassed. 'It wis like this, sir. Ah wis jist takin' a wee donner when Ah saw Joshua here.'

'Why were you there, Sammy?'

'Ah wis jist curious, sir. After whit you said last night. Ah'm sorry. Ah wanted a wee keek.'

'Joshua, what were *you* still doing there?'

'I was hanging about, sir. To see what the polis were doing after you left.'

'Fine, Joshua. Carry on, Sammy.'

'Well, a fair crowd had gathered thegither. This was the back o' nine this morning. And as Ah said, Ah saw Joshua here, so Ah asked him whit wis going on. He telt me you'd been on the raid, so ye hud. And that a woman had been shot. And she'd later died.'

'Died? Mandel is dead?' I asked. 'She was barely wounded.'

Danny piped up. 'I spoke to Duncan this afternoon, Brodie. She died on the way to the hospital. She seems to have taken something. Duncan thinks a cyanide capsule. She was in convulsions in the ambulance.'

'Sammy, did you see something? Is that what you're telling me?'

'Ah wis standing there blethering away wi' Joshua and suddenly Ah saw a fella in the crowd. It wis a man Ah'd seen ower in Hope Street. That's ma patch, as you well know. The barber there had pointed him oot tae me. He said the fella had started coming in the shop aboot six months ago. He wis now as regular as clockwork, getting a shave every week and a haircut and dye job every fortnight.'

'A dye job, Sammy!'

'Aye. Seems he wis always flush wi' cash. A roll o' it. Always smoking best fags. Black Russians, apparently. And here's the thing: he telt the barber he was Swiss. Ah mean, Swiss, here in Glesga. C'mon. Anyways. It wis him. This fella in the crowd. He pushed his way tae the front, looking . . . no' curious or onythin' like the rest o' us, mair anxious, like. He wis asking questions aboot what had happened. Sounded awfie posh.'

'Or Swiss.' I turned to Joshua. His eyes were gleaming and he nodded. 'Did he look like any of the photos we have? Was it Suhren?'

His face screwed up. 'I couldnae really say. It's hard wi' dyed hair and that.'

'Don't worry, Sammy. Go on.'

'Then when they brought the woman oot on the stretcher there wis a bit of a commotion. The crowd a' trying tae get closer and see what wis happening. You know what crowds are like.'

'What happened?'

'We couldnae see much for a' the shoving and pushing. The polis pushed everybody back and they got the woman into the ambulance and away they went.'

'This man. Did you see him get close to the woman on the stretcher?'

'Ah couldnae right say, sir. It's possible.'

'What did you do then?'

Joshua cut in. 'We followed him, sir. Me and Sammy. Down to the river and across the suspension bridge to Carlton Place. We know his house now. We saw him go in the entry,' he said with triumph.

'That smart terrace by the river?' I asked.

Sammy responded. 'Aye. Best street in Laurieston, just by the suspension brig. The South Portland Street brig.'

'When does he get his next dye job?'

Sammy's face broke into a gap-toothed grin. 'The morn.'

By now the hall had filled and we were surrounded by the full complement of twitching ears plus Shimon and Isaac. There was only one missing.

'How's Bathsheba, Danny?'

'Fine. Patched up and off home. I told her on pain of not being allowed back to our soirées to stay home and rest tonight.'

I called them to order and recounted the events of the day, including getting wee Sammy to tell us about his tracking exploits. It didn't take long for Malachi to get to his feet.

'Colonel, sir. I mean Brodie. Ah thought you said no guns?'

'I had one for self-defence, Mal. I'm trained to use it. We don't have licence to arm the lot of you and let you loose. As it is, my police pal is less than happy about even me using a gun.'

'Are we going to ambush this guy tomorrow? Give him a real close shave, eh?'

'*You* are going to continue with your search, Mal. This one has to be taken alive. McRae and I will meet him and invite him to have a chat with us. He could be the opening we need. A real breakthrough.'

We broke up and Danny and I headed back to Sam's. We agreed on our tactics for the morning and then turned to the issues that seemed to nag at us both.

'You seem a wee bit better, Brodie. More like you.'

'Despite being knackered? It's been a long day.'

'A good day.'

'Aye, it has. What you said last night. About the panics I've been getting. It feels a bit easier.'

'Don't you get too bouncy. It takes a while. One forward two back. But maybe it's a start. I was told it's about knowing *why* you panic. Once you understand, you're less feart.'

'It's no surprise I get bad dreams. The stuff I saw. But what have I to panic about?'

'You tell me. But take this morning; you can panic like that any time as far as I'm concerned.'

'That wasn't panic. It was fast reaction.'

'Fast shooting. By the way, I'll need a gun.'

'No you won't.'

'If that woman had a weapon, sure enough so will this bloke we're after. I need a gun.'

'I only have my service revolver.'

'There's a locked case in my bedroom.'

'There are a couple of guns that belonged to Sam's father.'

He said nothing.

'Danny? Todd would have a heart attack. And when he recovered he'd lock us both up.'

'I'd rather end up in the clink than dead, if it's all the same to you.'

I glanced at him, seeing again in the soft glow of the lamps the sharp cheeks and focused stare of the young man I'd collided with in Tobago Street nick more than a decade ago. I knew that look. There was no argument I could make, that anyone could make, that would have diverted him.

FORTY-FIVE

I fought myself awake until I'd broken clear of the clutches of my night-time furies. I lay gasping for air in a shivering dawn. As Danny said, sometimes it was one forward two back. Maybe I could cut it to one back.

The window was opaque with sworls of frost, like a giant thumbprint on the glass. I gathered the quilt round my shoulders like a shawl and padded across the carpet to perch on tiptoe on the cold linoleum. I formed an eye hole with my hot breath and peeked out. Huge soft feathers were tumbling and wheeling and settling. The road was obliterated, the world deadened.

The whole house was a mausoleum. We were trying to save coal. Already rationed, the deliveries weren't getting much beyond the mine-head. Large chunks of Scotland had become impassable, and people were freezing to death. No wonder they were hijacking coal trains.

I checked the time. Seven thirty. I got dressed and went downstairs. Danny's hat and coat had already disappeared. He'd gone on ahead. Probably stopping at Bathsheba's to see how she was.

Sam joined me for the first cup of tea.

'What are you up to, the pair of you?' Sam asked.

'We're meeting a man by the river.'

She eyed me speculatively. 'I heard about the shooting yesterday. Is this linked?'

I nodded.

'Just make sure you only hit the baddies.'

'I'm hoping I won't have to fire.'

'Me too. What about Danny? Is he armed to the teeth?'

I sighed. 'I gave him my gun. My army gun. I'll use the Webley.'

'God, I wish you hadn't told me.'

'In truth, I could do with someone at my back.'

'I know, I know. Look, I'm glad he came up. But he worries me. I get the impression he's even less biddable than you. And that's saying something.'

'He was a bit wild before. And I think that knock on the head lifted another layer of restraint.'

Sam rolled her eyes. 'Oh, good. That puts my mind at rest.'

I couldn't don enough clothes to keep out the chill. Wrapped like a mummy I ventured out. I took giant steps like Wenceslas but there was no one to fill my tracks. I had to be at the rendezvous point by eleven o'clock. I was early.

From my vantage point at the railway station entrance I could see across to the barber's. Despite walking up and down and slapping my hands together I could feel the cold creeping up my limbs in slow paralysis. On the other corner, in a shop doorway, looking equally frozen, was wee Sammy. His face was buried in a huge scarf and his body looked twice its normal width. A fag hung from his mouth and sent small puffs of grey into the air, as though Sammy ran on steam.

We watched customers come and go with fresh-shaven faces and short back and sides bared to the freezing air. But no sign of our man. Finally, fifteen minutes later than his supposed normal time, he emerged. I saw Sammy stiffen and fling away his fag. The man turned his head one way and then the other before heading south down Hope Street towards the Clyde. Sammy nodded my way and fell in behind the man, but some fifty steps behind. I set out after them on the other side of the road.

We came to the Broomielaw. Ahead, blocking the view of the river, were the lines of goods sheds. The man turned left and under the railway bridge, then on into Clyde Street. He hesitated for a moment and I thought he might go via Glasgow Bridge to Carlton Place, but he kept going, presumably preferring the scenic route. Sure enough, he crossed the street between the goods sheds, aiming for the suspension bridge. At this point Sammy just kept walking along Clyde Street while I hurried to close the gap on the man. The pavements were piled high with snow and the paths were a good foot deep in packed snow and ice. My feet slithered as I darted over the road. Timing was everything.

I got on to the footbridge with the man about twenty yards ahead of me. Even the slim walkway between the great sway of supporting cables was thick with snow. I peered past the man. Barely visible on the far side a figure had just started walking towards us. With luck and timing we would intersect with the target about halfway over. I quickened my step and felt inside my coat for the big revolver. Its weight and feel gave me confidence. For a moment the target turned round but I kept walking. He didn't speed up. Didn't run. But we were closing on each other.

Now I could see the face of the man walking towards us. Danny was trying to look nonchalant but instead looked like a man trying to look nonchalant. I hoped it didn't matter. I'd also hoped no one else would be on this frozen walkway into the Gorbals. But just then another two men started towards us from behind Danny. Under their snow-covered hats and scarves they were laughing and talking. I caught a glint of specs on one of them.

I looked behind me. Nobody. I left my glove in my coat pocket, reached inside my coat and pulled out the Webley. I was within ten feet of the man. Now I could see how tall he was. My height, and at least as big. Suhren's height. He was slowing. He was slowing because Danny had drawn his gun and was walking smartly towards him with it held out straight in both hands, pointing directly at the man's body. I moved a little to the right so that if Danny's finger twitched I wouldn't take a stray bullet.

I called out in German, 'Stop!' and closed the gap to within three feet. 'Stop! Hands up!'

Danny was nearly in his face now and I saw the man's shoulders slump.

I called out, 'Keep the gun on him. I'll frisk him.' I pocketed mine and used both hands to run over the man's clothes from top to bottom. I swung him round to pat down his front. Disappointment washed through me. Not Suhren. His face was contorted with rage.

'Who are you? I will call the police.'

I replied in German. 'We *are* the police. Sort of.'

Then relief kicked in. Not Suhren but one of the other officers. I had his photo. He was smiling in it, pleased with himself. His SS officer's cap perched at a rakish angle, Iron Cross dangling round his throat, set off by the SS flash on one collar and the three pips over two bars on the other.

'Danny, let me introduce you to Hauptsturmführer Klaus Langefeld, Senior Adjutant, Auschwitz concentration camp.'

'Are you sure, Brodie?' asked Danny.

'As sure as we're standing here.'

I saw the man's face sag, knowing the game was up.

'Stand in to the side, Langefeld. Let these men pass. Then we'll be on our way.'

I glanced up. The two men coming towards us had stopped laughing. Had stopped walking. They now stood either side of Danny. Christ. Langefeld had an escort! Idiot, Brodie! Why hadn't I foreseen that?

The one with specs had a gun pressed against Danny's head. The other opened up his coat and raised a Tommy gun.

He swung it at me. It didn't have to be precisely targeted. At this range it would hit everything in a ten-foot swathe. I braced myself. There was no time to dive off the bridge. Could I get to him after the bullets ripped into me? Stay alive long enough to break his neck?

Tommy gun tipped his hat back. I'd seen those eyes, that dark skin, among the platoon staring out at me last night. The two men Malachi had brought along. What the hell was going on?

Behind me, I heard running steps and another three men came panting up to stand behind me. Not my rescue party. They all carried pistols. All wore scarves high on their faces. One of them had an eye patch.

'Mal! You bloody idiot! Put that away! We've got this under control.'

'Sorry, Brodie. He's ours. Take their guns!' Malachi called.

The one holding the pistol to Danny's head reached out and took Danny's gun – *my* gun – from his outstretched hands. Rough hands grabbed my arms and pulled the Webley from my pocket. Mal took both pistols and quickly and efficiently emptied the shells from each and pocketed the cartridges. He tossed the guns on to the snow.

'Get him out of here.'

Mal's two sidekicks put their guns away, moved forward and grabbed the prisoner. For a moment my eyes met Langefeld's and I saw fear had replaced the anger. For the first time he spoke in German to me.

'What's happening? Who are these men? Are they yours?'

'They're Jews, Hauptsturmführer Langefeld. Angry Jews. I advise you to cooperate.'

Then he was bundled away back towards the city, so that only Malachi was left, pointing his gun at Danny and me. Slowly he lowered it.

'I'm sorry, Brodie.'

'I doubt that. But you will be. What are you going to do with him?'

'Get him to talk. Get him to tell us where the others are.'

'And if he doesn't?'

He shrugged. 'He will.'

'We'll come after you, Malachi.'

'I don't care, Brodie. I really don't care.'

He turned and walked away from us, sure that we'd do nothing to stop him. Danny and I picked up our useless guns and brushed the snow off them.

'Bugger,' said Danny softly. 'Will you call Todd or me?'

'I'll call him. We might be able to salvage something out of this mess. Let's go find this man's house. We'll tell Todd to meet us there.'

FORTY-SIX

As we walked over the bridge we saw Sammy scampering along the path to intersect with us. He must have belted along Clyde Street over Victoria Bridge and back to Carlton Place. He was red-faced and bouncing up and down when we met him.

'Did you get him? Whaur is he?'

'Malachi and some of his pals took him.'

'*Whit?*'

'Don't ask. Come on. Show me his entry.'

Danny and I had talked about ambushing him at his house, but decided we'd be better off sandwiching him on the bridge. It was the right call but the wrong result. The ambushers ambushed.

'Ower there. That's his entry. But I don't know the nummer of his flat.' Sammy pointed at a smart black door in the long sandstone façade of townhouses facing the river. There would be four, possibly six in the entry.

'Sammy, can you go and phone the police? Ask for Inspector Duncan Todd. Tell him Brodie would like him to join him as soon as he can. Give him this address.' I pointed at the black door. Sammy leaped into action, heading for the police box at the end of the bridge.

Danny and I crossed the road, walked up to the black door, opened it and stepped into a well-kept, stone-flagged corridor. Two doors faced each other on the ground floor and presumably there were two on the next. There were knockers in the centre of each door and name plates beneath. We knocked on McKinley, then Cousins. Nothing from the first, then footsteps from Cousins's door. We listened as chains rattled and locks clunked.

'Yes?' said a querulous wee man rubbing at a thin, nicotined moustache.

'Sorry to bother you – Mr Cousins? We're looking for a foreign gentlemen living in the building.'

'Well, there's an Englishman up the stairs, heh, heh, heh,' he kechled away at his own wit.

'Anyone else?'

'You'll be talking about yon Mr Schwarz. Swiss, so he is. He lives up the stair. Number four. But he's no' in. I heard him go oot. He goes for his haircut on a Thursday. This is Thursday, isn't it?'

We were already on the stairs.

'Aye, him and his wife are baith oot . . .'

We stopped and slowly walked back down.

'His wife?' asked Danny.

'Aye. A nice wummin. She goes out to work in the morning. She'll be back later, nae doot. Though I thought I heard somebody come and go earlier. Look, who are you fellas anyway? Are you the polis?'

'The police are on their way. Aren't they, Sammy?' I called out to the head that had just poked round the front door.

'Jist coming, they said. And they also said, tell Brodie to do nothing till Inspector Todd gets there. *Absolutely bloody nothing*. Those were the exact words I was to say.'

Danny and I climbed the stairs and sat down on the top one, side by side.

'Could we have the wrong man? I mean – *a wife*?' asked Danny.

'It's possible. But it's also possible that he's hooked up with one of the others. A good alibi.'

'Or maybe just sex.'

'There's always that.'

We smoked in silence until we heard the clanging bell, then doors slamming, then a small army invading the entry. Duncan Todd rounded the corner of the stairwell, panting for breath. He stopped and held us with his stare.

'Will you look at the pair o' ye. Ah hope you've touched nothing!'

'As if, Duncan. As if,' I said.

He climbed past us. 'Which door?'

'I'd suggest the one with the foreign name. Schwarz.'

'Have you chapped?'

'We were told to do nothing. We did nothing.'

Todd gave us a look. Then he hammered on both doors. Nothing from either.

'Do you have a warrant?' asked Danny.

'Aye, so stand back. I'm going in.' He walked back a couple of paces on the landing, ready to charge down the door. Danny spoke up.

'Duncan? If you'll give me a couple of seconds, I can save you dislocating your shoulder.'

Danny stepped forward and pulled out a small bundle from inside his coat. He unwrapped it and chose a sharpened screwdriver and bent nail. I'd forgotten his SOE training. So had Duncan. He stood shaking his head as Danny fumbled at the double lock. It was less than a minute before the door swung open. Danny stood aside and made a mock bow for Todd to enter first. I followed him into a spacious hallway and on into an even more spacious sitting room with views out on to the river. A shelf of books spoke of a pleasant lifestyle, one I could envy.

'Very nice,' said Danny, stroking the back of a good soft couch. 'The Third Reich must have a good pension scheme.'

'A golden one,' I said.

The three of us, quietly and methodically, took the flat

apart. It was quickly clear that a couple lived here. We found women's clothes – smart and cared-for – hanging in a wardrobe. Women's toiletries crowded the bathroom. A woman's scent tantalised our nostrils. But it was the paperwork that should offer the cornucopia. If there was any.

We found nothing. Tucked away in the bottom drawer of the sideboard in the bedroom, under a pile of women's silken underwear, were two cardboard files. Both were empty.

'Brodie?' Danny called out from the sitting room. He was kneeling by the fireplace, poking at a small mound of fragments. 'He's burnt them,' he said superfluously. 'He saw the Mandel woman get picked up.'

'He must have kept something. Some sort of ID. Ration book. That sort of thing,' I suggested.

'Probably had them on him.'

I gazed round the room. 'Try the books and down the back of the chairs.'

Danny started on the furniture, plunging his hands down the sides and back, then tipping them up and examining the underneath. I began rifling the books. Nothing.

'But you're sure it was this SS guy, Langefeld, Brodie?' asked Duncan.

'Positive.'

'Any ideas then about the woman?'

'Hard to say. Mandel is accounted for, leaving three possible women's names from the first list. But I still think the first dozen have left these shores. In which case we might just have found one of the unnamed women from the second list. What did you find at Mandel's house, Duncan?'

He shrugged. 'Nothin' much. Her passport. A few bits and pieces of supporting documents.'

'What sort? Anything to point us at a local connection?'

'Naw. Just the same sort of bumf you got from Dragan.'

I glanced at Danny. Todd was holding out on us, maybe still upset at our cavalier approach. We hadn't told him about this ambush. Why should he tell us what he'd found? We were given no time to probe him.

'Now, the pair of you, what happened on the brig? How did you cock things up so much? Do you know who took this guy Langefeld? Sit down and talk to me.'

We sat, and while Todd's uniformed men did a last search of the flat, Danny and I told him how we'd been outmanoeuvred.

'What do you think Malachi is going to do to the Kraut?'

'Make him say where the other rats are hiding.'

'Then what?'

'Then they'll go after them.'

'Shit.'

'Shit indeed, Duncan.'

'Do you have any idea where Malachi will be?'

We shook our heads.

He stood up. 'Right, we'd better get going.'

'What about this woman?'

'Ah was planning to leave a couple of men here.'

'We'll stay,' I offered. Danny stared at me; then he nodded. Duncan looked at the two of us.

'That'll save me two officers. Any chance you can take her alive, boys? Or is that asking too much?'

FORTY-SEVEN

He left Danny and me sitting there. Soon, unprompted, we each picked up a book and began reading. It had been a while since I'd read *People of the Mist*. It still gripped the boy in me. We read as the daylight faded and the gas lamps were lit outside.

'Do we close the curtains and put on a light?' asked Danny.

'What would *she* expect? Let's assume she doesn't know her boyfriend's been lifted.'

'She'd come home to a cosy house with a fire and lights on.'

'Sure that's not just to make you comfortable?'

We grinned at each other and set to. We drew the curtains and built and lit a fire. We lit the gas wall lights and trimmed the flames to give us a nice glow to read by.

'Find any booze?' I asked.

'Brandy? There's a bottle in the cupboard.'

'I think we're allowed a medicinal drink on duty,' I said as I splashed some of the dark, heady liquid into two tumblers. We sniffed and tasted appreciatively.

'They were gie good to themselves,' said Danny.

'Maybe it helped them sleep.'

'I don't think they had problems sleeping. Not like you, Brodie.'

'I'm a sensitive soul.'

'You've talked about interrogating these sods afterwards. Did you go to a camp?'

'All the interrogations were in tents at the British lines.'

'So you didn't actually visit a camp?'

'I suppose I took a look.'

'Did you go inside?'

'I must have. Yes.' Why was he pushing this?

'Which camp?'

'Well, Belsen was the nearest.'

'Christ, Douglas, did you go inside Belsen or not?'

'I don't recall much. It was a crazy time.'

'Douglas, it's not something you forget. It's not something you're unsure of. Think back. Did you go inside a camp?'

'For God's sake, what does it matter?' I took a big pull at my glass.

He spoke quietly and slowly. 'Take your mind back. You were detached from your brigade. Who did you report to? Where? Don't speak. Just think about it.'

He watched me, saw me remembering.

'Now, which camp did you visit?'

'Belsen. It *was* Belsen. All right? Now, are you satisfied?' Why was I so angry with him?

'There was barbed wire. And big gates. They all had them. Do you remember walking in through the gates? What was it like?'

'*You* know what it was like, Danny.'

'I had time to get used to it – if you like. Who did you see first? Who was the first person you met? What was *he* like? What was *she* like?'

Why did this matter? Yet it seemed to. To Danny and to me. But I had no clear memory of it. What was the last thing I could recall? The jeep. I remembered bumping along in the jeep. I had a driver. It was an open jeep; we were passing long lines of tall wire. I could see huts behind the wire. Smoke was drifting across our path. So was a smell. I put my hand up to my nose.

We came to a gap. The huge wooden gates were wide open. Inside, stick people sprawled or stumbled about among the fit young soldiers. The stick people moved like dying spiders. Some of them wore striped pyjamas. Some appeared to be naked. The driver stopped just inside the gates. I got out. The smell was very bad now. Filth and sweat mixed with carbolic soap and antiseptic. The reek of fires drifted across. It stung the nostrils. I took out a hankie and held it to my face and was ashamed of my weakness. No one else was so prissy.

'It's a' right, sir. You'll get used to it.' It was an army sergeant, a Jock. He was carrying two boxes each with a red cross on the side.

I stood, rooted to the spot in stupefaction. Nothing made sense. Not these tattered skeletons, some moving, some still. So I didn't see the figure until it was next to me. I jumped. It was a woman. Had been a woman. Her eyes were out of proportion to her skull. Her skin was smudged and wrinkled. She bared her teeth. The ones she had left were brown and thin.

'Help,' she croaked. Then she fell towards me. I put my arms up but she slid through them, like a collection of coat hangers. She crumpled at my feet, a puppet whose strings were cut. She lay still, her mouth grinning up at me. Then her eyes went blank.

I lifted my head and realised Danny was watching me, silently. My tears said it all.

'I'd forgotten, Danny.'

He nodded. 'You hadn't, Douglas. You really hadn't.'

FORTY-EIGHT

Danny got up, flung a rug at me from the couch and found one himself. We sat huddled up like two old men left to rot at a nursing home. Twice we took turns to go into the back kitchen and make some tea while the other kept silent watch in the front room. We added brandy to it to sweeten it. We found some bread and a tin of corned beef and wolfed down thick sandwiches. By midnight it was clear she wasn't coming back, but we couldn't risk missing her. We turned out the lights and hunkered down in our chairs and slept fitfully till the morning.

We struggled to our feet and stretched our stiff limbs. Sam would be worried. Duncan had promised to give her a call to let her know what we were doing, but even so. It had been a long day and a longer night. Danny looked as though he'd spent it on a park bench. I didn't want to hear his thoughts on me, but I could see a mirror of my image in his red eyes.

I peeked out between the curtains. There had been another dump in the night. All landmarks except the trees had been obliterated. I rubbed at the opaqueness but it was outside.

We closed the door behind us, left the entry and stepped out into the new snow up to our knees. I took out a cigarette and stuck it between my lips. Then I threw it away, unlit. My mouth already tasted like an ashtray.

'Your beard's red,' Danny commented.

'So's yours,' I replied, rubbing my face.

'So's my hair. Yours is dark.'

'The beard's from my mother. The hair's from my dad. You've just never seen me unshaven.'

'What now?'

'Let's see if we can find Malachi.'

We trudged up to Sam's through deep drifts. The gangs of council snow clearers had given up the Sisyphean challenge. We might as well have been on the Fenwick Moors rather than Argyll Street. We were in time to join Sam for breakfast tea, toast and jam before she headed to Edinburgh's high court for a preliminary hearing. Assuming the main line was open. We fell into chairs around the kitchen table, exhausted by our struggles.

'You look like wrecks.'

'You fair know how to bolster a man's self-esteem,' said Danny.

'It's her trademark.'

It was hard to argue with her analysis. We told her what had happened since we set out yesterday morning to trap Langefeld – as we now knew him.

'This woman? Did you check the bra size? Dress size?'

Danny and I looked at each other. In our mind's eye each of us was sensuously handling the silk knickers and slips. Too distracted to have Sam's practical vision.

'Er, no. Not exactly. She wasn't big. I mean we're not talking about giant bloomers or the like. About your shape, Sam.' The kitchen went quiet as the implications of my last comment sank in. Her smile had fangs.

'Well done, *detectives*.'

I called Todd from the hall phone before heading up to shave and change.

'Good idea, Brodie. Good thinking.'

'It was Sam's idea.'

'Woman's insight. We need more of that in the force. I'll get one of ours straight round there. In the meantime . . .'

'Yes?'

'Ah owe you an apology. Ah was keeping you in the dark.'

'About what you found at Mandel's place?'

'Ah knew you'd noticed. The thing is we've got a lead. Of sorts. I've arranged a meeting. The day. It's important, Brodie. And you need to come open-minded.'

'When am I not?'

'Aye well, see you do. Meet me here at Turnbull Street at eleven o'clock. On the dot. This is important. Very.'

I was there at quarter to. I stood between the columns of St Andrew's in the Square looking across to the familiar red sandstone of Central Division. I didn't miss it. I finished my fag and crossed the road. I walked into the front desk and found Duncan already pacing up and down.

'Good. Come on.' He grabbed me by my arm and hauled me back out of the door.

'Where are we going, Duncan?'

'You'll see. Just promise me this, Brodie. Best behaviour. No taking the piss.'

'About what? Are we seeing the Pope or something?'

He looked at me queerly. 'Shut up, Brodie. I said no piss-taking. OK?'

We walked – marched is the more the word – down Turn-bull Street and into Glasgow Green. We pressed south and west towards Saltmarket. By the time we were walking along Clyde Street, I was beginning to guess where we were going.

'Are we no' too late for mass, Duncan?'

He stopped dead. 'See! Ah telt ye. Yer taking the piss, Brodie.'

'Just tell me where we're going, then.'

He took a deep breath. 'St Andrew's Cathedral.'

'To see?'

'Donald Campbell.'

'As in Donald Campbell, Archbishop of Glasgow?'

'The very man.'

'Duncan, it's too late for me. You'll never get me to confession.'

We stood eyeball to eyeball; Duncan fuming and anxious, me taking the piss and wishing I wasn't. But unless he explained, this was what he was going to get.

He sagged. 'It's about the papers. On the woman, Mandel. I contacted his grace and he asked me to visit. With you.'

'*His grace*? Is that what you have to call him?'

'And *you*. Unless you want me to arrange for your body to be found floating by Dumbarton Rock.'

'Would *sir* not do?'

'Fuck's sake, Brodie!'

'Why me?'

'I made the really stupid mistake of mentioning you. Besides, he seems to know about some of the stuff you've been up to. Now can we get a move on? We'll be late.'

As we walked I tried to recall what little I knew of the Archbish. He'd been in the job a couple of years and, as his name suggested, he'd previously held the bishopric of Argyll. Campbell country. Sam would be pleased.

As we neared the cathedral I couldn't help glancing across the Clyde to Carlton Place.

'Did your policewoman get the knicker size?'

Duncan sighed. 'Aye, she did. Petite, apparently. Which narrows it down to half the wee women in Glasgow.'

'Maybe so, but how many wearing real silk?'

We wrenched our minds from the secular as we turned into the cathedral frontage. I was reminded what a little gem it was. Nothing on the grandiose scale of some English or French cathedrals, just a beautifully proportioned church with a central portico and high stained-glass window above. On either side of the door were tall, slim towers with slender shafts thrusting up from the corners of the steep slanting roof. A priest was waiting for us. We were shown into a small study and invited to take a seat. He took our coats and hats.

'His grace will be with you shortly.' He bowed and left us alone.

Within a few minutes the rear door opened and a man walked in. He was wearing a plain dark cassock surmounted by a huge cross on a chain.

Duncan and I got to our feet. Duncan shot forward and knelt. The Archbishop stepped forward, pressed the back of his hands to Duncan's face, allowed him to kiss his ring of office before getting him to his feet. He turned to me. He could see I wasn't going to bow the knee.

'Colonel Brodie, thank you for coming. I hope you don't mind this invite?'

His voice still held the lilt of the Highlands and the Isles.

'Not at all, your grace.'

He beamed at me. 'Please drop the title. I hope we can be informal, just the three of us.'

I saw Duncan's face redden. His indoctrination hadn't prepared him for anything but 'his grace'. And Donald Campbell pointedly hadn't indicated how we *should* refer to him. I decide to use no honorific whatsoever.

'Now shall we all sit?'

His non-grace took his seat behind the plain wooden desk. We sat opposite. We waited while tea was brought and his secretary had left us.

'Mr Brodie, this is a delicate matter. I am asking for your complete discretion. You are not of our faith' – he indicated Duncan – 'so I am relying on your word as an officer and a gentleman. Is that fair?'

'So you wouldn't trust me if I was a mere corporal?' I saw Duncan put his hand to his face.

Into the strained silence I went on, 'Is this about the Vatican connection with escaped Nazis?'

FORTY-NINE

The Archbishop stared at me for a long moment. 'Inspector Todd said you were direct. Yes, it is. Or rather it's about the *supposed* connection.'

'Do you mean the documents are fake?'

'Not necessarily. They could be real but might simply have been misused, do you see?'

'If we are to be open with each other, then I need to know what documents we're talking about. If they are the ones Duncan found at the dead woman's house, I haven't yet seen them.'

They glanced at each other briefly and Todd nodded in acquiescence. The Archbishop pushed his chair back and pulled out a drawer in his desk. He took out some papers and placed them on top. 'Please,' he said, indicating them.

I walked over and picked through the papers. There weren't many. A passport like the others, but also letters with seals similar to the ones I'd seen over two months ago taken by Malachi from Dragan's house. I held up the one with the seal of the Vatican on it and the signature under the printed name and seal of the Austrian Bishop Hudal.

'Does Bishop Hudal exist?' I asked.

'Most certainly. He is the rector of the Pontficio Istituto Teutonico di Santa Maria dell'Anima in Rome. It is a seminary for Austrian and German priests.'

'And has he been arranging escape routes – rat lines – for Nazis?'

The Archbishop folded his fingers together and said carefully, 'Some escape routes were set up during the war. For our own people. For persecuted churchmen. To help them get out of the occupied territories during the war. It seems perhaps these routes have been compromised.'

'By Bishop Hudal?'

'Perhaps.'

'Are you saying that someone else might be using the bishop's signature and stamp?'

The Archbishop twisted in his chair. His eyes flicked to Todd's. 'We are not certain.'

'It's an uncertain world. But tell me, why am I here? What do you want from me?'

'I want you to know – believe it if you will – that here in Scotland the Catholic Church plays no part in these so-called rat lines.'

'So they exist but outside your control. I see.' My sarcasm must have stung. It brought colour to Campbell's cheeks and a groan from Todd.

'You don't, do you, Brodie? Why should you?'

I waited. The Archbishop got up. We began rising too. I assumed the audience was over and that I was about to be thrown out for failing to take the word of a bishop of Rome. And for being chippy.

'No. Sit, please,' he said and moved round from behind his table. He walked over to a small painting on the wall next to his desk. It showed Paul, kneeling and blind, while a great light shone down on him.

'You know this scene?'

'The road to Damascus.'

'I'm not going to make simplistic parallels, Brodie. But let me at least throw some light on this matter.' He walked over to the window that gave out on to the side passage of the cathedral. He turned and looked at me. His face was contorted with anguish. 'I hear your friend McRae was in Dachau?'

I nodded.

'These stories of Nazi concentration camps. The stories of mass murder of our brothers in Christ, the Jews. They are *our* stories, Brodie. Thousands of my Catholic brothers were murdered by Hitler's gangs.' His Highland accent was growing stronger as he talked, the lilt making the words sing.

'Ask your friend McRae about the priests who died alongside him. They were gathered in Dachau from all over Europe and were slaughtered there. I am telling you that your enemy is mine. Nothing, *nothing* would have made me give them assistance to escape justice.'

I noticed the tense he was using. 'You sound as though there was temptation.'

His face darkened even more. He nodded. 'Christ himself would struggle with the choices. Nazism or Communism? Stalin is as much a persecutor of the Church as Hitler. Two years ago – shortly after I was appointed here – a representative of Rome called on me. He was the envoy of Cardinal Eugène Tisserant.'

'French?'

'Yes. And anti-communist.'

'Calling on the Auld Alliance?' I said with incredulity.

'You might say that. The cardinal had been approached by certain Argentinian cardinals. They were offering to establish escape routes to South America for French anti-communists.'

'And for anti-communist read Nazi?'

'He made a powerful argument. A subtle argument. Let me paraphrase. Communism's implacable goal is to wipe out religion. The Red Army is Satan's hordes. We cannot afford to be too selective as to who would serve with us under Christ's banner. Indeed, if we are clever, we can stand to one side and let the Bolsheviks and Fascists fight each other to extinction.'

'Total war doesn't work that way. There are no sidelines.'

'You're right, Brodie. That is the pragmatic objection. But there is also the moral one. I wrestled with this proposal for a day and a night. But in my heart I had already instantly decided. This was a squalid argument and a squalid bargain.'

'You refused to help.'

'Yes.'

'But *someone* accepted? Someone locally.'

'It seems so.'

'Do you know who?'

'Not the name.'

'But . . .?'

'The envoy said that America was on *our* side. His side. Against communism. That they wanted selected senior Nazis – scientists, doctors, spies – to help them in this new war.'

'So the local contact is an American?'

'A senior officer of some sorts.'

'In Glasgow?'

'At the airport. At Prestwick Airport.'

I stared at the Archbishop, then at Duncan. It was so obvious that it felt as if I was having my own Damascene enlightenment. I'd flown into it barely a fortnight ago. Prestwick had been a major allied hub for war planes throughout the war. Hundreds of freight and bomber flights every day poured in from America and Canada. The US Air Force had based a huge staff there marshalling forces for D-Day and beyond.

The airport was only eight miles from Kilmarnock. I remembered coming home on leave once and taking the train down to watch flight after flight roaring over the white beaches of Troon and Monkton. Now Prestwick was the booming heart of civilian transatlantic passenger flights. It was never fog-bound and offered a short direct hop to and from America's east coast. A perfect escape route.

FIFTY

I walked back to Central Division with Duncan.

'Did you know all this beforehand, Duncan?'

'Nup. I was dumbfoonert. Ah just had a wee chat with my own priest about the Vatican letter and next thing it's a holy summons.'

'At confession? I thought that was sacrosanct? No clyping even to an archbishop.'

'It was outside the confessional, I'll have you know.'

'Well, I'm sure you've earned yourself an indulgence or two.'

'Don't mock, Brodie. That's as near as Ah'll get to the top man.'

'God?'

'Ye cannae help yersel', can ye?'

'What are you going to do about the American connection?'

'What am *Ah* gonnae do? What do you suggest? Raid Prestwick Airport? Just roll down there wi' a fleet o' Black Marias and lift every Yank in sight. Is that the plan?'

'It's pretty desperate, isn't it?'

'Aye, it is.'

'We have to do *something*. This stinks.'

'To high heaven. But I assume it's occurred to you that it might be sanctioned?'

'By our own government? Yeah. Nothing surprises me any more. But Sillitoe would have said something. Surely.'

We walked back through the park and up Turnbull Street. Ahead of us was a small group of people. They seemed excited. As I got closer I recognised some of them, one especially. Rabbi Silver.

'Maurice, what's going on?'

'Brodie! It's Shimon and Isaac! They've taken them!'

'What! What are you saying? Who's taken them?'

The crowd re-formed round Duncan and me. To one side was a red-faced police sergeant.

Duncan pressed forward. 'What's going on, Sergeant?'

'Sir, these men say they got a phone call. Someone claiming they've kidnapped two of their pals.'

Maurice Silver cut in. 'They called the synagogue. Said they'd taken Shimon from his shop in Candleriggs and Isaac from his place and were holding them until we freed the man on the bridge, they said. They said they were both going to die unless they got *their* man back. We checked both shops. They're empty. But they'd carved a swastika on the counters. The two families are in a terrible state. Brodie, who is this man they want to trade for our two?'

'Yes! Who is this?' The little crowd of onlookers were shouting and shoving and working themselves into a real lather.

'Quiet!' I called. I tried to clear my head though it was fizzing with anxiety. 'Listen. Danny and I captured a Nazi on the South Portland Street Bridge yesterday. But Malachi Herzog showed up with armed men and took him from us. We don't know where they've taken him. We searched the man's house and found he was living with a woman. She was out and never came home. She must have found out her boyfriend had been taken. I assume she told her pals.'

Duncan took over. 'Right, you lot, I want the rabbi inside, and we'll take proper statements. The rest of you, on about your business. We'll handle this.'

Inside, in the dark vestibule of the police station, my heart was hammering its way out of my chest. I had to think, had to calm the panic. How the hell did they know about Shimon and Isaac? Both leaders of the groups that first got me involved? And one a dear friend? It seemed a very targeted bit of pressure. I put in a fast call to Sam's house and got Danny. I gave him the gist, and then I listened to Maurice as he gave us more details.

'I took the call at the synagogue, in my office.'

I asked, 'What did he sound like? The caller?'

'Like he was reading a script and putting on an accent.'

'A Scottish accent?'

'The other way around. Like a Scot putting on a German accent.'

'Did he mention the man's name? This Nazi we caught?'

'No. He called him the man on the bridge and also the man from Carlton Place.'

Duncan and I looked at each other.

'Tell us exactly what was said.'

'That we had to put the man back at the bridge. By himself. No police. They will be watching. By no later than six o'clock. Or they will kill Belsinger and Feldmann.'

'Six o'clock? When? Which day?'

Maurice looked surprised. 'Today. He said today, Brodie.'

We wasted precious time while Todd and his sergeant debated their next action. They summoned other officers to a review meeting. All so familiar. When you didn't know what to do next, you held a meeting. I took Rabbi Silver to one side and sat with him.

'We *have* to find Malachi.'

'I know, I know.'

'Any ideas?'

'No. Nothing. I don't know where he lives.'

'What about Rabbi Leveson at Garnethill? Will he know?'

'I will ask him. I'll phone him right now.'

'Hmm, I assume Malachi wouldn't be holed up in his own house. What about the pub I met him in? Would they know?'

'It's possible.'

'It's a start. Look, the best place for you is back at the synagogue. Stay next to the phone. I'll keep in regular contact.' I looked up. Danny was panting towards us. He arrived and I grabbed his arm. 'Don't stop. Let's go.'

Outside and away from the front of the police station, I asked, 'Did you bring them?'

'Why do you think my coat's clunking?'

We skulked between the pillars of St Andrew's in the Square while Danny slipped me the big Webley. He drew out my service Enfield. He passed me a fistful of ammunition and we both loaded up. We looked like assassins preparing to slaughter a priest. The mood I was in, if that's what it took, so be it.

'Where are we going?'

'A pub.'

'Good. I could murder a beer.'

'It's Malachi's local. Brown's.'

'The Catholic pub? Will they let us in?'

'Why do you think we've got guns?'

We splashed through puddles and running gutters all the way to the Barras. A brief thaw had set in, at least for a day. It meant we arrived at Brown's with our trouser cuffs soaking, our coats flapping and sweat wetting our hat-bands.

'Do we do this like Cagney? Crash through the doors, guns blazing?' he asked.

'We could. Or we could just walk in,' I said and pushed the saloon door open. It was lunchtime and there were a handful of drinkers at the bar. No hush fell. It was already morgue quiet. The barman barely looked up. We strode in and plonked our hats on the bar. The barman languorously lifted his head from the paper and stood up straight.

'Aye, boys, what'll it be?'

'Where's Mal?' I asked. 'Malachi Herzog.'

'Never heard o' him, pal.' He smirked at his two customers and settled back down to his paper.

I sighed and turned to Danny. I had no time for games. 'Looks like Cagney wins.' I took out my gun from my coat pocket and laid it on the counter with a good solid thunk. It got better attention. The two customers were off their seats in a trice and would have been out the door if Danny hadn't been standing between it and them with his gun trained on them.

'I'll ask you one more time. And if you don't start telling me something useful, then I'm going to come round the bar and shoot you in the knees.'

His face spoke for him, as did the nod.

'Good. Where's Malachi?'

I could see him struggling for spittle. His Adam's apple bobbed and then he found a voice. 'He isnae here.'

I shook my head. 'I can see that. Where is he?'

'There's a snooker place. Doon the road. Jake's. Try there.'

I got the address from him plus a promise not to call ahead to Jake's. To help him keep his word, I tore out the phone wires in the back room.

FIFTY-ONE

We hurried round to Jake's. It was an upstairs room above shops south of Barrowland. This time we took Danny's preferred approach. I hit the door with my shoulder, opening it enough to let Danny burst through first, gun in hand. I dived after and to his left, pointing my revolver round the small room. There were two snooker tables and only one man. He wasn't playing. He'd been sitting with his feet up on a table, balanced on the back legs of his chair. He was clutching a newspaper. Behind him was a door. Loud music was blasting out from within. It didn't seem like a tea dance. The chair dropped and he sprang to his feet, reaching for the shotgun lying along the green baize.

'Don't do it!' I shouted.

He froze and Danny ran forward to sweep up his weapon. I saw his eyes flicker to the door behind him.

'Don't think about it!'

I kept up my momentum and when I reached him, I grabbed him and forced him on to his knees. I put the muzzle of my gun against his head. His face was strained with fear. I grabbed his jacket collar and forced him lower so that his head was under the table.

'Crawl.' I said. He did. 'Stop. Stay there.' I turned to the door and nodded to Danny. The music was still blasting out. The Ink Spots by the sound of it. Danny grinned and took a run. He hit the door with enough force to smash it open and carry him through. I was right behind him with my gun high and looking for targets. What we saw when we crashed inside pulled us up short – and explained the noise.

It was like a scene from the Gestapo manual. A wireless was blasting from a side mantelpiece. Dead ahead, a man sat bare to the waist in a chair. His arms were tied behind him and his head lolled on his chest. Blood poured from wounds and bruises on his face and torso. A man in shirtsleeves was wiping a blade with a cloth. A second was playing with what looked like a heavy cable. They were the two men Mal had brought the other night to one of our platoon meetings. Paulus and Emmanuel. Hungarians supposedly. Irgun or Stern Gang more like.

They'd frogmarched Langefeld from the bridge. They had the solemn air of professionals practising their art. The one with glasses looked quite professorial, his Ph.D. in applied mechanics.

Mal himself was sitting to one side, slumped in a heavy armchair, rubbing his eye patch. His face was haggard and pale. He didn't seem surprised to see me.

'Ah, Brodie. You're just too late.'

I looked at the slumped man. His chest wasn't moving. I walked over to the mantelpiece and swept the wireless off it. Its cable snapped and the Bakelite smashed to fragments on the floor. Silence filled the room. I turned.

'Oh, *shit*, Malachi! What have you done?'

He stirred himself. 'I've killed a filthy Nazi, that's what. And we've learned a lot about the others. That's what I've done.' Defiance was trying to replace despair in his face. I wasn't going to help. The consequences of Langefeld's death raged through me in a mix of terror and anguish.

'Look at you. The three of you. No better than the man you've just murdered! I hope you think it's worth it. And come to that, who the hell are you two?'

I pointed my gun at the silent pair either side of the dead man. The torture professor had been edging towards a low table next to Malachi. It held three pistols.

'Oh, go for it, pal. The mood I'm in, I'd shoot you out of hand. Who are you?'

Professor moved back to be closer to his friend.

'Who are they, Mal? Where did you find them?'

Mal tried a death's head grin at me. 'They are the new Jews, Brodie. Jews that fight back. *Israelis.*'

'There's no such place. Not yet.'

Mal tapped his head. 'In here. And when we throw your troops out of our country, our nation will come alive again.'

Danny stepped forward and spoke to them in what I now realised was Hebrew. I caught only some of the words: *Irgun Zvai Leumi*.

The professor shrugged. I wasn't surprised, except by the reach of this Jewish terror brigade.

I heard the words *Ava Kaplan*. Danny frowned and swung his gun round to point at the man slumped in the chair. The exchange grew more heated. I heard words for murder and stupidity. Danny was clearly haranguing them for their brutality.

I'd had enough. 'Danny, skip it. We've no time for this.' I walked over to the table and picked up the three guns. I stuffed them in my coat pockets. 'Did you tell them about Shimon and Isaac?'

'No.'

I faced Malachi. 'They've taken my friend, Isaac Feldmann. And Shimon Belsinger. Taken them hostage.' As I said it, I thought: *And now they're going to kill them. Now they're going to kill Isaac.*

Malachi lurched forward. 'What?'

'Langefeld was living with a woman. We assume another Nazi. She got away. She and her cronies kidnapped our men. We had a phone call this morning.'

He asked, 'What do they want?' But he knew. He knew.

My voice was flat, defeated. 'You know what they want, Mal. What they *wanted*.' I nodded at the man in the chair. 'We were to deliver Langefeld – presumably breathing and in one piece – back at the bridge by six o'clock this evening.'

He glanced at his watch.

'Too late for that, Mal. Unless you're any good at resurrections.'

'Wait. Wait! We can find them. Find the others!'

'Do you have names? Addresses?' There might be some hope.

His face dropped. 'No. Not quite. Not . . .'

'Then what *did* you get? *For the lives of our friends?*'

Mal sank back in his chair and held his face in his hands. After a moment he took them away.

'He told us he was stuck here in Glasgow. Just like you said. Like Mandel. Like Dragan. They had enough gold to last for a while but were waiting for the go-ahead from their controller. He arranged for their passage to New York or Boston or sometimes straight on to South America. By plane or sometimes by boat.'

'Did he say why they were stuck?

'No.'

'Did he give the name of the controller?'

Mal shook his head.

'Did you find out where Suhren is holing up? Or any of the others? Are they together?'

He waved his hand.

'Anything? *Any* clues at all?'

'He mentioned Prestwick. But that's obvious, I guess.'

'Where do you think *you're* going?' I asked, turning my gun on the two Israeli gunmen. Both were putting on their jackets and heading to the door.

The professor spoke in English. 'We are finished here. We are going.'

'No you're bloody not!' I stood in front of him aiming at his chest.

The professor said something. Danny tensed and lowered his gun. 'Let them go, Brodie. They're no use to us.'

He was right. But I was just ready to shoot *somebody* for *something*. I nodded and dropped my gun. The two men brushed past me and were gone.

'How come you know Hebrew?' I asked.

'University of Dachau. A specialised vocabulary, mind.'

'I can imagine.'

He looked hard at me. 'I doubt it, old pal. You get a different perspective, inside.'

'What did he say, Danny? I heard them mention Ava Kaplan. Your girl.'

He looked at me with anguish. 'They know of her. He said: *If you love her, you'll let us go.*'

FIFTY-TWO

We found a phone box.

'Duncan, it's Brodie.'

'I hope you've some good news.'

'Mostly bad, some good.' I told him where to find Malachi and the dead man, and that there were two Jewish gunmen on the run. When I finished there was silence for a long moment.

'You mentioned good news? Were you lying to make me feel better?'

'We took their guns.'

'Brodie. This city's awash wi' bloody guns. If they've got cash, they'll have guns before the night's oot.'

'Any news from the kidnappers?'

'Nothing. Not a damn thing. All we can do is wait.'

I checked my watch. Two o'clock. Four hours to the deadline. I left the phone box and joined Danny. It was getting darker. The temperature was dropping and it had begun snowing again. I felt I was drowning in a rising tide of bleakness. Danny must have seen it on my face.

'There's nothing we can do about it.'

'Story of my life.'

'I'm saying it's not your fault, Douglas.'

'Does that make it better?'

'No, but you don't have to take the blame. You might as well tell it to stop snowing.'

303

For want of anything smarter to do, I called Maurice Silver and asked him to round up our gang and get them out on the frozen streets to see if they could see or hear anything. Danny set off to find Bathsheba. I trudged back to Sam's to await calls. All thought of going after Suhren and company had been pushed out of my head. All I could see was Isaac.

All I could think about was the years of friendship and comfort. After my own father had died and I'd first come up to Glasgow University, Isaac and his wife Hannah had filled a hole. I hadn't realised how large the hole was at the time, or how needy I must have appeared. In my first year studying German I'd been drawn to the babel of accents in the Gorbals. My stumbling attempts at communicating with this gruff tailor led to my first cup of coffee. Then soup. Then being gathered into his family's embrace as if I'd know them since birth.

I sat in the kitchen watching the clock arms swing round. Finally it struck six and I was left with no sensation of whether Isaac and Shimon were alive or not. Surely a wound would open in my heart if they'd killed him? I clung on to the notion that no news was good news. That it would serve no useful purpose killing either man. They were just bluffing and, having now called it, there was no point in following through with their threat.

Sam came home and I told her the situation. She took my hand and sat quietly with me.

It was nearly eight in the evening when Danny himself summoned me from a phone box. I left Sam to mind the phone in case there were any more developments and plunged out into the bleak night. It wasn't just the cold that now numbed me.

Danny and Bathsheba met me just south of the People's Palace. She had her arm in a sling. We didn't speak as they walked me down between the high banks of ploughed snow towards the St Andrew's suspension bridge that flew out across the frozen Clyde, into the Gorbals.

Ahead, Lieutenant Lionel Bloom and his five old warriors were standing on the path, smoking and stamping their feet. Their breath swirled above their swaddled heads. They nodded towards a line of footprints cutting through the high snow bank and leading a short way into the deep drifts. I followed their eyes and saw a dark bundle framed by the white. I walked towards it.

I kneeled down beside Isaac. He was flat on his back, gazing sightless at the echoing sky. The snow was trampled round about him. There was a black halo round his head where his hot blood had melted the snow. The remnants of a huge icicle lay shattered by his ear. His smart jacket and waistcoat were shredded and torn where knives had entered. To finish the job? Anger at losing Langefeld? Or just for the fun of it? I pulled the jacket over his bare chest and tried to close his eyes but they were stiff and unyielding.

I looked back at the path. Danny McRae was clasping Bathsheba to his thick coat. Under his hat-brim his eyes were filled with pity. For Isaac and perhaps also for me.

Bathsheba's face seemed twisted by sorrow and anger, as though she couldn't believe the horror of it. I certainly couldn't. For four months now I'd been chasing my own phantoms while people died around me. People I was being paid to protect. I'd been too slow or too dumb to prevent their murder. Now my friend had joined their ranks.

'Any sign of Shimon, Danny?' I called.

'He's safe though not very sound. They beat him up pretty badly then dumped him on Rabbi Silver. And before you ask, he says they wore caps, and scarves round their faces.'

'How many?'

'Three or four. And a woman.'

Some flashing lights caught my eye, back towards the People's Palace. Soon I could make out a hurrying group of policemen. As they drew closer I could see they were led by Duncan and Detective Chief Inspector Walter Sangster. They stopped in a panting group by the path and played their torches on me.

Sangster called out. 'Brodie! Get yoursel' over here and stop messing up a crime scene!'

I took a last look at my old friend, stood up and walked towards the path. Duncan just shook his head at me as I got close.

'Late as usual, Sangster,' I got in, before he started on me.

He stood in my way, his sharp eyes seething with bile. He hissed, 'I don't give a shit if you are pally with the Chief, Brodie. I've a bloody good mind to put you under arrest.'

'For what? Doing your job for you?'

'If we find a single fingerprint of yours on that body, I'll see you swing, Brodie, so help me God.'

I stepped closer, my hands coming up. Danny pressed between us and faced me. 'Come on, Douglas. Let's go. Say nothing else.'

'Oh, Christ! McRae too!' Sangster had spun Danny away from me and was nose to nose with him. 'Trouble comes in pairs. And they don't get any more troublesome than you twa! The same goes for you, McRae. If I find you've been involved in this in any way, you're for the high jump. Now, bugger off and let the real police do this properly.'

I took Danny's arm and marched him away. Bathsheba scampered after us. The others caught us up. I clasped the old lieutenant's shoulder.

'Lionel, can you get the word round the others? Tell them I want a full turn-out for him.'

'Yes, sir.' They picked up speed and by the time we'd left the park, they'd disappeared into the frozen alleys of the city.

We hauled ourselves back to Sam's house. We brought Bathsheba with us to thaw her out and to work out what to do next. Sam was home and drew us in and held me for a while when I told her about Isaac. I felt her weeping softly against my chest and didn't care about my own tears.

We hung our dismal coats and hats on the hall stand and piled down into the kitchen. I brought through some coal from the cellar and stoked the fire up on the range. We sat round its life-giving glow while steam rose from our trousers and Bathsheba's skirt. Sam pressed tea on us, and cut up some Dundee cake, another Izzie Dunlop special. The trappings of a wake.

I thought about the times I'd sat with Isaac in the back room of his shop, and how, before the war, his wife Hannah used to fuss about us and force-feed me spiced honey cake and kugel. I kept going over and over in my mind what I could have done differently. How I could have saved him. But it's hard to counter sheer malevolence. Why Isaac? Why my friend? Was he deliberately chosen because of that? In that case who would have known?

My thoughts were derailed by Sam sticking a large glass of Scotch in my hand. Danny received his like a sacrament, and drank deep. The girl wouldn't indulge but guzzled down two bowls of hot broth under the mothering attentions of her hostess. She'd been shy at first with Sam, gazing about her at the high ceilings and splendid staircase. By the fire-light, her eyes glowed like huge pools of oil. Danny couldn't take his gaze off her. Sam noticed and shared small smiles with me.

'Where do you live, Bathsheba?' Sam asked.

'Anderston.'

'With your parents?'

She shook her long dark hair. 'An aunt. Sort of. My parents didn't make it.'

'Does your aunt have a phone?'

She looked wary. 'No, but the woman in the next house does. Can I call her and say I'll be late?'

'Of course. But if you like, I'll speak to your aunt and say you're staying here tonight. I can put you up on the couch upstairs. It's far too late and far too cold to be out one second longer. Is that all right?'

Bathsheba looked panicked and shook her head. 'No, no. I couldn't put you out. And I have to get to work in the morning.'

'What do you do?'

'I'm a nurse.'

'Good for you. Now look, it really is late. If you won't stay, let's call your aunt and then a taxi.'

While they were out, I turned to Danny.

'She's lovely, Danny, and she seems pretty interested in you.'

'It wouldn't be hard to be interested in her.'

I refilled our glasses. It set Danny off again.

'Look, Dougie, about Isaac. You cannae carry his death on your shoulders. We're up against evil. We don't always win.'

'Just once would do. Lately it's been one-way traffic.'

'We're getting closer.'

'All I know is I've lost a friend. The world lost a good man. In exchange for what? A war criminal? There is a rat-line unit operating here. There is a controller, probably American, running a team who handle the human parcels. And I'm going to find them and take them apart.'

'Wait a minute! Why do you think it's a Yank we're looking for?' He looked startled, as well he might.

'Blast! Sorry. I haven't told you about my meeting with Duncan's boss this morning.'

'Sangster?'

'His spiritual boss.' I told Danny about the Archbishop's protestations of innocence. Danny's eyes grew wider.

'You believe him?'

I shrugged. 'He's an archbishop.'

'If they can lie about transubstantiating wafers into flesh, they can lie about anything.'

'Not a lie, surely. Just a belief.'

'You're too generous, Douglas. But he was right about the priests. The Germans sent them to Dachau from all over. There were a couple of thousand, maybe more. Mainly Poles. They had their own barracks and mostly didn't have to work. But they still died. About half of them, they said.'

'So Rome is hardly likely to side with the Nazis.'

'The Catholic Church is the great survivor. It bends and shifts to suit the times. Given a choice between Hitler and communism – well, I can imagine there would have been advocates in both camps.'

'Like Bishop Hudal handing out refugee papers? But Donald Campbell wasn't seduced.'

'So he says.' He held up his hand to stop my argument. 'Let's assume he's right. That there was – is – an American involved. I'm not surprised one wee bit.' I could see he was excited; his brain was running hot as he turned things over.

'What?'

'I need to tell you a wee bit more about Eve Copeland. In Berlin she tracked down a bigwig Nazi; the guy who'd killed her folks. Unfortunately the Yanks had put him in place. A stooge in a key job.'

'She killed him? Your kind of woman, Danny.'

'She didn't think so. Anyway, for that and some other stuff, they got gie upset with her. They set their new outfit on her. The Central Intelligence Agency, or CIA. Bit like MI6 but competent. And ruthless.'

'You think the CIA are involved here?'

'It has their dirty prints all over it. It's what they *do*, Douglas. Look, I've got a contact in our intelligence service. Gerry Cassells was a senior officer in SOE and got absorbed into MI6 after the war. I'll call him on Monday. MI6 have the links to the CIA.'

'Why would he help?'

'Ah, that's another wee story I haven't told you about. One of the coppers I tangled with in London ended up as liaison between the CIA, MI6 and Scotland Yard. A right bastard.'

'Dare I ask what happened to him?'

'He was murdered.'

'Please don't tell me you did it.'

'No. But I know who did and I might be able to make a trade.'

FIFTY-THREE

B y the time Sam and Bathsheba rejoined us the taxi had arrived. We saw Bathsheba into it, paid the driver in advance and waved her off. Danny wanted to go with her but she refused to put him out. We reconvened round the kitchen table, enjoying the warmth from the range and soup. I brought Sam up to date with the day's events, including my encounter with the Archbishop. But the conversation kept veering back to Isaac.

'Why him? Why such a good man?'

'He's a prominent Jew, Douglas. His synagogue is just round the corner from Carlton Place,' suggested Sam. 'Maybe they knew him? Maybe Langefeld bought a coat or something from him. Did you check his clothes? And labels?'

'Sam, it's a great thought. Like checking the woman's clothing. That could be the connection. Tenuous, but we've nothing else to go on.'

We lapsed into silence. Later, in bed, holding Sam to me, and knotted up inside, I thought about our earlier conversations and stifled the one idea that kept trying to prod its way fully into my consciousness.

Jewish law requires burials to be scheduled as soon as possible. But the next day was their Sabbath, and it wasn't until Sunday that we were able to bury Isaac. Even then it took considerable exhortation by Rabbi Silver to get the police to release his body to the family.

It was a long desolate drive out to Riddrie Cemetery. The snow lay deep against gravestones. The ground was so frozen that the gravediggers had had to build fires on the earth to break it up. Dig a foot, light a fire, dig another. When we got there the hole was ready but all round the snow was melted and the earth scorched. Though I noted from the sacking that still hung from it that they'd taken care not to harm the gravestone already in place: Hannah, beloved wife of Isaac, taken in '43 by TB.

Sam, Danny and I weren't the first. There was already a big crowd by the grave site from his synagogue and also from Garnethill. Shimon stood huge among them and nodded at me. Lionel and his men were there, ramrod straight. All they lacked were rifles for the salute. Alongside them were the rest of my platoon. Shortly, the funeral horse and cart drew up with Rabbi Silver and Isaac's family walking behind. Amos and his sister Judith led the group, supported on either side by their spouses. Walking between Amos and Judith and holding their parents' hands were two small children: Amos's daughter and Judith's son. They too linked hands. Judith also clutched a small shy girl to her shoulder. Though I hadn't seen Judith in years I recognised instantly – and with a pang – the unmistakable eyes and features of her mother. There were a dozen or so others behind them; relatives who'd also set up home here.

As instructed by Rabbi Silver, Shimon and I joined the cortège. Together with Amos and three members of the Great Synagogue congregation we shouldered the coffin and brought it gently to the graveside. We laid our light burden down by the edge of the deep rectangle, on top of three good ropes. The simple service began. I remembered Isaac's explanation and how similar it was to our Protestant service.

Amos started, "'The Lord is my shepherd; I shall not want . . .'"

The rest of us joined in the familiar psalm:

> *'He maketh me to lie down in green pastures;*
> *He leadeth me beside still waters.*
> *He restoreth my soul . . .'*

The mourners recited a blessing and Isaac's children ripped the lapels and the pockets of their clothes. The *Kriah*.

Maurice Silver talked simply and eloquently of Isaac Feldmann's life. A good life. The life of a good man. Then he led them in the recitation of the *Kaddish*.

"'Exalted and sanctified be his great name . . .'"

'Amen.'

"'In the world that in the future will be renewed . . .'"

We took up the cords again and lifted the coffin over the grave and began to lower it. It bumped and swayed and finally settled in the cold earth. We mourners took turns to tumble icy clods into the grave. With some prodding from their parents, and the passing of some objects to them, Isaac's grandchildren stepped forward. Judith's son held a tiny teddy bear and Amos's daughter a doll. They threw them on to the plain wood casket.

Finally the crowd formed a tunnel and the family walked through it taking handshakes and kisses and hugs as they departed. The *Nechama*. I held my hand out to Amos. He looked at me and nodded in just the way his father used to. His wife smiled at me from his side.

'There is nothing to stay for now, Mr Brodie.'

I glanced down at his daughter who was staring big-eyed up at me. 'Her?'

'She will eat oranges every day.' He smiled down at her, a promise made.

I nodded at the grave. 'Him?'

Amos shook his head. 'He was talking about coming too. When we got settled. Said his old bones could do with some sun.'

And now they'd never feel it. I turned to his sister. 'What about you, Judith?'

She hefted her babe to the other shoulder and touched the child's blond hair. A faint light came to Judith's cold cheeks. 'We are staying. We will look after him.' Her gaze flicked down to her son standing beside her, then up to her husband. Their blue eyes and fair colouring spoke volumes. I smiled. I shook Amos's hand and embraced Judith and they were past. For the family, the seven days of mourning – *Shiva* – would start now.

We had no time to mourn.

Sam, Danny and I drove home in silence and took strong drink, but it wasn't strong enough.

First thing Monday morning, Danny called his SIS contact, Major Gerry Cassells, from the house. It was a long call, and from the kitchen Sam and I could hear Danny's voice sometimes pleading, sometimes cajoling. He came back down.

'Right. He says he'll get back to us. It'll take a few days.'

I headed into the newsroom with little enthusiasm for turning out copy that had anything to do with Isaac. But once Eddie learned that I'd been at the heart of events, he all but threatened me with my cards unless I coughed up a front-page story for Tuesday's edition. I did, but steered it down the path of a one-off attack by an anti-Semite. I made no mention of rat lines, far less a possible American controller or a Vatican connection. For which latter omission I got a grateful call from Todd and a discreet thank-you note from St Andrew's Cathedral within hours of the paper hitting the streets.

There was also the worry that if the truth got out, the American controller would scarper. I very much wanted to confront him. Almost as much as I wanted to find Langefeld's lover and her murdering pals. Find Suhren.

By Wednesday, every newspaper had banner headlines about an anti-Semitic murder. Still no mention of the Nazis at large. I guessed Malcolm McCulloch was keeping a lid on that angle.

I'd barely got my feet under my desk when I was called to the phone. It was Danny.

'Cassells has just been on. He's got a name!'

'The American?'

'The Yank. The dirty Yank! Major David bloody Salinger, United States Air Force. He runs the supply-control unit for the Yanks at Prestwick.'

'I bet he does.'

'Shall we go?' Danny's voice was breathless, like a wee boy with a plan for mischief.

'I'm beginning to sympathise with Duncan Todd. Go? As in, just breeze in and – what exactly?' Having voiced the idea myself to Todd a few days back, I'd swung round to a more practical view of the barriers. No police warrant card. No jurisdiction over an allied military unit.

'We can't just sit on our arses, Brodie!'

'Let's talk tonight.'

That evening when I got home, Sam backed me up.

'What would you charge Salinger with, Danny?'

Danny bristled. 'War crimes, Sam. Salinger is as bad as any in your dock at Hamburg.'

'He's an ally,' she said.

'Not when he's shielding the enemy! And Salinger is a pretty German-sounding name if you ask me.'

'That's ridiculous, Danny. America is full of German stock. They've been fighting Nazism as hard as we have.'

'Fair enough. But we should still go after him.'

'What's your proof, Danny?' she persisted.

'Major Gerry Cassells, SIS, says so. And if you'll recall, so does the Archbishop of Glasgow!'

'Would you get either of them in the witness stand?'

Danny shrugged. I took over again.

'OK, what *do* we do? Tell the police? I could have a word with McCulloch. But what would *he* do? It's not in his jurisdiction. Get him to phone the local PC in Monkton and ask him to pop along on his bike to the airport and arrest the top brass?'

'What about your pal in MI5?' asked Danny.

'Actually I was wondering why Sillitoe wouldn't know already, if your man in SIS knows?'

'MI5 handles the local British action. SIS – or MI6 – covers the foreign stuff. Cassells explained it all to me.'

'They don't share information?'

'Not if it lost them an edge. Seems they'd rather share with the Russians than each other. It's all about budgets, Brodie.'

'So, should I tell Sillitoe or not?'

Sam said, 'Why not?'

Danny agreed.

'Fine,' I said, 'but that might not get us anywhere. We still have this woman on the loose. And we know she's not alone.'

'In the meantime,' said Danny, 'can I just remind you that you're a bloody half-colonel. Use your authority! Why don't we just visit Major Salinger and shake his tree a bit.' He had that light in his eyes again. But his comments stung. As they were meant to. He knew I preferred action to reflection. I made one last half-hearted attempt.

'That sounds like a crystal-clear objective. How will we know his tree has been shaken?'

'If a Nazi drops out?' he replied with a grin. 'And may I suggest, *Colonel*, if we are heading down to Prestwick, you press your uniform?'

'Only if you give back my gun.'

FIFTY-FOUR

We set off early next day. I decided to postpone calling Sillitoe until after we'd seen Salinger. I'd have more to tell him. And he might have tried to stop me. It wasn't a repeat of the journey Sam and I had taken – so long ago it now seemed. There was no staff car picking us up at Sam's house and whisking us to the airport. No military driver to salute and help us on board.

Partly this was because we weren't heading there in an official capacity. Partly because the direct route over the Fenwick Moors from Glasgow to Prestwick via Kilmarnock was under ten feet of drifting snow. We could have borrowed Sam's car and gone round the coastal route via Greenock, but it would have taken all day and there was some doubt about the link between Greenock south to Ardrossan.

We took the train. Snowploughs had reopened the Glasgow–Paisley route two days ago and it would take us on down through Beith and Dalry, then over to the coastal track through Irvine, Troon and into Monkton. It was a five-minute taxi ride from there to the airport.

Danny and I sat opposite each other in the overheated carriage.

'I like the outfit, Brodie. Less fussy than either of our Highland kit.'

'It still feels strange. Especially knowing that the last man who wore it is dead.'

'Any bullet holes?'

'He'd have been in combat gear.'

'Are those his medals?' He pointed at the ribbons on my chest.

'No. Mine.'

Danny whistled. 'How did you get the MC?'

'A long story.' I paused. 'Actually it's a short one. We were pinned down for days outside Caen. I threw a tantrum and charged a tank.'

He grinned. 'And there's me thinking you were always the cool head.'

'I have my moments.'

We could have changed at Irvine and caught the train across to my home town of Kilmarnock, but there was no time. Besides, my mother would have had a heart attack. We reached Monkton by one o'clock and got a ride in the local taxi that plied between the station and the airport. The only part of the journey that became familiar was stopping at the gatehouse to the military part of the airport. But this time no one was expecting me. I wound the window down as the RAF Regiment guy stepped forward.

'Lieutenant Colonel Brodie for Major David Salinger.'

'Sir!'

His arm shot up. I returned the smart salute as best I could in the back of the Austin 10.

He looked at his watch. 'Straight over to the officers' mess, sir. You should find the major still at lunch.' He pointed at a low brick building which ran along the airfield perimeter. It would house staff offices too, I guessed. We drove over, pulled up, I paid the driver and we walked into the building. A white-jacketed, white-gloved catering corps sergeant was passing.

'Two for lunch, sir?'

'Yes, thanks, Sergeant. We're also looking for Major Salinger.'

'He's just finished, sir. He's taking coffee in the bar. Do you want to see him before or after lunch?'

'I think after, don't you, Captain McRae?'

Danny's eyes widened at my use of his old rank. 'Sounds good to me, *sir*.'

We handed over my cap and Danny's hat and coat. We entered the dining room, which had pretensions to be an officers' mess room but looked merely like the inside of a Nissen hut with cloth-covered tables. But the food was good and we scoffed the lot. A waiter took my name for the visitors' book, assuming I would be signing for it against some travel chit. We didn't drop the pretence. The sergeant came up at the end of the meal.

'I mentioned to Major Salinger that you hoped to see him, sir. He's still in the bar if you'd like to join him?'

'Perfect, Sergeant. Please lead the way.'

We grabbed our headgear and Danny's coat on the way. It was nearly two o'clock. The bar was empty apart from one officer in USAF uniform. He was bald and wore rimless specs. He got up as we entered and came towards us, smiling, with his hand out.

'Colonel, I'm David Salinger. Welcome to Prestwick.'

'Thanks, Major. This isn't my first time.' We shook.

'You've transited through here before?'

'A few times. Last time, three weeks ago. Coming back from Hamburg.' I didn't enlighten him about my earlier trips. Once on a borrowed bike and umpteen times on the Troon train with my bucket and spade for a day at the beach. 'Can I introduce Captain Daniel McRae, formerly Scots Guards and SOE?'

Did I see Salinger's eyes flicker at the mention of the SOE? They shook hands.

'Shall we sit down, gentlemen? How about some coffee? It's from Cuba.' He leaned over the table and pushed a box towards us. 'As are the cigars. Can I offer you one?'

'Coffee, yes please. But it's too early in the day for cigars. Thanks.'

We exchanged small talk until the coffee was brought and we were left alone.

'Now then. How can I help, gentlemen?'

I gave it a beat, then, 'We want to talk about your escape route for Nazis.'

His cup didn't tip, didn't even clatter. He eased it back from his mouth and carefully placed it on the saucer. Then, just as carefully, he placed them on the table.

'Forgive me, Colonel. I don't know what you're talking about.' He smiled indulgently.

I smiled back. 'Let me help. I mentioned Hamburg. I was there for the Ravensbrück trials. The Nazi trials. Some of the Nazis were missing. They'd escaped through *Rattenlinien* – rat lines that run through Prestwick Airport.'

He laughed. 'I'm sorry, Colonel, I've never heard of these – what do you call 'em? – rat lines?'

'How about Vatican letters of transit? Ever heard of Bishop Alois Hudal? Cardinal Tisserant?'

'I have no idea what you're talking about, Colonel. Is this a joke? Am I being set up by my buddies?'

'No joke, I assure you. Do the following names sound familiar: Suhren, Langefeld, Mandel, Draganski . . .'

As I reeled them off, Salinger sat in the armchair, his fingers together in points, the eyes behind the glasses staring at me unblinking. I came to a halt and waited.

He shook his head. 'Nope, nothing. What do you want, Colonel?'

'Do you read the papers, Major?'

'*New York Times.*' His voice had gone soft.

'I'm sure you'll have glanced at the local headlines in Scotland. At the end of last week a man was kidnapped and murdered. Not just a man; a good man. A dear friend of mine. His body was found on Glasgow Green. What the papers didn't say was that it was in retaliation for the killing of one of your Nazis by a Jewish hit team. Ring any bells?'

His eyes didn't blink behind his smart specs. He asked again, even softer this time: 'What do you want, Colonel?'

'We want to know where to find Sturmbannführer Fritz Suhren, former commandant of Ravensbrück. We want the names and whereabouts of the other Nazis at large including Hauptsturmführer Langefeld's lover. And when we have all that, we want to rip up this end of the rat line. No more Nazis heading off to a sweet life in South America. Not through *my* country.'

He was silent for a long moment; then he pulled himself up in his chair. His voice strengthened. 'Who sent you? Who are you working for?'

'If you'd answer some of my questions, I might answer yours.'

Danny cut in. 'Tell us, Major, can you be in the CIA and a serving officer at the same time?'

He peered at us slowly though his glasses. Then he got up. 'Gentlemen, I think we're done here. If you'll excuse me, I have work to do.'

Danny was also on his feet. And pointing a gun at Salinger. Sam's Webley looked huge in his hand.

'Now that's veeery stupid,' said the Major.

'No, what's very stupid is not answering our questions,' said Danny, settling his stance and supporting his gun hand with his left. His voice had the ring of calm certainty of the slightly deranged. From Salinger's viewpoint the gun would look like a small cannon. For the first time, Salinger's façade cracked a little.

Danny continued: 'You see this scar, Major? I earned it in France. From the Gestapo. They made it worse during my sabbatical in Dachau. And here's the thing: after I got back they gave me months of psychiatric treatment. Because I used to do crazy things. *Apparently*.' He shrugged. 'I don't recall *every* silly wee thing I did. But I know it included shooting the man who framed me for murder. Funnily enough,' he mused, 'he was a major too. British Army. But hie, I'm not choosy.'

Salinger's eyes were growing wider. I decided to help things along.

'I'm afraid it's all true, Major. Captain McRae is as controllable as a bucket of frogs. Crazy enough to shoot his old boss. Crazy enough to shoot an American officer who was helping Nazis use his country as a staging post.' I sighed. 'If he's caught, McRae will just get hospitalised for a while then let out again. Mad as a hatter. But my kind of mad. The choice is yours. Sit down and talk or get a bullet in the head.'

'Not the head, Colonel. I wouldnae start there,' said Danny, pointing his gun lower.

I looked at him, and then turned to the major and shrugged as if to say, *What can you do with a lunatic?*

The major was gulping and I could see a sheen of sweat form on his lip and forehead. He swallowed and found his voice. It was less certain now.

'This is such a big mistake. You guys have no idea what you're doing.'

'The mistake would be yours. We know what we're doing. We want to know what *you're* doing.'

He thought for a moment and nodded. We took our seats again and he began to talk. Danny encouraged him by keeping his gun trained on his gut. Salinger confirmed what we knew, or guessed. That he'd been seconded to the CIA to perform this service.

'This order came from the top, Colonel. And I mean the top. That means your government knows all about it, don't you think?'

I feared he was right. 'Keep going.'

He knew it sounded bad but it was pragmatism at work. Didn't we realise who the new enemy was? Didn't we hear

Churchill's iron curtain slamming down across Europe? We'd seen how the Commies had fought: mercilessly and with zero regard for their own casualties. The West was next.

'Hell, you English fought the French a dozen times. Now you're allies.'

'We're not English,' Danny interrupted.

'OK, OK, you Scots fight alongside the English and the Irish, for God's sake. What does it matter? This is the here and now!' He jabbed the arm of his chair for emphasis.

'Why did the conveyor stop?'

'Excuse me?'

'Last year. The rat line got stuck.'

He shrugged. 'Change of policy. You know how that goes.'

'Tell me.'

'My predecessor wasn't doing enough – how shall we put it? – sifting.'

'Any old Nazi got through?'

'That kinda thing. We decided we should be a bit more selective.'

'Useful Nazis, as opposed to plain old sadistic murderers.'

'Broadly.'

'How many got a home run before this change in policy?'

'Before I came on board, about a dozen.'

'But you let another batch get this far.'

He looked pained. 'Not our idea. The guy on the continent just dumped them on us.'

'How many in the second batch?'

'Eight, I guess.'

'You guess? You don't seem to be giving this your full attention, Major. Let's drop all the moral arguments. What we're dealing with here is murder. Some of the guys in *your* team have committed murder on our soil. We want them in custody. And if you have had any hand in the business we want you in custody too.'

'Wait a minute. Just a goddamn minute! You can't touch

me. My government would come down on yours like a ton of shit. You Limeys won't know what hit you—'

'Spare us the threats, Salinger. We can account for three of the second batch of eight: Mandel, Draganski and Langefeld. All three dead. Correct?

'If you say.'

'We also know three of the names of SS officers from the delayed batch: Fritz Suhren, Rudolf Gebhardt, Siegfried Fischer. Are those correct?'

'Could be.'

'Could? Let's assume so. We want their local identities. And where we can find them. That leaves two unnamed women. We want them identified and located. Help us and we'll leave you alone. I'll put the word up the line and let my government handle you any way they want to.'

'Why the hell should I?'

I nodded towards Danny who was playing with the gun in his lap. 'Maybe I'll just leave you two alone for a while. See what transpires.'

Danny looked up and grinned. It wasn't a nice grin.

Salinger said, 'All right. I can give you details. But they're back in my office.'

'Where's your office?'

'Just along the corridor. Next building.'

Danny and I looked at each other. Was he bluffing? Playing for time? Luring us into a trap? Maybe all of the above.

'Let's go,' I said. 'Captain McRae, please walk behind us with your gun under your coat.'

We walked through the officers' mess and into a long corridor. We passed open rooms and offices, and as we walked we got deeper and deeper into what seemed to be American territory. The uniforms were US Army or Air Force. The salutes came thick and fast. And somewhere in that progress, Salinger must have given a signal. We stopped outside an office with his name and title on the glass panel.

'Here we are, gentlemen.'

He turned the handle and walked in. We followed and found two US Marine rifles sticking in our ribs.

FIFTY-FIVE

ehind us were running steps and shouts. More rifles and
pistols were jammed in our backs.

Salinger called out: 'Take their weapons and cuff them.'

A US Marine sergeant asked, 'Sir! Please, sir! This one's a
senior British officer. Cuff him too?'

'Cuff him, Sergeant. I have reason to believe he's imper-
sonating an officer. Take them both down to the brig and lock
them up. We'll do some checking of their credentials.'

He stood in front of me. 'You don't get it, do you? This is
World War Three, fellas. Time to choose sides.' He turned to
his sergeant. 'Take them away.'

We had a hard bed each. And one toilet and basin. We sat
facing each other, heads in hands.

'You're going to have to stop pulling a gun on people.'

'It works.'

'Unless they have more guns than you.'

'True, Brodie, true.'

'You *are* bloody mad, you know.'

'I thought you were overdoing that point, frankly.'

'Not nearly enough.'

The hours drifted by. Meals were brought to us, and tea,
but no one came to ask us questions. We shouted at the
guards to bring the most senior British officer at the airport.
Or to allow us one phone call. But nothing. We were simply

ignored. They were well trained. We made ourselves as comfortable as possible on the bunk beds and eventually drifted off to sleep.

The clanging of the cell door shot me upright.

'Colonel Brodie. Mr McRae. You can go now.'

A fresh-faced USAF lieutenant was standing at the cell door. He was holding it open. Danny and I struggled to our feet. I felt like death. Danny looked like it. I walked over to the sink and slunged some water on my face, feeling the coarse bristles grate and scratch. I wet my hair and brushed it back with my hands. While I was putting on my uniform shirt and tie, and lacing my shoes, Danny went through the same performance. Unshaven, but with some semblance of smartness, we walked out of the cell into the harsh corridor lights. We followed the lieutenant. As we passed our Marine captors I looked for some remorse in their faces but saw only blankness. But that's Marines for you.

We were taken back to Salinger's office. He wasn't there. Sam was. She had the long-suffering look of a mother whose kids had gone off the rails again. Summoned to the local nick to get another ticking off from the desk sergeant.

'Morning, *gentlemen*. Do you know I've been up half the night worried about you? I've been moving heaven and earth – not to mention several tons of snow – to find you?'

'Sam, I'm sorry. It got – we got—'

'Waylaid? That's for sure.'

'Where's Salinger?'

Sam looked behind us at the young officer.

'Sir! Major Salinger took the evening flight.'

'To where?'

'London, sir. Our embassy. He'll be there by now.'

I faced Sam. 'How did you get us out?'

'In case it slipped your mind, *Colonel* Brodie, I'm an advocate. I phoned the Procurator Fiscal at five o'clock. He was very grumpy. But he made some calls. And I phoned Iain. He's ahead of us in Hamburg. The wires have been buzzing between him and certain government departments. Anyway, strings were pulled and here you are. Here *we* are. I hope it was worth it?'

'Let's get out of here and we'll talk. How did you get here?'

'I drove. The coast route. It's just been opened.'

'Good grief, Sam. In the dark? With the snow and ice?'

'I'm not a daft wee lassie, Brodie.'

'No, you're not, Samantha Campbell. No, you're not. Shall we go?'

She'd had enough driving and put me behind the wheel with Danny bundled in the back. We headed straight north, following the Ayrshire coast up through Irvine, Saltcoats and Ardrossan. The sea churned grey and white on our left, dashing itself in spume and spray on the black rocks. Our windscreen blades kept sticking with the weight of new snow, and we had to get out and clear them.

'Do you think summer will ever return, Sam?'

'Nup. This is it. We've been bad and God is punishing us.'

I told her how little we'd got from Salinger and what a wasted journey we'd all had.

'It's not a waste, Brodie. You've just got rid of the controller of this end of the Scottish rat line. He's been hauled off to London. He won't be back. How can you dismiss that?'

'He's out of our reach now. That's how. And we know little more about who his local operators are or how to find them.'

We fell out of the car at Sam's, groaning with stiffness. The house was a cold shell and the three of us huddled in our coats until we'd got a fire going in the kitchen. We took turns thawing out limbs in front of it while sipping hot toddies.

Later, I was sitting on my bed, wrapped in my quilt, thinking through the consequences of my actions. I had no doubt the wires would be buzzing between Whitehall and

Washington. I was probably facing a court martial for threatening an allied officer.

Sam slipped in to join me. She took a side of the quilt and we huddled together. It was a timely moment.

'Sam, you know what a cynical, suspicious old sod I can be?'

'Only too well. In my experience, it's what gets you into – and out of – trouble.'

'Right then, hear me out and then I'll ask you to do a couple of things for me. Unless you think I've completely lost my bearings . . . or my marbles.'

FIFTY-SIX

Saturday morning began with racing engines, banging car doors and shouting. It didn't sound like a neighbourhood party. When I looked at my watch, it said six o'clock. Sam had gone back to her own room.

The sounds were somehow familiar. As I dragged myself up and over to the window, banging started on the front door. I keeked out to see a police car and two canvas-topped lorries slewed across the snow-clad road and soldiers running forward and taking up positions. American soldiers. Four went down on their knees, rifles to their shoulders, aiming at our front door and windows. They saw me and instantly raised their aim. Several wore MPs' helmets, the rest were Marines. The banging got louder, and then a loudhailer started up. The voice was American.

'Colonel Douglas Brodie, you will come out with your hands up. We are acting under orders from your government.'

There was a pause and another voice took over. I knew it.

'You heard, Brodie. Come out before they come in for you. No guns.'

I pulled back the curtains and threw up the window. I stuck my head out. 'Sangster, if you don't shut up, I'll call the police and get them to remove you for disturbing the peace.'

'Oh aye, very funny, Brodie. But you'll no' be laughing in a minute when I send these boys in. By the way, there's more of them roon' the back.'

'This is total bullshit, Sangster. American troops have no right whatsoever to be threatening British citizens. Whose authority?' Just then another black uniform walked forward.

'That would be *my* authority, Colonel,' said Chief Constable Malcolm McCulloch.

I gazed down at him, wondering whom I could trust any more. 'I thought we were on the same side, Malcolm? OK, here's what'll happen. You will give me, Miss Campbell and Mr McRae ten minutes to get dressed. Then we will invite you, Chief Constable, to join us for a wee chat so we can sort out what seems to be a gross misunderstanding.'

McCulloch joined the American officer – a lieutenant of Marines – and together with Sangster had a heated conversation.

McCulloch turned and looked up at me. 'Brodie, you have no idea how serious this is. We will give you *five* minutes; then you will open the door and let me and Lieutenant Osborne here come in. We will be joined by two armed Marines. We know you have guns. If there is any sign of you using them, the Marines are ordered to open fire. Is that clear?'

'Ten minutes and we'll put the kettle on.'

He paused for a beat, looking over to the Marine officer. He nodded. Reluctantly.

'Ten minutes. No tricks or, as sure as I'm standing here, these boys will come in shooting. Is that clear?'

Behind me, I could hear doors banging; then Sam and Danny burst into my room. I leaned out the window and called out, 'Clear.'

I slammed the window down and turned to the ashen-faced Sam and the red-faced McRae.

'This must be about Salinger. Let's get dressed and find out. Sam, is there someone you can call? Someone very senior?' She nodded.

'Danny, if you so much as think about drawing a gun I will personally blow your head off. Are we clear?' He nodded.

They dispersed to their rooms. I dressed hurriedly. In the circumstance I thought I might as well meet uniform with uniform and pulled on my khaki. I put my .38 in my bedside table and unclipped my holster to show it was empty. I met the other two in the hall. Sam was on the phone, talking fast. She finished. I glanced at my watch. One minute to go.

'I got the Procurator Fiscal. Again. He and I used to get on like a house on fire. Until two days ago. Nevertheless he's on his way. I don't know if he's more angry with you or the Americans.'

'Well done, Sam. Shall we meet in the dining room?'

They nodded and I started unbolting the door. The guns and uniforms were waiting. I stepped forward and stood foursquare on the doorstep. I stared straight at the bull-necked young Marine officer whose pistol pointed at my stomach.

'Lieutenant Osborne. Don't you normally salute a senior officer?' Before he could react, I turned to McCulloch. 'Chief Constable, if you'd like to follow me, the owner of this house, *Advocate* Samantha Campbell, will receive you in the dining room. Mr McRae and Miss Campbell are already waiting for you. Wipe your feet. This had better be good, gentlemen.'

The lieutenant was red-faced with the internal conflict between saluting me or shooting me. I simply turned smartly on my heel and marched down the hall towards the dining room, feeling my shoulders twitching. Behind, there was a scuffling, then a rush of footsteps. The lieutenant ordered his men to take up position in the hall. The door was open and Danny and Sam were standing at the far end of the table, near the window. I walked over and joined them. We faced the visitors. McCulloch came in first, followed by the officer, then Sangster. Two armed Marines crowded at the door, unsure of where to point their weapons.

'Lieutenant, please note I am unarmed.' I showed him my empty holster. 'Can you please lower your weapons and ask your men to step back into the hall? We can then sit and have a civilised discussion.' I waited. The officer's jaw clenched so tight I thought it would snap.

'Oh, for God's sake, Lieutenant, put your guns away,' said McCulloch.

'Sir, no, sir! Due respect, sir! I have orders to search the house.'

Sam walked round the table and faced the young officer. She had on her icy-cool face. I almost felt sorry for the boy.

'Lieutenant, this is *my* house. You are on private property. In Scotland, not Tennessee. Please put your gun down.'

Slowly, under her unswerving blue gaze, he lowered his gun to his side.

'Thank you. Now, before you move another inch, I want to see warrants and written orders from someone very senior indeed. Preferably with a royal seal. I've already summoned the Glasgow Procurator Fiscal. He'll be here shortly. As you should know, Chief Constable – assuming you've got the right house – I am a member of the Faculty of Advocates in Scotland. Unless I get a sensible explanation – from *one of you* – in the next thirty seconds, I will have you and your armed guard here in front of a high court judge before you can say Liberty Bell.'

The Chief Constable had his cap off and was looking decidedly pale. 'Miss Campbell, my apologies. Let's sit down and we'll explain. Lieutenant, just take a seat and stop huffing and puffing, will you?'

We all sat. Sam waved her hand regally across the table at the men. 'Chief Constable?'

He pointed across the table at me and Danny. 'These two men – Colonel Douglas Brodie and Mr Daniel McRae – attempted to kidnap an American major at Prestwick Airport two days ago. Is that correct?'

'Kidnap is a bit strong, Chief Constable,' I responded. 'We were drinking coffee in the officers' mess, having a wee chat with the major about escaped Nazis and such stuff. Along the lines of my private conversations with you.'

McCulloch's lips thinned. 'One of you drew a gun, I believe? You tried to coerce the major into some form of admission.'

'Is that reason enough for a re-enactment of D-Day?' I said.

He shook his head. 'That's something for later debate. It's not why we're here.'

'Can you get to the point, please?' Sam said.

'Major Salinger had you arrested and imprisoned overnight. He then took the last flight from Prestwick to London.'

'That's what we were told,' I said.

'Major Salinger was abducted in London yesterday morning.'

FIFTY-SEVEN

'**O**h God,' I said. 'How? Where?'

'From a flat used by visiting senior officers and embassy officials.'

'And you think he's *here*?' Sam demanded. 'That's why you wanted to search my house? Are you completely daft, Chief Constable?'

'Sir! Permission to search the house, sir!' The lieutenant's Pavlovian response made us all stare at him.

'Oh, shut up, Osborne!' said McCulloch. 'Do you really think Miss Campbell is hiding your missing major under her bed?'

We all waited for the lieutenant to reply. I thought he might burst.

'Don't know for sure, sir. Just following orders, sir.'

Sam got to her feet. There was a scramble by all the men to get to theirs.

'Lieutenant, I admire your persistence. You must follow orders. Even if they're silly. So you have my permission to go and look under my bed. In fact, all our beds. Apologies in advance for the stoor. It's my housekeeper's day off.'

The lieutenant's mighty jaw was working overtime. I wondered if he thought *stoor* could be dangerous, as if Sam had booby-trapped the beds instead of merely failing to dust them. He looked at the Chief Constable and then back at Sam, racked with indecision, afraid if he left the room the Limeys would gang up on him. She waved the backs of both hands at him.

'Off you go. And take your nice soldiers with you.' She pointed at Sangster, who flinched. 'I'd like you to go with them, Chief Inspector, to make sure they don't stick bayonets into my feather pillows.' Sam sat back down. 'Now then, Chief Constable, tell us all the details, and we'll see if we can help.'

The lieutenant gave a smart salute to the room in general, made a heel-clicking about-turn and started shouting orders at his men. Sangster rose to his feet, grabbed his cap and went after them. They set off up the stairs, shouting as they went, watching out for stoor. Sam abandoned her serene air.

'Malcolm, I am going to have you nailed to the door of the high court for this. That circus outside my house at this time on a Saturday morning? That was simply unnecessary and I won't stand for it. Every neighbour for miles around will have dived back into their air-raid shelter. What a fuss! Now, tell us everything, and make your case well.'

The Chief Constable ran his finger round his choking collar and explained. After Salinger had had us arrested he'd phoned his embassy and told them he needed to visit urgently. He'd flown down that night, and stayed at the embassy flats nearby. Yesterday, as Danny and I were being let out of the Prestwick military nick, Salinger was walking round to the embassy for a nine o'clock meeting when he was coshed and bundled into a Harrods van. According to two passers-by, it was driven off at high speed. It wasn't deranged customer service by the store; the van had been stolen earlier. It was found abandoned at Regent's Park later in the morning. There had been no sign of Salinger since.

Sam heard McCulloch out and, before I could make the same point, said: 'Malcolm, I think you'll accept that Douglas and Danny have a cast-iron alibi for their whereabouts yesterday morning at the time of the kidnap.'

McCulloch was hating this. He knew he was on a hiding to nothing.

'Miss Campbell, of course I accept your argument. But I had no choice this morning. This came down from the Home Secretary's office, via MI6 and the Scottish Secretary. In person. I have to play along. Follow orders.'

'You sound as hidebound as Osborne! But he's got an excuse. He's a US Marine.'

McCulloch swelled. 'You do realise this is a major international incident? And that it's surely stretching coincidence to have Major Salinger threatened one day by Brodie and McRae, and being abducted the next. At the very least there's a connection!'

I cut in. 'Malcolm, while the Neanderthals are upstairs kicking up dust, can I just confirm you're aware that Major Salinger is the local controller of the Scottish rat line? He's the one you and I have been after for weeks now.'

'I was told you'd say that, Brodie. The Secretary of State was told you don't have proof.'

'Has he spoken to Sillitoe? Have you?' Then I remembered I hadn't called Sillitoe. Blast. Did he know?

McCulloch shook his head. 'As you can imagine, I've not had much time between getting shouted at by two government ministers and having the US Marine Corps banging on *my* front door at four in the morning.'

'You want proof? I'd start with a word – a quiet word – with Donald Campbell. Aye, him, the Archbishop of Glasgow.'

McCulloch wiped the deepening lines on his brow.

'Then call Sillitoe and say MI6, his sister service, is keeping information from him about the CIA. The Americans are running operations in Scotland to give their pet Nazis a second life in South America.'

Just then, Sangster and the Marines arrived.

McCulloch asked, 'Well, Lieutenant, did you find anyone?'

'No sign, sir. But I found these.' He reached forward and put my service revolver and Sam's father's Webley on the table. He reached behind and was handed the two beautiful

Dickson shotguns. He looked like a bulldog who was expecting a pat on the head for fetching some sticks.

'That's my service revolver, Lieutenant. The one that fits this empty holster. That belongs to the British Army. I'll take it now.'

'And those are my father's guns,' said Sam. 'If you've broken into my gun cupboard to get them, I will bring charges against the US Army of breaking and entering, and theft. Now put them down!'

'I can't do that, ma'am. I had orders to secure all weapons.'

'To steal? I think not. Put them down,' she said in that quiet, steely courtroom manner that cut the legs off hostile witnesses.

I backed her. 'Lieutenant, you're off your base under civilian orders. That means the Chief Constable here. You've searched the house, found nothing, so you can now report back to your senior officers you've successfully completed your mission. Put the shotguns and my handgun on the table and leave.'

'Oh, for God's sake, do it,' ordered McCulloch.

In the grey light of a soggy dawn we waved the whole pack of them off and retired to the kitchen. I undid my tunic. Tea was made and poured. It was barely seven o'clock but it felt like midday.

'Poor bloody Salinger,' said Danny. There wasn't much sympathy in his voice.

'Think it's Irgun again?' I asked.

'Racing cert, don't you think?'

'How the hell would they know?' I asked. 'I mean, how would they know it was Salinger, and how would they know where he was?'

'I'm betting Langefeld told Malachi and the two Irgun guys more than Mal told us,' said Danny.

'Could be. But even if they had a name, how would they know he'd gone to London?'

'Maybe they hung about Prestwick? Maybe they were watching the US embassy in London once they had a name? These guys are good. The King David bombing was well planned.'

'I might give Duncan a call. Find out where they're keeping Malachi. Suggest they have a word with him about Langefeld. About what they forced from him.'

'Oh, bugger!' said Sam. 'Douglas, didn't I tell you? Malachi's got his first hearing on Monday.'

'Do you think we should go?'

'I've no choice.'

'Why?'

'He asked me if I'd represent him.'

'You can't! You're – I don't know – involved.' I struggled to get my head round the mess.'

'No, I'm not. You are. I'm going to have to call you – and Danny – as a witness.'

'This is madness, Sam. I'm going back to bed. It's clear I'm in the middle of nightmare. Maybe if I lie down I'll wake up and this morning will all have been a terrible dream. Ouch! What did you pinch me for?'

'You're awake.'

FIFTY-EIGHT

I t seemed all the more important that I spoke to Duncan Todd. He wasn't surprised to hear from me. I got him at his home late morning. I was happy to interrupt his day off.

'I shouldnae even be speaking to you,' he said.

'You knew we were going to be raided this morning by your boss and his boss and half the US Marine Corps?'

'Ah heard about it half an hour ago. The station called me. You boys sure know how to cause a fuss.'

'*Us?* We were just following leads, Duncan. And as you'll recall, you and *his grace* gave us one of our strongest ones. So don't play the bloody innocent with me, old pal.'

'Fair enough, Brodie. But it's no' roses around the station either. They say Sangster is having his tenth fit of the day. Ah don't think he likes an early rise.'

'Neither do I! McCulloch must have known it was a wild-goose chase, Duncan. We were four hundred miles away from Salinger when they took him.'

'Right enough, Brodie. But it's hard to think when you've got half the government shouting doon the phone at you in the middle o' the night. And you can see there might be a connection between you and the galloping major.'

The weekend drifted by in a haze of fruitless conjecture and sleep catch-up. I planned to get down to the court early on Monday, wondering what charges would be brought against

Malachi Herzog. Abducting a Nazi? Torturing a Nazi? Murdering a Nazi? And did it matter if he was a Nazi or not? Was it still a crime regardless of the moral depravity of the kidnapped, tortured and murdered? Of course. But . . .

On Monday morning I called into the newsroom to let Eddie know what was happening and to suggest he hold the front page for Tuesday. I made it round to the Sheriff Court at nine thirty. Sam had gone on ahead of me. The hearing would be at ten. I was loitering with a fag in my mouth outside the courtroom when I heard the police wagon arrive. Soon a pair of policemen marched Malachi along the corridor towards me. Mal was handcuffed and the police were either side of him, holding his upper arm.

Suddenly the structured scene dissolved. At first I wasn't sure what was happening. Two figures crashed out of the toilets. They wore flat caps and scarves round their mouths. Each was swinging a pickaxe handle. Simultaneously a second pair of masked men dashed in from the corridor behind Malachi. The two police stood no chance. They barely had time to shield their heads with their arms before they were clubbed down without mercy by the first two at the scene. I spun my fag away and started running towards them, wishing I had a gun. The two others had grabbed Malachi and were dragging him backwards on his heels like a bag of coal. Mal saw me running towards him and shouted, 'Help, Brodie! Help!'

The two who'd felled the police turned to face me and began to raise their weapons. I hit the one on the left in a tackle that would have stirred the crowd at Murrayfield. We went down in a welter of flailing arms, legs and club. Then the second pickaxe handle entered the fray. It took me across the shoulder and side of my head. I fell off the man I'd pinned down and rolled as far and fast as my dazed head would let me. I was lucky. Man number two didn't follow through with the brain strike. He would have killed me.

As I struggled to my hands and knees I was dimly aware of the pair of them running away. Other voices were now taking up the cry. I was helped to my feet by a policeman.

'Where did they go? Did you see?' I shouted at him.

'Down there, sir.' He pointed to a corridor off left.

I felt at my head. My hand came away bloody.

'Come on, Constable.' I lurched off in the direction he'd pointed. He grabbed me back.

'Sir, sir! They could be armed. Leave this to the police.'

'Well, get after them, man!'

'There's four of them. I need reinforcements. They could be armed!'

'For fuck's sake, Officer, don't be such a jessie!' I wrenched my arm free and staggered off round the corner after them. The corridor stretched a hundred yards. There was no sign of anyone. Then, about three-quarters of the way along, a door burst open and the four men broke out. They looked towards me and then ran in the opposite direction. I must have looked tough.

The constable caught up with me. 'That's the back way out, sir!'

Shit. They'd got away. But they hadn't got Malachi. I ran down the corridor and skidded to a halt at the door of the Gents' toilet. It was still swinging on its hinges.

I pushed at it and went in. I could at least soak my head in cold water. But I lost interest in that when I saw Mal. His tongue was sticking out, as though he was saying *boo*. But his one good eye was bulging. And his toes were two feet off the ground. A rope went up and over a pipe near the ceiling. One end was tethered to a handrail by the urinals. The other was round Mal's neck. By the time we'd got him down it was way too late. They'd broken his neck with the first yank on the rope.

I stuck my head in the basin and let the blood flow down the drain. Someone handed me a towel. I looked up into the mirror. Sam stared back at me.

'The Nazi brigade or the Jewish terrorist boys?'

'Hell, Sam, pick a card. It could be the CIA, MI6 or the Norman Conks for all I know. But at least you've got the rest of the day off.'

I got a lift to the infirmary from one of Duncan's men in a squad car. They put half a dozen stiches in my scalp, scalded me with iodine, gave me a handful of aspirin and pushed me out. I went back to the newsroom with a very different story to tell. I didn't know where to start with the Salinger piece so I didn't. It was still too hot a potato. But I had an eye-witness scoop at this morning's debacle in the Sheriff Court.

I tugged the draft column out of my typewriter just as Elaine came to my desk. Elaine had taken over secretarial duties for me. Morag no longer felt it necessary to brandish her engagement ring at me now she'd converted intent into substance. In fairness she'd been gushingly grateful at getting my congratulatory telegram. All the way from Hamburg.

'You've got a woman on the line. Says it's your *landlady*.' She made it sound like a clandestine call from my secret lover demanding an afternoon assignation. Which would be nice. Unlikely, but nice.

I handed her my draft column and picked up the phone. 'Samantha?'

'Meet me at Kelvingrove Art Gallery.'

'Now?'

'Right now, Douglas. I've got news.'

I splashed through the slush until I could get to the tram-line. I took the top deck and sat gazing out of the window at the melting city around me. Rivers coursed down the streets. Mini-icebergs blocked the gutters. The blackened ramparts lining the pavements were dissolving.

Were these our worldly sins flushing down the streets? Was that our conscience thawing? Our remorse awakening?

Was there a huge tidal wave of guilt and contrition about to break over Blythswood Hill and carry us all into the Clyde and then out to sea, to cleanse our sins and renew the cycle?

Or was it just concussion?

I got off at the gallery and walked up the steps into the great gaudy hall. Sam was sitting on a bench waiting for me. She saw me coming and gave a little smile, but it was half-hearted and tentative. I guessed that she had nothing to smile about. That she'd carried out the mission I'd given her and the news was bad. I sat beside her and took her right hand and squeezed it. Her left held a piece of paper.

'You had the day off, Sam. You should have put your feet up.'

'Your mistrust was well founded, Douglas.'

'You found her house?'

She shook her head. 'I found *a* house. It's not the one Danny knows.'

'The tenements in Anderston?'

'That's the address he gave the taxi driver the other night.'

'But?'

'Before we called the taxi, she phoned her aunt's neighbour to pass on the message not to worry. I noted the number. It wasn't deliberate. Numbers just stick with me. I called it this morning and spoke to a woman. Said I had the number but had forgotten the address. She said a man had called with the same problem. Anyway it's not in Anderston; it's further over, in Finnieston. I went round there. Quite a smart building. Three floors, each with two flats. The neighbour with the phone was very helpful. She pointed upstairs to where the aunt lives. But she said no one had been home for days.'

'No one? Neither her nor her niece?'

'Just said there was only one woman living there, though she was rarely there. Her niece sometimes rang to speak to her. Sometimes the niece stayed the night.'

'Did the neighbour describe this *aunt*?'

'An English lady, she thought. Neat. Middle-aged. Very polite.' Sam shook her head. 'I knocked on the door and waited a while. Nothing. So I went round to the house Danny knows in Anderston. Rougher place. I just started knocking on doors. I got two neighbours at home. Old gossips.'

'Lovely. I like gossips.'

'They confirmed a girl used the flat. The description fits. They knew her as Miss Goldstein. A nurse, they said, though they'd not seen the uniform. She lived alone, but was often not there. They speculated that she was some sort of fancy woman. That a man rented the place and it was for romantic dalliances.'

'Any sign of this man?'

Sam smiled ruefully. 'A couple of times. They described seeing a red-haired man with a big scar on his head. But they were disappointed to report he never stayed the night.'

'Danny getting about, eh? So we have two houses, with Bathsheba and her aunt flitting between. But who is Bathsheba?'

'That's what I'm coming to. I got this telegram from Iain today.' She handed me the paper.

I smoothed the crumpled yellow sheet on the bench and read the pencilled words: 'Records Ravensbrück camp show one Bathsheba Goldstein stop 48-year-old Jewess from Vienna stop Admitted camp 25 June 1943 died typhus 12 January 1945 stop Hope helps stop Iain Scrymgeour'.

I looked up. 'Who is she?'

'And what do we say to Danny?'

We walked up the steep streets to Sam's house. We tried out theory after theory but none of them made sense. Or rather, only one made sense and it was too gut-churning to articulate until we'd tried all the others.

'Is it really such an unusual name, do you think?' Sam suggested.

'I have no idea. But you'd need strong-minded parents to call your daughter after the woman who enticed King David to murder his favourite general.'

'Giving her the benefit of the doubt, does her story work? Could she have been lying low in Paris through the war? You took French at Glasgow as well as German.'

'I never tried French on her. Never any need.'

'But she got herself shot while facing that Nazi woman, Mandel. That puts her on our side, doesn't it?'

'She spoke Polish to her, Sam. I don't know what they said. Then Mandel killed herself with a cyanide pill. Where did she get it?'

'Good God. Are you saying *she* gave it to her, Douglas?'

'I'm not closing off any idea.'

'Your boys spotted Langefeld in the crowd. I thought he got the pill to Mandel?'

'We don't know. The question is: how did he know to be there? Who told him?'

'But why would she get so involved with you and Shimon Belsinger? Oh, I see . . .'

'It's the perfect place to hide. Right in front of us. And it means she could see exactly what was going on.'

'And tell the others?'

'One of whom was Langefeld. Another is this *aunt* of hers.'

We were silent for a while as we zigzagged our way up the steepness of Park Street. We got our breath back on the flat at the top of the terrace and looked out over the park. Patches of grey-green were being uncovered at the top of the great white hollow. The trees were now bare and wet. Was it conceivable that they'd leaf? That the world would come back from the dead?

Sam quietly asked, 'So you think it was her?' She knew what had been drumming through my mind for days.

'Someone knew how much Isaac meant to me. Someone tried to use that – use *him* and Shimon – to get me to free

347

Langefeld. It points to someone in the Jewish platoon. It could have been any one of them.'

'But it would have been simpler to have warned Lange-feld.'

I nodded. 'I told the boys the night before the ambush. Everyone who was there knew about it. All they had to do was contact Langefeld that night and we'd have lost him.'

'Bathsheba wasn't there.'

'No, she wasn't.'

FIFTY-NINE

Sam was wearing galoshes but the slush and blocked gutters and pockets of deep snow had got over the tops and inside. My leather shoes might as well have been cardboard. We poured the water out at the door and squelched into the hall. Danny's coat and hat were hanging up, dripping. His outdoor shoes were sitting in a pool of water under the coat rack. We looked at each other, knowing we couldn't duck this moment.

Sam called out, 'Danny. We're home.'

There was silence for a moment, then: 'I'm down here,' from the kitchen.

Sam and I stripped off our outer clothes and padded down. She pushed open the door and said a quiet 'Oh' before I followed her in.

Danny was sitting at the table. In front of him was a mug and a gun. Opposite him sat Bathsheba. Her mouth was gagged. Her eyes were huge and appealing. Her arms seemed to be restrained behind her.

'Come in, come in. The kettle's no' long boiled,' he said. He pushed the Webley towards me. 'Here you go, Brodie. Keep an eye on her and I'll make some more tea.'

'Danny, what the hell . . .?' started Sam.

'Oh, do I need to explain? I'm sure you smart pair are already in the know. The lovely Bathsheba here is playing for the other side. Aren't you, hen?'

Bathsheba made mewling noises and shook her head at us.

Sam and I slid into seats facing the girl.

'Tell us, Danny. Tell us what you know,' I asked.

He clattered the kettle on to the ring and lit the gas. He turned back to us.

'It's my modest nature, Brodie. I'm not the prettiest boy in town, especially with this side parting. And I was just always a bit surprised at this lovely wee burd throwing herself at me.'

'Hardly grounds for tying her up and poking a gun at her.'

'Agreed. It was a couple of other things. In Dachau, as you ken, I picked up some German, some Hebrew and Yiddish. But there were a lot of Poles about, including all yon Polish priests the Archbishop of Glasgow mentioned to you.'

'So you know Polish?'

'I have a few words. Enough.'

I looked at the girl. 'What did she say to Warden Mandel?'

'I didn't get everything. But outside the door, this lady here seemed to be asking Mandel to trust her. That it would be all right. Then Mandel fired the shotgun. When we got inside, Mandel accused her of being after her gold. Like *Klaus*. Presumably Klaus Langefeld. This one said she was being stupid. That Mandel was going to be tortured and hanged. Mandel said the same would happen to her. She would see to it. That's when our girl here slapped her.'

'You could interpret it differently,' I said. 'She could just have been following our line, but a bit more enthusiastically.'

'Possible. That's what I thought at first. But then we find Mandel takes a pill or is given a pill and, boom, she's gone. And Langefeld is skulking about the scene. We have a story that fits.'

'Tell us.'

'Mandel was spending too much, throwing her gold around. Imperilling the rest of them and the network. Langefeld tried to stop her. That was the argument the old boy said he overheard. Girly here is on Langefeld's side and chooses not to warn Mandel we were coming. She was happy for Mandel to get taken and planned to make sure she didn't talk. She didn't expect the shotgun. Which is why she skelped Mandel. When she had her in a clinch, she probably convinced Mandel that a cyanide pill was preferable to swinging from a rope. She would have slipped it into her blouse when they were rolling around the floor.'

'That's a lot of speculation, Danny. Anything else?'

Danny filled the teapot with tea leaves and then boiling water. He hefted the still steaming kettle, as though he was minded to pour it over the girl's head. She was watching it, panic-eyed.

'Lots. She was the only one of our gang that wasn't at the meeting that night, the day Mandel got taken. So she didn't know her pal Langefeld had been spotted. So she couldn't warn him.'

He put the kettle down. Bathsheba – or whatever her name was – quietened. She sat staring at Danny with furious eyes as though she could torch him into silence with her gaze.

Danny went on. 'The first time she knew about it was when I met her that morning, wasn't it, darlin'? There's a café in Anderston we've met in before. She was there that morning. Stupid old me told her what we were planning. She was shocked. She said how worried she was for me. How dangerous it was. Now I know why she was shocked. She tried to get to Langefeld's flat to warn him, but it was too late. He'd already gone off for his haircut. But it gave her enough time, didn't it?'

Sam asked, 'Enough time for what?'

'To clear out her own papers,' he replied.

'She was Langefeld's woman?' Sam said.

Danny smiled. 'Exactly. Christ, I'm such an eejit. I took her round to the flat in Anderston a couple of times. Even met her there once. By arrangement with her. But it was really a cover. Her wee love nest was in Carlton Close. Wasn't it, *liebchen?*'

'How do you know for sure, Danny?'

'Because you and I waited all bloody night for the mystery woman to show at the flat, and she never did. How did she know? Because stupid me telt her, that morning.'

Our gaze was drawn back to her. Her eyes had filled as Danny had been piling up the case. Now they overflowed. Soulful beauty is a powerful weapon. It would have softened the hardest heart. Normally. Danny supped his tea.

'Spare us, sweetheart. You're for the high jump.'

'In the meantime, Danny, what about this so-called aunt?' I asked. 'Any ideas?'

He shook his head. 'Nup. I called her number and went round there.'

'So I heard. I must have just missed you,' said Sam.

'No sign of auntie. As you've found out too. Shall we summon Duncan? Ask him to bring a warrant to knock down auntie's door?' he said.

'Certainly. And tell him to bring some handcuffs.' I nodded at the girl. 'Have you found out her real name? Sam, tell him what you found about the real Bathsheba Goldstein.'

'She was a Jewess from Vienna. Aged forty-eight. They took her to Ravensbrück. She died early in '45.'

'But her identity seems to have escaped.' I looked at the woman who'd called herself Bathsheba. 'Were you one of the kindly nurses working in the camp, I wonder?'

She said nothing, just stared at me, her face streaked, her eyes red.

'Can we take the gag off, Danny?'

'Help yourself. Watch she doesn't bite.'

I walked round and untied the dishtowel that was tight round her head. She spluttered and shook her long dark hair. I wanted to stroke it. I wanted to throttle her. I wanted to

walk out and get some fresh air. I sat down next to her, noting
that both wrists were tied to the chair back.

'Bastards!' she spat. 'Bloody bastards!' Then switched to a
stream of German invective that would have got me a clip
round the ear back in university. I let her rant for a minute
or two without even slapping her. Finally she stopped, chest
heaving.

'Did you arrange the murder of Malachi? What's your
name?' I asked.

This time she did spit. I lifted my hand. She flinched.

'Brodie!' said Sam. 'Don't! You'll get nothing from her.'

It was too easy to get into the habit of slapping Nazi
women. I was already ashamed of myself for even thinking of
doing it. Even for Isaac. Especially for gentle Isaac. I lowered
my arm and got up.

'I'll call Duncan. Then we discuss next steps.'

SIXTY

Duncan was round in ten minutes, bell clanging on his squad car. The neighbours would be getting a petition up.

I briefed him in the hall and he sent two uniforms down to bring up the girl. The struggle had gone out of her, but her look of sheer malevolence required no words. Duncan charged her with enough crimes to see her hanged and sent the car off without him. We went back down to the kitchen together and took stock with Sam and Danny.

'That was very nearly a decent piece of detective work, boys. Some of my teaching stuck after all.'

'Is this you taking the credit again, Duncan?' I asked. 'You've already had one promotion out of me.'

'Can ye no' take a compliment, Brodie? Anyway, was she pretending to be a nurse here?'

'That's the one thing that checks,' said Danny. 'She claimed to be working at the Glasgow Cancer Hospital. I phoned them. They do have a Nurse Bathsheba Goldstein on the books.'

'My God, Danny! Do you know where that is?' asked Sam, beating me to it.

He looked puzzled. 'If I did, I've forgotten.'

'It's on Hill Street. Opposite the Garnethill synagogue.'

It was cause enough to break out the whisky. To help us think. The four of us reconvened in the lounge with full tumblers and shortbread to soak it up.

Duncan started. 'Was it just coincidence, do you think? The hospital opposite the synagogue?'

'What would she have gained by arranging it that way?' Danny asked.

'Hiding in the open, surely. She stole the identity of a real person, like Draganski. Remember Dragan? When she got here, with a name like Bathsheba, it was better to hide among the Jewish community,' I suggested.

'Joining your hunting party, Douglas, was deliberate,' said Sam.

'Risky but smart. It meant they were always one step ahead of us. They were stuck here and must have felt the net closing. With Salinger out of action, the escape route is truly cut off. Caged rats.'

'Is that why they killed Malachi, do ye think?' asked Duncan. 'What else did he learn from torturing Langefeld? Did he get more names? An address? Did he find out about Salinger?'

We sat quietly sipping our Scotch and digesting the options.

'Let's agree what we do know,' I said. 'A man like Malachi attracts a lot of enemies. Mal was either murdered for what he knew or what he did. Revenge for Langefeld? We don't know if the four men who snatched him were the same crew that kidnapped Shimon and Isaac. Or if they were Nazi runaways or members of Irgun.'

'You've got ma heid spinnin', Brodie. Why would Jewish terrorists do him in?' asked Duncan. 'I thought he was on their side?'

'I think Mal did get more out of Langefeld. A pointer to Suhren, their king rat? Irgun seem to want Suhren as badly as we do. They didn't want Mal blabbing about it to the authorities before they get hold of him. But it could have been some other gang with a grudge.'

'Och, don't tell me there's another crew of bampots out there, Brodie. Somebody we huvnae heard of yet.'

'A good cop keeps an open mind, Duncan. That's what you taught us,' I went on. 'We also know there's another woman out there. Bathsheba's – or rather the woman we thought was Bathsheba – her "aunt". Is she a Nazi on the run? Or just a helpful local? Is she the Leith contact point?'

Duncan was holding his head in his hands at the thought of the spreading ripples. I lobbed another stone in his pond.

'We need to find her before they restart the rat line.'

'Or there's another death,' added Sam.

'Christ!' Duncan muttered.

A little later, when both the whisky and the shortbread ran out, we drew lots. Danny and Duncan lost out and were sent off into the damp night on a sacred mission. Within the hour they returned triumphant, with four fish suppers and two bottles of Bell's. We tucked in.

Much later, we poured Duncan into a squad car that he'd summoned. *A wee perk o' the job, lads.* The rest of us went to our separate rooms for separate nights of troubled dreams.

For penance in the morning I should have done an extra ten lengths at the Western. But it was still closed. In lieu, I filled my stomach with four oblongs of grilled Ulster Fry in a floury bap. The result was I felt much better when I reached my desk than I had any right to. The good feelings didn't last long. Eddie lounged over the filing cabinet holding a long streamer of tickertape in one hand.

'This just came in, Brodie. Seems your Jewish pals are holding this Yank. Threatening to shoot him unless . . .'

'Unless what, Eddie?'

'They didnae say. In fact it seems that's what the *unless* is aboot. They will reveal *something* unless the Americans stop doing whatever it is they huvnae revealed. If you follow. Any guesses?' He looked at me knowingly.

'Oh, yes, Eddie. I can guess.'

'Can we run wi' it? Or are you going tae go all secret agent on me?'

I got up and stood behind my chair to think better. Eddie waited. I came to a decision.

'Can we do an evening edition, Eddie?'

His eyes gleamed just like the old Eddie's. 'Is it that good, Brodie?'

'It's big. Big as it gets. Give me an hour.'

It took three drafts with much blue-pencilling from both Eddie and Sandy Logan to get the words right. There were also calls upstairs to let the directors know what we were doing and to get their permission to run a special. They wanted to see a draft first. Then they wanted to see me.

Eddie and I were ushered into the boardroom on the fifth floor for a hastily convened meeting. I found myself facing Alec Gillespie, the Chief Executive, across the table. Four of his fellow directors lined the sides of the dark oak table. The smoke from two pipes and three cigarettes made the air opaque.

'Mr Brodie,' asked Gillespie. 'Is this true?' He waved my draft article.

'Yes, sir.'

'You're really saying that there are escaped Nazis living in Glasgow, and that they've been behind the spate of murders in the Jewish community? And' – he looked down – 'this operation has been run by the United States military out of Prestwick Airport?'

'Yes, sir.'

'Hell's teeth, man. Can you prove this?'

'If you mean, can I table evidence that would stand up in court, I doubt it. The question is, can the government *dis*prove it?'

Gillespie tapped his fingers on the table while he thought. Then he reached out and pulled the snake of tickertape towards him.

'And this American major who's been kidnapped, he was running the show here? This is what the terrorists are threatening to reveal?'

'I believe so, sir.'

'What happens if we run this?'

'To Major Salinger? We can't be sure. But if we don't, we can be pretty certain that the Americans will refuse to agree to the kidnappers' demands. They will never admit they're helping some Nazis escape while they're busy hanging others in Nuremberg. Whereas if *we* disclose it, the Jews will get part of what they want and they might release Salinger unharmed.'

'But the Americans will deny it and our government will get it in the neck. Then *we'll* get it in the neck.'

One of the other directors – Hamilton, I think – leaned across the table.

'Alec, we're a newspaper. This is news. Big news. We cannae miss this chance.'

Gillespie looked round the table. He got nods from the three others. A smile lit his face. He looked as though he'd been waiting for this moment all his days.

'Mr Paton, don't just stand there, roll the presses!'

SIXTY-ONE

We didn't have enough material in the main article to publish a full paper. We got a couple of other journalists to knock out some fillers on the weather and sport. And we always had a spare couple of cartoon strips for such an eventuality. But I sat with Sandy and concocted a chain of linked columns that traced the pattern of events since the first inkling of something dark happening. We reminded the readers of the various murders and how we could now reveal their connections. We flung in some photos from my SS scrapbook and tossed around some lurid headlines.

I wrote about the goings on at Prestwick Airport. How it had been taken over by the Americans and how it was being used as a staging post for Nazi war criminals to swan out of the country and on to a nice life in the free world. I considered presenting Salinger's arguments about combating the rise of communism to see what reaction we'd get, but then I realised I knew what the man on the Govan tram would say. *Whit? Are ye aff yer heid? We jist fought a bloody war against they bastards. An' noo ye want to be pals wi' them? Away tae hell . . .*

The end result was a ten-pager whose front page ran under the banner 'NAZIS AMONG US'.

By six o'clock the paper-sellers were calling out the latest from every street corner in Glasgow: *Latest, latest, read all about it! Nazi gang in Glasgow! Nazi murderers in Glasgow! Special edition! Read all about it!*

And they did . . .

I was exhausted by the time I got home clutching a copy of the special. But Sam had beaten me to it. She was in the lounge, sipping tea, the paper folded on the side table beside her.

'Do you think this was wise?' She pointed at the paper. 'I mean, aren't you going to get shouted at by – oh, let me think – everybody? It's already on the wireless.'

'Sticks and stones.'

'It's the stones that worry me. Not to mention the knives and guns.'

'Samantha, I'm fed up being on the back foot. Let's see what reactions we get.'

The phone rang. We smiled at each other.

'That'll be for you,' we said together.

I broke first.

I went down to the hall and picked up the phone.

'Colonel Brodie, please hold the line.'

Oh, God. Still a colonel then.

Then: 'Brodie? It's Percy Sillitoe.'

'Sir.'

'Have you any idea how upset our best friends are?'

'No, sir.'

'This is at Foreign Sec level, Brodie. They are – *we* are, it is only fair to say – pissed off at the very highest level. Especially my sister service.'

'Sorry to hear that, sir.'

'You should have consulted me before telling the world that the Americans are protecting former Nazis.'

'You would have stopped me.'

'Damn right I would.' Then his voice dropped. 'So I'm glad you didn't.'

'Sir?'

His voice lost its hectoring tone. 'You're a man after my

own heart, Brodie. Act first, apologise afterwards. That's how I cleaned up Glasgow in the thirties. With your help. And *your* bravado has got a result. MI6 has coughed up a name, Brodie. Along with their heart's blood and spleen. Bloody games they play. Anyway, we have a name and details of the top Nazi that Salinger was trying to get out of the country.'

'Suhren, I presume, but why are the Americans helping?'

'On the one hand they can openly and publicly deny their role in helping Nazi war criminals escape. They will want you to withdraw your outrageous claims. But at the same time they can quietly tell the kidnappers you have the person they want and get Major Salinger back.'

'But I don't.'

'Well, it's time you did, isn't it? And I have news for you. It's not Suhren.'

'What!'

'Apparently the former commandant of Ravensbrück missed the cut. The Yanks changed their mind about letting him through. He had nothing they wanted.'

My brain did a flip. 'But Suhren came here. He left Cuxhaven for Leith about a year ago.'

'He did, but the Americans were already reviewing policy. Re-assessing criteria, shall we say. Hence the pause in the conveyor belt. Suhren's arrival simply confirmed their doubts. His skills – running a concentration camp, for God's sake – were not required in the New World. And the man was a loose cannon. Wanted the emperor treatment. Fine food, wines, brandy. Wouldn't lie low. Quite delusional.'

'Fits with Odette Sansom's description. Where is he now?'

'Sailed away under his own steam. They think he found his way to France.'

'Damn! So who *is* the chief rat? One of the other medics? Rudolf Gebhardt? Siegfried Fischer?'

'Neither. I'm afraid they both caught a ride to the Americas.'

'Useful Nazis?'

'Apparently. They did some interesting research into eugenics and how to survive dips in the North Sea.'

I was struggling to take it in. 'So who's left?'

'The mystery woman. The one you call Auntie.'

'Name?'

'Dr Herta Kellerman. She was a senior doctor at Auschwitz and, before that, Ravensbrück, where she trained. You'll have a photo and full details first thing in the morning. I have a courier on his way.'

'I assume she was no angel of mercy?'

'Hardly. She carried out experiments on wounds. You would know how easily wounds go septic on the battlefield.'

I surely did. I'd seen more than my share of men weeping as they were hauled away to have a leg or arm amputated a few days after a minor shrapnel wound. If they were lucky.

'What did she do?'

'Experimented with a stuff called sulphanilamide. Seemed to have some success with it. Huge potential.'

'We used sulfa. So did the Yanks. Poured it over everything. But it was hit and miss. We lost thousands of fighting men from minor wounds that went bad.'

'You can see why our friends across the water were interested.'

'So she was testing this stuff on the German soldiers?' It was a stupid question. I knew the answer but just didn't want to hear it.

'Not on their own troops, Brodie. The good doctor tested it on the camp inmates. Injected them with spores of tetanus and gangrene. And just to make certain, cut them open and filled the wounds with dirt and glass and metal. To simulate a battlefield injury. Then she waited till the rot set in and tried to arrest it with varying amounts and forms of sulphanilamide.'

'Good God!'

'No, he wasn't. Not in the camps, Brodie. You know that.'

I felt a bubble rise in my chest. My heart was hammering. Not again. Not now. I focused on what he told me. Concentrated on the next steps.

'So Salinger was lying. They restarted the rat line for the select few. Why didn't Kellerman get passed on to the Americas?'

'We don't know. The Yanks didn't say.'

'Why don't the Yanks go get her themselves?'

'Because they don't want to have anything to do with her. Not after your newspaper revelations. As I said, they're going to deny everything.'

'Well then, we can call on Malcolm McCulloch and his merry men.'

'Brodie, you can't sidestep this. We don't want a hue and cry. Any more than we have already. *You* need to find her. Bring her in.'

'Where do I start? Where is she now? Does she have a new name?'

'At this stage all I know is she's still calling herself doctor. More details in the morning.'

'She's practising?' I felt the last piece click sickeningly into place.

'Apparently. The Glasgow Cancer Hospital.'

Of course. 'Did she bring a colleague with her? From the camp?'

'Oh, yes. The woman you handed over to McCulloch? Bathsheba something? Seems she was her assistant. Real name Martha Haake, a nurse at the camp.'

'Salinger knew all this. He was playing with me. Did our American friends tell you about the others? The ones who murdered Isaac Feldmann, kidnapped Belsinger? Who hanged Malachi? Are they the same team?'

'They knew nothing, I'm afraid, Brodie.'

'But likely to be armed. At least with pickaxe handles.'

'You should assume so. And because of that, Brodie, I'm giving you authority to arm up to six of the men in this ragtag army of yours. Do any of them know how to handle weapons?'

'I know just the ones, sir. Where will I get the arms?'

'McCulloch. I'm calling him now. Good luck, Colonel.'

SIXTY-TWO

I stood for a long time in the hall, long enough for Sam to poke her head out the lounge door and ask if I was all right. It jolted me out of my bleak reverie.

'That was Sillitoe.'

'Did he shout at you?'

'Funnily enough, no. We have a name. I think the phrase is: *the game's afoot.* I'll be up in a tick. I need to make a call.'

I was hanging up when Danny came in. I joined Sam in the lounge and waited till Danny was with us to tell them about Sillitoe's call.

Danny was galvanised. 'This is it, Douglas! Let's go!'

'Go where, Danny? It's ten o'clock at night.'

'The hospital, of course.' He was on his feet and pacing.

'She will be long gone. She must be the woman living at the flat in Finnieston. And she hasn't been seen since we uncovered Bathsheba – sorry, *Haake*. Besides, we're waiting for a photo and more details from Sillitoe in the morning.'

'There's no harm in ruling out the hospital where . . . where Haake worked.' His face twisted. He'd shown little emotion other than anger over Bathsheba. I wondered how he was really taking it?

Sam said, 'Douglas is right, Danny. It'll keep till the morning. And what about these others? The four who killed Isaac and Malachi. Same four? Who are they? Where are they? Are they standing guard round this woman?'

'On that last point, Sillitoe's authorised me to arm some of our team. I've asked them to meet me here first thing. Then we'll do some planning.'

I slept badly and woke early when I heard the letterbox snap and something hit the wood floor of the hall. I went down to retrieve it and sat in the kitchen studying the papers and the photo. The door opened and Sam came in wearing her dressing gown.

'Tell me,' she said.

'She's got a passport in the name of Dr Heather Coleman. Funny how people don't want to get too far from their own name. Before the war, she did her medical training in Berlin and then four years at Imperial College and at Guy's Hospital in London. Native German speaker but also Polish, French and, of course, from her stint in London, fluent in English.'

'And now working in a cancer hospital. *Our* cancer hospital.'

'Here she is.' I slid the photo across to her. It showed an attractive woman in her forties. Dark brown curls and dark eyes. Smiling, good teeth. A woman you could pass in the street and say good morning to, confident you were dealing with someone who shared your standards and beliefs. A good citizen with a nice friendly name. A chameleon. A werewolf.

We got dressed and waited for the day to start up. By now, with all the door-crashing and kettle-whistling and wireless-hissing, Danny would be up and about. In fact, he was usually about long before this. Sam took a cup of tea up to knock on his door. She came back down with it, her face full of concern.

'He's not there, Douglas. His bed hasn't been slept in.'

I punched the table. 'The eejit! He couldn't wait. Had to go out and check the hospital.'

'And the gun is gone. The Webley.'

'The *bloody* eejit. Well, he either found her or, more likely, failed to find her. Either way he should be back before long. Let's get some toast.'

Danny wasn't back by seven thirty. I tucked my service pistol in my coat pocket and headed out for a rendezvous at Central Division with six old warriors.

They were waiting for me as I marched up. All six of them. Three threw away their fags as I approached. Former lieutenant Lionel Bloom came to attention and threw a smart salute, which was fine, as he was wearing a Glengarry. So were the others. It was the only bit of uniform they'd managed to muster. For combat tunics they'd substituted donkey jackets with good leather shoulder and elbow patches.

They would do. Would have to do. We might be facing four armed men, ready to defend Kellerman to the death. And with Danny gone off half-cocked who the hell knew what had been stirred up?

'Good morning, Lionel, gentlemen. Let's get you fixed up.' I entered the station and found Duncan leaning against the counter chatting to the desk sergeant, and holding a sheet of paper.

'Well, if it isnae Colonel Bogey and the Home Guard.'

'I thought Sillitoe would assign someone competent to help me. Oh, well, Duncan, shall we get going?'

The desk sergeant led the way, followed by Duncan and me.

'Can Ah jist say, Brodie, this is the stupidest order Ah've ever been given.' He waved the paper at me.

'McCulloch?'

'Sillitoe to McCulloch to Sangster to me. Are you really gonnae gie these guys guns? They're peching just keeping up wi' us. Ah cannae see them belting aboot in a shoot-out. Far less hand-to-hand combat.'

'They at least know which end the bullet comes out and how to point them. These guys were going over the top at

Ypres when you and I were in our prams. Don't knock them, Duncan.'

We walked down a rabbit warren and eventually came to the small police armoury. The sergeant opened the heavy metal door and Duncan and I walked inside. It was a small room with a table and one wall filled with police Webleys and a handful of shotguns, two of which had their barrels shortened.

'These don't look standard issue.'

'Confiscated.'

I chose the two sawn-offs and four revolvers. 'Lionel? Can you send your men in one by one, please.'

The sergeant issued a weapon to each plus a box of bullets or shotgun cartridges. Each man signed for his arms and seemed immediately familiar with their weapon.

I had them line up outside the armoury door.

'Gentlemen, I don't want to see these weapons on display. We don't want to scare the public. Can you please find somewhere to tuck them out of sight. I'd put the revolvers inside your donkey jackets or down the back of your trousers. Keep mind, the Webleys don't have safety catches. Don't blow your bums off.'

The two men with shotguns looked for help.

'Inside your jackets, gents. There should be enough room in your poacher's pocket.'

They grinned and tucked them away out of sight. Duncan stood shaking his head and muttering, 'Bloody daft, so it is. Bloody daft.'

I ignored him. But he had a point.

'Let's go, boys.'

SIXTY-THREE

Other than an extra 9,994 men, the Grand old Duke of York had nothing on me and my donkey-jacketed army. I marched them up and marched them down the Glasgow streets, and then finally up Garnethill. En route I explained to Lionel and David Doctorow, his old sergeant, what was happening and what I planned. They in turn made sure the others knew their roles.

I passed round the photo of Kellerman so they all knew who to look out for. I warned them about the four men who'd raided the Sheriff Court with the sole aim of shutting up poor Malachi, for good. I had no idea who they were or why they'd done it. Nor did I know if they were armed or not. If they were Kellerman's protection team they could be waiting for us at the hospital.

At the top of Hill Street there was a good bit of wheezing around me and I gave them five minutes to have a smoke and get their breath back. Ahead and on the left was the synagogue, its windows glittering in the morning sun that filtered through the rain clouds. Directly opposite and ironically close stood the long low sandstone building of the cancer hospital. There was no sign of Danny. What the hell was he up to? *Where* was he?

We moved forward, me in front and by myself, Lionel and two of his men on the left pavement and the other three led by Doctorow on the right. I had no sense of an ambush in place. But then, despite what Roy Rogers or Dick Tracy may have us think, you never do with the best-set ones.

I deployed my men at either corner of the hospital and marched straight up the short driveway and into the reception hall. I smiled at the lady behind the desk.

'I wonder if you can help me? I'm looking for Dr Heather Coleman.'

Her sweet young face brightened up. 'Dr Heather? Oh, she's one of our favourites. Always such a smile.' She lowered her voice. 'They say she's brilliant.'

'That's interesting. Why do they say that?'

'She's that good with the patients. And an awfie good surgeon. Anyway, everyone seems to be looking for her today. You've just missed her.'

'Who? I mean who was looking for her and where is she now?'

'Let me see.' She looked at her reception book. 'A Mr McRae. He asked for a Dr Herta Kellerman. I said he must be confused. He must mean Dr Heather Coleman. She was due in about eight for the day shift.'

'But you say I've just missed them?'

'He waited over there and spoke to her when she came in. Ah didnae hear what was said but it looked like a wee bit of an argument.'

'Then what?'

'Next thing, him and the doctor are heading out the door.'

'Thanks, lass. You've been a great help.'

I darted for the door. For a moment I couldn't think where to start looking. They could be anywhere. Holed up in Glasgow? Trying to leave it? Why?

I called Lionel over. 'Get your men. Split them up and have them cover the main stations and the passenger terminal down at the docks. See if there's a ship leaving this morning. You're looking for Danny McRae and the woman.'

'She was still here?'

'*Was* is the word, Lionel. We just missed her. I'm heading back to Miss Campbell's. Call me there with any information. Go!'

Lionel rounded up his lads and set off at the double. I turned right and began striding downhill. My brain was racing. Why was Kellerman still around? Didn't she know her pals had been taken? What the hell was Danny up to? Would he shoot her out of hand? Was he still angry over Bathsheba? Had he had a relapse? God, I hoped not. He was my example, my hope.

Back home I waited for news, pacing the hall. The call came just before noon.

'It's Lionel Bloom, sir. I'm at Central Station. They're on the London train. We spotted McRae and the woman in the crowd, then lost them. But we caught sight of them heading down platform nine just before they closed the gate.'

'What time does it get into London?'

'Seven o'clock tonight. Euston.'

'No sign of the other four?'

'Nothing, sir.'

I hung up and stood thinking and calculating. The simplest thing would be to phone Sillitoe and arrange a reception. But Danny's behaviour had thrown me. Was he losing his mind again? And what did it foretell for me? I needed to confront him. Personally.

Sillitoe told me I could call for any help I needed. Anything. I did.

SIXTY-FOUR

There were trains every half-hour to Kilmarnock. By one thirty I was being dropped at Prestwick Airport by the local taxi firm. The Dakota was waiting for me, engine running. We landed at RAF Hendon just after four and I was sitting in Euston Station supping a bowl of soup by five. All the time in the world. For thinking.

Euston. Back where I started, a year ago. Dragged north to Glasgow to try to save an old pal from a hanging. It was how I'd met his advocate, Samantha Campbell. Met and fell for a hard-to-live-with, independent lady with troubles of her own. Lately I'd begun to think the feelings were reciprocated. But did we have any future? She was a career girl and I was back in the army. Seconded to MI5, for God's sake, moonlighting from my job as a reporter on the *Glasgow Gazette*.

Meantime my old buddy and alter ego had appeared like a ghost at my own funeral to draw me back from my dalliance with the shades. He'd talked about his own mental battles and how he'd overcome them. Had he just lost the fight? Or had he been more in love than he said with the girl who called herself Bathsheba? It was a terrible twist. Had it derailed him?

If he hadn't gone doolally, what the hell was he up to? Trying to gain kudos for delivering Kellerman? But to whom? Was it somehow linked to the murder of Malachi? What secrets did Malachi have? Why was he silenced? Punished, *pour encourager les autres*? Who were the *others* in this context? Was it the protective ring round Dr Kellerman? Or some fresh trouble I couldn't even think of? My brain seethed.

On the whole it's best not to have time to think.

I was waiting by the barrier as the train pulled up in a huge belch of steam and a final convulsive tug from the giant brakes. I was part concealed by the welcoming crowd and I had my hat down on my brow and my coat collar up.

I saw the pair of them amidst the arriving throng, McRae holding her tightly by the arm. She was smaller than I expected. Petite even, dark-eyed, quite pretty. Not at all like a fiend who carried out medical experiments on prisoners.

But then I froze. Just behind, flanking the happy couple, walked two men. Their eyes glanced left and right, front and back. I saw the glint of glasses and knew it was the professor and his silent pal. The two Jewish terrorists who'd tortured Langefeld to death at Malachi's bidding. Irgun Zvai Leumi.

My mind reeled. Then I understood. They had a gun on Danny. They'd been waiting for him at the hospital. That made brutal sense. I reached inside my pocket and fingered the cold steel of my own weapon. I wasn't going to lose out again to this pair. But this was no place for a shoot-out. Maybe I could create a diversion so Danny could break loose?

I withdrew further into the shadows, running through the permutations, trying to work out my best tactic. I'd had a long-enough flight and nearly two hours of waiting at the station to think of a plan. I'd squandered it all, gambling on a spur-of-the-moment idea to hit me when I was faced with the situation on the ground. I hadn't bargained on Irgun and two captives.

They were getting close. Soon they'd sweep past. I abandoned subtlety and took the full-frontal approach. I strode forward, head down, and straight into the slight figure of Dr Herta Kellerman.

I hit her with my left shoulder with enough force to carry her backwards and out of Danny's clutches. She was light enough to be ripped off her feet. I had my left arm round her waist and her head buried in my chest so that it would look like a passionate embrace, taken to extreme. I kept going in this wild tango, punching a hole between the two startled Irgun agents and then through the onrushing crowd.

I said to her in German, 'If you value your life, Frau Doktor Kellerman, don't scream, just hang on.'

I felt her gasp and then her arms came up to clutch my shoulders as she hung on for dear life. We'd made ten yards before I heard the shouts behind me. I swept to the right and burst into the ladies' waiting room. It was empty. I dropped her on her feet, dragged her to the far end and pushed her behind me. We were cornered but at least they couldn't get behind me. I drew my gun.

'Hold me!' I shouted and turned to face the music, gun levelled on the door.

The two agents barged in, pistols up and pointing at me.

I shouted. 'Stop! Close enough!' Kellerman's arms were grabbing at my waist, her head buried in my back. She was sobbing.

The two men froze and stood poised, knees bent and guns in both hands, with me at the apex of their crossfire. Then Danny dashed in and stood panting between them, gun in hand. Aimed at me.

'What the fuck are you doing here, Brodie? What the fuck are you playing at?' he screamed.

It hit me like a bucket of ice water. My breath stopped. Then I found my voice.

'You eejit, Danny! What are you doing with this pair? Whose side are you on?'

The three men moved apart, widening their angle, with Danny in the centre. He kicked the door shut. Through the dirty windows I could see the crowd dissolving, too intent on getting home to notice what we were doing. Within a few seconds we were alone in this stuffy crucible.

The one I thought of as *Professor* called to Danny in Hebrew.

I guessed what they were saying.

Danny replied in English. 'Don't you bloody dare! Nobody shoots! Put your bloody guns down! Do you think he's here alone?'

As he said this, Danny lowered his own gun and stood up straight. Slowly the Irgun men let their hands fall. I kept mine up, aimed at Danny's belly. Danny walked forward until he was six feet away. Until I could see his eyes. They were red raw.

'Haven't slept much, old pal?' I asked.

He shook his head. 'You can't stop us.'

'Us? Are you really with this pair of killers? What the hell's going on, Danny?'

'You can't stop me, Brodie,' he repeated.

'Sure I can, Danny. You know I can be as daft as you at times. This is one of those times. Tell me what's going on? Were you coerced? *What the hell happened?*'

His expression twisted. 'Why are you saving this woman? This – monster!'

'I'm saving her for a trial. What were *you* planning?'

A hard grin came over his face. 'Oh, we've got a trial in mind too.'

'*We?* You and this pair of sadists? Was it going to be trial by torture? Application of pincers, cutting off bits until she talked? What's she going to say? Sorry!'

'We'll see, won't we?'

'You're a bloody Scot! A wee Protestant boy from Ayrshire. Like me. That's who *you* are. That's your "we". What are you doing with these sods, for God's sake?'

Behind Danny, the door began to open. A porter? The police? A woman's head appeared. A mass of striking auburn hair under a beret. It was the ladies' waiting room. I hoped she'd take one look and go and get the police. Instead she opened the door wider, slipped in and closed it behind her.

Danny's face had lit up. She came up beside him and took him by the arm.

'You came,' he said, as though she might not have done.

'I promised.'

Realisation dawned like a hammer striking a gong.

'Ava Kaplan? Or do you prefer Eve Copeland?' I asked. Danny's Jewish paramour. The one who'd thrown him over. The girl in Berlin. Member of the Israeli negotiating team at the UN.

She turned her great dark eyes on me. 'And you must be Douglas Brodie. Danny's talked about you.'

I turned back to Danny and asked him softly, '*This* was the bargain? This is what it was all about? Since when, Danny? When did the treachery begin?'

'Does it matter?'

'You came at Sam's request. Didn't you?'

'Sort of. I called her. I saw the Glasgow papers. So did Eve and her friends. They contacted me.' He shrugged. 'It was a conjunction of interests.'

'A conjunction of interests? What bullshit is that? It was betrayal! You said you came to help me!'

He winced with every word. Eve put her hand on his shoulder and turned to me.

'We're taking Herta Kellerman to Israel. She'll be tried there. By the people *she* tortured. It's our right, *Colonel* Brodie. All you big boys – Americans, the British, Russians, even the snivelling French – are having their show trials. The Jewish nation has a bigger stake than anyone. We will show the world we can administer justice.'

'How many hangings will *that* take?'

Her eyes blazed. 'It will tell the ones that got away that we're coming after them. There's no hiding place.'

I lowered my gun and gently unhooked the fingers of the woman cowering behind me. I drew her to my side. She was shaking from top to toe.

'Dr Kellerman. *Dr Kellerman.*'

She turned and spoke to me in soft German. 'What's going to happen to me? Are you going to give me to them? They will kill me.'

'Frau Doktor Kellerman, if you did all that you're accused of, it's not a matter of whether you will be killed. It's who will do it, and when.'

She held my gaze for a long moment, and then nodded. 'Yes. I know that.'

'Why didn't you run? You knew we'd taken Langefeld and his woman.'

I saw her take a deep breath and steady herself. She brushed hair from her forehead. She spoke loud enough to be heard by Danny and Eve.

'Martha Haake wasn't his woman.'

I gazed down at her. 'It was *you* living with Langefeld?'

'Do you think Nazis can't fall in love, Mr Brodie?'

'So you stayed for Langefeld. The Americans didn't want him. They wanted you. Why didn't you bugger off after this pair killed your precious Klaus?' I pointed at the Irgun agents. 'The net was closing, yet you went back to the hospital?'

Her dark eyes filled. 'I'm tired, Mr Brodie. Tired of it all. I did good work at Glasgow. I helped people. It was what I trained for. Do you understand? What I did in the camps was to help people. *My* people. I hope you never have to choose, Mr Brodie.'

I stared at her, trying to equate this little woman with her crimes. Then I thought of her latest atrocity. Anger bubbled up.

'And you traded Isaac Feldmann for your lover. You killed my friend!'

She pointed at the Irgun agents. '*They* killed *Klaus*!'

Bleakness washed over me. Danny betrayed me for his woman. Kellerman murdered Isaac for her man.

'An eye for an eye, *Doctor*? Is that your medical ethics?'

Her shoulders slumped. I grabbed her, shook her.

'The Nazis who helped you kill Isaac – are they the same four who killed Malachi? Where are they?'

Her mouth lifted at the corners in a condescending smile. 'Still in Glasgow, I imagine. Where they belong.'

'What do you mean?'

'We have like-minded supporters everywhere.'

The man with the music-hall German accent who phoned Rabbi Silver demanding we free Langefeld.

'*Blackshirts?* Mosley's boys?'

She shrugged. 'Everyone takes sides.'

I pushed her away.

'Heard enough, Brodie?' asked Danny. 'We need to get going.'

I looked down on Kellerman, weighing up her crimes against the good she was doing in Glasgow. Weighing up Israeli justice against our own. Asking myself was I really ready to have a shoot-out with my terrible twin.

'Take her.'

Kellerman's mouth opened and closed as if to make one last plea. She searched my face, seeing my answer. She just nodded. Then she turned and walked forward into the ambit of Danny and the Irgun agents.

'Shall we go?' she said.

Danny spoke briefly to the two men. They opened the door, shepherded her through and began walking her down the platform. Danny followed for a few steps, finishing his instructions. For a moment, I was left with Ava Kaplan. I spoke softly.

'Do you love him?'

She made a maddening, noncommittal face and my anger at Danny dissolved.

'The poor bastard. At least be kind to him.'

She held my gaze; finally she nodded. And the moment was gone. Danny returned and took her hand. His face was a mix of emotions. When he looked at her, it opened up. Would I have done this for Sam? Then he looked at me . . .

'Brodie? Brodie, I'm—'

'—an eejit. Bugger off, Danny.'

Absolution wasn't within my gift.

The pair turned and walked away, hand in hand. I stood and watched until they got to the barrier. Danny glanced back. I thought he was going to wave. Then he was gone.

AUTHOR'S NOTE

There are many historical truths in this story.

Glasgow had a population of over 12,000 Jews in 1946, many living in the Gorbals, and some speaking Scots-Yiddish. If you thought Glaswegian was hard on the ears . . .

In 1923 the League of Nations handed Great Britain the poisoned chalice of administering the mandate for Palestine. It was a thankless task made miserable in the post-war, post-Holocaust era when the surviving ranks of European Jews sought refuge in their 'Promised Land'. The poor British squaddie was piggy-in-the-middle between Arabs and Jews. Our soldiers were bombed, shot and assaulted right up to May 1948 when the United Nations permitted the creation of the state of Israel. And then things went downhill . . .

Rat lines were a system of escape routes for Nazis and other fascists fleeing Europe at the end of the Second World War. They ran from Germany through Italy, Austria and Franco's Spain to safe havens in South America, the USA and Canada. Escapees included Dr Josef Mengele and Adolf Eichmann. The organisers of these rat lines included US intelligence agencies, fascist organisations such as the Croatian Ustashe, and senior churchmen such as Bishop Alois Hudal in Rome, Cardinal Eugène Tisserant of France, Cardinal Antonio Caggiano of Argentina, and Father Krunoslav Draganovi of Croatia.

The wartime Special Operations Executive was blessed with some extraordinarily courageous and daring young women. They were led by Vera Atkins and included Odette Sansom, GC. After her capture Odette survived Ravensbrück by keeping her head and maintaining the fiction that she was married to a relative of Winston Churchill. She avoided the wretched fate of her fellow SOE agents in Ravensbrück: Cicely Lefort, Violette Szabo, Denise Bloch and Lilian Rolfe.

Malcolm McCulloch was Chief Constable of Glasgow from 1943 to 1960. He succeeded Sir Percy Sillitoe (Chief Constable 1931–43), who went on to become head of MI5 (1946–53).

Donald Campbell was Archbishop of Glasgow from 1945 to 1963 and had nothing whatsoever to do with rat lines, Scottish or otherwise.

The winter of 1947 was the worst in the twentieth century. It was bloody cold.

Irn Bru was spelled Iron Brew until 1946. Its sales were suspended during the war because of rationing.

The rest of this story is fiction . . . more or less . . . but it all adds up to a greater truth.

Trials for War Crimes and Crimes against Humanity

From the end of the Second World War in 1945 until 1949 a number of war crimes trials took place across Europe. Among them were:

Belsen trials: British Military Court, Lüneburg. First trial 17 September to 17 November 1945. Second trial June 1946.

Nuremberg trials: trial of major war criminals before the International Military Tribunal, Nuremberg, 20 November 1945 to 1 October 1946. Subsequent trials took place up to April 1949.

Ravensbrück trials: British Military Court, Curiohaus, Hamburg. Seven trials in total from December 1946 to July 1948. The first ran from 5 December 1946 to 3 February 1947.

Verdicts and Sentences

Pilgrim Soul is peopled with fictional and real-life characters. Where I have invented a 'baddie' I've used an amalgam of names and vile deeds drawn from real life, e.g. Dr Herta Kellermann is a composite of Doctors Herta Oberheuser and Ruth Kellermann, both of whom conducted foul medical experiments at Ravensbrück. For her sins Oberheuser spent a mere seven years in prison before becoming a family doctor; Kellermann was never imprisoned. As for the other real Nazis I've deployed in my novel, these were their fates:

Suhren: Sturmbannführer [Major] Fritz Suhren, Camp Commandant Ravensbrück 1942–5. Also served at Sachsenhausen 1941–2. Escaped from American custody in 1946, recaptured in France in 1949. Hanged in Fresnes Prison, Paris, in 1950.

Schwarzhuber: Obersturmführer [Lieutenant] Johann Schwarzhuber, Deputy Camp Commandant Ravensbrück January–April 1945. Also served at Dachau, Sachsenhausen and Auschwitz-Birkenau. Convicted of war crimes, hanged May 1947.*

Hellinger: Obersturmführer [Lieutenant] Dr Martin Hellinger, Camp Dentist Ravensbrück 1943–5. Also served at Sachsenhausen and Flossenbürg. Sentenced to fifteen years' imprisonment, released 1955.

Ramdohr: Ludwig Ramdohr, Gestapo Officer Ravensbrück 1942–5. Convicted of war crimes, hanged May 1947.*

Binz: Oberaufseherin [Chief Warden] Dorothea Binz, Ravensbrück 1939–45. Convicted of war crimes, hanged May 1947.*

Bösel: Aufseherin [Warden] Greta Bösel, Ravensbrück 1944?–45. Convicted of war crimes, hanged May 1947.*

Haake: Nurse Martha Haake, Ravensbrück 1943–5. Tried in the fourth Ravensbruck trial May–June 1948, sentenced to ten years' imprisonment, released on health grounds 1951.

Grese: Aufseherin [Warden] Irma Grese. Warden at Ravensbrück, Auschwitz and Belsen, convicted of war crimes and crimes against humanity in the Belsen trials, hanged 13 December 1945.*

* Hanged by the busy British executioner, Albert Pierrepoint, in Hamelin Prison, Germany. Pierrepoint's final tally of Nazi executions was around two hundred.

Big thanks to:

Sarah Ferris, first reviewer, cheerleader and reality checker. Richenda Todd, editor and producer of silk purses from sow's ears. Helen Ferris, CPsychol, for expert advice on post traumatic stress. Tina Betts, persevering literary agent and supporter. Tony Hanley for racing tips. The Rev John Bell of the Iona Community for his observations about Glasgow and human frailty. Sara O'Keeffe and Team Corvus for unstinting enthusiasm for 'Brodie'.

Read on for more of Brodie's adventures in

GALLOWGLASS

He's dead. It says so in his own newspaper, the *Glasgow Gazette*. A brief editorial describes the tragic death of their chief crime reporter and staunchly defends him against the unproven charge of murder. It's a brave stance to take, given the weight of evidence. The death is confirmed in the tear-streaked faces of the women by the freshly dug grave. It is spelled out in chiselled letters on the headstone, glistening oil-black in the drizzle:

> Douglas Brodie
> Born 25 January 1912 –
> Died 20 July 1947

Just four weeks before, a senior banker was kidnapped. His distraught wife pleaded with Brodie to deliver the ransom money and free her husband. The drop went wrong, disastrously wrong. Brodie was coshed in the kidnappers' den. He woke with a gun in his hand next to a very dead banker with a bullet in his head. The police, led by Brodie's old foe Sangster, burst in and arrested Brodie.

The case is watertight: the bullet comes from Brodie's revolver, the banker's wife denies knowing Brodie, and Brodie's pockets are stuffed with ransom notes. Samantha Campbell deploys all her advocacy skills to no avail. It looks like her lover is for the long drop. But in an apparent act of desperation – or guilt – Brodie cheats justice by committing suicide in his prison cell. Is this the sordid end for a distinguished ex-copper, decorated soldier and man of parts?

Coming from Corvus in
April 2014

GALLOWGLASS

DOUGLAS BRODIE BOOK 4

"The merciless Macdonald,
Worthy to be a rebel, for to that
The multiplying villainies of nature
Do swarm upon him, from the Western isles
Of kerns and gallowglasses is supplied."

Macbeth, Act I, Scene II.
William Shakespeare

ONE

He was dead. It was announced in his own newspaper, the *Glasgow Gazette*. Instead of the usual crime column, there was a brief editorial. It described the tragic death of their chief crime reporter and staunchly defended him against the unproven charge of murder. It was a brave stance to take, given the weight of evidence against him.

Finally and conclusively, his death was confirmed in the tear-streaked faces of the women by the freshly dug grave. It was spelled out in chiselled letters on the headstone glistening oil-black in the drizzle:

Douglas Brodie

Born 25 January 1912 –
Died 20 July 1947

'A man's a man for a' that.'

In the circumstances there were only three mourners: a frail white-haired woman in a veiled hat sheltering under a black umbrella held aloft by a younger, taller woman. She too wore a veil so that only the tufts of the blond hair on her pale neck were on show. The third was a man in a wheelchair, hat pulled down over his drawn face, rain dripping from the brim onto the oilskin which covered his arms and body. The minister had abandoned them after a desultory oration by the graveside. It had taken some persuasion even to get

Douglas Brodie consigned to this cemetery. There had been an embarrassed debate with the kirk and the corporation about using a Christian burial site for the internment of a man with double black marks against him: an alleged murder and a confirmed suicide.

The threesome started to turn and shuffle their way back down the path. The women clutched each other for support on the wet tarmac. The seated man birled his wheelchair round and kept pace with the women as they headed towards the gate and the big funeral car waiting for them. It took a while and considerable manoeuvring to get the chair packed into the boot and the three mourners ensconced in the car. Once seated, they closed the window between themselves and the driver. Then they were off into the steady downpour, the windscreen wipers thumping back and forth, like a metronome.

'Are you all right, Agnes?' said Samantha Campbell. 'It's over now. We can get on.'

The old woman sniffed and wiped her nose and eyes with her hankie.

'Ah never thought I'd see the day. It's not right for a son to go before his mother.'

Sam patted her hand and turned to the man sitting facing them.

'I hope you haven't overdone it, Wullie. Can you get that soaking cape off? Dry out a bit?' She reached to help him pull it over his head and drop it on the floor.

'That's better. I'm fine, lassie.' Wullie McAllister, some-time doyen of crime reporting at the *Glasgow Gazette*, reached into his jacket, pulled out his pack of Craven A, lit up and drew luxuriously on a cigarette.

They were quiet for a bit, then Agnes spoke.

'Such a poor turnout, as well.'

'You can hardly blame them, Agnes. We asked for privacy in the announcement.'

'Ah suppose so, Samantha. All the same.'

'He wouldnae have wanted a fuss. You know what Brodie's like,' said Wullie.

Agnes persisted. 'Not even his old regiment. There should have been a piper.'

Wullie blew out smoke.

'Mrs Brodie, funerals are dreich enough affairs without *The Flowers of the Forest* making our ears bleed.'

Again, silence left them with their thoughts until they began the climb up to Park Terrace and Sam's home.

'It would never have happened if he'd got through to me that night,' said Sam.

'You can't blame yourself, Samantha. Douglas wouldn't have listened to you anyway. He was as stubborn as his faither.'

'Still, I might have persuaded him. It could have turned out differently. . .'

Danny McRae Book 1

TRUTH DARE KILL

THE WAR IS OVER. But there are no medals for Danny McRae. Just amnesia and blackouts; twin handicaps for a private investigator with an upper-class client on the hook for murder.

Danny's blackouts mean that hours, sometimes days, are a complete blank. So when news of a brutal killer stalking London's red-light district starts to stir grisly memories, Danny is terrified about what he might discover if he delves deeper into his fractured mind.

Will his past catch up with him before his enemies can? And which would be worse?

A fast-paced crime-thriller, by the author of the 2011 kindle sensation, *The Hanging Shed*, a Douglas Brodie investigation.

Praise for Gordon Ferris:

'Ferris is a writer of real authority, immersing the reader into his nightmare world... Everything speaks of an original voice.' Barry Forshaw, *Independent*

'Electrifies readers... A rising star of Scottish literature.' *Scotsman*

'Great feel and authenticity... terrific.' Val McDermid

Danny McRae Book 2

THE UNQUIET HEART

LONDON 1946. Danny McRae is a private detective scraping a living in ration-card London. Eve Copeland, crime reporter, is looking for new angles to save her career. It's a match made in heaven… until Eve disappears, one of McRae's contacts dies violently and an old adversary presents him with some unpalatable truths.

McRae's desperate search for his lover draws him into a web of black marketeers, double agents and assassins, and hurls him into the shattered remains of Berlin, where terrorism and espionage foreshadow the bleakness of the Cold War. And McRae begins to lose sight of the thin line between good and evil…

The thrilling sequel to *Truth Dare Kill* by the author of the 2011 kindle publishing sensation, *The Hanging Shed*.

Praise for Gordon Ferris:

'The word of mouth hit that is leaving its fellow thrillers in its wake. Ferris is a wonderfully evocative writer.' *Observer*

'Great feel and authenticity… terrific.' Val McDermid